MEETING &
FISHING
THE HATCHES

MEETING & FISHING THE HATCHES

Charles R. Meck

ILLUSTRATIONS BY **Dennis Bender**

STEPHEN GREENE PRESS

PELHAM BOOKS

THE STEPHEN GREENE PRESS/PELHAM BOOKS

Published by the Penguin Group
Viking Penguin, a division of Penguin Books USA Inc., 40 West 23rd Street,
  New York, New York 10010, U.S.A.
Penguin Books Ltd., 27 Wrights Lane, London W8 5TZ, England
Penguin Books Australia Ltd, Ringwood, Victoria, Australia
Penguin Books Canada Ltd, 2801 John Street, Markham, Ontario, Canada L3R 1B4
Penguin Books (N.Z.) Ltd, 182-190 Wairau Road, Auckland 10, New Zealand

Penguin Books Ltd, Registered Offices: Harmondsworth, Middlesex, England

First published in 1977 by Winchester Press
This revised edition published in 1990 by The Stephen Greene Press/Pelham Books
Distributed by Viking Penguin, a division of Penguin Books USA Inc.

10 9 8 7 6 5 4 3 2 1

Photographs by the author
Line drawings by Dennis Bender

Grateful acknowledgment is made to the publishers of the *Miscellaneous Publications of the Entomological Society of America* and *Transactions of American Entomological Society* for permission to use their copyrighted material.

Library of Congress Cataloging-in-Publication Data
Meck, Charles R.
  Meeting & fishing the hatches : a fly fisher's guide to hatches
throughout the United States / by Charles R. Meck : illustrations by
Dennis Bender.
     p.   cm.
     Includes bibliographical references.
     ISBN 0-8289-0727-7
     1. Trout fishing—United States. 2. Fly fishing—United States.
3. Insects, Aquatic—United States. 4. Fly tying. I. Title.
II. Title: Meeting and fishing the hatches.
SH687.M36 1990
799.1′755—dc20   89-39282
                                                         CIP

Printed in the United States of America
Designed by Deborah Schneider
Set in Times Roman by CopyRight
Produced by Unicorn Production Services, Inc.

CONTENTS

To Shirley, Lynne, and Bryan
for their encouragement

ACKNOWLEDGMENTS

I have seen numerous fly-fishermen anxiously attempt to identify emerging mayflies. Sure, many of these cursory observations might be accurate, but the only certain method of identification is by a skilled entomologist's examining a male spinner in the laboratory. In preparing this book, I have relied heavily on these experts who are adept at mayfly identification. I have been fortunate to have the complete cooperation of one of these experts, R. Wills Flowers of Florida A&M University. Wills identified some of the Eastern and many of the Western species and suggested several changes in chapters 3 and 4. Without his assistance, especially in identifying troublesome mayfly species, this book might never have been completed.

The late Charlie Brooks of West Yellowstone, Montana, reviewed, commented on, and suggested changes in the Western hatches. Without Charlie's help, the Western stories and hatches would have been much more difficult to complete.

In Pennsylvania I had assistance from Greg Hoover of the Pennsylvania State University. His aid and encouragement were invaluable in the preparation of this text.

Dennis Bender, also with Penn State University, prepared the illustrations in the book. There are many others who have helped; to all of them, I say thanks.

PREFACE

With the advent of high energy costs, today's fishermen may feel a pinch in their travel plans to their favorite fishing spots. However, with better planning to fish the hatches, fly fishermen, at least, can enjoy those less frequent trips with more success.

The purpose of this book is to provide North American fly fishermen with information on some of the most important mayflies, stoneflies, and caddis flies and their probable emergence times. The inexperienced fly fisherman especially needs guidelines to aid him in his pursuit of a new sport. This book will not tell you how to fly-fish, but it will tell you what fly to use, when to use it, and why you're using it.

All too often we do little or no advance planning when hatches of insects appear on the water, and when trout feed voraciously on naturals. Do you want to increase your chances of success? Then plan ahead—schedule your trips to meet the hatches. Be prepared to fish while the hatch is in progress with an artificial that imitates the actual insect. The answer to meeting and fishing the hatches is planning, planning, and more planning. This book will help you in planning, organizing, and scheduling your future fishing trips. Then you too can enjoy the success usually associated with fly fishing when insects appear on the surface.

Admittedly insect hatches are not the only complexity that troubles many new fishermen. Fly-fishing has an intimidating mystique. Many of us would like to try it as a new skill, but when we observe the "expert" displaying his adroitness, we give up without even trying. This is a pity, for fly-fishing is not difficult.

The techniques of presentation can be acquired by anyone—and without a book. Presentation and casting are skills and like most other skills can best be learned through practice.

Meeting and fishing the hatches, however, is not a skill but a body of knowledge, and it can be learned from a book. This book doesn't deal with the mystique of fly-fishing. Rather, it attempts to simplify the subject by pinpointing one specific but troublesome aspect: the imitation.

Another aspect of fly-fishing that I do not discuss is its history and the texts associated with it. The evolution of fly fishing is an entertaining subject, and an understanding of it can help even the angler, but it has been presented many times by many other authors and need not divert us from our topic.

As you read this book, you'll almost immediately note a strong personal bias on my part. I find that enticing a trout to the surface with a lifelike dry fly is much more enjoyable, rewarding, and challenging than any other type of fishing. Granted, an expert nymph fisherman will take more and larger trout day after day, year after year, than any angler relying solely on dry flies. But when fishing a weighted nymph, you lose the same thrill you forfeit when using garden hackle or spinner, you lose the ultimate thrill: that split-second sensation when trout meets fly in full view. However, if you're a wet-fly fisherman and converting you to the dry fly is out of the question, then you can tie all the patterns discussed in the following chapters as downwinged wet-fly versions.

You'll note too as you read that I have included some new untried recommendations and virtually untested hypotheses. There is other material that, although not new, is presented in a new way. Dividing the hatches into morning, afternoon, and evening is a new approach to the problem of meeting and fishing the hatches. Chapter 9 is devoted to meeting the "unhatches" and suggests possible flies to use during this period.

I have done my best not only to cover the subject but to contribute to it. I hope that the next time you find yourself in the midst of a hatch of emerging insects, and with the appropriate imitation on your tippet, it will be this book—not just good luck—that has put you there. And, of course, I wish you good luck too.

MEETING & FISHING THE HATCHES

CHAPTER 1

GENERAL RULES FOR MEETING THE HATCHES

You're on the most productive pool of your favorite stream, and a hatch appears. The mayfly resembles a Pale Evening Dun or Sulphur, so you check your fly box for an appropriate imitation. The closest artificial you have is a size 12 Light Cahill; the mayfly would more appropriately be imitated by a size 16 Pale Evening Dun. You hurriedly cast in the direction of five rising trout. The first two trout rise to the imitation but refuse it. Finally you hook a trout! Many more casts over rising—but no more success. You decide you'll quit for the day, angry at yourself for not being better prepared with proper dry flies.

Sure you fished when a hatch appeared. But were you prepared for it? Suppose you had planned to meet this specific hatch, and you had some prior, basic knowledge of hatches.

Let's look at the same hatch with some planning on your part. You've looked forward to this trip for a long time. You've planned the trip to be on your favorite stream when the Pale Evening Dun appears. You're prepared for the hatch with plenty of size 14, 16, and 18 Pale Evening Dun imitations. A half-hour after you arrive at the pool, the expectant mayfly emerges. Several trout feed in front of you on sluggish naturals, and you begin casting in their direction. After twenty minutes, you've hooked and released four heavy brown trout. You move downstream toward several other feeding fish and experience the same success there. What a memorable day!

This latter example clearly depicts meeting and fishing the hatches: scheduling your trip at a certain time and date for an anticipated hatch with the appropriate imitation. If you follow the rules provided later in this chapter for fishing the hatches, you too

might experience the latter series of events more often.

Meeting and fishing the hatches offers many advantages. First, it should increase the number of fish you catch. With some knowledge of the hatches, you'll be prepared with an imitation resembling the emerging dun or mating spinner. Furthermore, during this anticipated hatch, trout are more likely to be feeding.

Second, fishing the hatch is extremely important for the novice fisherman. I know of no better way for a beginner to get hooked on fly-fishing than to experience a fantastic insect emergence and the concomitant success of matching the hatch.

Watching several hatches progress encouraged me the first few times I met them.

Many years ago, before I knew what words like *hatch, dun, spinner,* and even *mayfly* meant, I encountered the Green Drake (*Ephemera guttulata*) on Penns Creek in Pennsylvania. It was only an accident that I decided to fish a pool near the town of Coburn. When I arrived at the stream, I saw twenty cars parked near the stream and assumed the state had recently released trout. As I collected my gear out of the car, I noticed that not one of the more than two dozen fishermen was actively casting; all of them were resting near the bank. The anglers huddled in clusters of twos and threes, apparently discussing strategy. This prodded my curiosity, so I stopped and talked to a couple of them.

"Why isn't anybody fishing?" I inquired.

"Gotta wait until the shadfly gets thicker," one man near me replied.

I didn't want to appear ignorant, so I stood back and carefully surveyed the stream. Five to ten large, dark insects flew toward trees on the far shore. Only an occasional trout rose for these large morsels. At 8:00 P.M. all hell broke loose; hundreds of these insects now rested on the surface, and thirty to forty trout actively fed on the laggards.

"They're working, they're working," shouted several fishermen above and below me. They all immediately jumped to their feet and started casting toward rising fish.

This was my introduction to fishing the hatches, and I was totally unprepared—but I was impressed, so I decided to stay and observe.

I was fortunate enough during the hatch to be near a true expert fly-fisherman. This man cast a Green Drake imitation flawlessly over one rising trout after another. He caught more trout that evening than I normally caught in an entire year. He promptly released most of these trout back into the water to fight another time, to rise during another hatch. He kept only one huge dark brown trout that weighed close to 4 pounds.

Through more than two hours of light, half-light, and darkness, I observed and conversed with the adept fly-fisherman. I was curious to discover his success. I knew it took time to learn to cast as capably as he did, but there seemed to be much more.

"You have to be at the right place at the right time and fish the hatches," he said, as he disassembled his fly rod in front of his car lights.

"That's easy to say," I said, "but how do you know when, where, and what hatches will appear?"

"Well that's where experience helps. You should familiarize yourself with some of the common hatches and when and where they'll appear."

These astute words fell on my deaf ears; within a week I was back to my normal fishing with spinning rod in hand.

It took another so-called coincidence or another accident rather than knowledge before I became a true convert to the when and where of a common hatch.

This next fortuitous event occurred almost one year later, again in June. I had coaxed a friend, Lloyd Williams, to resume fly-fishing after a hiatus of twelve years. Tom Taylor also accompanied us to a small mountain stream in north-central Pennsylvania, Hoaglands Branch. As usual I used my spinning rod with a Mepps spinner and had a few trout flash at the lure, but I didn't hook any. About 6:00 P.M. we decided to travel downstream to a large, open pool formed by the confluence of Hoaglands Branch and Elk Creek. Here we sat and chatted, mostly about our lack of success that day. Lloyd said that if that afternoon was any sample of the fishing to come, it would probably be twelve more years before he purchased another license.

About 7:00 P.M. some large cream duns started emerging. I didn't know what they were at the time, but they were probably *Stenonema* subimagos. The hatch became heavy, and by chance we had Light Cahills to match the hatch effectively.

When several trout started surface feeding, all three of us hustled toward the stream and cast to the rising fish. We netted and creeled trout after trout until we ran out of imitations. We had begun the hatch with five dry flies; now all were mutilated beyond recognition. However, before our abortive finish, I had caught my limit of eight trout. This was a momentous evening for all of us but especially for me. I have never cast my spinning rod over trout since I experienced that hatch those many years ago.

After the second accidental meeting-and-fishing-the-hatch episode with the Light Cahill, I recalled and reviewed the advice the expert had given me a year earlier on Penns Creek. His suggestion—that I should familiarize myself with some of the common hatches and when and where they'll appear—evolved into four rules, which I follow rigidly when I want to meet and fish a specific hatch: (1) *select a common mayfly, stone fly, or caddis fly;* (2) *choose a probable date the common species emerges;* (3) *look for the hatch on a good stream;* and (4) *fish the stream at the proper time.* All four rules are equally important to follow; if you miss one, you'll likely miss the hatch; if you execute all, you very well may meet the hatch.

Let's look at each of the rules in some detail.

1. When attempting to fish the hatch, *select a common and fishable species of mayfly, caddis fly, or stone fly.* Some mayflies, caddis flies, and stone flies inhabit more streams than other species. Why? There are probably many limiting characteristics; the following are just a few:

a. Nymphs of many species have exacting habitat requirements. Nymphs of *Hexagenia, Ephemera,* and other genera in the Family Ephemeridae seek out bot-

Figure 1. Big Fishing Creek near Lamar in central Pennsylvania is an example of a good stream. On the stretch pictured, good hatches of *Ephemera guttulata* (Green Drake), *Litobrancha recurvata* (Brown Drake), *Ephemerella subvaria* (Hendrickson), *Paraleptophlebia guttata* (Dark Blue Quill), and many more appear.

toms of mud, silt, gravel, or other similar material to borrow. These species are found in numbers only in streams that meet their requirements. When conditions are right, however, hatches of this family can be truly phenomenal.

Other genera like *Baetis* and *Isonychia* have no such habitat requirements and swim about freely on the bottom. These two genera should be found in a wider range of waters than the burrowers—though they too have requirements, like the need for fast water.

Other nymphs like those of the Family Heptageniidae usually cling to rocks in fast to moderate water. If these features are missing or minimal, the hatches will be lacking or unimportant.

b. Some species can apparently withstand pollution more readily than other species. *Epeorus* species are common only in cold, rapid, and highly pure waters. Conversely, both *Stenacron interpunctatum canadense* (Light Cahill) and *Ephemerella rotunda* (Pale Evening Dun) appear to be able to withstand some pollution— or at least they return more quickly to a stream just emerging from pollution. This comes from no scien-

tific study but my own observations. These two species produce heavy hatches on two central Pennsylvania streams—Spring Creek and the Little Juniata River— that are just returning from extensive periods of severe pollution.

c. Finally, other mayflies like some *Potamanthus*, *Stenonema*, and *Ephoron* species develop on large rivers usually too warm to be permanent trout streams and not the typical water to which we are accustomed. Still other species are found mainly on slow water and on ponds and lakes. Members of the Genus *Callibaetis* are important on many Western lakes. And there are others (most of those listed in Chapter 3 in the Emergence Chart) often found on typical trout streams.

But there's the question: why is a species of mayfly found on one stream and not on another when both are in close proximity and similar in characteristics? This apparent inconsistency has bothered me on many occasions. Let me cite one. There are two Bald Eagle Creeks in the Bald Eagle Valley in central Pennsylvania; one flows northeast (NE) and the other southwest (SW). Although they flow in opposite directions, both begin in the same swampy area near Port Matilda. In late August, eight miles downstream from its source, the Bald Eagle Creek (NE) has an impressive hatch of the huge *Hexagenia atrocaudata* (Big Slate Drake). No such hatch apparently occurs on the other Bald Eagle Creek (SW). I have observed the latter stream night after night between 6:00 P.M. and 7:00 P.M. and have not sighted one spinner of the species. Here are two streams, approximately the same size, both beginning in the area, and having similar characteristics—but one has a good hatch of *Hexagenia atrocaudata* and the other apparently has none.

A species must be more than common; it must be fishable. That is, the species must be slow enough in its takeoff from the water's surface to encourage trout to surface feed. What's the use of imitating a species with a dry fly when trout rarely get an opportunity to observe the dun on the surface, let alone seize the natural? Several years ago a friend wanted to show me an exceptional hatch on a local stream in late August. I decided to go because it was the last week of the season, and I was curious about the hatch. Around 7:30 P.M. thousands of duns from all sections of the stream emerged—but not one trout showed. Why? It was a *Heptagenia* species, and like most other *Heptagenia* species, it rose rapidly from the surface, rarely if ever pausing to rest before flying. Here's a classic case where a nymphal pattern takes precedence over the dry fly. Weather often affects whether the hatch will be fishable. Meet a Hendrickson hatch on a cold, blustery day, and many of the duns will be unable to become airborne. Fish that same hatch on a warm spring day and few duns will delay their flight.

I've seen many hatches like the *Heptagenia* species over the years: indescribably prolific emergences but *not fishable*. If you plan to use dry flies, the dun's ability to escape from the water's surface is an important aspect to consider. In Chapter 2 we rate duns (and spinners) subjectively, according to their speed of takeoff from the water. Usually the slower the takeoff, the more fishable the hatch.

Summary for Rule 1: Choose a *common* and *fishable* mayfly or caddis fly species that can be found on most streams, or at least choose one that might be common to the stream, river, or lake you plan to fish.

2. *Choose a probable date* the common species emerges. Nature works in orderly ways. As the forsythia begins blooming in late April in central Pennsylvania, the Hendrickson begins its annual appearance. When the locust tree is full of fragrant, white blossoms, the Green Drake is leaving its graveled aquatic habit and emerging on the surface. Look at the Brown Drake as another example. When the peony blooms in late May in central Pennsylvania, this burrower emerges. In Michigan and Wisconsin the peony blooms a week or two later. The Brown Drake also appears in the Midwest a week or two

later than it does in the East. On Henry's Fork the Brown Drake usually makes its annual appearance in late June or early July. I'll never forget the evening near Pond's Lodge when I left the river after a tremendous Brown Drake hatch. As I headed back to the car, I noticed that peonies in the ranger's yard were in full bloom. Many plants and animals, including mayflies, caddis flies, and stone flies, appear with some scheduled regularity year after year. Scientists call this relationship phenology. However, emergence does vary to a limited extent for the same species in different locations and may deviate from year to year even on the same stream.

Emergence of the same species can vary considerably in different locations, especially as you travel north or south. The Hendrickson (*Ephemerella subvaria*) commonly begins emerging in central and northeastern Pennsylvania about April 23. As you travel north, this species consistently appears · later and later. On the Delaware River, Beaverkill, and Willowemoc, you'll encounter the same species about four or five days later. Conversely, as you travel south, the same dun is likely to emerge earlier than April 23. The Emergence Map (Chapter 2, figure 2) is a rough guide to compensate for north-south emergence variations.

There are even discrepancies in beginning emergence dates from year to year on the same stream. A colder-than-average March or April might cause hatches to be later than normal. Warmer-than-average temperatures during 'these two months might produce premature appearances.

Species affected most by variations in temperature, and therefore most difficult to predict accurately, are usually the earliest ones like the Quill Gordon and the Hendrickson. Hatches after June (except for the Green Drake and a few others) don't appear to be affected as much by weather variations. (These later hatches do alter their emergence and spinner fall time with changes in the weather.)

A species also can appear later in the season as you move upstream. The Green Drake presents a good illustration of this on Penns Creek. The Drake first appears on the lower stretch near the town of Weikert around June 1 (plus or minus seven days). Within seven to ten days the hatch travels 15 miles upstream to Coburn. Usually about the time the Drake has ended on Penns Creek, it just begins on one of its tributaries, Elk Creek. And when the hatch has ended on Penns Creek, it usually just begins on Big Fishing Creek in nearby Clinton County.

The Western March Brown presents another example of those mayflies appearing later in the season as you move upriver. Ken Helfrich of Eugene, Oregon, guides the lower end of the McKenzie for the hatch from February to April. When May arrives, he often meets and fishes the same hatch 30 miles upriver on the McKenzie near Vida or Blue.

Figure 2. The Willowemoc at Roscoe, New York, is a good example of Rule 3: selecting a good stream.

The Pale Morning Dun varies its emergence from river to river. Hatches may occur on near-coastal Oregon rivers like the McKenzie in April and May, whereas the same species might not appear until mid-June on the Metolius River in central Oregon. Hatches on Henry's Fork often appear near the end of June. In July and August you'll encounter the same hatch on the Bighorn and the Kootenai, both in Montana.

I state these examples to show that emergence of the same species does vary considerably even on the same stream, in the same year—and it varies even more on different streams. You can utilize this information to your advantage. When fishing the Green Drake, or for that matter any other common hatch, if you don't know ahead of time where the hatch is on a specific date, start at the lower end of the stream. Check the trees carefully for resting duns and recently matured spinners, and query local fly-fishermen to ascertain exactly where the hatch is. If the hatch has not yet begun, you can remain on the lower stretch, hoping that night will be the beginning of a big hatch.

Buss Grove and his friends, with many years of ex-perience in fishing the Green Drake, use this knowledge to their advantage. They begin fly-fishing near Weikert on Penns Creek, fish the hatch upstream for the next week or two, then move to Big Fishing Creek for that Green Drake hatch. When the emergence wanes on Big Fishing Creek, Buss travels to Pine Creek to fish over the same species there.

With a little knowledge, you can meet and fish short-emergence species for a relatively long period by moving with the hatch—first upstream and then to another stream where the species appears later.

Summary for Rule 2: Emergence dates for many mayflies are predictable if you *select a good average date for a particular stream*. Always be prepared with other artificials in case the species you plan to fish is not emerging. And always remember: *emergence dates are only rough guides and never should be adhered to rigidly*.

3. Look for the hatch on a *good stream, river, or lake*. The opening story about the Green Drake is a good example of the importance of stream selection. Had I been on most other streams, I would not have found this species.

A good stream has varying characteristics to hold a large variety of species. It has fast, moderate, and slow stretches of water, and its bottom contains rocks, pebbles, and silt for a diversity of nymphal life. Some of our so-called trout streams are at best marginal for nymphs because they're polluted. Don't expect sizable hatches on questionable waters. Rather, when you plan to fish a hatch, try to be on a fertile, unpolluted stream. *Even a good stream doesn't contain all species*. Learn which waters contain which hatches, and record the information for future trips.

If you plan to fish one of the *Callibaetis* hatches prominent in the West after May, look for the hatch on slow-moving water or in a lake or pond. I've fished several small lakes near Kalispell, Montana, in July when the air was filled with these Speckle-Winged Duns. Look for these mayflies on dams, ponds, and lakes and on slow stretches of rivers.

I've had some fishermen tell me that using emergence dates to fish the hatches is futile. They were on a good stream at what they thought was the proper time and date, but they didn't see a specific insect appear. Remember: not all insects emerge on all streams. Remember too that hatches vary greatly in intensity from stream to stream, and even from stretch to stretch on the same stream.

Find out from other fishermen which mayflies and caddis flies prevail on your favorite streams. Then plan your trips to those streams for those hatches. After a couple of years of observation, you'll be aware of which waters contain which hatches.

When hatches occur in June, July, and August, a "good stream" is not only one that has a large variety of hatches but also one that is cool enough to encourage trout to surface feed during hot summer months. If a species occurs on your favorite stream but the water is too warm for trout, look for the species on a colder one. The experience with the Yellow Drake in Chapter 4 depicts this incident readily. What good is a tremendous hatch if water temperatures are too high to produce a good response?

Summary for Rule 3: *Select your stream carefully* for a specific mayfly and choose one with a variety of hatches.

4. Fish at the *proper time* for a specific hatch. You can be on an ideal stream at a good date expecting a common hatch and still not meet the mayfly. Why? Maybe it's the wrong time of day. If I had been on Penns Creek in the opening story at noon, I probably would not have experienced the enormous hatch of Green Drake duns that I saw at 8:00 P.M. If you look for a great hatch of Yellow Drakes at any time other than 8:00 P.M. to 9:30 P.M., you'll probably not see any, or at best only a few. Fish the Brule in Wisconsin on an early May morning, and you'll probably see few Hendricksons. If you're on Henry's Fork in late June at 5:00 P.M., you've probably missed the Western Green Drake for the day.

Figure 3. Rusty Gates on the Au Sable in Michigan—another good stream.

Because many fly-fishermen are creatures of habit, "proper time" may be difficult to heed. They're creatures of habit because they customarily fish the same time each day. One friend fishes only Saturday mornings, and another fishes only evenings. Although both are excellent fly-fishermen, they'll miss some of the good hatches throughout the season because of their fishing habits. To fish the hatches, you must be willing to alter your time to that of the hatch time of the species you wish to meet.

Let me cite an example. One early August evening several years ago, I appeared on Big Fishing Creek near Lock Haven. It's unusual to meet another fly-fisherman at that time of year, so when I saw one nearby, I approached him to find out how he was doing. He complained that most of the fly hatches had ended and that this would probably be his last time out this year. After about a half-hour's discussion, I asked him to fish one more time and to meet me next morning on the stream at 7:00 A.M.

That morning was preceded by a late-evening

thunderstorm, and when we met the next morning, the water was a bit discolored. By 7:30 A.M. we saw a few Blue Quills (*Paraleptophlebia guttata*) and Pale Olive Duns (*Tricorythodes attratus*) emerging. A half-hour later, emergence of the latter species was in full swing, and hundreds of spinners had already moved upstream, just above the surface.

It was now 8:30 A.M., and we hadn't yet cast a line. Soon female *Tricorythodes*, spent after laying their eggs, floated past us by the hundreds. Now several trout started feeding on the spent imagos. Jim quickly tied on one of the female spinner imitations, the Reverse Jenny Spinner, and cast three or four times to the nearest rising trout and caught it. Ten minutes later he hooked another, just as the fall subsided.

"I guess we can leave now," Jim said.

"No, let's wait another hour or so."

"Why? The spinners are gone and the trout have quit feeding."

"There should be another mayfly species hatch around 11:00 A.M.," I said.

We then moved upstream to a fast shallow riffle where I had seen a decent hatch of Blue-Winged Olives (*Drunella cornuta*) emerging the past couple of days, and we sat and chatted. Although this species normally appears from the end of May to early July, it continues in more limited numbers on Big Fishing Creek until September.

By 10:45 A.M., a few duns had appeared, and within fifteen minutes, a second major hatch had occurred. Only a couple of trout rose to take the escaping duns, however, since the subimagos of this species depart rapidly from the water's surface. Jim earlier had tied on a size 14 Blue-Winged Olive and now started casting. Another half-hour and the emergence dissipated but only after he had caught and released two more trout.

I state this story mainly to convey to you that the time of day is extremely important when fishing the hatches. Here was a good fly-fisherman who because he fished at inappropriate times in early August diminished his chances of success *by not fishing* over trout rising to a specific hatch.

Summary for Rule 4: *Fish the time of day a specific mayfly, stone fly, or caddis fly is most likely to emerge.* Remember that on cloudy days, evening hatches may occur during the day. Also with species like *Tricorythodes*, the time of the spinner fall varies with the type of weather. On hot, humid August days, the spinner fall might last only fifteen minutes and occur as early as 7:30 A.M. On cooler overcast days the fall might last for more than an hour and occur near 9:00 A.M. Tricos that appear in mid-September might not fall until after 11:00 A.M. Hendricksons on a warm day might appear as early as 8:00 A.M. or as late as 6:00 P.M.

Are these the only rules you need to fish the hatches? No; there are others, although they are not as important as the four just discussed. For instance, many mayflies emerge on fast, moderate, or slow stretches only. You should know this so that you can be at the proper place on a stream. And some duns rest longer before escaping than others.

Spinners also vary in their importance. Some females rarely fall to the surface, and others do so in great numbers. I have never seen a Great Red Spinner (*Stenonema vicarium*) fall to the surface of any Eastern or Midwestern stream or river. Anglers often confuse another closely related spinner (*Stenonema pudicum*) with the Great Red Spinner. *S. pudicum* does fall on occasion.

Don't forget that your favorite hatch might appear on one part of a stream or river and not another. I fished for two days one September looking for a Trico hatch on the main stem of the Au Sable. The third day I found a heavy one on the North Branch of the Au Sable.

You'll see some of the duns and spinners assigned a rating in the Emergence Chart. These numbers should help guide you to the more important species.

Do these four major rules of meeting and fishing the hatches really work? Can they aid you in catching more fish? The only way you'll know is by trying the method several times. Let's take a sample hatch and spinner fall and follow them through the four rules.

For our example for the East and Midwest, we'll select the Hendrickson (as the female dun is known) or the Red Quill (the male dun of *Ephemerella subvaria*). First and foremost, this species conforms with the requirements of Rule 1: it is *common* and *fishable*. You can find the Hendrickson on hundreds of streams and rivers in the East—the Beaverkill, Ausable, and Delaware in New York; the Battenkill in Vermont; the Brodhead, Pine, Upper Allegheny, and Caldwell Creeks in Pennsylvania. But the hatch also occurs on many Michigan rivers, including all of the Au Sable branches west to the Brule in Wisconsin. The Hendrickson is a very common species.

Let's also look at a hatch that emerges on Western rivers at the same time the Hendrickson appears in the East and Midwest. Those fortunate enough to meet and fish the Western March Brown on near-coastal rivers in Oregon will probably experience a memorable fishing event. The March Brown is extremely common in the Willamette River drainage area in central Oregon. It appears there for such an extensive time that meeting the hatch is usually no problem. We'll select the McKenzie River near Eugene, Oregon, as the river where we plan to fish the hatch. We'll select the same time, late April and early May, to meet the hatch on the McKenzie River.

Fish small streams or large rivers in early spring in the East and Midwest, and you're likely to encounter the Hendrickson hatch. Not only is it common on many trout waters, but it is fishable on most occasions (see Chapter 3). Since the species appears on many cool spring afternoons, many of the duns ride the water for long distances before taking flight. Trout seem to sense that this is the harbinger of things to come and eagerly devour duns, even in the chilly April waters. Another asset when meeting and fishing while this hatch appears is that it usually emerges in large numbers. Furthermore, the hatch can occur on any given day for an hour or more. The same can be said of the Western March Brown. It too appears in heavy numbers at about the same time of day as the Hendrickson.

Rule 2 suggests we select a good average *emergence date* for the Hendrickson and Western March Brown. Selecting a good emergence date for the Hendrickson is risky since the hatch appears on any selected stream for at most two to three weeks in late April and early May. Also, typical spring temperatures might delay or antedate the hatch.

I've seen Hendricksons appear on the Beaverkill as early as April 21 and as late as May 8 however, selecting a date as early as April 21 is hazardous. The Emergence Chart in Chapter 2 suggests April 23 as the average beginning emergence date. We'll opt for April 25 on the Loyalsock and April 28 on the Beaverkill, and May 1 on the Au Sable and Brule rivers. By selecting these later dates, the hatch might have appeared the past couple of days and trout might have become accustomed to the insect.

Since the Western March Brown begins appearing in late February, we can be certain that it should appear on April 28.

Rule 3 recommends that we look for the hatch on a *good stream*, *river*, or *lake*. Better than hoping the hatch occurs is to know ahead that it does appear on the stream you plan to fish. You might be able to discover this information ahead of time by quizzing local fishermen. The Hendrickson appears on many small, midsized, and large streams. For our examples, we'll select the Loyalsock Creek in north-central Pennsylvania, the Beaverkill in New York, the Au Sable near Grayling, Michigan, and the Bois Brule near Brule, Wisconsin. For the Western March Brown, we'll select the McKenzie River a few miles upriver from where it enters the Willamette at Eugene, Oregon.

Finally, Rule 4 suggests that you select an optimum *time of day* the species might appear April 25 to April 30. Although some Hendrickson and Western March Brown duns appear as early as 10:00 A.M. or 11:00 A.M., most appear from 2:00 to 4:00 P.M. To be prepared, we'll plan to be on the stream by noon at each location.

If you've followed all four rules, you should meet a hatch of *Ephemerella subvaria* and *Rhithrogena morrisoni*. More important, you'll be prepared with proper imitations to fish while the hatch occurs. Cold weather, rain, high murky water, and cloudy skies— any of these or a combination can alter the predicted emergence and create a problem. Remember too that unusually warm weather can dramatically change the time of the hatch.

You can meet spinner falls too. In fact, many spinner falls can be more productive than dun emergences. They can be more productive since imagos often mate and lay eggs in a short, concentrated period. However, females of many species drop their eggs from several feet above the water and are not accessible as food.

For our example we'll select the Trico (*Tricorythodes* species). Species of this genus are found from coast to coast on small streams and large rivers. Spinners fall every morning from mid-July until mid-September and even later on some rivers. Although these mayflies rarely exceed 4 mm (size 24), they fall in numbers heavy enough to bring trout to the surface. Therefore, the spinner is *common and fishable* and conforms to Rule 1.

We'll choose to meet the Trico spinner on August

Figure 4. The West Branch of the Delaware River above Hancock, New York. Although it has limited access, it is a fine example of a river with good hatches.

10 (Rule 2), on the McKenzie in Oregon, the South Platte in Colorado, the North Branch of the Au Sable in Michigan, and the Beaverkill in New York (Rule 3), and be on the stream or river at all locations by 7:00 A.M. (Rule 4). If all four variables go as planned, we'll be on the stream prepared to fish while a spinner fall occurs.

What about other species? Two suggestions should help you utilize the four rules to meet them. First, use the Insect Emergence Chart in Chapter 2 for three of the four rules (emergence date, common and fishable species, and emergence time). The third rule, selecting a good stream, is up to you. Second, keep a record of all insect activity on your favorite stream.

RECORDING THE HATCHES

Up to now we've discussed thoroughly the four rules for meeting and fishing the hatches. But what about some locally significant hatches that I have not listed? Furthermore, when do species listed here emerge in your locality? You can increase your knowledge immensely by keeping records of all fishing trips and the mayflies, caddis flies, and stone flies you encounter.

But immediately another question crops up: "How do I know what species is emerging?" If you feel the hatch is an important one, you might capture a male dun and attempt to identify it by using the procedure in Chapter 3 or, better, have it identified by an entomologist. If you can't do either, describe the coloration of the hatch and list a pattern that imitates it.

Keep records, logging every pertinent piece of information you feel is necessary so you can meet and fish the hatch annually.

Recording relevant information worked for me on a troublesome hatch I met several years ago. Five years ago I recorded a large *Hexagenia* species on the Cherry Run section of Penns Creek. I carefully noted all the information about this unusual spinner. This species is unusual because it appears late in the season and also because the spinner appears above the water at 6:15 P.M. and just as abruptly disappears at 6:45 P.M. I meticulously noted all necessary information in my diary on that first meeting night. Since I didn't capture any of the male imagos, I couldn't have the species identified.

Five years later I returned to the same spot on the same day, August 25, determined to snare some of the large male spinners if they appeared. I arrived at Johnson's Camp at 5:30 P.M. and scanned the air above the water for any large mayflies; no *Hexagenia* spinners had yet appeared. By 6:16 P.M.—and not much before—several dark-reddish-brown spinners appeared from their resting areas on giant oaks, high above the stream, and headed for the pool.

By 6:30 P.M. thousands of these huge spinners saturated the air, carrying out their predestined mating flight. I busily swung an insect net at some of the lower imagos, determined to capture several for positive identification. For what seemed like hours I was oblivious to signs of trout rising to the spent female spinners. However, trout must have fed on the spinners upstream because I heard gulping and splashing sounds most assuredly coming from rising fish. Finally, I caught several of the giant *Hexagenia* males and secured them in a killing solution. I looked at my watch. It was now 6:45 P.M., and only a dozen or so males remained in the air. All the females apparently had completed their reproductive cycle and died. The few remaining male spinners now headed toward trees on the far shore.

Here was a spinner I hadn't seen in five years—but because I had recorded the important information on its emergence when I first saw it, I was able to observe it again. More important, I saw the mating display five years later on the same day at the same time. By the way, the species has been identified as *Hexagenia atrocaudata*, and it can provide some great late-season fly-fishing on our larger streams.

Yes, meeting and fishing the hatches does work—and it can be even more successful if you keep a record of the hatches. To record pertinent information, I use a Keuffel and Esser Weatherproof Level Book. Orvis and other fine sporting goods stores stock other logs. Here's an example of a record for the Hendrickson and Western March Brown hatches we discussed:

Date	Time	Stream	Imitation	No. of fish caught
April 25	2 P.M.	Loyalsock	Hendrickson	5
May 1	2 P.M.	Au Sable	Hendrickson	8
May 1	2 P.M.	McKenzie	Western March Brown	15

Insects Seen	Water Temp.	Air Temp.	Weather
East—Loyalsock			
Ephemerella subvaria	52	60	Clear
Epeorus pleuralis			
Paraleptophlebia adoptiva			
Midwest—Au Sable			
Ephemerella subvaria	50	58	Clear
Paraleptophlebia adoptiva			
West—McKenzie			
Rhithrogena morrisoni	49	49	Drizzle

CHAPTER 2

INSECT EMERGENCE

Much of a trout's diet consists of three orders of insects: Ephemeroptera, or mayflies; Trichoptera, or caddis flies; and Plecoptera, or stone flies. The percentage of the three food sources varies considerably among the different species of trout. Paul Needham, in *Trout Streams*, indicates that brown trout appear to prefer mayflies (including nymphs and adults), whereas brook trout in the same stream prefer caddis flies. In studies, rainbow trout select mayflies slightly more than caddis flies. Needham's figures are:

	Mayflies: nymphs and Adults	Caddis Flies: larvae and Adults
Brook trout	19%	43%
Brown trout	79	9.5
Rainbow trout	37	19

We can see that mayflies make up a large portion of a trout's diet. Since trout eagerly take both nymph and adult, it's important to understand the life cycle of the average mayfly (Figure 1).

The female mayfly spinner, or mature mayfly (scientists call the spinner an imago), mates with the male spinner, usually over fast stretches of a stream and most often in the evening. The male appears over the stream first, waiting for the female spinner. After mating, the female deposits her fertilized eggs by one of three methods: (1) flying just above the surface, (2) sitting or dipping on the surface, or (3) diving underwater. After the egg laying is completed, many females fall onto the water, usually with wings spent (flat on the surface). Later in this chapter we rate many of the spinners according to their availability as a source of food for trout. This is an important

concept because when trout feed on natural spinners, they often take artificials imitating the dead imagos.

Nymphs hatch from the fertilized eggs in a couple of weeks. The nymph spends approximately a year (there are exceptions in the Family Ephemeridae) in slow, medium, or fast stretches on rocky or muddy bottoms; many species are specific in their habitat. After almost a year of growing and shedding its outer covering many times (instars), the nymph is ready to emerge.

After several false dashes, the nymph reaches the surface. Here it sheds its nymphal skin dorsally (a few do this on the bottom of the stream) and becomes a dun (often called a subimago). Many of these duns, including the Quill Gordon (*Epeorus pleuralis*), Yellow Drake (*Ephemera varia*), and Green Drake (*Ephemera guttulata*), have difficulty leaving the water and ride the surface for some distance before taking flight. These duns are especially important to imitate with dry-fly patterns.

When the dun finally becomes airborne, it usually heads for the nearest tree or a bush close to the stream. Duns emerging early in the season sometimes rest on sun-warmed rocks or debris next to the water to protect themselves from early-season freezes.

Although a few genera (*Tricorythodes, Caenis,* and *Ephoron*) change from dun to spinner in an hour or less, and a few never change (*Ephoron* female), in most genera the transformation requires one or two days. With a final molt, the dun shucks its outer covering and reappears over the water as a more brightly colored mayfly with clear, glassy wings. These spinners then meet and mate to complete the life cycle.

Thus, there are three stages of the mayfly on which trout can actively feed: the nymph, dun, and spinner. Trout discriminate little and take either male or

11

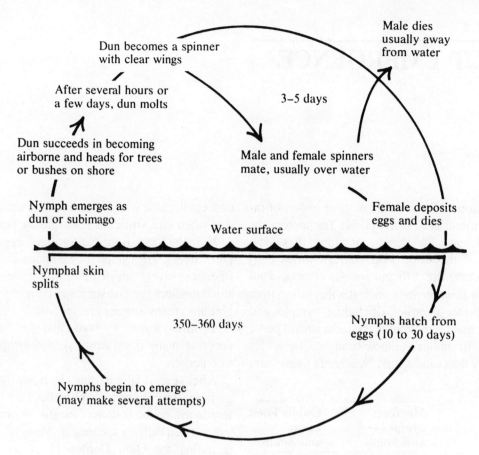

Dun becomes a spinner
with clear wings

After several hours or
a few days, dun molts

3–5 days

Male dies
usually away
from water

Dun succeeds in becoming
airborne and heads for trees
or bushes on shore

Nymph emerges as
dun or subimago

Male and female spinners
mate, usually over water

Water surface

Female deposits
eggs and dies

Nymphal skin
splits

350–360 days

Nymphs hatch from
eggs (10 to 30 days)

Nymphs begin to emerge
(may make several attempts)

Nymphs are either burrowing, rock clinging, or free-swimming
and feed on bottom for approximately a year

female nymph and dun. With the third phase, the spinner or imago, the female is devoured more often than the male. In many species, the female dies spent on the water after completing her egg-laying task. The male, conversely, often leaves the stream area after mating and frequently dies over land.

The longer the mayfly dun or spinner is on the water, the better are the chances for surface feeding by trout. This length of time on the water is critical for fishermen using floating imitations. With some mayflies—some of the *Heptagenia* species and the Big Slate Drake (*Hexagenia atrocaudata*), the dun escapes so rapidly that few trout feed on them. The Green Drake (*Ephemera guttulata*) and many other species are just the opposite: they take off sluggishly from the surface, often resting on the water for quite

some distance. These laggards are important to imitate with dry-fly artificials. (We'll discuss time spent on the water in more detail later in this chapter.)

The emergence of many duns is sporadic; that is, they do not appear in concentrated numbers, and few trout rise to the naturals. However, many spinners of these same sporadic species often fall in large enough numbers in a short period to create rises. Often the spinner falls of sporadic species are concentrated, occurring for an hour or less in the evening.

Fishing some hatches can be unpredictable; you might be late for the peak of the subimago by a couple of days. In these instances, being prepared with imitations of the spinner of the species can turn a frustrating experience into a successful one.

Two years ago, several of us met at Penns Creek

during the Green Drake hatch. As often happens with this species, we arrived a couple of days too late to experience a major emergence; only a few duns appeared that evening. However, around 8:30 P.M., Lloyd Williams pointed to thousands of white-bodied spinners moving toward the stream. By 9:00 P.M. there were literally thousands of spinners, slowly and methodically moving upstream, 10 to 15 feet above the surface. There were so many spinners on wing that we could actually hear a humming sound.

Within fifteen minutes after mating, spent females floated past us in enormous numbers. Scarcely a square inch of water was not covered with these dead spinners. I could hear trout gulping loudly, taking in two, three, even four naturals on each rise. It was difficult to catch these trout now because it was totally dark. Besides, how can a trout select your imitation in the midst of thousands of naturals in the same area?

This story is a good case in point: when fishing the hatches, have imitations handy of both dun and spinner. As with the dun, I rate the spinner according to its importance as a source of food later in this chapter.

Up to this point I have mentioned little about caddis flies. As streams become polluted, caddis flies take on added importance. This order might be able to withstand a greater degree of pollution than some other orders of aquatic insects, especially mayflies.

Unlike the mayfly, the caddis goes through a complete metamorphosis. It has a pupal stage that lasts a couple of weeks. After the male and female mate, the female dives underwater and deposits the eggs. Some species drop the fertilized eggs in flight like many mayflies, and others swim underwater to place them. The eggs develop in a few weeks, and the newly hatched larvae build cases to protect their fragile bodies. Unlike the mayfly nymph, which has a hard outer covering called an exoskeleton, the caddis larva has only a thin integument covering the greater part of the body. Only the legs and head of the larva are heavily protected (sclerotized), and these parts usually extrude from the case.

To construct a covering, the larva uses sand, pebbles, stone, sticks, or any number of other things found in a stream. Each genus is usually specific in selecting building materials. In some genera, however, the larva moves about freely and has no case. An example of the latter is the Green Caddis (*Rhyacophila lobifera*); imitations of this larva usually work well.

Most species, however, do build cases. The Grannom (*Brachycentrus fuliginosus*) builds its case of sticks and is usually found in backwater areas of streams. Another important caddis, the Dark Blue Sedge (*Psilotreta frontalis*), found most often in fast water, builds its case of sand and pebbles. Several genera like *Hydropsyche* and *Chimarrha* are called net spinners and build small, fibrous nets that serve to collect food.

As the larva feeds and grows, it adds to its case. About two weeks before it emerges as an adult, it goes into a pupal stage. When the adult develops, the case (in this stage called a cocoon) is almost completely closed except for a small hole, which allows some water to enter. After about two weeks, the pupa, encased in a protective membrane, swims to the surface. At the surface, it breaks the covering membrane and flies to the shore.

Adults usually live longer than mayfly adults—perhaps a week or more. Since emerging adults are capable of mating, no change occurs from dun to spinner as it does in mayflies. At the time of emergence and during the egg-laying process, trout seize emerging adults eagerly. Since the wings of the adult are folded back over the body in a tentlike fashion, the wings of imitations, wet or dry, should be shaped similarly. Wet-fly patterns imitating the emerging caddis perform exceptionally well during a hatch.

TERRESTRIALS

There are many insects that do not live in water but at some time are found near or on the water. Terrestrials, as these forms are called, can be especially plentiful on warm, blustery summer days. Beetles, ants, crickets, grasshoppers, two-winged flies, and leafhoppers take on added importance as a source of food during days such as these. Gusty winds sometimes transport terrestrials to strange aquatic environs.

The grasshopper and cricket are visitors to trout waters but usually only in limited numbers. Ants, however, especially the winged varieties, and beetles

Figure 5. Two effective terrestrials are the beetle (left) and the ant (right).

occasionally land on the surface in large enough numbers to produce a typical hatching situation. Imitations of ants and beetles are often difficult to follow on the water but can be extremely effective. Needham, in *Trout Streams*, indicated that beetles, ants, grasshoppers, and two-winged flies make up 85 percent of the total true terrestrial food (this does not include adult mayflies, caddis flies, or stone flies) taken by brook trout.

Ken Sink of Indiana recently asked me to tie him a dozen grasshopper imitations and gave me a copy of the pattern he wanted tied. The terrestrial had an olive yellow polypropylene body and yellow-dyed deer hair to imitate the wings, legs, and head. The deer hair on this pattern is tied on just like the Muddler Minnow. The finished pattern looks a lot like the Letort Hopper, without the wings. I dubbed this new pattern Ken's Hopper (after Ken Sink).

I tied a few of the hoppers for myself but didn't use them for more than a year—not until I traveled to the Arkansas River just below Buena Vista, Colorado. On a recent trip to Colorado, Ken Walters and Bob Newell of Denver suggested that I try this swift, treacherous river in central Colorado. Ken operates the Flyfisher Limited in Denver, and Bob is a skilled entomologist and especially knowledgeable on the Trico hatches in Colorado. Bob now lives in Anchorage, Alaska.

I selected an area of the Arkansas just above Brown's Canyon. I tried several standard patterns but had only meager success. In frustration, I selected one of the hopper patterns I had tied a year earlier. Wind gusts on this dangerous river reached 40 miles an hour that afternoon. There were extensive grasslands on either side of the river, and I saw many grasshoppers moving about on this mid-August day.

I greased the hopper with plenty of Gink, tied it onto a 15-foot leader, and began skittering it across the fast water. I gave the terrestrial a series of short jerks to imitate the natural on the water.

I extended the fly rod and took advantage of the gusting wind and long leader. On the second cast, a small brown trout, barely 10 inches long, hit the hopper. A couple of more casts with moving retrievals and another brown hit the terrestrial. This fighter measured over 15 inches long. Then several more casts, and another brown splashed at the pattern. After a couple of dozen casts, I greased the hopper with more Gink to keep it floating in this swift water.

During my three-hour trip to the Arkansas that afternoon, I didn't see one trout rise. But with action imparted to the hopper, I caught more than twenty brown trout on the Arkansas, some up to 3 pounds.

Another exciting pattern to copy terrestrials is the Poly Beetle (see tying instructions in Chapter 5). I first had an opportunity to test this new pattern on the sandy-bottomed Manistee River near Frederick, Michigan. Throughout the afternoon in late August, the Poly Beetle caught brook trout up to 12 inches long.

The Poly Beetle floats high, takes a lot of punishment, and presents an excellent beetlelike silhouette. All afternoon on the Manistee, the pattern caught trout.

Ants also make up a portion of the trout's diet, particularly around the end of August. This is the time when dark brown winged varieties are common on many streams. A few years ago I traveled to the Cherry Run section of Penns Creek on August 25 to meet and fish an exciting hatch of *Hexagenia atrocaudata*. When I arrived at the long, quiet pool, I saw thousands of winged ants on the water. The water temperature was about 73 degrees that late afternoon, and only four or five trout fed on the displaced terrestrials. I selected a dark brown winged imitation but caught only one small brown trout that afternoon. Ant imitations are often extremely difficult for the fisherman to detect on the water. Mike O'Brien adds a small piece of white poly to the top of the ant so it's more readily seen. Barry Beck adds a piece of orange poly to his patterns.

AQUATIC BEETLES

Usinger, in *Aquatic Insects of California*, indicated that there are 5,000 species of aquatic beetles (order Coleoptera). This number does not include the terrestrial beetles, which only occasionally wander onto the water. In this number we include only species that spend at least part of their life cycle under water. If aquatic beetles are so widespread, then it should make sense that they are underrated as a source of trout food.

The life cycle begins when the female deposits her eggs beneath the surface. The eggs hatch into larvae shortly. Most of these larvae have gill filaments and respire like mayfly nymphs. The next two stages, however, the pupa and adult, depend on atmospheric air for respiration. The pupa usually crawls out of the water but remains nearby for this resting stage.

Many adults spend their complete life cycle underwater, coming to the surface only to capture needed air under their wings. Other adults spend their final stage completely out of water.

Various stages of the beetle become available as potentially important sources of trout food; the larvae, the pupae, and the adults provide nourishment. Not much has been written about this order of insects and its significance to trout fishermen; more will probably be mentioned in the future. If you want to be innovative, here's an area where there's a need for some creative patterns. For example, we find *Psephenus* species larvae or "water pennies" in numbers on the undersides of rocks in many of the fertile limestone streams in central Pennsylvania. Bob Murphy first brought this unusual creature to my attention. He had caught several large trout on those streams, and their stomachs contained many of these larvae. His problem was to tie a good imitation of the larval stage. Since the larva is flat and round, it is difficult to tie with conventional methods. This example illustrates the diversity of possible imitations for aquatic beetles.

NOTES ABOUT THE INSECT EMERGENCE CHART (EASTERN)

The Insect Emergence Chart should be of special interest to you when attempting to meet and fish the hatches. Most of the species listed are mayflies, although there are a few stone flies and caddis flies. An explanation of the chart's column heads follows.

SCIENTIFIC AND COMMON NAMES

Most mayflies, stone flies, and caddis flies have common names that refer to the coloration of the insect. Some are named for their creators or for well-known fishermen. Still other common names have come intact from England. This last type of acquisition has created, along with incorrect nomenclature, a strange conglomeration of artificials. These artificials appropriately match species on English waters but do little for Americans on our streams. Even with this lack of consistency, however, most common names suggest a pattern for the emerging dun or spent spinner.

EMERGENCE DATE

Those dates listed in the chart are **approximate** beginning emergence dates for the duns in central Pennsylvania. Spinner falls usually occur one to three days after the dates listed for the duns. Remember that beginning emergence dates, even on the same stream, can vary from year to year by as much as two weeks. (*Caution:* The dates, times, and body colorations listed in the next few chapters can be extremely variable. Dates and times are provided only to suggest crude estimates to you.)

The map in Figure 2 suggests possible emergence dates for your area. The map is a very rough guide; it is not meant to be a scientific tool to follow rigidly. The lines used in the map correspond to degree-days. Each line represents a difference of approximately 500 degree-days per year. Degree-days are determined by taking average daily temperatures and, if that average is below 65, by accumulating that number for a 365-day span. It stands to reason that an area having more degree-days (colder) should have later hatches of a species.

To plot degree-days in your area obtain a copy of the U.S. Department of Commerce's state-by-state guide, "Decennial Census of the United States Climate—Heating Degree Day Normals," from your local Weather Bureau Office. The number of degree-days for central Pennsylvania (our zero point) is approximately 6,500 (or an average of 18 degrees per day per year). Most degree-days occur from November through April.

TIME OF DAY THE LARGEST HATCHES EMERGE (DUNS) OR FLIGHTS TAKE PLACE (SPINNERS)

All times listed are in daylight saving time. Time of day can vary considerably, especially on overcast days. Some species are specific in their emergence time, and others appear over a long period of time— that is, they are sporadic. Species like *Epeorus pleuralis* (Quill Gordon), *Ephemerella subvaria* (Hen-

drickson and Red Quill), and *Ephemera varia* (Yellow Drake) usually emerge for a short, consistent period. This short period is usually two hours or less and seldom varies in its beginning and ending time. But preface the Hendrickson hatch with a few unseasonably warm spring days and see what happens. After a series of warm days on central Pennsylvania's Bald Eagle, I've seen the Hendrickson appear as early as 9:00 A.M. The hatch had completely ended an hour later. On Michigan's Au Sable after a few warm days, I've seen Hendricksons and Red Quills appear after 5:00 P.M.

Other species, although they vary in timing, emerge in numbers large enough to be called a hatch (sometimes a large hatch). Examples are *Ephemera guttulata* (Green Drake), *Stenacron interpunctatum canadense* (Light Cahill) and *Stenonema fuscum* (Gray Fox), and many other species. The Light Cahill and Gray Fox might begin emerging at 3:00 P.M. or 4:00 P.M. in numbers and on another day may not appear until later. Some caddis flies too fall in this variable category. The Green Caddis (*Rhyacophila lobifera*) and Grannom (*Brachycentrus fuliginosus*) too can fluctuate in their appearance from day to day.

NYMPH IS FOUND IN FAST, MEDIUM, SLOW, OR ALL TYPES OF WATER

This column indicates in what part of the stream to find the emerging duns. If you're looking for a hatch of *Tricorythodes stygiatus*, don't go to a fast mountain stream. Conversely, if you're searching for the Gray Fox or American March Brown, don't fish a slow, meandering stream void of any fast stretches. It's important not only to plan the time of day and time of year but also to find a type of stream that provides suitable habitat for that species.

NYMPH BURROWS IN MUD, CLINGS TO ROCKS, OR SWIMS FREELY

This column is fairly self-explanatory. Some nymphs live on rocks (like those in the Family Heptageniidae), some burrow in mud, silt, gravel, or sand (most of those in the Family Ephemeridae), still others spend most of their nymphal life swimming about freely (the Family Baetidae). You might say at this point, "So

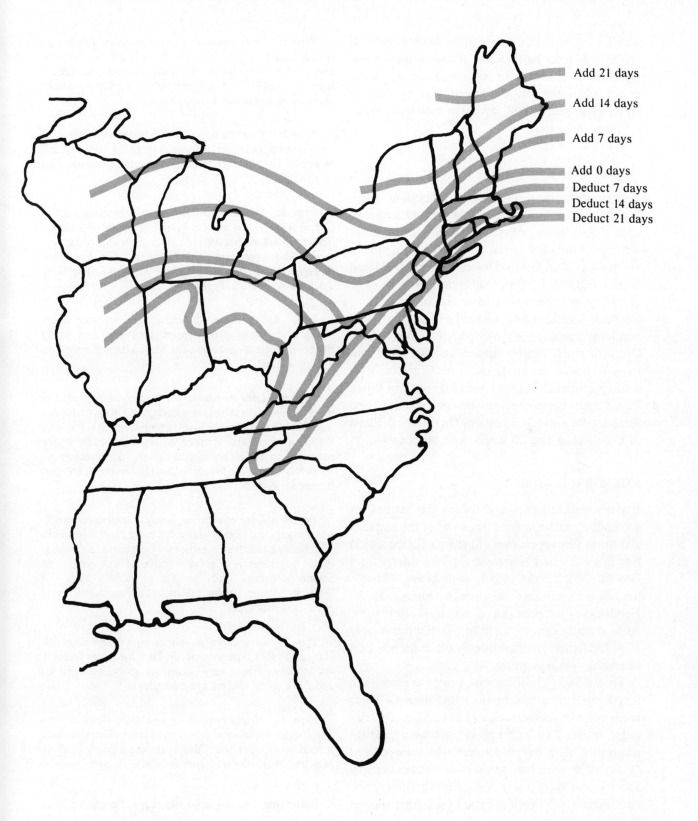

Add 21 days

Add 14 days

Add 7 days

Add 0 days
Deduct 7 days
Deduct 14 days
Deduct 21 days

what? How will this information help?" Well, if you're looking for the Green or Yellow Drake (Family Ephemeridae), search for water that contains some gravel on its bottom. If you're trying to locate a *Stenonema* species, look for fast or moderate, rocky stretches of a stream.

HOOK SIZE

Size of imitations can be very important when duplicating mayflies. It's always a good idea to have several sizes of an imitation available since size of naturals of the same species may vary from stream to stream. The Green Drake, American March Brown, and Pale Evening Dun appear to vary in size according to the fertility and/or size of the stream. On Penns Creek, the Green Drake is usually 18–22 mm long, whereas the same species on White Deer Creek, a much smaller stream, is only 16–18 mm long. To imitate the Drake on Penns Creek calls for a size 8 artificial; a size 10 would do well on White Deer Creek. On most rivers you can copy the Trico spinner with a size 24 imitation. On the South Platte in Colorado, a size 20 works well on occasion.

EMERGENCE TYPE

If you've been meeting and fishing the hatches for some time, you've noticed that some of the mayflies and caddis flies appear over a longer part of the season than others. Some *Tricorythodes* species emerge from late July until mid-October, with heavy, fishable hatches each morning they appear. Others, like the Hendrickson, appear for a much shorter time; heaviest hatches emerge from late April through early May, and fishable hatches usually occur for less than two weeks on any stream.

The following classifications, geared to emergence length, are very arbitrary, since one stream's major hatch might be another's minor hatch. Also, a species might emerge for a longer period on one stream than on another. Many marginal waters, which are polluted to varying degrees, have sparse or no hatches of many species. Although there are great variations, the emergence types might aid you in selecting species to meet and fish.

Type 1: *Short duration, heavy emergence.* Emergence occurs usually at a highly specific time for two weeks or less on the same stream. Each day this type appears, it does so usually in large numbers. The Brown Drake (*Ephemera simulans*) fits this type.

Type 2: *Short duration, sparse emergence.* These insects never appear plentiful and emerge for only a couple of weeks. The stone fly *Isoperla signata* (Light Stone Fly) is an example.

Type 3: *Medium duration, heavy emergence for two to four weeks, then a short period of sparse emergence.* These individuals emerge in heavy numbers for two to four weeks. This is preceded and followed by a period of sparse emergence, which lasts a couple of weeks. The Hendrickson represents Type 3.

Type 4: *Medium duration, sparse emergence throughout.* These insects appear for two to four weeks but never in great numbers. The March Brown represents a Type 4 emerger.

Type 5: *Long duration, heavy emergence for four or more weeks, then a sparse emergence for several additional weeks.* Emergence in this group is heaviest for more than four weeks and is preceded and followed by a long period of sparse emergence. Sulphurs like *Ephemerella rotunda* and the Pale Morning Dun (*Ephemerella inermis*) belong to Type 5.

Type 6: *Long emergence, heavy emergence throughout.* Emergence occurs daily for more than five weeks with heavy hatches on almost every appearance. *Tricorythodes stygiatus* is a good example of this type, with hatches occurring daily for six or more weeks. The Western March Brown (*Rhithrogena morrisoni*) also represents this type.

Type 7: *Long duration, sparse emergence throughout.* Hatches of this type may occur daily for many weeks— six or more—but in very limited numbers. Some *Baetis* and *Callibaetis* species are examples.

Type 8: *Heavy hatches two or more times a year.* Some species like some *Baetis* and *Pseudocloeon* produce several broods per year. You might see a heavy hatch in May and then another hatch in late September.

Following are some of the ways the emergence-type classification can be used:

Easiest category to meet: Type 6.

Most important groups to imitate: Types 1, 3, 5, 6, and 8.

Most difficult type to predict accurately: Types 1 and 2

Least important categories to imitate: Types 2, 4, and 7.

SPORADIC AND CONCENTRATED

Some species appear in a short, concentrated hatch. Others may emerge throughout the day (or evening) and not at any predictable time: they are sporadic. The most important duns to imitate (if their rating is low) are those that appear at a concentrated, scheduled time.

Immediately following the type number of each dun is the letter *S* (sporadic), *C* (concentrated), or *S&C* (sporadic and concentrated). The last designation indicates that the dun sometimes appears sporadically and other times as a concentrated hatch.

RATING

Duns and spinners are rated from 1 to 10. Duns are rated depending on their characteristic takeoff from the water's surface. Species with a rating from 1 to 5 are important to imitate in the dun or subimago stage. Those with a rating of 6 to 10 are less important, since they rarely, if ever, pause on the surface before taking flight. Although the duns of a species might be of questionable importance, the spinner or imago stage of the same species might be rated lower and therefore be important to copy. Species toward the high end of this subjective scale might better be matched by nymphs than by dry flies.

This rating system is subjective because it's based on my own observations and not on any concise scientific study.

Spinners are also rated from 1 to 10 but by different criteria. Although emergence of a species (dun) may be sporadic and appear in small numbers throughout the day, the spinner fall can be concentrated into an hour or two, most often in the evening. After the female mates with the male, it typically deposits its eggs in one of several methods. Many species of a genus deposit eggs in the same manner.

Following are some of the methods by which females deposit eggs:

1. Female intermittently lands on the surface for a couple of seconds, extrudes some eggs, takes off, then repeats the process (some *Stenonema* species, *Heptagenia* species, and *Epeorus* species).

2. Female intermittently dips or touches the surface and immediately takes off (*Leptophlebia* species, some *Stenonema* species, and some *Epeorus* species).

3. Female carries an egg sac and drops it from just above or on the surface (some *Stenonema* species, some *Tricorythodes* species, and *Ephemerella* species).

4. Female usually rides the surface until all eggs are extruded (*Ephemera* and *Hexagenia* species).

5. Female dives beneath the surface to deposit eggs (*Baetis* species).

6. Female drops eggs from several feet above the water (*Paraleptophlebia* species and *Isonychia* species).

As with the dun, the importance of the spinner varies greatly from species to species. Probably the main group to imitate, according to their method of depositing eggs, is category 4. Least significant are those species that drop their eggs several feet above the water, category 6 (still, many of these females find their way to the water's surface).

I have rated spinners too according to their importance as a source of food for trout. This rating is based on some extent on their method of depositing eggs. Again, those rated from 1 to 5 are the most important species to imitate.

Although two species deposit eggs in the same manner, they may be rated differently. Females of one species might die spent on the surface, whereas females of another species might die over land. Furthermore, *Heptagenia marginalis* will never be as important as *Stenonema fuscum* because the latter usually falls in enormous numbers, whereas the former does so in restricted numbers.

Most caddis flies escape rather rapidly from the surface. Adult stone flies too are often not readily available to surface-feeding trout since they emerge on rocks, emergent logs, bridge abutments, and so on. Therefore, I have rated few of these aquatic orders in the Insect Emergence Chart. When many of these insects return for their egg-laying phase, however, they can be important to meet.

NOTES ABOUT THE INSECT EMERGENCE CHART (WESTERN)

If emergence dates can vary by two, three, and even four weeks in the East and Midwest, the dates listed for Western species can be off by five or more weeks. *Emergence dates for Western species are only crude guides and should never be adhered to rigidly.* Because of water-temperature differences, a species might have completed its annual hatch on a relatively warm Western stream, whereas on a colder river, the hatch might not occur for another month. Moreover, these two streams might be only a few air miles apart. The Upper Madison River and the Gallatin River are excellent examples of this latter diversity.

You'll note in the Emergence Chart (Western) that I've included temperature and elevation ranges for most of the Western species. These ranges, as well as the emergence dates and times, are very crude. However, all variables do aid fishermen in meeting and fishing the hatches by helping them pinpoint streams, locations, and approximate days and times for many species.

Most of the column heads are similar to those in the Emergence Chart (Eastern and Midwestern). Those that are different or require further explanation are discussed below. Emergence types are not listed at all because of the extreme variability of many Western hatches.

EMERGENCE DATE

Emergence dates listed for Western species are usually the earliest dates that hatches of a given species appear. In several cases where I have not determined the beginning date, I indicate this in a footnote. A few hatches begin before the dates listed in the chart (in addition to those listed with an asterisk).

The West has many exceptions. A mayfly species may appear on coastal or near-coastal waters in April or May, whereas on Rocky Mountain waters the same species might emerge in June or July. The Western Green Drake appears on the McKenzie and Metolius rivers as early as May. On Henry's Fork in Idaho, the same species appears toward the end of June.

Look at the variation in emergence dates for the Brown Drake (*Ephemera simulans*) from East to West. This is one of a handful of species found in all three regions of the United States. In the East, the Drake appears near the end of May. On Michigan and Wisconsin rivers, this same hatch emerges the first two weeks in June. On Henry's Fork in Idaho, the Brown Drake often emerges at the end of June or early July.

Most hatches continue to appear well past the date listed in the chart. The Gray Drake (*Siphlonurus occidentalis*) and Gray Fox (*Heptagenia solitaria*) are excellent examples. The Gray Drake begins its annual emergence around July 5 (although a few emerge before that date), but the majority don't appear until early August. Another example is the Gray Fox. I have suggested a beginning date as July 5; however, hatches of this species may occur as late as early September on some rivers. Moreover, the hatches and spinner falls encountered of *Heptagenia solitaria* are extremely heavy in late summer.

APPROXIMATE ELEVATION

The elevation of a stream has an effect on which species it contains. Much of the basic information on elevation, and for that matter water temperature also, has been adapted from Steven Jensen's *The Mayflies of Idaho* and modified from my personal observations. As with emergence dates, elevation ranges listed in the chart are imperfect and will be modified with further observations.

Following is a breakdown of the elevation ranges:

High (H): Mayfly species is often found on streams with elevations of more than 7,000 feet.
Moderate (M): Mayfly species is often found on streams with elevations ranging from 4,000 to 7,000 feet.
Low (L): Mayfly species is often found on streams with an altitude lower than 4,000 feet.
All (A): Mayfly species is often found on streams at all elevations.

Although I have listed a species as one that appears on streams at high elevations, the species could well appear on streams at moderate elevations—and it might emerge on streams at all elevations. Remember too that some Western rivers range in elevation from high (above 7,000) in their upper reaches to low (lower than 4,000) in their lower sections. The Yellowstone River is a good example.

APPROXIMATE WATER TEMPERATURE

Water temperature also affects which streams a species inhabits and when this species will emerge (emergence date). Again, the temperature ranges for species listed in the chart will be modified with future observations.

"Water temperatures" refers to temperatures at the time a species emerges. Water temperatures rise above or fall below those listed on the river that a particular species inhabits.

Following is a breakdown of the water temperature ranges for the various mayfly species:

Warm (W): Mayfly species often emerges in water at temperatures higher than 65 degrees.
Moderate (M): Mayfly species often emerges in water at temperatures between 55 and 65 degrees.
Cold (C): Mayfly species often emerges in water at temperatures lower than 55 degrees.

Nothing is sacred about the elevation or temperature ranges used. Many species emerge in two ranges of temperature and two elevation classifications. Species that do emerge in a wide range of elevations and water temperatures are usually among the more common species.

Look at *Ephemerella inermis* as an example of a very common species. The Pale Morning Dun inhabits streams at all (A) elevations with water temperatures below 65 degrees (C&M). On almost every occasion I have fished Western waters after mid-June, I have fished while a hatch, though sometimes sparse, emerged. I have encountered this mayfly on Clark Fork below Missoula (elevation, 2,900 feet; water temperature, 57 degrees); on the Bitterroot (elevation, 3,400 feet; water temperature, 54 degrees); and on Henry's Fork (elevation, 6,100 feet; water temperature, 60 degrees). Of course, we take for granted that we're on the stream from late morning until early evening in late June or July (possibly earlier and later).

RATING

Rating the value of duns and spinners is even more subjective with Western species than it is with Eastern and Midwestern species. Again, using *Ephemerella inermis* as an example, the dun of this species would have a rating of 2 on the Railroad Ranch of Henry's Fork; on the Bitterroot, the same species has a rating of 3.

If I have observed a species in only limited numbers or not at all, I have not attempted to suggest a numerical rating for the species. In those cases the space is left blank.

INSECT EMERGENCE CHART (Eastern and Midwestern)

Scientific and Common Name M = Mayfly C = Caddis fly S = Stone fly	Emergence Date (dates are only rough guides and should not be followed rigidly)	Time of Day Largest Hatches Occur (Duns) or Flights Take Place (Spinners)
Capnia vernalis (S) Little Black Stone fly	March 1	Morning and afternoon

Baetis tricaudatus (vagans) (M)
  Dun: Little Blue-Winged Olive Dun
  Spinner: Rusty Spinner
	April 1	10:00 A.M.–6:00 P.M.

Strophopteryx fasciata (S)
  Early Brown
  Stone fly
	April 10	Afternoon

Paraleptophlebia adoptiva (M)
  Dun: Dark Blue Quill
  Spinner: Dark Brown Spinner
	April 15	11:00 A.M.–4:00 P.M.
		Heaviest: 2:00–4:00 P.M.
		Spinner: 4:00–7:00 P.M.

Epeorus pleuralis (M)
  Dun: Quill Gordon
  Spinner: Red Quill Spinner
	April 18	1:00–3:00 P.M.
		Spinner: 11:30 A.M.–2:00 P.M.

Siphloplecton basale (M)
  Dun: Great Speckled Olive Dun
  Spinner: Great Speckled Spinner
	April 18	1:30 P.M.

Brachycentrus numerosus (C) Grannom	April 23	Morning and afternoon

Ephemerella subvaria (M)
  Male dun: Red Quill
  Female dun: Hendrickson
  Spinner: Red Quill
	April 23	2:00–4:00 P.M.
		Spinner: 3:00–8:00 P.M.

Leptophlebia cupida (M)
  Dun: Black Quill
  Spinner: Early Brown Spinner
	April 25	2:00–4:00 P.M.
		Spinner: 1:00–6:00 P.M.

Chimarrha atterima (C) Little Black Caddis	April 26	11:00 A.M.–6:00 P.M.
Psilotreta species (C) Tan Caddis	April 26	Morning and afternoon
Isoperla signata (S) Light Stone fly	May 8	Afternoon

Ephemerella rotunda (M)
  Dun: Pale Evening Dun
  Spinner: Pale Evening Spinner
	May 10	2:00–8:00 P.M.
		Spinner: 6:00–8:00 P.M.

Pseudocloeon species (M)
  Dun: Blue Dun
  Spinner: Rusty Spinner
	May 10	Afternoon and evening

Nymph/Larva Found in Fast (F), Medium (M), Slow (S), or All (A) Types of Water	Nymph Burrows in Silt or Gravel (M), Clings to Rocks (R),[21] Swims Freely (F), Lives in Vegetation (V), or Detritus (D)	Hook Size	Emergence Type: Sporadic (S) or Concentrated (C)	Rating Dun	Spinner	Species Found in East (E) or Midwest (M)
F	R	18	1 (C)	2		E&M[22]
A	F	16–20	3 (S&C)	3	5	E&M
F	R	14	4 (S&C)			E&M
A	F	18	1 (C)	1	4	E&M
F	R	14	1 (C)	2	8	E
S&M	V	10 or 12	1 (C)	3	7	E&M
		14	1 (C)	2		E&M
A	R	12–16	3 (C)	2	4	E&M
S	F	12 or 14	4 (S)	6	4	E&M
F	R	16	1 (C)			E&M
F		14	1 (C)			E
F	R	12 or 14	4 (S)			E
A	R	14 or 16	5 (C)	2	3	E&M
S&M	F	20	5 (S&C)	2	7	E&M

Scientific and Common Name M = Mayfly C = Caddis fly S = Stone fly	Emergence Date (dates are only rough guides and should not be followed rigidly)	Time of Day Largest Hatches Occur (Duns) or Flights Take Place (Spinners)
Rhyacophila lobifera (C) Green Caddis	May 10	4:00–9:00 P.M.; caddis fly appears later (around dusk) in June and July
Baetis flavistriga (phoebus) (M) Dun: Little Blue-Winged Olive Dun Spinner: Rusty Spinner	May 10	Morning
Brachycentrus fuliginosus (C) Grannom	May 10[1]	Evening 3:00–7:00 P.M.
Stenonema fuscum (M) Dun: Gray Fox Spinner: Ginger Quill Spinner	May 15	Dun emerges sporadically throughout chance of heaviest hatches 4:00–8:30 P.M. Spinner: 7:00–8:30 P.M.
Baetis quebecensis (M) Dun: Little Blue-Winged Olive Dun Spinner: Rusty Spinner	May 15	Morning Evening
Ephemerella septentrionalis (M) Dun: Pale Evening Dun Spinner: Pale Evening Dun (3)	May 18[1]	8:00 P.M.
Heptagenia aphrodite (M) Dun: Pale Evening Dun Spinner: Pale Evening Dun[2]	May 18[1]	8:00 P.M.
Ephemerella invaria (M) Dun: Pale Evening Dun Spinner: Pale Evening Spinner	May 20[1]	3:00–8:00 P.M. Spinner: 7:00–8:30 P.M.
Stenonema vicarium (M) Dun: American March Brown Spinner: Great Red Spinner	May 20	10:00 A.M.–7:00 P.M. Spinner: 8:00 P.M.
Symphitopsyche slossanae (C) Spotted Sedge	May 23	1:00–6:00 P.M.
Eurylophella (Ephemerella) bicolor (M) Dun: Chocolate Dun Spinner: Chocolate Spinner	May 25	Late morning and early afternoon Spinner: Evening
Stenonema modestum (M) Dun: Cream Cahill Spinner: Cream Cahill Spinner	May 25	Evening
Siphlonurus quebecensis (M) Dun: Gray Drake Spinner: Brown Quill Spinner	May 25	Evening
Stenonema ithaca (M) Dun: Light Cahill Spinner: Light Cahill	May 25	Evening

Nymph/Larva Found in Fast (F), Medium (M), Slow (S), or All (A) Types of Water	Nymph Burrows in Silt or Gravel (M), Clings to Rocks (R)[21] Swims Freely (F), Lives in Vegetation (V), or Detritus (D)	Hook Size	Emergence Type: Sporadic (S) or Concentrated (C)	Rating Dun	Spinner	Species Found in East (E) or Midwest (M)
F	F	14	5 (S&C)			E&M
All	F	20	3 (S)	3	7	M
F		12	1 (C)			E&M[22]
F&M	R	12	3 (S&C)	4	2	E&M
All	F	20	5 (S&C)	3	7	E&M
F&M	F	14 or 16	1(C)	5	7	E
F	R	16	1 (C)	5	7	E
A	R	16 or 18	5 (S&C)	3	5	E&M
F&M	R	12	3 (S)	3	9	E&M
F	R	14 or 16	1 (C)			E&M
F&M	A	16	3 (S&C)	4	4	E&M
F&M	R	14 or 16	7 (S)	5	4	E
M	F	14	1 (S&C)	4	7	E&M
F	R	12 or 14	3 (S&C)	4	6	E

Scientific and Common Name M = Mayfly C = Caddis fly S = Stone fly	Emergence Date (dates are only rough guides and should not be followed rigidly)	Time of Day Largest Hatches Occur (Duns) or Flights Take Place (Spinners)
Isonychia sadleri (M) Dun: Slate Drake Spinner: White-Gloved Howdy	May 25	Evening
Epeorus vitreus (M) Male Dun: Light Cahill Female Dun: Pink Cahill Spinner: Salmon Spinner	May 25	Evening
Stenacron interpunctatum (M) Dun: Light Cahill Spinner: Light Cahill	May 25	Evening
Stenacron interpunctatum canadense [4] (M) Dun: Light Cahill Spinner: Light Cahill [3]	May 25	Sporadic during day but mainly 6:00–8:30 P.M. Spinner: 7:00–9:00 P.M.
Litobrancha recurvata [4] (M) Dun: Dark Green Drake Spinner: Brown Drake	May 25	1:00–8:00 P.M. Spinner: 7:00 P.M.
Ephemera simulans (M) Dun: Brown Drake Spinner: Brown Drake	May 25	8:00 P.M.
Ephemera guttulata (M) Dun: Green Drake Spinner: Coffin Fly	May 25	8:00 P.M.
Stenonema modestum (M) Dun: Cream Cahill Spinner: Cream Cahill Spinner	May 25	Evening
Drunella (Ephemerella) cornuta (M) Dun: Blue-Winged Olive Dun Spinner: Dark Olive Spinner	May 25 [1]	Sporadic during day Morning with a possible spurt at 11:00–noon Spinner: 7:00–9:00 P.M.
Isonychia bicolor (M) Dun: Slate Drake Spinner: White-Gloved Howdy	May 30	Sporadic, but mainly 7:00 P.M. Spinner: 8:00 P.M.
Ephemerella needhami (M) Dun: Chocolate Dun Spinner: Chocolate Spinner	May 30 [1]	Afternoon (early) and morning (late) Spinner: afternoon and evening
Ephemerella dorothea (M) Dun: Pale Evening Dun Spinner: Pale Evening Dun	June 1 [1]	8:00 P.M.
Serratella (Ephemerella) deficiens (M) Dun: Dark Blue Quill Spinner: Dark Brown Spinner	June 1	Evening

Nymph/Larva Found in Fast (F), Medium (M), Slow (S), or All (A) Types of Water	Nymph Burrows in Silt or Gravel (M), Clings to Rocks (R),[1] Swims Freely (F), Lives in Vegetation (V), or Detritus (D)	Hook Size	Emergence Type: Sporadic (S) or Concentrated (C)	Rating Dun Spinner		Species Found in East (E) or Midwest (M)
M&F	F	12	5 (S&C)	5	5	E&M
M&F	R	14	4 (S)	4	7	E&M
M&F	R	14	3 (S&C)	4	6	E&M
F&M	R	12 or 14	3 (S&C)	3	4	E&M
S	M	8 or 10	4 (S&C)	4	5	E&M
S&M	M	10 or 12	1 (C)	3	2	E&M
A	M	8 or 10	1 (C)	1	1	E
F&M	R	14 or 16	7 (S)	5	4	E
A	F	14	1 (C&S)	3	5	E
F	F	12	5 (C&S)	5	5	E&M
A	V	14 or 16	1 (S&C)	4	5	E&M
A	F	16 or 18	5 (C)	3	3	E&M
S&M	F	20	4 (C)	5	7	E&M

Scientific and Common Name M = Mayfly C = Caddis fly S = Stone fly	Emergence Date (dates are only rough guides and should not be followed rigidly)	Time of Day Largest Hatches Occur (Duns) or Flights Take Place (Spinners)
Paraleptophlebia mollis (M) Dun: Dark Blue Quill Male spinner: Jenny Spinner Female spinner: Dark Brown Spinner	June 3[1]	10:00 A.M.–4:00 P.M.
Hexagenia limbata (M) Dun: Great Olive-Winged Drake Spinner: Great Olive-Winged Spinner	June 5	Dusk to dark
Paraleptophlebia strigula (M) Dun: Dark Blue Quill Male spinner: Jenny Spinner Female spinner: Dark Brown Spinner	June 5	Early morning to mid-afternoon
Attenella (Ephemerella) attenuata (M) Dun: Blue-Winged Olive Dun Spinner: Dark Olive Spinner	June 5[1]	Sporadic during day often with a heavy burst at 11:00 A.M.
Isoperla bilineata (S) Yellow Stone fly	June 5	Morning and afternoon
Alloperla imbecilla (S) Little Green Stone fly	June 5	Morning and afternoon
Psilotreta frontalis (C) Dark Blue Sedge	June 8	8:00 P.M.
Leptophlebia johnsoni (M) Dun: Iron Blue Dun Male spinner: Jenny Spinner Female spinner: Blue Quill Spinner	June 9[1]	11:00 A.M. Spinner: Evening
Drunella (Ephemerella) lata (M) Dun: Blue-Winged Olive Dun Spinner: Dark Olive Spinner	June 12	Morning and afternoon
Serratella (Ephemerella) simplex (M) Dun: Blue-Winged Olive Dun Spinner: Dark Olive Spinner	June 15	Morning (sometimes afternoon) Spinner: Evening
Baetis brunneicolor (M) Dun: Little Blue-Winged Olive Dun Spinner: Rusty Spinner	June 15[24]	Morning and afternoon Spinner: evening
Stenacron interpunctatum heterotarsale (M) Dun: Light Cahill Spinner: Light Cahill	June 15[1]	Evening
Heptagenia marginalis (M) Dun: Light Cahill Spinner: Olive Cahill Spinner	June 15[2]	8:00 P.M.

Nymph/Larva Found in Fast (F), Medium (M), Slow (S), or All (A) Types of Water	Nymph Burrows in Silt or Gravel (M), Clings to Rocks (R),[1] Swims Freely (F), Lives in Vegetation (V), or Detritus (D)	Hook Size	Emergence Type: Sporadic (S) or Concentrated (C)	Rating Dun	Spinner	Species Found in East (E) or Midwest (M)
A	F	18	3 (C)	2	7	E&M
S	M	8	1 (C)	2	2	M
A	F	18 or 20	3 (S&C)	3	5	E
A	F	14 or 16	3 (S&C)	5	7	E
F&M	R	14	3 (S)			E
F&M	R	16	3 (C&S)			E&M
F		12	1 (C)			E&M
A	F	14 or 16	3 (C)	5	8	E
A	F	16	3 (C&S)	3	2	E&M
A	V	20	3 (C)	2	2	E&M
A	F	18 or 20	3 (C&S)	3	7	M
M&F	R	14	7 (S&C)	4	4	M
F&M	R	12	7 (S)	9	3	E

Scientific and Common Name M = Mayfly C = Caddis fly S = Stone fly	Emergence Date (dates are only rough guides and should not be followed rigidly)	Time of Day Largest Hatches Occur (Duns) or Flights Take Place (Spinners)
Stenonema pulchellum (M) Dun: Cream Cahill Spinner: Cream Cahill Spinner	June 15[2]	Sporadic, from midday to evening Spinner: evening
Siphlonurus alternatus (M) Dun: Gray Drake Spinner: Brown Quill Spinner	June 15	Morning and afternoon
Ephemera varia (M) Dun: Yellow Drake Spinner: Yellow Drake	June 22[2]	8:00–9:15 P.M.
Heptagenia hebe (M) Dun: Pale Evening Dun Spinner: Pale Evening Dun	June 22[1,2]	8:00 P.M.
Paraleptophlebia guttata (M) Dun: Dark Blue Quill Male spinner: Jenny Spinner Female spinner: Dark Brown Spinner	June 25[1,2]	Sporadic during day Spinner: morning and afternoon
Potamanthus distinctus (M) Dun: Golden Drake Spinner: Golden Spinner	June 25	9:00 P.M.
Tricorythodes stygiatus (M) Dun: Pale Olive Dun Female spinner: Reverse Jenny Spinner or Trico Spinner Male spinner: Dark Brown Spinner	July 15[2]	7:00–9:00 A.M. Spinner: 8:00–11:00 A.M.
Tricorythodes attratus (M) Dun: Pale Olive Dun Male spinner: Dark Brown Spinner Female spinner: Reverse Jenny Spinner or Trico Spinner	July 15[2]	7:00–9:00 A.M. Spinner: 8:00 A.M.
Caenis species (M) Dun: Little White Mayfly Spinner: Little White Spinner	July 15	Evening
Isonychia harperi (M) Dun: Slate Drake Spinner: White-Gloved Howdy	July 20[1,2]	Sporadic during day, but mainly 7:00 P.M.
Baetis pygmaeus (M) Dun: Little Blue-Winged Olive Dun Spinner: Rusty Spinner	August 1	Morning and afternoon

Nymph/Larva Found in Fast (F), Medium (M), Slow (S), or All (A) Types of Water	Nymph Burrows in Silt or Gravel (M), Clings to Rocks (R)?[1] Swims Freely (F), Lives in Vegetation (V), or Detritus (D)	Hook Size	Emergence Type: Sporadic (S) or Concentrated (C)	Rating Dun	Spinner	Species Found in East (E) or Midwest (M)
F&M	R	12 or	7 (S)	6	4	E&M
S&M	F	10	3 (S)	2	4	M
S	M	10 or 12	5 (C)	3	5	E&M
A	R	16	6 (C)	9	5	E&M
A	F	18	5 (C)	4	8	E
S&M	M	12	3 (C)	4	5	E
S	F	24	6 (C)	3	1	E&M
S	F	24	6 (C)	3	1	E
S	D	26	5 (C)	4	6	E&M
F	F	12	5 (S&C)	5	8	E&M
A	F	22	3 (C&S)	3	7	M

Scientific and Common Name M = Mayfly C = Caddis fly S = Stone fly	Emergence Date (dates are only rough guides and should not be followed rigidly)	Time of Day Largest Hatches Occur (Duns) or Flights Take Place (Spinners)

Ephoron leukon (M)
    Dun: White Mayfly
    Spinner: White Mayfly
	August 15	7:00 P.M.

Ephoron album (M)
    Dun: White Mayfly
    Spinner: White Mayfly
	August 15	Evening

Hexagenia atrocaudata (M)
    Dun: Big Slate Drake
    Spinner: Dark Rusty Spinner
	August 18	8:00 P.M.
		Spinner: 6:00–7:00 P.M.

Nymph/Larva Found in Fast (F), Medium (M), Slow (S), or All (A) Types of Water	Nymph Burrows in Silt or Gravel (M), Clings to Rocks (R),[21] Swims Freely (F), Lives in Vegetation (V), or Detritus (D)	Hook Size	Emergence Type: Sporadic (S) or Concentrated (C)	Rating Dun	Spinner	Species Found in East (E) or Midwest (M)
S&M	M	12–16	3 (C)	5	2	E&M
S	M	12	3 (C)	4	3	M
S	M	6 or 8	3 (S&C)	9	5	E&M

INSECT EMERGENCE CHART (Western)

Scientific and Common Name M = Mayfly C = Caddis fly S = Stone fly	Emergence Date (dates are extremely variable)	Time of Day Largest Hatches Emerge (Duns) or Flights Take Place (Spinners)

Rhithrogena morrisoni (M)
   Dun: Western March Brown
   Spinner: Western March Brown
	February 25[4]	Afternoon

Baetis tricaudatus (M)
   Dun: Little Blue-Winged Olive Dun[2]
   Spinner: Light Rusty Spinner
	April–October	Morning and afternoon[1]
		Spinner: early morning and evening

Baetis intermedius (M)
   Dun: Little Blue-Winged Olive Dun
   Spinner: Dark Rusty Spinner
	April–October	Morning and afternoon
		Spinner: early morning and evening

Ephemera simulans (M)
   Dun: Brown Drake
   Spinner: Brown Drake
	May 25[3]	Evening

Ephemerella inermis (M)
   Dun: Pale Morning Dun[5]
   Spinner: Pale Morning Spinner[5]
	May 25[4]	Morning, afternoon, and evening
		Spinner: morning and evening

Pteronarcys californica (S) Salmon Fly	May–July	Emergence often occurs in the morning; egg laying can occur almost any time of the day or evening

Brachycentrus species (C)
   Dark Gray Caddis
   Dark Brown Caddis
	April–October	Egg laying can occur almost any time of
		day—sometimes in the morning on colder
		streams but often in the evening on many
		streams

Rhyacophila species (C) Green Caddis	May–October	Variable

Baetis bicaudatus (M)
   Dun: Pale Olive Dun
   Spinner: Light Rusty Spinner
	June–October	Morning and afternoon
		Spinner: morning and evening

Calineuria californica (S) Golden Stone fly	June–September	Afternoon
Hesperoperla pacifica (S) Willow Fly	June and July	Variable

Callibaetis nigritus (M)
   Dun: Speckle-Winged Dun
   Spinner: Speckle-Winged Spinner
	June–September	Late morning

Paraleptophlebia heteronea (M)
   Dun: Blue Quill
   Spinner: Dark Brown Spinner
	June 1	Morning and afternoon

Nymph/Larva Found in Fast (F), Medium (M), Slow (S), or All (A) Types of Water	Nymph Burrows in Silt or Gravel (M), Clings to Rocks (R), or Swims Freely (F), Lives in Vegetation (V), or Logs (L)	Approximate Elevation at Which Hatch Occurs: High (H), Moderate (M), Low (L), or All (A)	Approximate Water Temperature When Hatch Occurs: All (A), Cold (C), Moderate (M), or Warm (W)	Hook Size	Rating	
					Dun	Spinner
F&M	R	L	C&M	14	1	7
M&F	F	A	A	18	3	7
M&F	F	M&H	A	18 or 20	3	7
S&M	B	M	M&W	10	3	2
A	LR&V	A	C&M	16 or 18	2	6
F	R			4	8[6]	2[7]
				12–16		
				12–16		
M&F	F	A	C&M	20	2	6
F	R			6	3	
F	R			6	8[8]	2
S	F	A	M&W	14	3	3
M&F	F	M&H	A	16	3	

Scientific and Common Name M = Mayfly C = Caddis fly S = Stone fly	Emergence Date (dates are extremely variable)	Time of Day Largest Hatches Emerge (Duns) or Flights Take Place (Spinners)
Cinygmula ramaleyi (M) Dun: Dark Red Quill Spinner: Red Quill Spinner	Late May and early June	Late morning Spinner: midday
Drunella (Ephemerella) grandis (M)[23] Dun: Western Green Drake Spinner: Great Red Spinner	June 5	Late morning and afternoon Spinner: evening
Serratella (Ephemerella) tibialis (M) Dun: Red Quill Spinner: White-Gloved Howdy[10]	June 5	Midday Spinner: evening
Hexagenia limbata (M)[11] Dun: Michigan Caddis or Great Olive-Winged Drake Spinner: Michigan Spinner	June 12	Dusk and later
Callibaetis coloradensis (M) Dun: Speckle-Winged Dun Spinner: Speckle-Winged Spinner	June 12	Late morning and early afternoon
Epeorus longimanus (M) Dun: Quill Gordon Spinner: Red Quill Spinner	June 12	Late morning and afternoon
Drunella (Ephemerella) doddsi (M) Dun: Western Green Drake Spinner: Great Red Spinner	June 15	Late morning and afternoon
Drunella (Ephemerella) flavilinea (M) Dun: Blue-Winged Olive Dun Spinner: Dark Olive Spinner	June 15	Morning and evening (heaviest hatches seem to appear in the evening)
Heptagenia elegantula (M) Dun: Pale Evening Dun Spinner: Pale Evening Spinner	June 20[12]	Late afternoon and evening Spinner: evening
Baetis hageni (parvus) (M) Dun: Dark Brown Dun Spinner: Dark Brown Spinner	June 20	Late morning, afternoon, and early evening Spinner: early morning and evening
Ephemerella infrequens (M)[13] Dun: Pale Morning Dun[14] Spinner: Rusty Spinner[14]	July 1	Late morning and afternoon Spinner: morning and evening
Paraleptophlebia memorialis (M) Dun: Dark Blue Quill Spinner: Dark Brown Spinner	July 1	Morning and afternoon S&M

Nymph/Larva Found in Fast (F), Medium (M), Slow (S), or All (A) Types of Water	Nymph Burrows in Silt or Gravel (M), Clings to Rocks (R), or Swims Freely (F), Lives in Vegetation (V), or Logs (L)	Approximate Elevation at Which Hatch Occurs: High (H), Moderate (M), Low (L), or All (A)	Approximate Water Temperature When Hatch Occurs: All (A), Cold (C), Moderate (M), or Warm (W)	Hook Size	Rating Dun Spinner	
M	R	M	C&M	16 or 18		
M	VR	L&M	C&M	10 or 12	2	
M&F	R	M&H	C&M	16 or 18	3	
S	M	L&M	M	8	2	2
S	F	M&H	C&M	16	3	3
M&F	R	M&H	C&M	12 or 14		
M&F	R	A	C&M	10	2	
S&M	F	M&H	C&M	14 or 16	2	4
S&M	R	L&M	M&W	14	4	5
M	F	L&M	C&M	20	1	6
M	LR&V	L&M	C&M	18	3	5
S&M	F	A	C&M	18	3	5

Scientific and Common Name M = Mayfly C = Caddis fly S = Stone fly	Emergence Date (dates are extremely variable)	Time of Day Largest Hatches Emerge (Duns) or Flights Take Place (Spinners)
Rhithrogena futilis (M) Dun: Quill Gordon Spinner: Quill Gordon	July 1[15]	Late morning and afternoon Spinner: evening
Cinygmula reticulata (M) Dun: Pale Brown Dun Spinner: Dark Rusty Spinner	July 5[15]	Late morning and afternoon Spinner: early morning
Paraleptophlebia vaciva (M) Dun: Dark Blue Quill Spinner: Dark Brown Spinner	July 5	Morning and afternoon
Heptagenia solitaria (M) Dun: Gray Fox Spinner: Ginger Quill Spinner	July 5[16]	Late afternoon and evening Spinner: late morning and evening
Epeorus albertae (M) Dun: Pink Lady Spinner: Salmon Spinner[17]	July 5	Evening
Paraleptophlebia debilis (M) Dun: Dark Blue Quill Spinner: Dark Brown Spinner	July 5[18]	Morning and afternoon
Siphlonurus occidentalis (M) Dun: Gray Drake Quill Spinner	July 5[19]	Late morning and afternoon; heaviest appear around 3:00 P.M. Spinner: morning and evening; evening seems to be heavier
Cinygma dimicki (M) Dun: Light Cahill Spinner: Light Cahill	July 5[15]	Evening
Timpanoga (Ephemerella) hecuba (M) Dun: Great Red Quill Spinner: Great Brown Spinner	July 5	Evening[20]
Rhithrogena hageni (M) Dun: Pale Brown Dun Spinner: Dark Tan Spinner	July 10	Late morning and afternoon Spinner: morning and evening
Ameletus cooki (M) Dun: Dark Brown Dun Spinner: Dark Brown Spinner	July 10[15]	Late morning and afternoon
Rhithrogena undulata (M) Dun: Quill Gordon Spinner: Red Quill or Dark Red Quill [13]	July 10[15]	Morning and afternoon Spinner: afternoon and evening

Nymph/Larva Found in Fast (F), Medium (M), Slow (S), or All (A) Types of Water	Nymph Burrows in Silt or Gravel (M), Clings to Rocks (R), or Swims Freely (F), Lives in Vegetation (V), or Logs (L)	Approximate Elevation at Which Hatch Occurs: High (H), Moderate (M), Low (L), or All (A)	Approximate Water Temperature When Hatch Occurs: All (A), Cold (C), Moderate (M), or Warm (W)	Hook Size	Rating Dun	Spinner
M	R	L&M	C&M	12	3	4
M&F	R	M&H	C&M	14	7	4
A	F	A	M	18	3	5
M	R	M&H	C&M	12 or 16	4	2
M	R	L&M	A	12	5	4
S&M	F	L&M	M	18	2	
S	F	A	C&M	10 or 12	3	5
S&M	R	A	M	12	5	3
M	R	L&M	M&W	10	3	
M&F	R	M&H	C&M	12 or 14	5	
A	F	A	M	14	6	3
M	R	L&M	C&M	12	5	3

Scientific and Common Name M = Mayfly C = Caddis fly S = Stone fly	Emergence Date (dates are extremely variable)	Time of Day Largest Hatches Emerge (Duns) or Flights Take Place (Spinners)

Tricorythodes minutus (M)
  Dun: Pale Olive Dun
  Male Spinner: Reverse Jenny Spinner or
    Trico Spinner
  Female Spinner: Dark Brown Spinner
	July 15	Morning

Drunella (Ephemerella) coloradensis (M)
  Dun: Dark Olive Dun or Autumn Green
    Drake
  Spinner: Dark Brown Spinner
	August 1	Midday
		Spinner: evening

Ephoron album (M)
  Dun: White Mayfly
  Spinner: White Mayfly
	August 15	Evening

Paraleptophlebia bicornuta (M)
  Dun: Dark Blue Quill
  Spinner: Dark Brown Spinner
	September 10	Morning and afternoon

Dicosmoecus species (C) October Caddis	October 10	Late morning, afternoon, and early evening

[1]Heaviest hatches of many Western *Baetis* species occur in the afternoon; spinner falls are usually heaviest in the evening.
[2]Little Brown Dun might be a more appropriate name.
[3]Appears on Henry's Fork in late June.
[4]Species may appear for many days.
[5]Since color varies tremendously, there might be more appropriate local names.
[6]Rated at emergence time.
[7]Rated at egg laying time.
[8]Refers to emergence; spinner refers to egg-laying.
[9]Species most often appears on Henry's Fork and the Madison from middle to late June.
[10]Common name taken from the Eastern *Isonychia* spinner.
[11]Important species in the Midwest; only locally significant in the East and West.
[12]Species appears in heaviest numbers in August and continues emerging into September.
[13]Color of species varies considerably.
[14]Since color varies from stream to stream, patterns may not be appropriate for your stream.
[15]Hatches may occur before date listed.
[16]Species emerges in heavy numbers into September.
[17]Male is lighter.
[18]Hatch continues into October.
[19]Heavy hatches occur in August.
[20]Species may appear at another time of day in heavier numbers.
[21]For many species in the Family Ephemerellidae R (Rocks) refers to gravel.
[22]Midwest has closely related species.
[23]See discussion of subspecies.
[24]Also appears in heavy numbers in September.

Nymph/Larva Found in Fast (F), Medium (M), Slow (S), or All (A) Types of Water	Nymph Burrows in Silt or Gravel (M), Clings to Rocks (R), or Swims Freely (F), Lives in Vegetation (V), or Logs (L)	Approximate Elevation at Which Hatch Occurs: High (H), Moderate (M), Low (L), or All (A)	Approximate Water Temperature When Hatch Occurs: All (A), Cold (C), Moderate (M), or Warm (W)	Hook Size	Rating Dun	Spinner
S	F	A	M&W	24	3	2
M&F	R	M&H	C&M	12	3	7
S	M	L&M	M&H	12	4	3
S&M	F	L&M		18	3	3
L&M	C&M			12	2	

CHAPTER 3

A PRIMER ON THE HATCHES

Why should you worry about scientific names for mayflies? All you want to do is enjoy yourself with a great leisure-time activity—fly-fishing. Besides, it's hard work to learn those names.

I'm certain that this is the opinion of many fly-fishermen—but let me cite an incident that points to the need for at least a basic knowledge of insect classification.

I had heard for years that Pine Creek in north-central Pennsylvania had an unbelievable hatch of Green Drakes and that few fly-fishermen actually fished while this hatch appeared. The night before, I had fished the same hatch on Penns Creek. On a 2-mile stretch of that latter stream, I had counted over two hundred fishermen. I enjoy fishing, but I detest crowded conditions. I was determined that I would fish on a different and far less crowded stream tonight—Pine Creek, for example.

Jim Heltzel and I traveled to Pine Creek that evening. We stopped at a local store near Cedar Run and inquired about the fishing.

"The Green Drake's on heavy—you'll have a good night tonight," one local fisherman reported.

Great! We were well prepared for the expected hatch. I had tied a dozen imitations of the Green Drake and the Coffin Fly Spinner just the night before. Now all we had to do was wait until 8:00 P.M. or a little later, and then we'd meet and fish the hatch.

Pine Creek is a massive river, even larger than the Beaverkill. We stared at a section of the stream from the high bridge crossing Cedar Run. How would we ever successfully fish this water?

Since there was no action on Pine Creek, we moved up Cedar Run to explore it. This fantastic freestone water, loaded with stream-bred browns, has incredible hatches of many mayfly species. As we arrived at the first pool 100 yards upstream from Pine, we noted thousands of Ginger Quill Spinners already high over a fast-water section preparing for their final ritual before death.

Trout rose to a variety of insects on that first pool, but we wanted to investigate this fertile stream more fully, so we moved upstream several hundred yards beyond the pool. Here, in the fast water, and about 5 to 10 feet above the surface, we saw clouds of Dark Olive Spinners (*Drunella* species). Trout rose throughout the 200-yard stretch above us, and we caught trout after trout on the Dark Olive Spinner.

The sun set behind the huge canyonlike wall to the west, and now the water chilled the early June air. As I looked up toward the cliff on the far side, I saw a few large dark brown spinners now positioning themselves 30 feet above the stream.

As Jim and I retraced our steps back downstream to Pine Creek, we noted that these dark brown spinners became more numerous. These huge imagos began to puzzle me as we arrived on Pine Creek. Were they Great Red Spinners (*Stenonema vicarium*)? Where were the Green Drakes? It was now past 8:00 P.M. These brown spinners became more numerous. Thousands and thousands flew 20 to 30 feet above the river. Shortly, spent females landed on the surface—first a few and then many. Large trout sensed the almost unending food supply and fed freely on the spent spinners.

I still didn't know to which species these imagos belonged, but I hurriedly tied on one imitating *S. vicarium* (similar to the Great Red Spinner). Besides,

Figure 7. An *Ephemera simulans* female dun (Brown Drake). On Pine Creek, this species is sometimes incorrectly called the Green Drake.

Figure 8. A female dun of *Ephemera guttulata* (Green Drake).

I was in a hurry to fish the spinner fall, though I still didn't know what spinner it was. Now fifty large trout surfaced freely in front of Jim and me. I fruitlessly cast the dry fly toward the largest of these trout and after ten minutes finally caught a heavy brown about 16 inches long. Eight other trout seized our imitations that evening before dusk and darkness finally ended our fishing.

Just before we left the stream, I was able to capture one male and one female spinner. I was amazed, puzzled, curious, and frustrated at the spinner fall and our inability to do well while it occurred. When we got back to the car, I carefully examined the spent spinners. They were Drakes, but they were imagos of *Ephemera simulans*—Brown Drakes, not Green Drakes. Now I knew why we hadn't caught more trout: we had been casting dark-brown-bodied dry flies over those educated trout, while they captured naturals with tannish yellow bodies.

On our way back home, we stopped in the same local store that we had before the hatch that evening. Some of the locals talked freely about the great "Green Drake" spinner fall they had just experienced. Green Drake? Yes, that's how some of the local fishermen refer to the Brown Drake on Pine Creek.

If only one of those fishermen who told me about the hatch had also indicated which species it was. If only fishermen would use scientific names, especially in cases where one common name describes, many times inadequately, several species. Because of the frequent inaccuracy of common names—and for many other reasons—you should learn the scientific names of the more important species, especially those capable of producing fishable hatches in your locality.

To start with, you should understand the relationship of aquatic insects to the total fauna. Mayflies, caddis flies, and stone flies are members of the Class Insecta. Class Insecta belongs to the Phylum Arthropoda, and all phyla are components of the Animal Kingdom.

If we look at the Brown Drake (*Ephemera simulans*, to be precise) as an example, we should be able to see more clearly just how it is that mayflies fit into the scheme of things:

Kingdom: Animal (all animals from one-celled to humans)
Phylum: Arthropoda (animals that have outer skeletons called exoskeletons)
Order: Ephemeroptera (all mayflies)
Family: Ephemeridae (nymphs usually are burrowers; in adults longitudinal vein M_2 is bent sharply toward Cu at its base)
Genus: *Ephemera* (forewing darkened or heavily spotted)
Species: *simulans* (differentiated by the coloration of various body parts and the shape of the penis—the Brown Drake)

The subdivisions become more specific as we descend the hierarchy and less specific as we ascend. Each part of the hierarchy contains a degree of relationships. The affiliation at the top is very general, but as one progresses from kingdom to species, the relationship becomes highly specific.

The basic unit in the classification system is species. A species is sometimes divided into subspecies. When this occurs, the subspecies is listed as *Drunella grandis grandis*, with the last of the three names referring to the subspecies. Usually only members of the same species can mate and have offspring. Usually several species (sometimes only one)

belong to the same genus. In our sample genus, *Ephemera*, we also have *Ephemera varia* (Yellow Drake), *Ephemera guttulata* (Green Drake), and others. The genus of a mayfly is much easier to determine than is the species and more difficult to ascertain than family.

The next rung up the ladder is the family. The family of a mayfly is easier to determine than is the genus. In our example, the genus *Ephemera* belongs to the Family Ephemeridae, or the true burrowers. In addition to *Ephemera*, other genera, such as *Hexagenia* and *Litobrancha*, belong to the Family Ephemeridae.

Ephemeridae is one of at least seventeen families of the Order Ephemeroptera (mayflies) found in the United States. Below are some of the more common families and genera, along with some of the characteristics of each. Under each genus, I have attempted to list the most common species. This is by no means a complete list, and many others can and do produce fishable hatches. I also have tried to indicate where these hatches are found: *E* for species found in the East; *M* for those found in the Midwest; and *W* for those found in the West. A word of caution: although the species is supposed to be common in your area, there's a good possibility that it might not exist in any numbers on your favorite stream.

FAMILY EPHEMERIDAE

Most members of this family inhabit slow to moderate stretches of streams, rivers, and lakes and ponds. Most nymphs burrow in mud, silt, or fine gravel. Duns usually appear, and spinners fall at dusk or later from late May until mid-September. This family contains many of the largest mayflies in North America. Ephemeridae species are separated from other families by the bent path of vein M_2 in the forewing (Figure 3).

GENUS *EPHEMERA*

This genus contains moderate to large (10–25 mm) gravel-burrowing nymphs. Most species emerge and fall (spinners) at dusk, and many continue well past dark. Wings on duns and spinners are heavily spotted, and all adults have three tails—unlike members

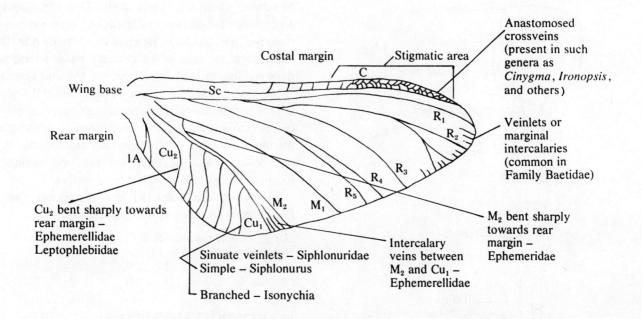

Anastomosed crossveins (present in such genera as *Cinygma*, *Ironopsis*, and others)

Costal margin

Stigmatic area

C

Wing base

Sc

R₁

R₂

Veinlets or marginal intercalaries (common in Family Baetidae)

Rear margin

1A

Cu₂

R₃

R₄

R₅

M₂

M₁

M₂ bent sharply towards rear margin – Ephemeridae

Cu₂ bent sharply towards rear margin – Ephemerellidae Leptophlebiidae

Cu₁

Intercalary veins between M₂ and Cu₁ – Ephemerellidae

Sinuate veinlets – Siphlonuridae
Simple – Siphlonurus

Branched – Isonychia

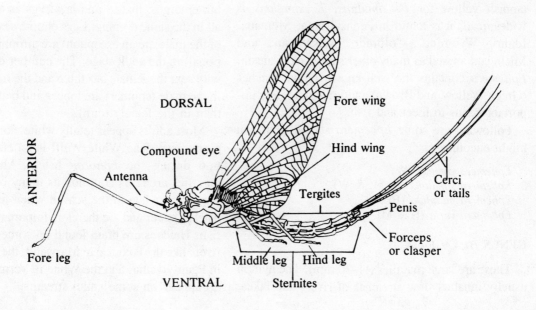

DORSAL

Fore wing

Hind wing

Compound eye

Cerci or tails

Antenna

Tergites

Penis

Forceps or clasper

Fore leg

Middle leg   Hind leg

Sternites

VENTRAL

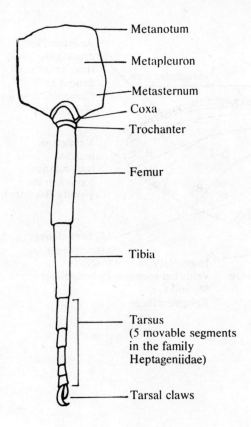

Metanotum

Metapleuron

Metasternum

Coxa

Trochanter

Femur

Tibia

Tarsus
(5 movable segments
in the family
Heptageniidae)

Tarsal claws

of the genus *Hexagenia*, which have no spotting and only two tails. Sternites (underside of abdomen) vary in color from pale cream for *Ephemera guttulata* to tannish yellow for *E. simulans*. *E. simulans* is widespread; it is found in Pennsylvania, Montana, Idaho, Wyoming, Colorado, Wisconsin, and Michigan, as well as many other states, and Canada. *Ephemera* contains the well-known Drake hatches (Green, Yellow, and Brown) and is an extremely important genus to meet and fish.

Following are some *Ephemera* species that you might encounter:

Ephemera compar (W)
Ephemera simulans (E, M, & W)
Ephemera guttulata (E)
Ephemera varia (E & M)

GENUS *HEXAGENIA*

These are large mayflies (14–30 mm). The nymph usually inhabits slow stretches of rivers and lakes, or ponds, where it burrows in silt. Dun emergence and spinner fall often occur at dusk or later and continue well past that time. Wings of the duns are heavily barred, and the veins of the spinners' wings are often dark reddish brown. In all species, the middle tail is reduced to a barely visible vestige, and only two tails are prominent. *Hexagenia recurvata* is now placed in a new genus, *Litobrancha*. Although members are large, I have seen only *H. limbata, H. atrocaudata*, and *L. recurvata* produce fishable hatches (or spinner falls) on trout waters.

Following are some of the *Hexagenia* (and *Litobrancha*) species that might appear:

Hexagenia atrocaudata (E & M)
Hexagenia munda (E & M)
Hexagenia limbata (E, M, & W)
Litobrancha recurvata (E & M)

FAMILY POLYMITARCIDAE

This resurrected family includes mayflies with nonfunctional legs. Until recently these species were included in the Family Ephemeridae.

GENUS *EPHORON*

These medium-sized (6–12 mm) burrowers frequent large and medium-sized streams. Duns of these species emerge most abundantly in July, August, or September in the evening. The female never molts but emerges, mates, and lays eggs as a subimago— all in the same evening. Legs of both sexes (front legs of the male are an exception) are atrophied (nonfunctional) in the adult stage. The number of tails differs with sex; the female has three and the male two. Tails in the male (spinner) are longer and better developed than in the female (dun).

Most adults appear totally white, sometimes with a gray cast. The White Wulff is an effective imitation during the *Ephoron* hatch. Although these mayflies aren't as common as many other species, they appear late in the season when few other true hatches occur and are therefore important to meet and fish. Hatches are often found on some of the larger rivers like the Potomac in Maryland, the Susquehanna in Pennsylvania, and the White in Vermont. Hatches do appear on some small streams.

MEETING AND FISHING THE HATCHES

Following are the common *Ephoron* species:

Ephoron album (M & W)
Ephoron leukon (E & M)

FAMILY POTAMANTHIDAE

Until recently *Potamanthus* species also were included in the Family Ephemeridae. However, *Potamanthus* nymphs are not true burrowers, and adults can be separated from the true burrowers by the branching of the first anal vein in these species. Only one genus is in this family.

GENUS *POTAMANTHUS*

These moderate-sized (9–16 mm) nymphs are sprawlers rather than burrowers, although they inhabit the same areas of a stream as the true burrowers (Ephemeridae). Duns emerge and spinners fall at dusk or shortly thereafter, and all have white, cream, or creamish yellow bodies and wings, sometimes with tan shading on the abdomen.

Fishermen commonly call mayflies of this genus Golden or Cream Drakes. Wing venation and body shading are important in separating species.

Following are some of the *Potamanthus* species that might produce fishable hatches.

Potamanthus distinctus (E)
Potamanthus rufous (E & M)
Potamanthus verticus (E & M)

FAMILY CAENIDAE

Members of this family are often found in quiet water, where the nymphs move about freely in debris, trash, or silt. These diminutive mayflies rarely exceed 6 mm. Dun emergence and spinner fall occur at evening, dark, before morning, or in the early morning hours. Most species appear after June. Members of this family are separated from other families by the size of the ocelli (simple eyes located between the compound eyes); these ocelli are at least half the size of the compound eyes (Figure 6).

GENUS *CAENIS*

These tiny mayflies are rarely longer than 5 mm and inhabit lakes, ponds, and slow stretches of streams. Adults are white, cream, or buff-colored and usually appear at or shortly before dark. Duns change to spinners shortly after they emerge, and these imagos meet at dark or in the early morning hours to mate. Spinners are strongly attracted to light, and thousands can be seen near lighted areas at night.

Following are *Caenis* species that you may encounter:

Caenis anceps (E & M)
Caenis simulans (E, M, & W)

I have seen *Caenis anceps* emerge by the thousands in late July and August on Spruce Creek. To imitate this mayfly, one would have to use a size 28 or 30 hook, which is almost impossible to use effectively.

FAMILY TRICORYTHIDAE

Until recently members of this family were included in Caenidae; however, *Tricorythodes* adults have claspers with three distinct segments (parts), compared to one in *Brachycercus* and *Caenis*.

GENUS *TRICORYTHODES*

We find these tiny (3–5 mm) but important species on small streams like Falling Springs in south-central Pennsylvania and on large ones like the Beaverkill and the Loyalsock in the East, the Au Sable and Namekagon in the Midwest, and the Colorado, McKenzie, and Wood in the West. Duns often emerge in the morning, molt to spinners almost immediately, and mate within a couple of hours. Male and female spinners often fall spent to the water, so it's important to have imitations of both sexes on hand. All species have three tails. Most Tricos can be copied on a size 24 hook. The Tricos I've seen on Colorado's South Platte River near Deckers can be imitated with a size 20 Trico.

Some *Tricorythodes* species that seem to be common and can produce fishable hatches are:

Tricorythodes attratus (E & M)
Tricorythodes minutus (E & W)
Tricorythodes stygiatus (E & W)

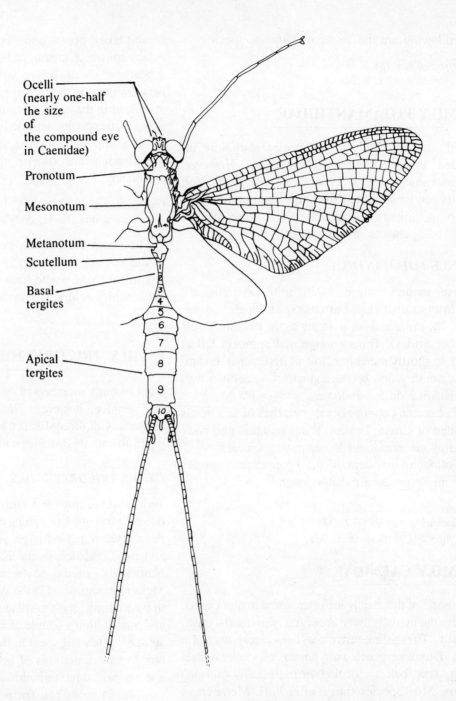

Ocelli
(nearly one-half
the size
of
the compound eye
in Caenidae)

Pronotum

Mesonotum

Metanotum

Scutellum

Basal
tergites

Apical
tergites

FAMILY EPHEMERELLIDAE

Until a few years ago this family contained only one genus, *Ephemerella*. This one genus has been split into *Ephemerella*, *Dannella*, *Drunella*, *Attenella*, *Eurylophella*, *Serratella*, and *Timpanoga*. The family is still separated from other families by the few cross-

veins adults have in their forewings, by the two long intercalary veins between M_2 and Cu_1, and by the bent path of vein Cu_2 (Figure 3). The three tails present on all members are often extremely weak on subimagos or duns. For the fly fishermen *Ephemerella* and *Drunella* contain the most important members of the genus.

GENUS *EPHEMERELLA*

Members of this genus range in size from 5 to 14 mm. The genus contains many of the more common members of the family. Most of the "sulphurs" and "pale morning duns" belong to *Ephemerella*. The abundant Hendrickson is also a member.

Some of the more common species are:

Ephemerella dorothea (E & W)
Ephemerella inermis (W)
Ephemerella infrequens (W)
Ephemerella invaria (E & M)
Ephemerella needhami (E & M)
Ephemerella rotunda (E & M)
Ephemerella septentrionalis (E)
Ephemerella subvaria (E & M)

GENUS *DRUNELLA*

Body length of the members of this genus usually ranges from 6 to 15 mm. Fly fishermen call many species in this group blue-winged olives. Important mayflies in the East, Midwest, and West are found in this genus. *D. cornuta* produces major hatches on many Eastern waters. *D. lata* can be found on many Midwestern and some Eastern streams.

D. grandis and its subspecies and *D. doddsi* produce the famous Western Green Drake hatches in the West. *D. grandis grandis* is found in southwestern Oregon, southern Idaho, western Wyoming, most of Utah, Nevada, western Colorado, northeastern Arizona, and northwestern New Mexico. *D. grandis ingens* is a more northern subspecies found in western Montana, northern Idaho, western Washington, central and northwestern Oregon, and central California. *D. grandis flavitincta* is a coastal and near-coastal subspecies found in the western parts of Oregon and Washington. *D. grandis ingens* (*glacialis*) is found on rivers in Montana like the Bitterroot and Flathead. This subspecies is a darker, almost slate-gray species, with a heavy olive green cast.

D. grandis grandis, found on the Fryingpan in Colorado, contains more olive green and less gray. Below Reudi Reservoir, Green Drakes on the Fryingpan emerge well into August because of the bottom release.

Some of the more common *Drunella* are:

Drunella coloradensis (W)
Drunella cornuta (E & M)
Drunella cornutella (E)
Drunella doddsi (W)
Drunella flavilinea (W)
Drunella grandis flavitincta, ingens, and grandis (W)
Drunella lata (E & M)
Drunella longicornis (E)
Drunella walkeri (E & M)

GENUS *EURYLOPHELLA*

These are moderate-sized mayflies ranging from 6 to 11 mm in length. Anglers call some of the members of the genus "chocolate duns." Species of this genus are usually found in the East and Midwest. Often imitated with size 16 or 18 hooks, these mayflies frequently appear at midday. Some common members are:

Eurylophella bicolor (E & M)
Eurylophella funeralis (E & M)
Eurylophella aestiva (E & M)

GENUS *DANNELLA*

Entomologists have placed only two species in this genus and only one, *D. simplex*, is important to fishermen. Members are small with body lengths near 6 mm. *D. simplex* has been overlooked in angling literature but produces explosive hatches in mid-June.

Dannella simplex (E & M)

GENUS *SERRATELLA*

Members of this genus are usually small, ranging from 4 to 9 mm. *S. deficiens* is small, dark, and important to imitate. Some of the more common members are:

Serratella deficiens (E & M)
Serratella tibialis (W)

GENUS *CAUDATELLA*

Members of this species are found in the West and range in size from 5 to 11 mm. The most important members are the three subspecies of *C. heterocaudata*.

GENUS *TIMPANOGA*

This genus holds one Western species, *T. hecuba*. There are two subspecies *pacifica* and *hecuba*. *T. hecuba* is a fairly large (size 10 to 12) mayfly.

FAMILY LEPTOPHLEBIIDAE

These small-to-moderate sized (6–14 mm) nymphs prefer lakes or ponds or slow-to-moderate stretches of streams. Subimagos of most species appear dark brown or dark grayish brown, and most imagos are dark brown or reddish brown. Fishermen call the male imagos of many species of this family Jenny Spinners. These males have an abdomen of white or amber with the last few segments dark brown. The family is separated from others by the bent path of vein Cu_2 in the forewing (Figure 3).

GENUS *LEPTOPHLEBIA*

Many duns of these species appear around noon or shortly after. Both dun and spinner have three tails. The middle tail of the male is almost always only one-third to two-thirds as long as the outer ones. Dark-brown or black imitations (Early Brown Spinner and Black Quill) work well when a hatch or fall of this genus occurs.

Some of the more common *Leptophlebia* species are:

Leptophlebia cupida (E & M)
Leptophlebia johnsoni (E)
Leptophlebia gravastella (W)
Leptophlebia nebulosa (E, M, & W)

GENUS *PARALEPTOPHLEBIA*

These small- to moderate-sized (5–9 mm) nymphs can tolerate much more current than *Leptophlebia* and are therefore more common on trout streams and seem abundant on many smaller streams. Fly fishermen match the dun effectively with the Blue Quill or Dark Blue Quill and the female spinner with the Dark Brown Spinner.

The dark-grayish-brown duns often appear during the morning or early afternoon. Male spinners have a characteristic undulating mating flight and are active from morning until early evening. Fishermen sometimes confuse these spinners with the smaller *Tricorythodes*.

The genus *Paraleptophlebia* contains many species that on occasion can produce fishable hatches. Among some of the more common examples of these species are the following:

Paraleptophlebia adoptiva (E & M)
Paraleptophlebia bicornuta (W)
Paraleptophlebia debilis (E, M, & W)
Paraleptophlebia guttata (E & M)
Paraleptophlebia heteronea (W)
Paraleptophlebia memorialis (W)
Paraleptophlebia mollis (E & M)
Paraleptophlebia packii (W)
Paraleptophlebia strigula (E)
Paraleptophlebia vaciva (W)

FAMILY BAETIDAE

Nymphs are free swimming, highly streamlined, and range in size from 3 mm in species like *Pseudocloeon* to 10 mm in *Callibaetis*. Nymphs vary in their habitat from ponds and slow-water stretches, where we find species like *Callibaetis*, to fast water, where several species of *Baetis* live. This family is separated from others by veinlets (small free veins) on the margins or the forewing, which is characteristic of the genus *Baetis*. Some members of the family (*Cloeon* and *Pseudocloeon*) lack hind wings.

GENUS *PSEUDOCLOEON*

These are small mayflies but sometimes extremely important to match. Species of this genus can be separated from *Baetis* by the absence of the hind wing and from *Cloeon* by the two veinlets between the longitudinal veins (*Cloeon* has one).

Species of this genus often produce two or three broods a year. Duns emerge on Eastern and Midwestern waters on many cold May afternoons and evenings. They also appear in late September and early October in the afternoon. Fishermen can match many of these species with a Blue Dun (size 20–24) and a Rusty Spinner for the spinner.

Some of the more common *Pseudocloeon* species are:

Pseudocloeon anoka (M)
Pseudocloeon edmundsi (W)
Pseudocloeon carolina (E)
Pseudocloeon futile (W)
Pseudocloeon cingulatum (E)
Pseudocloeon parvulum (E & M)
Pseudocloeon dubium (E & M)

GENUS *BAETIS*

These small (3–7 mm) nymphs often inhabit shallow-water areas of streams. Many duns of this genus rest for protracted periods before taking flight. Therefore, although they're extremely small, many of these species are important for the fly-fisherman to imitate. Furthermore, many of these species, including *Baetis hageni (parvus)*, a common Western species, emerge on midsummer afternoons, a period often void of other mayfly species.

Duns usually have dark gray, dark brown, or tan bodies, often with an olive cast, in contrast to the rusty brown or dark brown bodies of the imagos. The Blue Dun, Blue Upright, and Blue-Winged Olive Dun are used to match the subimago. Many male spinners resemble some of the *Paraleptophlebia* species and have abdomens with the middle segments almost colorless (hyaline). *Baetis* species are difficult to separate. The venation of the hind wing and the presence of projections on that wing are important factors to consider in determining species.

Some common species are:

Baetis bicaudatus (W)
Baetis brunneicolor (M)
Baetis tricaudatus (vagans) (all)
Baetis flavistriga (levitans and quebecensis) (E & M)
Baetis hageni (parvus) (W)
Baetis flavistriga (phoebus) (M)

Note that the former *Baetis phoebus* and *Baetis levitans* have now been lumped together under *Baetis flavistriga*. *Baetis parvus* is now listed as *Baetis hageni*.

GENUS *CALLIBAETIS*

The free-swimming nymphs of this genus dwell in still water of permanent ponds and lakes or sluggish areas of streams. Many species develop from egg to adult in five to six weeks and consequently appear throughout the summer. Adult females live a week or more after mating. When eggs are finally deposited in still water, the young hatch out almost immediately.

Adults range in size from 5 to 10 mm. The female spinner has wings washed heavily with gray flecks. All species have two tails.

Following are some *Callibaetis* species that you might encounter:

Callibaetis coloradensis (M & W)
Callibaetis ferrugineus (E & M)
Callibaetis fluctuans (E & M)
Callibaetis nigritus (W)

GENUS *CLOEON*

Many members of this genus range from 3 to 8 mm. Although often overlooked as hatches, some *Cloeon* species can be important. Duns of some species closely resemble a size 24–26 Pale Evening Dun. Hatches of *Cloeon rubropictum* appear on July mornings just after the Trico spinner has completed its daily fall.

Some common species are:

Cloeon rubropictum (E & M)
Cloeon vicinum (E)

FAMILY SIPHLONURIDAE

Members of this family until recently were included in the Family Baetidae. It is now separated because all members have four segments on the hind tarsi (Baetidae members have three) and by the path of M_2 in the forewing (this vein is detached in Baetidae).

Siphlonurus and *Isonychia* (now in a new family) can be separated by the sinuate veinlets in the forewing—single in *Siphlonurus* and branched in *Isonychia* (Figure 3).

GENUS *SIPHLONURUS*

These moderate-sized (9–14 mm) mayflies are often called Gray Drakes by fishermen. Emergence for different species occurs throughout the season. *Siphlonurus quebecensis* appears near the end of May in the East and Midwest, *S. alternatus* emerges around the end of June in the same areas, and *S. occidentalis* appears on Western waters from mid-July into August. Species often emerge sporadically in the afternoon. Legs, wings, tails, and bodies of many species are dark gray, with the bodies ribbed slightly lighter.

Some of the more common *Siphlonurus* species are:

Siphlonurus alternatus (E & M)
Siphlonurus occidentalis (M & W)
Siphlonurus quebecensis (E & M)
Siphlonurus rapidus (E & M)

GENUS *AMELETUS*

Duns and spinners of these moderate-sized mayflies are usually brown or yellowish brown in general coloration. Some species of this genus are locally important in the West. I have noted only one species that appeared in fishable numbers in the West. That species, *Ameletus cooki*, can be important to imitate.

FAMILY OLIGONEURIIDAE

This new family has rather diverse genera. Nymphs contain two rows of long hairs on the forelegs. In adults the forelegs are shorter than the second pair and longitundinal veins are reduced or similar to *Siphlonurus*. The Genus *Isonychia* is extremely important to fly-fishermen.

GENUS *ISONYCHIA*

Recent studies suggest that some of these species may have more than one brood per year. This might indicate why Slate Drakes appear all summer and again in late September and early October.

These large, streamlined nymphs prefer rapid water. When emerging, nymphs often swim to shallow rapids, crawl onto an exposed rock, break their nymphal skin, and escape to a nearby tree.

Adults usually have dark forelegs and creamish hind legs. All have two tails. Duns often have slate-colored bodies, while spinners are dark maroon or dark rusty brown in color. The Slate Drake effectively imitates many species of this genus.

Some common *Isonychia* species are:

Isonychia bicolor (E & M)
Isonychia harperi (E & M)
Isonychia matilda (E)
Isonychia sadleri (E & M)

FAMILY HEPTAGENIIDAE

Nymphs of this rock-clinging family often dwell in moderate and fast water. All individuals have two tails. The tarsi on the hind legs have five movable parts, a distinguishing feature of this family (Figure 5). All adults have two pair of cubital intercalary veins in the forewing.

GENUS *STENONEMA*

Many species of this genus spend much of their nymphal life attached to rocks in moderate and fast water. Adults vary in size from 8 to 16 mm, and most have cream, yellow, or tan bodies. Legs of duns and spinners are cream or yellow with characteristic darker banding. Male and female of the same species often vary considerably in color, sometimes necessitating two patterns. Few *Stenonema* species are found in the West.

Species previously listed in the *interpunctatum* group of this genus are now placed in a new genus, *Stenacron*.

Some of the more common *Stenonema* species are:

Stenonema fuscum (E & M)
Stenonema ithaca (E)
Stenonema luteum (E & M)
Stenonema pulchellum (E & M)
Stenonema vicarium (E & M)

GENUS *STENACRON*

This genus holds many of the "light cahills." These can be separated from others in the family by the later clusters of spines on the penis in the male adult. Most species range from 8 to 13 mm long.

Some of the more common *Stenacron* species are:

Stenacron interpunctatum canadense (E & M)
Stenacron interpunctatum heterotarsale (E & M)
Stenacron interpunctatum interpunctatum (E & M)

Although we consistently refer to many *Stenacron* species throughout the text as *Stenacron canadense, Stenacron heterotarsale*, and so on, the proper nomenclature should be as indicated above. These mayflies, plus others, are considered subspecies of *Stenacron interpunctatum*.

GENUS *HEPTAGENIA*

Duns of this genus often escape rapidly from the surface when emerging, and therefore many duns are of questionable value to the angler. Spinners sometimes take on more importance because they characteristically rest on the surface while depositing eggs. Duns and spinners usually have bodies of cream, pale yellow, or tan, often with an olive cast. Some Western species like *Heptagenia solitaria* are more important than their Eastern counterparts because of their size and type of emergence. Fishermen imitate many species of this genus with the Pale Evening Dun or Gray Fox.

Some of the more common *Heptagenia* species are:

Heptagenia aphrodite (E)
Heptagenia diabusia (M)
Heptagenia elegantula (W)
Heptagenia hebe (E & M)
Heptagenia pulla (M)
Heptagenia solitaria (W)
Heptagenia walshi (E)
Heptagenia marginalis (E)

GENUS *EPEORUS*

These nymphs often inhabit fast, shallow sections of pure, cool water. Duns, when emerging, shuck their nymphal skin on the bottom of the stream or river rather than near or on the surface. Wet flies work well during emergence activity of these species. Many species (*Epeorus vitreus* and *E. albertae* are exceptions) have bodies of pale yellow to dark gray. Species are most important in fast-flowing trout streams of the East and West.

Some common *Epeorus* species are:

Epeorus albertae (W)
Epeorus deceptivus (W)
Epeorus pleuralis (E)
Epeorus longimanus (W)
Epeorus grandis (W)
Epeorus vitreus (E & M)

GENUS *RHITHROGENA*

Nymphs of these species usually cling to gravel in fairly fast current. Adults are often dark tan, dark gray, or dark brown. Species can be locally important, especially on Western waters. The forewings of spinners are anastomosed (netlike) in the stigmatic area.

Some common *Rhithrogena* species are:

Rhithrogena morrisoni (W)
Rhithrogena futilis (W)
Rhithrogena hageni (W)
Rhithrogena undulata (M & W)

GENUS *CINYGMA*

This is another genus of some importance on Western rivers. The cross-veins in the stigmatic area are also anastomosed, but the veins in that area are divided into two fairly even rows (*Rhithrogena* is not divided). *Cinygma dimicki*, which outwardly resembles *Stenonema fuscum*, is important on some Western streams.

GENUS *CINYGMULA*

Species of this genus are often found in moderate to small streams that are relatively cool. Wings of most members have a decided gray or yellow cast. Wings of the spinners are not anastomosed, in contrast to *Cinygma* and *Rhithrogena*.

Some common *Cinygmula* species are:

Cinygmula ramaleyi (W)
Cinygmula reticulata (W)

FAMILY METRETOPODIDAE

Nymphs of this family are streamlined and fairly large, ranging from 9 to 16 mm. *Siphloplecton* adults have heavily spotted forewings. Not until Greg Hoover identified *S. basale* on Clark Creek did I realize that this species emerged in heavy enough numbers to create a fishable hatch. Anglers often confuse this mid-to-late April hatch with the Hendrickson or March Brown.

There is only one common species:

Siphloplecton basale (E & M)

FAMILY BAETISCIDAE

These two-tailed adults are noted for their hump-backed appearance. Most are 8 to 12 mm long. The Genus *Baetisca* does produce hatches on some of the more acid streams in the Northeast and Midwest. Nymphs often crawl onto rocks to emerge similar to *Isonychia*.

One of the most common species is:

Baetisca laurentina (E & M)

MAYFLY IDENTIFICATION

When attempting to identify species, genera, and families of mayflies, entomologists use keys. When utilizing these keys, it's important to remember significant features of the adult male that differentiate it from other species. Following are some of the body parts of the adult that are important in identification.

1. Wings

   a. Forewing

      1. Color and shading of the parts
      2. Path of veins: branching of longitudinal veins
      3. Veinlets or intercalaries present or absent and number
      4. Stigmatic area: anastomosed and shaded

   b. Hind wing

      1. Present or absent
      2. Shading and coloration of veins
      3. Costal projections present
      4. General venation

2. Legs

   a. General coloration and markings; tarsal claws similar or dissimilar; number and size of tarsal segments; length of leg parts, especially forelegs; color of coxae and trochanters

3. Abdomen

   a. General coloration or shading; color and shading of each tergite; are spiracular dots present or absent, and what is the shape of these dots; markings, including dots and shading of ganglionic areas; shading around the pleural fold
   b. When working with the parts of the abdomen, it's important to know locations to which keys often refer. Such terms as *lateral, posterior, anterior, mesal, dorsal, ventral, apical,* and *basal* are especially important

4. Tails

   a. Number, general coloration, length, color at joinings, and the size of the middle tail

5. Thorax

   a. Coloration and shading of top (notum), sides (pleuron), and bottom (sternum). Color pattern of scutellum

6. Head

   a. Size of ocelli; shape and general color of the eyes; size of the eyes. Coloration and shading of head and antennae

7. Genitalia

   a. Forceps: number of segments, shape, and color
   b. Shape of penis; presence and location of spines; general coloration; any projections present

The number of tails a mayfly species has is helpful in identifying it. All mayflies have two or three tails, and although there are a few exceptions (*Ephoron*), all species of a genus have the same number of tails. Here is a list of mayfly genera according to the number of tails each has:

Two Tails	Three Tails
Baetis	*Caenis*
Callibaetis	*Ephemera*
Cinygma	*Ephemerella*
Cinygmula	*Ephoron* (female)
Cloeon	*Leptophlebia*
Epeorus	*Paraleptophlebia*
Ephoron (male)	*Potamanthus*
Heptagenia	*Tricorythodes*
Hexagenia	*Drunella*
Isonychia	*Attenella*
Litobrancha	*Eurylophella*
Pseudocloeon	*Serratella*
Siphlonurus	*Dannella*
Stenacron	
Stenonema	

Tails are extremely fragile; make certain when examining mayflies that none of the tails is broken.

Figure 13. A Yellow Drake dun, *Ephemera varia.*

Figure 14. A Yellow Drake spinner.

CHAPTER 4

MEETING A MAYFLY HATCH: THE YELLOW DRAKE

Up to this point we've discussed emergence and hatches as if you were completely familiar with them. This chapter is intended to clarify any question you might have about hatches. In it we examine the emergence characteristics of one species, the Yellow Drake.

Mayflies appear annually. Members of a species appear for a few days, a week, two weeks, or much longer. During this annual emergence period, many species appear in greater numbers on certain days and in reduced numbers on other days. We'll call this period of heavy emergence the *peak*. Probably the best time to meet and fish a hatch is at its peak. This peak emergence can occur for a short, medium, or long period. The peak dates may vary for a species from year to year but are often of the same duration on the same stream. Also the peak is usually preceded and followed by periods of sparser hatches. It is probably less important to meet and fish the hatch on these days. With some species, however, the period immediately after the peak, when the number of a species is waning, can be exceedingly productive.

The following study should place the concept of emergence in the proper perspective. A few years ago I visited the Bald Eagle Creek in central Pennsylvania almost daily to determine the peak period and emergence characteristics of *Ephemera varia*, commonly called the Yellow Drake by fishermen. I marked off a 200-foot slow to moderate stretch of stream and spent evening after evening carefully counting the number of *E. varia* subimagos (duns) emerging within that stretch.

Why did I select this species for this experiment? First and foremost, the Yellow Drake is large (13–17 mm) and fairly easy to identify in the air because of its pale yellow wings and body. Even in the half-light after 9:00 P.M., this pale yellow mayfly is relatively easy to see. Second, this species often concentrates its daily appearance from 8:30 P.M. to 9:15 P.M. (This time might vary east or west of central Pennsylvania because of an earlier or later sunset.)

Not only did I count the number of duns emerging during the observation period, but I also scanned the surface for signs of feeding trout. High water temperatures adversely affected this part of the study, since temperature readings from 68 to 75 degrees were common on the Bald Eagle Creek in late June and July. When the water temperature rises to the mid-70s, trout usually seek cooler environs. (I discussed this point earlier in connection with selecting a good stream.) What good is a dense hatch if high water temperatures discourage trout from feeding?

Figure 7 shows the number of duns appearing and the dates they emerged. I recorded seeing duns as early as June 16 and as late as August 6; however, duns probably appeared earlier and later than the observations indicate. The peak of the annual emergence for that year occurred from June 23 to July 5. Determining the length of a peak is somewhat subjective. Furthermore, many species probably don't display the drastic decline that the Yellow Drake did between July 5 and July 8. Peaks for some species may be much more difficult to determine. Other species might well be erratic, showing an increase

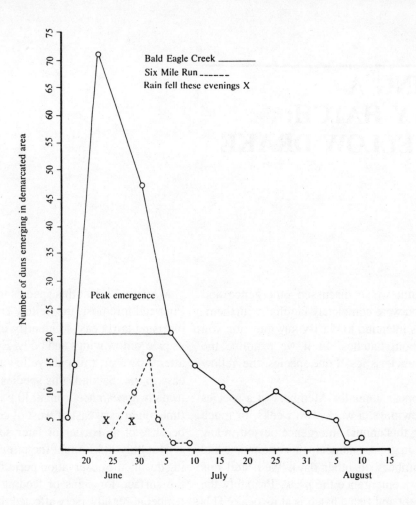

Number of duns emerging in demarcated area

Bald Eagle Creek _____
Six Mile Run _ _ _ _ _ _
Rain fell these evenings X

Peak emergence

20   25   30   5   10   15   20   25   31   5   10   15
June   July   August

after a decrease. A point worth noting is that the Yellow Drake has a longer emergence peak on Fishing Creek in northeastern Pennsylvania. On this latter stream, good hatches appear for two or more weeks.

Several evenings during the observation period, it rained. On most of these occasions, I noted only a few rain-soaked duns emerging. The highest number on any day was recorded on June 23, with seventy-two duns appearing in the 200-foot area. After the peak, for about three to four weeks, ten to fifteen duns emerged almost every evening. This latter phase, where only ten or so duns appeared, encompassed the last three weeks in July. Finally, only a few duns emerged nightly during early August.

But the reason for the study is to determine how trout react to the emergence, especially the peak. As early as June 18, I observed one large trout feeding on the lethargic duns. On June 23, the beginning of the peak, I noted only three trout taking duns on the surface. Remember, I commented earlier about the warm water temperatures and how these probably discouraged other trout from seizing duns on the surface. After the peak, in mid-July, I saw only one trout rise to the now-reduced hatch.

The same year I also counted duns of the same species on Six Mile Run on alternate nights and later in the season. This is a small, extremely cold mountain stream in central Pennsylvania just 15 miles north of the Bald Eagle Creek. But the elevation on the Bald Eagle Creek at the study site is 850 feet, whereas the altitude at the Six Mile Run study area is 1,790 feet—a difference of almost 1,000 feet. Six Mile Run is substantially slowed in its downstream movement by numerous beaver dams and other natural and man-made obstructions. These impoundments evidently slow this water enough so it can harbor a fair-sized *Ephemera varia* population. As it does on the Bald Eagle Creek, the Yellow Drake appears on Six Mile

Figure 16. The study site for the Yellow Drake on the Bald Eagle Creek. The branch in the foreground marks the end of the site.

Run most often from 8:30 P.M. to 9:15 P.M. You'll note in Figure 7 that the peak emergence occurred about a week later on this latter stream.

Although the water temperature never rose above 66 degrees in the study area on Six Mile Run, I saw only three trout rise for escaping duns during the peak. I presume this happened because of the relatively small number of emerging duns (seventeen was the highest number).

Time of emergence for this species is interesting. Most duns appear (in central Pennsylvania) between 8:45 P.M. and 9:15 P.M. A few come out before and some later, but the majority emerge in that half-hour. It's intriguing because the last swallow and flycatcher leave the stream near 8:45 P.M., and the first insect-eating bat appears on the stream around 9:15 P.M. A biological clock has instinctively alerted the majority of these slow-moving, easy-to-capture subimagos to emerge during that half-hour each night when the air is relatively free of winged predators.

Spinners too provide an important source of food for trout. The duns emerging last night and the night before become tonight's spinners. Imagos of some species are more readily available as food for trout than others. *Ephemera varia* exudes its eggs while riding on the surface and therefore is potential food for trout. In addition to counting duns each evening, I also tried to approximate the number of spinners above and on the water in the study area. The peak of the spinner fall occurred the evening of June 25.

A word of caution: emergence times can and do vary. I've seen our sample hatch on occasion appear in the morning. The time of emergence (and time of the spinner fall) can deviate considerably from the times listed in the Insect Emergence Chart. *Ephemera varia*, and for that matter most other species, may emerge earlier or later in your locality because of light differences between your stream and those in central Pennsylvania.

Peaks vary tremendously from species to species—even from stream to stream for the same species. Nonetheless, trout activity (surface feeding) is usually at its best during the peak of a hatch. The emergence dates listed in Chapter 2 are rough estimates of the earliest dates you might expect a peak to occur.

CHAPTER 5

A REALISTIC APPROACH TO IMITATING MAYFLIES AND OTHER AQUATIC INSECTS

I first attempted fly-fishing on a local, marginal stream in eastern Pennsylvania in the early fifties. Some prodding by several angler friends and stories of success with artificials they used motivated me into purchasing an initial selection of two March Browns. I chose the March Brown wet fly because one of the locals indicated that he had limited out the day before on the same stream with that pattern. These imitations had a brown partridge hackle, tannish body, brown tail, and dark-brown wings.

As luck would have it, I came home that day with three heavy trout, all caught on the March Brown. I lost the first artificial on an early cast and caught all three fish on the second and last imitation I had. That latter wet fly was badly mutilated after a couple of hours of fishing, so I decided to obtain more March Browns at another store on my way home.

"Do you have any March Brown wet flies?" I asked the owner.

"Yes," he said, and he opened a large box of patterns and pointed to some imitations with very dark-brown bodies.

"No. I want a March Brown with a tannish body."

"Only ones I have are these dark ones," the owner said.

In desperation I looked for any artificial that roughly matched my original March Brown. Finally, I selected several patterns the owner listed as Brown Mallards because they did look a bit like the March Browns I had purchased before.

I've been dismayed these more than thirty years by the tremendous number of artificials available to fishermen—but more than that, dismayed by the variation of patterns with the same name.

Do you want to be utterly frustrated sometime? Try this experiment next time you purchase artificials. Visit two sporting goods stores and order the same pattern at each. If the patterns are not supplied by the same tier or company, you'll probably note some differences in the "same" dry fly. Of course, the Light Cahill, Dark Cahill, Quill Gordon, and many, many other common patterns will vary little. But buy two March Browns, Gray Foxes, Slate Drake (I bet they don't have this one), or Yellow Drakes (they probably won't have this one either), and you'll notice that the patterns are probably not similar.

Purchasing a good caddis fly or stone fly imitation is even more difficult. Ask for an imitation of the Grannom or the Little Black Caddis. They probably won't have either. The same comment goes for the Early Brown Stonefly. Yet all of these, plus many others, work well during the hatches they match. All of these artificials should have wings folded down over the body like the natural.

Suppose you tie your own imitations. To find information on the suggested pattern, check Donald DuBois' book, *The Fisherman's Handbook of Trout Flies*. This excellent work codes fly patterns according to common names. Examine this volume for patterns of the American March Brown and March Brown, and you'll find sixteen separate patterns for the first and sixty-four separate patterns for the second. Thus for two common names, we have eighty different patterns from which to choose. Check five other texts or articles on fly tying or fly-fishing and you'll probably come up with five additional March Brown patterns. Granted, the differences may be slight, but they're still differences.

Let's look at one more pattern in DuBois's book: the Green Drake. He has sixty-seven imitations listed for this mayfly, with body materials ranging from white floss to green floss to yellow floss to brown raffia. Hackles in these patterns range from brown to ginger to green. It appears that one man's Green Drake is another man's March Brown.

Even if you copy the natural as carefully as possible in every detail and as realistic as the pattern might appear, it will not always work. Sometimes what seems like an exact imitation doesn't work during a hatch of naturals that the imitation seemingly duplicates. Recently Bill Kimmel of California State University and I traveled to Falling Springs near Chambersburg to meet and fish while a *Tricorythodes* species appeared. Clouds of spinners saturated the air, and many spent females were already drifting on the water. I tied on a spent-female imitation, hook size 24, and cast over twenty or twenty-five actively feeding trout. Cast after cast, for two hours, we fished over these trout until the spinner fall subsided—and we caught only two fish. I became so frustrated I grabbed one of the female spinners floating past me and placed it next to my imitation. Although the natural was infinitesimally smaller, the color and the appearance were very similar. Was it the tapered leader? I was using a 6X leader with a tippet diameter of .042. Would another pattern have been more effective? Maybe. I'd rather think that the trout that Bill and I were attempting to catch that day had been "fished over" by hundreds of other fly-fishermen. For two months this particular *Tricorythodes* species

had appeared faithfully daily, along with fly-fishermen matching it. After all those imitations cast over them, the trout had become highly selective. Besides, this is a "no kill" stream and probably most of the trout had been hooked and released several times. Well, anyway, you can't blame me for trying to rationalize!

PATTERNS

If the Green Drake artificial is supposed to imitate the *Ephemera guttulata* duns, why do imitations with the same name vary so greatly? There are many reasons, but here are three. First, some fishermen, although they see the natural hundreds of times, think a change in color here or there might produce a more effective imitation. Evolution, especially in fly patterns, is not always more useful or more successful.

It's a revelation to journey upstream and downstream on Penns Creek just before a hatch of Green Drakes to observe which artificial each fly-fisherman is using. Each fisherman has his own pet pattern. Invariably each fisherman relives accounts of success his Drake pattern has engendered. On these walks, before the hatch begins and while all other anglers are at streamside waiting for the emergence, I've seen a host of imitations. These patterns vary in hook size from 6 to 16 and in body color from green to bright yellow. Remember, all of these diverse imitations represent one species, which varies little from individual to individual.

A second reason for pattern variation might be that color in the same species does vary from location to location. Leonard and Leonard in *Mayflies of Michigan Trout Streams* suggest that *Stenacron canadense* (the Light Cahill) varies from cream to dark brown depending on the locale. Many other species also deviate in color from stream to stream.

Our early dependence on English imitations is a third explanation for the divergence in patterns. Along with the name *mayfly*, the English gave us such patterns as the March Brown, the Green Drake, and the Iron Blue Dun. These patterns, intended for use on English streams, only vaguely represent the mayfly for which they're intended in the United States.

There are other reasons for this evident diversity of patterns. Two fly tiers might use different materials for the wings or the body, for example, because one material might be more accessible than others.

The imitations listed in this chapter represent both the male and female dun of a species. If the two sexes vary in coloration, I have included both duns.

Only occasionally do male imagos take on importance as trout food. Therefore, I've included only one male spinner pattern, *Tricorythodes stygiatus*. This male spinner is short-lived (usually three hours or less) and sometimes dies in numbers over the water. Another male spinner, the Jenny Spinner, which represents many species (especially in the Family Leptophlebiidae), does find its way to the surface, on occasion.

MATERIALS

You'll note some changes in materials used for the imitations. For spent wings of the spinner, I like white or very pale gray polypropylene tied perpendicular and flat. This material is exceptionally buoyant, durable, and versatile and comes in almost any color.

Recently George Harvey, the dean of fly-fishermen, suggested using a few strands of Krystal Flash with the poly to copy the spent wings. Spinner imitations with the new material perform much better than without it.

In the patterns, I repeatedly recommend spin fur and hackle stems as appropriate body materials and mallard quill sections for wings. Spun furs are easy to find, easy to work with, and available in many colors (as is polypropylene). Hackle stems (peacock also), when stripped, effectively duplicate the ribbed appearance of many mayflies.

Most fly tiers loathe using mallard quill sections for wings. The main disadvantage of these is that they split easily after a few casts. You can overcome this problem by applying a drop of Pliobond adhesive to each wing. You can use hackle tips also for wings, but when you want a dark slate wing, you can't beat mallard sections. The dark slate color of the mallard quill is similar to the wing coloration of many mayflies, such as the Slate Drake, Blue-Winged Olive Dun, and Blue Quill. More recently I've switched to hackle tips on most size 16 and larger flies because the quill wings often twist many of the finer tippets. Even if I list mallard quill sections in the pattern descriptions, you might instead consider hackle tips or another material.

CAUTIONS IN IMITATING THE HATCHES

A word of caution in the following descriptions. What one person interprets as yellowish cream might be yellow or cream to someone else. Also don't forget that body color can vary radically for the same species on different streams. It can even vary for the same species on the same stream. Furthermore, a day or two after emergence, the coloration of the dun can darken, and the spinner too often becomes darker the longer it lives. Some *Baetis* species exemplify this color change. Immediately after changing from dun to spinner, many *Baetis* species have tannish brown abdomens. Two days after the change, the body has evolved into a very dark brown.

With all of these cautions in mind, and probably many others not mentioned, we can look at the natural and suggested imitation for the various species. I've recorded some of the more important species to imitate in the following section. I describe the dun and spinner on the left and suggest a pattern on the right. Immediately following the description of each species, I have listed commercial patterns to purchase, which may prove as effective, or nearly so, as the recommended imitation.

I have placed duns in approximate chronological order; those emerging early in the season appear first on the list.

You'll probably note changes in some of the common names. If a species has no common name, I have used a common name that usually describes its general coloration.

NATURALS AND IMITATIONS
(Eastern and Midwestern)

Each description that follows can be used for tying a wet or a dry fly. If you prefer using wet flies, substitute a heavier steel hook, less buoyant body material, and hen hackle for the tail and legs. If the pattern you want to copy calls for a deer hair tail and the natural has a tail that is amber mottled with brown, use fibers from a mallard or wood duck flank feather instead. Rather than use a body made of dubbed poly, you might substitute fur or any other material that tends to sink more rapidly to tie the wet fly. When the wings of the dun are dark gray and the dry fly calls for dark gray hackle tips, use mallard quill sections for the wet fly.

Don't overlook the emerging caddis pupa. During many caddis hatches, these pupal imitations have made the difference between a day of frustration and one of success.

If you use poly yarn and tie the wings spent on the spinner, you'll probably omit hackle on your spinner imitations.

ORDER EPHEMEROPTERA—MAYFLIES

Baetis tricaudatus (vagans)	Imitation — Little Blue Dun
Dun — 5-7 mm	Hook size — 16-20
	Thread — Gray
Wing — Medium slate gray	Gray hackle tips
Body — Dark slate, ribbed lighter, and with a decided olive cast	Gray muskrat dyed olive and dubbed or grayish olive polypropylene
Legs — Tannish gray with pale gray tips	Pale dun hackle
Tail — Gray	Dark dun hackle fibers
Spinner	Rusty spinner
	Thread — Brown
Wing — Glassy clear	Pale gray hackle tips or pale polypropylene, tied spent
Body — Dark rusty brown, ribbed with tan	Dark brown hackle, stem stripped
Legs — Dark grayish brown	Dark brown hackle
Tail — Dark grayish brown	Dark brown hackle fibers

Commercial pattern, dun: Blue Dun or Little Blue-Winged Olive Dun
Commercial pattern, spinner: Rusty Spinner or Red Quill

I have seen this species on central Pennsylvania waters as early as March 5 and on New York's Beaverkill by April 1. It's important to include patterns copying *Baetis tricaudatus (vagans)* at the beginning of the season. I've also encountered this hatch on the Au Sable in September. You'll see two broods of this species each year.

To get the proper color for the body of the dun, place a piece of dark gray muskrat fur in a hot (but not boiling) bath of Rit Olive Dye. Leave the fur in the dye for only a minute or two; then rinse the fur with cold water to set the dye. For dry flies, grayish olive poly copies the natural perfectly.

The dark brown body of the female spinner is ribbed with a lighter tan. To obtain this ribbed effect, strip a dark-brown hackle stem of its fibers and wind. As with the Red Quill body, place a drop of lacquer on the completed body to prevent it from splitting.

Caution: On some streams, this species appears as a larger (8–9 mm) mayfly early in the season. Later broods are smaller (6-7 mm).

Paraleptophlebia adoptiva, P. mollis,	Imitation — Blue Quill
P. guttata, and similar species	Hook size — 18
Dun — 6–9 mm	Thread — Gray

Wing — Dark slate gray	Dark gray hackle tips
Body — Dark brownish gray	Peacock quill (not from the eye)
Legs — Grayish tan with darker markings	Light to medium blue dun hackle
Tail — Grayish brown	Dark blue dun hackle fibers
Spinner	Dark Brown Spinner
	Thread — Dark brown
Wing — Glassy clear	Pale gray polypropylene tied spent
Body — Dark brown	Dark brown polypropylene
Legs — Dark brown	Dark brown hackle
Tail — Dark brown	Dark brown hackle fibers

Commercial pattern, dun: Blue Quill
Commercial pattern, spinner: Dark Brown Spinner

The legs of many *Paraleptophlebia* species appear lighter than others. When tying the lighter species, use a lighter dun hackle. Female spinners of most species have dark brown bodies, legs, and tails. Few commercial imitations have this dark brown combination. Artificials of the imago are extremely effective, especially early in the season. Make certain you carry copies.

Many male spinners have amber or white bodies, with only the last couple of segments dark brown. These male imagos are the familiar Jenny Spinners and are often confused with Tricos. Midwestern rivers like the Manistee in Michigan host hatches into September.

Epeorus pleuralis	Imitation — Quill Gordon
Dun — 9–12 mm	Hook size — 12
	Thread — Gray

Wing — Slate gray	Dark gray hackle tips
Body — Dark gray, ribbed faintly with lighter gray (some areas of body become almost olive gray)	Eyed peacock quill, stripped
Legs — Tannish gray with darker markings	Blue dun variant hackle
Tail — Dark gray	Dark blue dun hackle fibers
Spinner	Red Quill Spinner
	Thread — Brown
Wing — Glassy clear	White polypropylene, tied spent
Body — Reddish to tannish brown, ribbed finely with tannish cream	Dark reddish brown hackle stem, stripped
Legs — Grayish tan with reddish brown markings	Medium blue dun hackle
Tail — Dark brown	Dark brown hackle fibers

Commercial pattern, dun: Quill Gordon
Commercial pattern, spinner: Red Quill

Immediately you'll note a difference in the suggested pattern over what you're accustomed to seeing. The imitation I suggest has a gray hackle tip wing, not barred wood duck. The wings of the natural are actually dark slate, so why use wood duck? If you feel your artificial is not complete without the wood duck, include it.

Until a few years ago, I recommended using mallard quills to copy the gray wings on many mayflies. If you include quill wings on larger patterns (size 18 and larger), these quill wings tend to twist the leader, especially the new super-strong, finer leader available today. I've now almost exclusively resorted to hen hackle.

Siphloplecton basale	Imitation — Great Speckled Olive Dun
Dun — 13–14 mm	Hook size — 12
	Thread — Pale gray
Wing — Gray, barred	Mallard flank
Body — Pale gray	Pale gray polypropylene, dubbed
Legs — Medium gray	Medium blue dun
Tail — Medium gray	Medium blue dun fibers
Spinner	Great Speckled Spinner
Wing — Clear with some brown barring	Pale tan poly yarn
Body — Grayish cream	Pale gray polypropylene, dubbed
Legs — Dark gray with lighter areas	Bronze dun variant
Tail — Brownish blue	Bronze dun variant fibers
Commercial patterns, dun and spinner: none	

I met this hatch only recently. Greg Hoover of Hallifax, Pennsylvania, introduced it to me on Clark Creek near Harrisburg. This large mayfly appears early in the season, and many anglers confuse it with the Hendrickson hatch or the later March Brown. The Great Speckled Olive Dun is found on some larger Eastern and Midwestern streams.

Ephemerella subvaria	Imitation — Hendrickson (female); Red Quill (male)
Dun — 9–12 mm	Hook size — 12 (female); 14 (male)
	Thread — Tan
Wing — Slate Gray	Gray hackle tips
Body — Female: creamish to dark tan ribbed lighter (sometimes with pinkish cast) Male: pinkish tan with lighter ribbing	Female: Tan fox belly fur Male: Reddish brown hackle stem
Legs — Creamish yellow marked with tannish gray	Tannish gray hackle with a turn or two of dirty cream hackle
Tail — Dark tannish gray	Dark bronze dun hackle fibers
Spinner	Red Quill Spinner Thread — Brown
Wing — Glassy clear	White polypropylene tied spent
Body — Dark tannish brown ribbed finely with tan	Reddish brown hackle stem
Legs — Tannish gray with reddish brown markings	Bronze dun hackle
Tail — Tannish gray with dark-brown markings	Bronze dun hackle fibers
Commercial pattern, dun: Hendrickson (female); Red Quill (male) Commercial pattern, spinner: Red Quill Spinner	

Again I suggest a dark hackle tip for the dun rather than the usual barred wood duck. Wood duck, however, does work well for the spinner.

The body of the Red Quill is formed from a reddish brown hackle, stripped of its barbules. To tie the body, strip the stem, and place it in water for a few minutes to make it more pliable. Tie the tip of the stripped stem on the hook at the bend, and wind toward the eye. Using the tip of the stem first makes the rear segments appear smaller than the front ones, much the same as in the natural.

The female spinner imitation is usually called the Female Beaverkill or the Female Hendrickson. The pattern most suggested has a body of cream, ribbed with yellow. The spinners I've observed, however, possess a tannish brown body ribbed with tan. Use a brown hackle stem as the basis for the body rather than the "cream-with-yellow-ribbing." Granted, the coloration of this species varies from location to location, but I still think the Red Quill might be more appropriate. You can add a turn or two of yellow polypropylene at the tip to imitate the egg sac of the female spinner.

If you plan to fish the Au Sable River system in Michigan or the Brule in Wisconsin in early May, make certain you have plenty of these patterns with you. If the hatch hasn't ended before the trout season has begun, the Hendrickson is a major hatch on these rivers.

Caution: Individuals of this species vary considerably in body color and size from stream to stream. I've seen female duns that could have been copied with a size 16 hook. Caucci and Nastasi in *Hatches II* suggest that there are several subspecies of *E. subvaria*. My records support this theory.

Leptophlebia cupida	
Dun — 9–12 mm	Imitation — Black Quill
	Hook size — 14
	Thread — Dark brown
Wings — Medium to dark slate gray	Dark gray hackle tips
Body — Dark slate gray (with brown cast), ribbed lighter	Eyed peacock herl, stripped
Legs — Front: dark brown (almost black) Rear: dark tan	Dark brown hackle with a turn or two of tan hackle in the rear
Tail — Grayish banded with brown	Dark bronze dun hackle fibers
Spinner	Early Brown Spinner
	Thread — Dark brown
Wing — Glassy clear with some brown in stigmatic (front) area of wing	Pale tan polypropylene
Body — Dark reddish brown banded with pale yellow	Dark reddish brown polypropylene ribbed with pale yellow thread
Legs — Front: dark (almost black) Rear: dark tannish brown	Dark brown hackle
Tail — Dark grayish brown (almost black)	Dark brown hackle fibers

Commercial pattern, dun: Black Quill
Commercial pattern, spinner: Early Brown Spinner

This species, although not as common as many others discussed in this chapter, can be important in late April and May. The Black Quill is common on lakes and ponds and on slow stretches of streams. All duns I have observed escape rapidly from the surface. Except for cold spring days, this phase of the insect is of questionable value to imitate. The spinner is active all afternoon, and the female does fall spent on the surface. The latter is probably the more important phase to imitate.

Ephemerella rotunda	Imitation — Sulphur Dun
Dun — 7–9 mm	Hook size — 14 or 16
	Thread — Cream
Wing — Pale gray	Pale gray hackle tips
Body — Creamish yellow with distinct	Creamish yellow polypropylene dyed pale
olive cast (male is more tan)	olive
Legs — Pale creamish yellow	Cream hackle
Tail — Pale creamish yellow	Cream hackle fibers
Spinner	Sulphur Spinner
	Thread — Tan
Wing — Glassy clear	White polypropylene tied spent
Body — Tan (male is reddish brown)	Red fox belly fur
Legs — Tan	Pale ginger hackle
Tail — Tan with darker ribbing	Pale ginger hackle fibers

Commercial pattern, dun: Sulphur Dun or Pale Evening Dun
Commercial pattern, spinner: Sulphur Spinner or Pale Evening Spinner

The body of some duns of this species has a distinct olive cast. For the past few years, commercially tied patterns have contained the correct color pattern. Some of these mayflies on Michigan and Pennsylvania waters are tan rather than yellow.

The male of the species is effectively copied with a size 16 Red Quill. Rarely do male spinners fall to the surface, but on some evenings they do. Carry some size 16 Red Quills with you.

This species is as common in the East and Midwest as the Pale Morning Dun is in the West. You'll find great hatches on the Mossy and Smith rivers in Virginia north to the Oatka in New York and west to the Boardman, Au Sable, and Mamistee in Michigan; and the Namekagon near Hayward, Wisconsin.

Caution: Members of this species vary greatly in color and size from stream to stream.

Ephemerella septentrionalis	Imitation — Pale Evening Dun
Dun — 7–9 mm	Hook size — 14 or 16
	Thread — Yellow
Wing — White to creamish gray	Cream hackle tips
Body — Creamish yellow with orangish	Pale orangish yellow polypropylene
cast	
Legs — Creamish yellow	Cream hackle
Tail — Creamish yellow	Cream hackle fibers
Spinner	
Wing — Glassy clear	Same as dun
Body — Creamish yellow	
Legs — Creamish yellow	
Tail — Creamish yellow	

Commercial pattern, dun and spinner: Pale Evening Dun

This species looks exactly like *Ephemerella dorothea* except for its size and emergence time. *E. septentrionalis* usually emerges earlier in the year than the smaller *E. dorothea*. The species is fairly common on Eastern waters from mid-May to early June.

Duns tend to emerge near the edge of streams around 8:00 P.M. The Pale Evening Dun is effective during the hatch. You might, however, make a few imitations with white wings rather than the pale gray if you feel the small variation is important.

Heptagenia aphrodite and *Heptagenia hebe*
Dun — 6–8 mm (*H. aphrodite*) and 5–7 mm
     (*H. hebe*)
  Wing — Pale gray and barred
  Body — Creamish yellow with olive cast
     (*H. hebe* has no olive cast)
  Legs — Yellowish cream
  Tail — Creamish yellow

Spinner
  Wing — Glassy clear
  Body — Pale yellow
  Legs — Pale yellow
  Tail — Cream

Imitation — Pale Evening Dun
Hook size — 14 or 16

Commercial pattern, dun and spinner: Pale Evening Dun

I don't suggest a pattern for these species, since the Pale Evening Dun in the correct sizes should suffice.

Since most *Heptagenia* species alight from the surface rapidly, you might need an imitation of one very infrequently. These and similar-looking *Heptagenia* species can be found on many streams from late May until late September. Most duns have yellowish cream bodies (sometimes with an olive cast), cream legs with darker markings, cream tails, and medium gray wings. At least one *Heptagenia* species has a tan body.

H. aphrodite, since it appears in mid-May when temperatures in the evening cool quickly, often rests before takeoff. Species emerging in July and August escape much more rapidly.

Stenonema fuscum
Dun — 9–12 mm

  Wing — Pale yellow, barred, and with
     a grayish cast
  Body — Pale creamish yellow to tan
  Legs — Creamish yellow with darker
     markings
  Tail — Amber with dark brown markings

Spinner

  Wing — Glassy clear with dark brown
     barring and darker area in
     stigmatic (front tip) section
  Body — Grayish tan, ribbed with pale tan
  Legs — Grayish tan with dark brown
     markings
  Tail — Tan with dark brown markings

Imitation — Gray Fox
Hook size — 12
Thread — Cream
Pale yellow mallard flank

Creamish yellow angora, dubbed
Cream variant hackle

Ginger hackle fibers

Ginger Quill Spinner
Thread — Tan
Pale amber hackle tips

Tan peacock eye, stripped
Cream ginger hackle

Ginger hackle fibers

Commercial pattern, dun: Gray Fox or Light Cahill
Commercial pattern, spinner: Ginger Quill

This species has typical *Stenonema* leg coloration: pale creamish yellow legs with brown markings. To obtain the desired coloration with the dark markings, use a badger or natural cream variant neck. The badger neck is cream with a dark center, and the cream variant is cream with ginger or light brown horizontal markings. Both colors do an effective job, but I lean toward the cream variant. The Light Cahill is an adequate substitute during an emergence of *S. fuscum* subimagos.

This species is abundant on Wisconsin rivers like the Wolf and Prarie; on Michigan waters like the Boardman, Little Manistee, and Au Sable; and on Eastern streams like the Rapidan and Big Run in Virginia and the Schoharie and Ausable in New York.

Caution: Coloration of this species varies from stream to stream.

Stenonema vicarium
Dun — 10–16 mm

Imitation — American March Brown
Hook size — 10–12
Thread — Yellow teal or mallard flank dyed pale tannish yellow

Wing — Tannish yellow, usually heavily barred with profuse black markings

Body — Creamish tan to dark tan, ribbed faintly with reddish brown
Creamish tan polypropylene or fox belly fur, ribbed with brown thread

Legs — Cream with dark brown markings
Cream variant or creamish yellow hackle, with grizzly dark brown hackle fibers

Tail — Dark brown barred
Dark brown hackle fibers

Spinner
Great Red Spinner
Thread — Dark brown

Wing — Glassy clear, with brown markings, and a brown area in the stagmatic region
Creamish tan mallard flank or tan polypropylene tied spent

Body — Tan, ribbed with dark brown
Fox belly fur, dubbed, and ribbed with dark brown thread

Legs — Amber, with dark brown markings
Cream ginger and dark brown hackle mixed

Tail — Dark brown, mottled
Dark brown hackle fibers

Commercial pattern, dun: American March Brown
Commercial pattern, spinner: Great Red Spinner

Some members of this species can be correctly imitated with a size 10 hook; however, this larger hook is more difficult to float for any distance, and I recommend a size 12.

Teal flank feathers contain much heavier barring than mallard flank. The former therefore better duplicates the wings of the American March Brown.

I have never seen a female spinner, the Great Red Spinner, fall spent on the surface. A closely related species, *S. pudicum*, appears at the same time of year as does *S. vicarium*, and female spinners of the former species do become important to copy on rare occasions with a Great Red Spinner.

This species doesn't appear on as many streams as does *S. fuscum*. When it does appear, it can be important. The March Brown is fairly abundant on the Rapidan and Big Run in Virginia.

Caution: Color and size of individuals of this species vary considerably.

Stenacron interpunctatum canadense	Imitation — Light Cahill
Dun — 9–12 mm	Hook size — 12 or 14
	Thread — Pale yellow
Wing — Pale yellow, barred slightly	Pale yellow mallard flank feather
Body — Creamish yellow (female has orange cast)	Creamish yellow polypropylene (with orange cast to imitate female)
Legs — Creamish yellow, marked with dark brown	Cream variant hackle or creamish yellow with a turn of brown hackle
Tail — Creamish yellow	Creamish yellow hackle fibers
Spinner	Salmon Spinner (female)
	Thread — Yellow or pink
Wing — Glassy clear with faint yellow cast	Very pale yellow mallard flank feather
Body — Pale yellow (the female, with eggs, has a creamish orange cast)	Pale cream polypropylene
Legs — Creamish yellow, marked with dark brown	Same as dun
Tail — Creamish	Cream hackle fibers

Commercial pattern, dun: Light Cahill
Commercial pattern, spinner: Salmon Spinner or Light Cahill

The Light Cahill effectively copies both the male dun and spinner of this species. However, as with many *Stenonema* and other *Stenacron* species, male and female duns differ greatly in body coloration. The artificial for the female dun should contain a distinct orange cast to the body. Several other similar species have orange or pink bodies; it's important to have on hand dry flies copying these body colors.

Caution: Coloration of this species varies from stream to stream.

Litobrancha recurvata	Imitation — Dark Green Drake
Dun — 20–28 mm	Hook size — 8 or 10
	Thread — Dark gray
Wing — Black, heavily barred, with dark green reflections	Green teal flank feather
Body — Dark slate, ribbed finely with yellow olive	Dark gray polypropylene dubbed and ribbed with yellow thread
Legs — Front: dark brown Rear: tannish brown	Dark brown hackle
Tail — Black	Moose mane
Spinner	Brown Drake
	Thread — Dark brown
Wing — Glassy, heavily barred with dark brown	Brown teal flank
Body — Reddish brown, ribbed with yellow	Dark brown polypropylene ribbed with fine yellow thread
Legs — Dark brown	Dark brown hackle
Tail — Black	Black hackle fibers

Commercial pattern, dun: Dark Green Drake
Commercial pattern, spinner: Brown Drake

As with the Black Quill, this species does not often produce a fishable hatch. These mayflies tend to emerge around the end of May in small, cold streams containing some slow water. Duns appear as early as 1:00 P.M. I have seen hundreds of these duns emerge concurrently with Green Drakes on small streams. Bryan Meck fished when a heavy emergence of this species occurred and when the Dark Green Drake imitation worked well. After their mating ritual, female spinners ride the water spent for great distances. Note the change from the genus *Hexagenia* to *Litobrancha*.

Ephemera simulans	Imitation — Brown Drake
Dun — 11–15 mm	Hook size — 10 or 12
	Thread — Brown
Wing — Grayish tan with dark brown markings	Grayish tan flank feather
Body — Grayish tan (with yellow cast) with dark brown markings	Grayish tan polypropylene
Legs — Dark brown, with lighter markings on rear pair	Dark brown hackle with a few turns of ginger
Tail — Dark brown, ringed with tan	Dark brown deer hair
Spinner	Brown Drake Spinner
	Hook size — 10 or 12
	Thread — Brown
Wing — Glassy clear with dark brown markings	Pale tan polypropylene yarn with dark brown fibers tied upright or spent
Body — Dark tannish yellow with dark brown markings	Dark tannish yellow polypropylene
Legs — Same as dun	
Tail — Same as dun	

Commercial pattern, dun and spinner: Brown Drake or Ginger Quill

---

Don't be without imitations of the Brown Drake. *Ephemera simulans* is found in all three regions of the United States. It is common on Connecticut's Housatonic River, the upper Delaware River between New York and Pennsylvania, and many other Pennsylvania streams. In the East, the hatch appears the last week in May. In the Midwest, it appears on rivers like the Au Sable and Pigeon in Michigan. On the Brule and Namekagon in Wisconsin, the hatch appears most often in early June. In the West, you can expect to see hatches on Henry's Fork and the Wood River in Idaho and on the Firehole in Yellowstone Park. Hatches on Henry's Fork don't appear until the end of June.

The spinner has brown markings on both sides of its belly. To make these markings, I use a brown felt waterproof marking pen.

The Brown Drake usually appears for no more than three to five days. If you meet the hatch and carry the Brown Drake patterns, you're in for a memorable experience.

Eurylophella (Ephemerella) bicolor	Imitation — Chocolate Dun
Dun — 6–9 mm	Hook size — 16
	Thread — Brown
Wing — Slate gray	Dark gray hackle tips
Body — Chocolate brown	Chocolate brown polypropylene finely ribbed with lighter brown thread
Legs — Tannish brown	Tan hackle
Tail — Gray	Medium gray
Spinner	Chocolate Spinner
	Thread — Dark brown
Wing — Glassy clear	Pale gray polypropylene tied spent
Body — Dark chocolate brown	Dark rusty brown polypropylene dubbed
Legs — Dark brown	Dark brown hackle
Tail — Tannish gray	Pale gray hackle fibers

Commercial pattern, dun: None
Commercial pattern, spinner: Dark Brown Spinner

The Chocolate Dun copies several species in the Genus *Eurylophella*. These duns can be found on many streams in late May through June. Most often the naturals emerge around midday.

Isonychia bicolor, I. sadleri, rufa, matilda, and *harperi*	Imitation — Slate Drake
Dun — 12–16 mm	Hook size — 10–14
	Thread — Gray
Wing — Dark slate gray	Dark gray hackle tips
Body — Dark slate gray	Peacock (not from eye) stripped
Legs — Front: dark brown	One cream and one dark brown hackle
Rear pair: cream	
Tail — Medium gray	Medium blue dun fibers
Spinner	White-Gloved Howdy
	Thread — Brown
Wing — Glassy clear	White polypropylene or hackle tips tied spent
Body — Dark reddish mahogany	Dark reddish mahogany raffia
Legs — Same as dun	One cream and one dark brown hackle
Tail — Medium gray	Medium blue dun fibers

Commercial pattern, dun: Leadwing Coachman
Commercial pattern, spinner: White-Gloved Howdy, Mahogany Spinner

On several imitations listed, I've recommended using peacock fibers stripped. To tie the Slate Drake, take the fiber from the lower part of the tail feather. Fibers from this area don't contain the light and dark sides the eyed peacock has but rather a uniform dark slate color.

Fast-water versions of the Slate Drake are very effective. To tie the wings, use impala dyed dark gray, dark gray poly for the body, and pale gray deer hair for the tail.

Some Slate Drake species may produce more than one brood per year and become important on many Eastern waters again in late September and early October.

Ephemera guttulata	Imitation — Green Drake
Dun — 16–22 mm	Hook size — 8–12
	Thread — Cream
Wing — Yellowish green heavily barred with dark brown or black	Yellowish green mallard flank
Body — Pale cream	Cream polypropylene
Legs — Front: dark brown / Rear: cream	Two cream hackles in rear and one dark brown hackle in front
Tail — Dark brownish black	Dark brown moose or dark brown hackle stems
Spinner	Coffin Fly
	Thread — White
Wing — Glassy, but heavily barred and with a yellow cast	Pale yellow mallard flank or pale cream polypropylene
Body — Chalky white	White polypropylene or ten long white bucktail hairs
Legs — Front: dark brown / Rear: cream	Same as dun
Tail — Tannish mottled with dark brown	Ginger hackle stems, stripped brown of barbules, or light brown deer body hair

Commercial pattern, dun: Green Drake
Commercial pattern, spinner: Coffin Fly or White Wulff

For the female spinner, I suggest white polypropylene or white bucktail. John Perhach showed me an effective method of using the bucktail. Take about ten white hairs from a tail, and tie in by their tips at the bend of the hook. Wind over the extended body and forward toward the wing. Not only is the bucktail buoyant, but the chalky white color of the material is similar to the natural. White poly also copies the natural.

Use pale cream polypropylene to imitate the body of the dun. It's much more durable and buoyant than older materials like raffia. If you prefer an old method of tying an extended body, add a 3-inch piece of 20- or 30-pound monofilament line. To make the monofilament easier to secure to the hook, flatten the end to be tied with pliers. After you secure the line, take three very dark moose mane hairs or very dark brown hackle stems. If you use the stems, strip them of their barbules. Tie in the hairs or the stems by their butts. Now dub in the cream polypropylene or raffia midway on the shank. Wind the body material back over the extended body (monofilament) for an inch or two (depending on the size of the fly), and wind forward to the wings. Cut off the monofilament where the body ends, and shape the tail.

I've had more success recently with a wet-fly version of the dry fly. Often when naturals emerge and I have no success with a floating fly, I purposely sink the imitation. This often works.

Maryland streams like the Youghiogheny River, Big Hunting Creek, and the Savage River hold populations of this species. The Delaware River near Hancock, New York, and the Beaverkill near Roscoe, New York, contain excellent hatches.

Caution: Size and color of this species vary from stream to stream.

Epeorus vitreus	Imitation — Light Cahill (male); Pink Cahill (female)
Dun — 7–9 mm	Hook size — 14 or 16
	Thread — Cream
Wing — Pale grayish with yellow cast not barred	Pale yellow mallard flank
Body — Male: pale yellow; Female: pinkish cream; top has dark reddish brown markings (both sexes have an olive cast)	Pale yellow or pinkish cream (depending on sex) polypropylene (with a slight olive cast)
Legs — Creamish yellow marked with brown	Creamish yellow hackle
Tail — Dark grayish brown	Dark blue dun hackle fibers
Spinner	Salmon Spinner
	Thread — Salmon
Wing — Glassy clear	Pale gray polypropylene
Body — Pinkish red	Coral polypropylene
Legs — Creamish tan, barred	Cream ginger hackle
Tail — Creamish tan	Cream ginger hackle fibers

Commercial pattern, dun: Light Cahill
Commercial pattern, spinner: Salmon Spinner

I have encountered this species on Six Mile Run in north-central Pennsylvania, the Delaware River, and the Brodhead near Stroudsburg. The hatch on the Delaware and the Brodhead can be spectacular and important to match. Male and female body colors vary considerably.

Ephemerella invaria	Imitation — Pale Evening Dun or Sulphur
Dun — 6–9 mm	Hook size — 16
	Thread — Yellow
Wing — Pale to medium gray	Gray hackle tips
Body — Creamish yellow with heavy orange cast	Creamish yellow polypropylene orange cast
Legs — Creamish yellow	Creamish yellow hackle
Tail — Creamish yellow	Creamish yellow hackle fibers
Spinner	Pale Evening Spinner or Sulphur Spinner
	Thread — Tan
Wing — Glassy clear	White polypropylene, tied spent
Body — Orangish tan (tan without the eggs)	Tan polypropylene
Legs — Tan	Ginger hackle
Tail — Pale cream	Cream hackle fibers

Commercial pattern, dun: Pale Evening Dun or Sulphur Dun
Commercial pattern, spinner: Pale Evening Spinner or Sulphur Spinner

The body of this dun has a distinct orange cast. To copy the body color, soak white polypropylene in Rit Yellow Dye for five to ten minutes. This dye has a hint of orange, and when the material is saturated, it produces a body almost indistinguishable from the natural. Male duns are much darker than the females.

Wings for this imitation should be very pale gray, so select sections from the base of two mallard quills or very pale gray hackle tips.

Serratella (Ephemerella) deficiens
  Dun — 5–7 mm

This species can be copied with a Dark Blue Quill.

Tie the pattern on a size 20 hook, use a darker gray hackle for the legs and tail, and a dark gray stripped peacock herl from the base of the feather.

Ephemerella dorothea	Imitation — Pale Evening Dun
Dun — 5–7 mm	Hook size — 16 or 18
	Thread — Cream
Wing — Very pale gray	Pale gray hackle tips
Body — Creamish yellow	Pale yellow polypropylene
Legs — Pale yellowish cream	Yellowish cream hackle
Tail — Yellowish cream	Yellowish cream hackle fibers
Spinner	Pale Evening Spinner
	Thread — Cream
Wing — Glassy Clear	White polypropylene
Body — Creamish yellow	Creamish yellow polypropylene
Legs — Creamish yellow	Creamish yellow hackle
Tail — Cream	Cream hackle fibers

Commercial pattern, dun and spinner: Pale Evening Dun

This species is often placed with *Ephemerella rotunda* and *E. invaria*. *E. dorothea*, however, is usually pale yellow with little olive or orange cast, and it usually emerges later in the season than the other two.

Many Eastern and Midwestern streams and rivers contain good populations of this species. The North Branch of the Au Sable in Michigan holds a good number, as does the Delaware between New York and Pennsylvania.

Attenella (Ephemerella) attenuata	Imitation — Blue-Winged Olive Dun
Dun — 7–10 mm	Hook size — 14
	Thread — Olive
Wing — Dark bluish gray	Dark gray hackle tips
Body — Medium olive faintly ribbed and with a gray cast	Medium olive hackle stem or muskrat, dyed olive
Legs — Medium olive	Medium olive hackle
Tail — Grayish	Blue dun hackle fibers
Spinner	Dark Olive Spinner
	Thread — Dark brown
Wing — Glassy clear	Pale gray hackle tips
Body — Rusty brown with an olive cast	Dark brown fur with an olive cast
Legs — Tannish gray	Blue dun hackle
Tail — Tannish gray	Blue dun hackle fibers

Commercial pattern, dun: Blue-Winged Olive Dun
Commercial pattern, spinner: Dark Olive Spinner

I have seen this species on two occasions, both on the Beaverkill in early June. It appears to have an olive body with a distinct gray cast. You might want to use the same muskrat dyed olive suggested for some of the *Baetis* species.

Ephemerella needhami	Imitation — Chocolate Dun
Dun — 6–9 mm	Hook size — 16
	Thread — Dark brown
Wing — Dark slate	Dark hackle tips
Body — Chocolate brown, ribbed finely with tan	Dark brown polypropylene, ribbed with fine gold wire
Legs — Creamish tan	Cream ginger hackle
Tail — Medium gray	Medium dun hackle fibers
Spinner	Chocolate Spinner
	Thread — Dark brown
Wing — Glassy clear	Pale gray hackle tips
Body — Dark rusty brown	Dark brown polypropylene
Legs — Cream	Cream hackle
Tail — Tannish gray	Bronze dun hackle fibers

Commercial pattern, dun and spinner: Little Marryat

I have observed both dun and spinner of this species on small streams in late May and early June shortly after noon. Artificials imitating the dun have proved very productive during hatches of this species. *E. needhami* is found from Virginia to Wisconsin and north to Nova Scotia.

Stenonema pulchellum	Imitation — Cream Cahill
Dun — 9–13 mm	Hook size — 12 or 14
	Thread — Cream
Wing — Pale cream and very slightly barred	Very pale cream mallard flank feather
Body — Very pale cream, almost white	White or pale cream polypropylene
Legs — Pale cream with darker markings	Cream hackle
Tail — Pale tan	Tan hackle fibers
Spinner	Cream Cahill Spinner
Wing — Glassy clear with brown shading in stigmatic (front) region	Use dun imitation and substitute pale gray polypropylene yarn for the wings
Body — White (female with eggs has pale cream body)	
Legs — Pale cream with darker markings	
Tail — Pale tan mottled	

Commercial pattern, dun and spinner: White Wulff

Since dun and spinner of this species are similar except for wings, one imitation will suffice for both. Duns emerge sporadically during the day, with the heaviest appearances from 10:00 A.M. to 2:00 P.M. and again near dusk. The spinner can be an important source of food for trout. Spinners usually appear about 8:00 P.M., lay their eggs, and move back toward shore. While laying eggs, the female alights and rests briefly on the surface. Emergence begins about mid-June and continues through September in sparser numbers. The spinner of the species appears in the evening shortly before the Yellow Drake.

The Cream Cahill also copies many other cream *Stenonema* mayflies like *S. luteum* and *S. modestum.*

Heptagenia marginalis
Dun — 9–13 mm

    Wing — Yellow, slightly barred
    Body — Yellowish cream
    Legs — Yellow with grayish tan markings
    Tail — Dark brown

Spinner

    Wing — Glassy clear with some dark
          brown in stigmatic (front) region
    Body — Grayish cream (with faint olive
          cast)

    Legs — Front: dark grayish brown
          Rear: yellowish cream with darker
          markings
    Tail — Dark grayish brown

Commercial pattern, dun: Light Cahill
Commercial pattern, spinner: Light Hendrickson

Imitation — Light Cahill
Hook size — 12
Thread — Cream
Yellow mallard flank
Yellowish cream polypropylene
One cream and one blue dun hackle
Dark brown hackle fibers

Olive Cahill Spinner
Thread — Cream
Pale gray hackle tips or cream polypropylene
   yarn tied spent
Fox belly fur dubbed

Front dark brown hackle; rear cream hackle

Dark brown hackle fibers

The dun of this species is almost identical to the male of *Stenacron interpunctatum canadense*, and the imitation of the latter will prove effective for this species. The spinner, however, is probably the more important phase to copy. Although emergence of the dun is very sparse from its beginning in mid-June to its end in September, there are enough spinners over fast water to make it common and an imitation important. Female imagos are active about 8:00 P.M. and hover a few inches above rapids laying eggs. Since the adult is so near the water's surface, it is often difficult, or even impossible, to detect its presence. On several occasions I've observed trout jumping completely out of the water to seize the naturals. I've tied the spinner imitation with a very long hackle to attempt to duplicate the hovering spinner. Sometimes dragging the artificial upstream during this egg-laying flight can be effective. I incorrectly identified this spinner in the first edition as *Stenonema luteum*.

Drunella (Ephemerella) cornuta
  Dun — 7–10 mm

    Wing — Dark slate
    Body — Medium olive (may have grayish
          cast)
    Legs — Amber with olive cast
    Tail — Pale grayish olive

Spinner

    Wing — Glassy clear

    Body — Dark olive (male has brown-olive
          body)
    Legs — Dark olive brown
    Tail — Dark gray

Commercial pattern, dun: Blue-Winged Olive Dun
Commercial pattern, spinner: Dark Olive Spinner

Imitation — Blue-Winged Olive Dun
Hook size 14
Thread — Olive
Dark hen hackle tips or poly
Fox belly fur dyed olive

Ginger cream hackle
Pale blue dun hackle fibers

Dark Olive Spinner
Thread — Dark olive
Pale gray hackle tips or polypropylene,
   tied spent
Muskrat fur, dyed olive or dark olive
   polypropylene
Dark brown hackle
Dark blue dun hackle fibers

This species is highly important to imitate in the dun and spinner stages. Although the majority of these mayflies emerge in late May, you'll see stragglers until September. Meeting and fishing the dun most often occurs in the morning; the spinner is most active just at dusk.

Baetis species	
Dun — 4–6 mm	Imitation — Little Blue Dun
	Hook size — 20
	Thread — Olive
Wing — Medium gray	Mallard quills or gray hackle tips
Body — Medium olive	Muskrat, dyed olive
Legs — Creamish tan	Cream ginger hackle
Tail — Medium gray	Medium blue dun hackle fibers
Spinner	Rusty Spinner
	Thread — Brown
Wing — Glassy clear	Pale gray hackle tips
Body — Medium brown	Medium to dark brown polypropylene
Legs — Tannish	Dark ginger hackle
Tail — Tannish	Dark ginger hackle fibers

Commercial pattern, dun: Blue-Winged Olive Dun
Commercial pattern, spinner: Rusty Spinner

Although I have not yet had this species identified, it is an extremely important mayfly to imitate. The species appears on many streams in July during the afternoon and evening. Furthermore, the dun of the species rests a long time before taking flight. The pattern can be used for just about all of the *Baetis* species listed in the Insect Emergence Chart.

This species has a deeper olive color to its body than does *Baetis tricaudatus (vagans)*. To duplicate the body color, place the gray muskrat fur in Rit Olive Dye for several minutes.

The male spinner resembles the Jenny Spinners of the genus *Paraleptophlebia*.

Dannella (Ephemerella) simplex
Dun — 5–7 mm

To copy this species, use the same pattern listed for *Baetis* species. Tie the pattern in a size 20 or 22. If you locate this species, you're in for some great late-season fly-fishing. The hatch appears heaviest late in the morning beginning in mid-June. Duns often continue to appear until late afternoon.

Hexagenia limbata Dun — 17–26 mm	Imitation — Michigan Caddis Hook size — 6X Thread — Brown
Wing — Smoky gray with a distinct olive cast	Teal flank feather, dyed smoky gray and with an olive cast
Body — Yellowish brown, with dark brown markings on top (coloration of this species varies from tannish yellow to brown)	Yellowish brown polypropylene
Legs — Tannish yellow with darker markings	Cream ginger hackle with a couple of turns of brown
Tail — Brown	Brown hackle fibers
Spinner	Michigan Spinner Thread — Brown
Wing — Glassy clear with dark purple markings in the costal area (front area)	Mallard flank feather
Body — Varies from yellow to yellowish brown	Brownish yellow polypropylene
Legs — Front: dark brown Rear pair: yellow	One dark brown and two cream ginger hackles
Tail — Tannish yellow	Cream ginger hackle fibers

Commercial pattern, dun: Michigan Caddis, Great Olive-Winged Drake
Commercial pattern, spinner: Michigan Spinner

If you plan to fly-fish any one of dozens of Michigan rivers like the Au Sable, Pere Marquette, Manistee, or Boardman from mid-June to July, make certain you have imitations of the Michigan Caddis or Great Olive Winged Drake with you. You'll find this hatch important on the Brule, Wolf, and Namekagon rivers in Wisconsin. Usually activity begins after dusk.

Drunella (Ephemerella) lata Dun — 7–9 mm	Imitation — Blue-Winged Olive Dun Hook size — 16 Thread — Olive
Wing — Dark slate gray	Dark gray hackle tips
Body — Medium olive	Olive polypropylene, dubbed
Legs — Ginger with olive cast	Pale olive hackle
Tail — Gray with olive cast	Gray hackle fibers
Spinner	Dark Olive Spinner
Wing — Glassy clear	Pale gray polypropylene, tied spent
Body — Very dark olive	Dark olive poly
Legs — Very dark olive	Dark olive hackle
Tail — Very dark olive	Dark olive hackle fibers

Commercial pattern, dun: Blue-Winged Olive Dun
Commercial pattern, spinner: Dark Olive Spinner

This Blue-Winged Olive Dun appears on Eastern streams like Penns Creek in Pennsylvania and many of the Michigan streams like the Au Sable, Little Manistee, and Platte. In most areas, the hatch lasts for a couple of weeks. In the East, you'll encounter this Blue-Winged Olive Dun in later June and early July. In the Midwest, the hatch usually appears in mid-July.

The evening spinner fall can be spectacular with this species. Trout become extremely selective during the fall and refuse taking any spinner imitation except one with a dark olive dun body.

Ephemera varia Dun — 12–14 mm	Imitation — Yellow Drake Hook size — 12 Thread — Pale yellow
Wing — Pale yellow, barred	Pale yellow mallard flank
Body — Pale yellow	Pale yellow polypropylene
Legs — Pale yellow, front pair with darker markings	Creamish yellow with a turn of grizzly in front
Tail — Tan with darker markings	Pale deer hair
Spinner	Yellow Drake Spinner Thread — Pale yellow
Wing — Glassy clear with barring	Mallard flank or pale polypropylene, tied spent
Body — Creamish yellow	Pale creamish yellow polypropylene
Legs — Rear: creamish yellow Front: darker	Dun variant
Tail — Amber with darker markings	Dark deer hair
Commercial pattern, dun: Yellow Drake	

The Yellow Drake takes on importance in late June and early July on many Eastern streams like the Little Juniata River and the Beaverkill. You'll need this pattern on Midwestern waters.

Tricorythodes stygiatus and *T. attratus* Dun — 3–4 mm	Imitation — Pale Olive Dun Hook size — 24–26 Thread — Pale olive
Wing — Pale gray	Pale gray hackle tips
Body — Pale creamish olive (female); medium dark brown (male)	Olive green polypropylene (female); dark brown polypropylene (male)
Legs — Pale cream	Cream hackle
Tail — Cream (female); pale gray (male)	Cream hackle fibers (female); gray hackle fibers (male)
Spinner	Harvey Trico Thread — Dark brown
Wing — Glassy clear	White or pale gray polypropylene tied spent, with two or three strands of sparkle yarn
Body — Female: rear half of abdomen is pale cream and front half is dark brown	Rear half pale cream polypropylene, front half dark brown polypropylene
Body — Male: dark brown faintly ribbed lighter	Dark brown polypropylene
Legs — Female: pale cream Male: front are dark brown and rear are cream	Female, pale dun; Male, pale dun with a turn of dark brown in front
Commercial pattern, dun: Pale Sulphur Dun	

Many fly tiers have asked how to tie wings on a size 24 hook. I always say, "Very carefully." For the dun imitation, I use two hackle tips from a hen's neck, trim them to size, and tie them on.

Wing placement on spinner imitations is easier. Tie in the polypropylene perpendicular to and on the same plane as the shank of the hook. Wind over and around each wing to secure. Add a couple of strands of sparkle yarn. George Harvey first recommended adding sparkle yarn, and it really works. Try it especially after the hatch has been on a stream for awhile.

When tying the body of the female spinner imitation, take a piece of pale cream polypropylene, and tie it in at the bend of the hook. After making two or three complete turns with the pale cream, dub some dark brown poly, tie in, and wind up the shank to the spent wings.

Hexagenia atrocaudata	Imitation — Big Slate Drake
Dun — 16–26 mm	Hook size — 6 or 8
	Thread — Dark gray
Wing — Dark slate	Dark gray calf tail
Body — Dark slate (may be finely ribbed)	Peacock, stripped (take from bottom of herl)
Legs — Dark brown	Dark brown hackle
Tail — Dark grayish brown	Dark gray hackle fibers
Spinner	Dark Brown Spinner
Wing — Glassy clear with rear of front and rear wing ringed with dark brown	Brown mallard flank feathers or tan polypropylene
Body — Tannish yellow ribbed finely with dark brown	Tannish yellow polypropylene ribbed with with dark brown thread
Legs — Front: dark brown Rear: tannish yellow	One dark brown hackle in front and a tannish yellow one in the rear
Tail — Dark brown	Dark brown hackle fibers

Commercial pattern, dun: Dark Cahill
Commercial pattern, spinner: American March Brown

How do you tie a size 6 or 8 dry-fly hook to make it float consistently? That's difficult to do, but if you make the body of trimmed deer hair or poly, it will probably work. I prefer, however, to tie the imitation on a size 10 or 12 long shank dry-fly hook. I firmly believe that an imitation smaller than the natural emerging is much more successful than one larger than the actual mayfly. Don't overlook this late August species. Allentown, Pennsylvania, area fishermen look forward to hatch and spinner fall on the Little Lehigh Creek.

Ephoron leukon	Imitation — White Mayfly
Dun — 9–12 mm	Hook size — 14 or 16
	Thread — White or cream
Wing — Very pale gray	Pale gray hackle tips or pale gray polypropylene, upright
Body — Female: pale cream Male: white with rear two segments pale brown	Pale cream or white polypropylene Same
Legs — Front: very dark brown Rear: white	White hackle with a turn of dark brown in front
Tail — Pale gray	Pale blue dun hackle fibers
Spinner (male only)	
Wing — Clear	
Body — White (rear two brown)	
Legs — Front: dark brown Rear: white	
Tail — Pale gray	

Commercial pattern, dun and spinner: White Wulff or White Mayfly

Again one imitation should suffice for both dun and spinner. *Ephoron leukon* can be a locally important species in August and September. While finishing *Pennsylvania Trout Streams and Their Hatches*, I found twelve trout streams in Pennsylvania with White Mayfly hatches. When you discover a stream that contains these nymphs, you're probably in for some excellent late-season fly-fishing. This species is important on the Housatonic River in Connecticut and on the lower end of the Au Sable and Muskegon in Michigan.

The female never sheds its subimagal skin and therefore mates and lays its eggs as a dun. The male dun changes to the spinner stage almost immediately after emerging. Many times the male spinner carries the partially shed skin while in flight. The male is noticeably smaller and more streamlined than is the female. On some streams and rivers, a size 16 will copy the length of the male spinner.

Caution: The size of this species varies from stream to stream.

ORDER TRICHOPTERA — CADDIS FLIES

Rhyacophila lobifera	Imitation — Green Caddis
Adult — 8–12 mm	Hook size — 14–16[1]
	Thread — Green
Wing — Medium brown, heavily flecked	Brown deer body hair
Body — Medium green to grayish green	Green polypropylene
Legs — Tan	Tan hackle (optional with deer hair)

[1]Mustad 94840 recommended for imitations unless another hook is specifically mentioned.

Rhyacophila fuscula is another member of this free-swimming genus common on trout waters. You'll see this caddis emerging from June to September.

Brachycentrus fuliginosus and *B. numerosus*	Imitation — Grannom
Adult — 9–12 mm	Hook size — 12–16
	Thread — Black
Wing — Dark brown, heavily flecked	Dark turkey tail or dark brown deer hair
Body — Dark brownish black	Black fur dubbed
Legs — Dark brown	Dark brown hackle

Brachycentrus numerosus has two color phases. Don Baylor and others on the Delaware refer to the lighter phase as the Straw Caddis because of its tan body.

Symphitopsyche slossanae	Imitation — Spotted Sedge
Adult — 7–10 mm	Hook size — 14 or 16
	Thread — Tan
Wing — Tan, flecked	Pale deer hair
Body — Tan	Fox fur
Legs — Amber	Ginger cream hackle

Symphitopsyche bronta is common on Eastern waters from June to September. This caddis also has a tan body and is adequately copied by the same Spotted Sedge imitation.

Psilotreta frontalis	Imitation —Dark Blue Sedge
Adult — 10–12 mm	Hook size — 12
	Thread — Dark gray
Wing — Dark bluish gray	Dark bluish gray hackle tips or deer hair dyed gray
Body — Dark slate gray	Peacock herl (not eyed) or dark gray polypropylene
Legs — Dark brownish black	Dark brown hackle

A common Gray Caddis, *Psilotreta labida*, also appears in June.

Chimarra atterima	Imitation — Little Black Caddis
Adult — 6–10 mm	Hook size — 16
	Thread — Black
Wing — Medium gray	Medium gray mallard quills or dark deer hair
Body — Black	Black fur dubbed
Legs — Dark brown	Dark brown hackle

Many anglers confuse *Chimarrha atterima* with another size 16 Little Black Caddis, *Dolophilodes distinctus*. This latter species hatches year round. Don Baylor says that he finds *Chimarrha* on warmer areas of a stream and *D. distinctus* on cooler stretches of water.

Caddis Larva
Thread: Appropriate color (most often dark brown or black)
Body: Olive, green, brown, yellow, black, or tan fur dubbed and ribbed with fine wire, or use a rubber band of the appropriate color and tie in at the bend of the hook and spiral to the eye
Thorax: Dark brown fur, dubbed; or an ostrich herl, dyed dark brown, wound around the hook several times
Hook: Mustad 37160, sizes 12–18

Emerging Caddis Pupa
Thread: Same color as the body color selected
Body: Olive, green, brown, yellow, black, or tan fur or polypropylene nymph dubbing material
Wings: (Optional) Dark mallard quill sections shorter than normal and tied in on both sides of the fly, not on top
Legs: Dark brown grouse or woodcock neck feather wound around the hook two or three times
Hook: 37160, sizes 12 to 18

Strophopteryx faciata
Adult — 8–10 mm

Wing — Dark brown barred
Body — Dark brownish gray

Legs — Dark brown
Tail — Dark brown

Imitation — Early Brown Stone fly
Hook size — 14
Thread — Dark brown
Mallard flank feather dyed brown
Peacock (not eyed) stripped or brownish gray polypropylene
Dark brown hackle
Dark brown hackle fibers

Isoperla signata
Adult — 10–14 mm

Wing — Pale yellow barred

Body — Pale yellow ribbed with tannish brown
Legs — Cream ginger
Tail — Cream ginger

Imitation — Light Stonefly
Hook size — 12–14
Thread — Pale yellow
Mallard flank feather dyed pale tannish yellow
Pale yellow floss ribbed with tannish yellow
Cream ginger hackle
Cream ginger hackle fibers

Isoperla bilineata
Adult — 7–10 mm
Wing — Pale yellow
Body — Pale yellow
Legs — Creamish yellow
Tail — Yellow. Short

Imitation — Yellow Stonefly
Hook — 14 or 16
Pale deer hair, dyed yellow
Primrose polypropylene, dubbed
Pale yellow hackle
Very short yellow hackle fibers

Alloperla imbecilla
Adult — 6–8 mm
Wing — Pale green
Body — Bright light green
Legs — Pale green
Tail — Pale green

Imitation — Little Green Stone Fly
Hook — 16
Pale deer hair, dyed green
Green polypropylene, dubbed
Pale green hackle
Pale green fibers

Wings of stone flies are tied like caddis fly imitations. You can use deer hair to imitate the wings, legs, and tail by tying one small bunch of hair in just back from the eye. The Yellow Stone fly can be important on the Beaverkill in early June.

TERRESTRIAL IMITATIONS

Recently plastic foams like Polycelon have been introduced. This material is extremely useful when tying terrestrials and other patterns you want to float high. The material comes in an assortment of colors and can be used for mayflies and caddis flies, as well as crickets, ants, beetles, and grasshoppers. Even if you can't tie flies, you can shape this material and tie it on a hook. Barry Beck ties in a short piece of orange poly on top of some of the terrestrial patterns for better visibility.

Cricket Imitation
> Hook size — 10 Mustad 9672
> Thread — Black
> Wing — Black goose quills section tied downwing
> Body — Black floss or black angora
> Legs — Black deer hair spun around the hook, just behind the eye

The deer hair is buoyant and floats this large artificial rather well. The deer hair is spun around and clipped to form the head.

Grasshopper
> Hook size — 10–18 Mustad 9672
> Thread — Olive, yellow, tan or cream
> Wing — Medium turkey wing tied downwing
> Body — Tan, yellow, olive, or cream fur
> Legs — Brown deer hair tied similar to the cricket

Crowe Beetle
> Hook size — 14–18 Mustad 94840

Take a bunch of black deer body hair and tie on at the bend of the hook by the butt. After tying in the butt, wind the thread toward the eye of the hook. Now pull the tips of the deer hair up over the top of the shank. Tie in the tips just behind the eye and finish off, and clip off the end of the hair. If you want to imitate more closely the body coloration of the Japanese Beetle, you can use peacock for the body.

Poly Beetle

Gerald Almy in *Tying and Fishing Terrestrials* suggests that the Crowe Beetle doesn't seem to stand up to the punishment of many strikes. A new extremely simple pattern I developed does. To tie the Poly Beetle, use two to five strands (depending on the size hook you're using) of black poly yarn. Tie the yarn in well below the bend of the hook. Bring the yarn up over the top of the hook and tie in just behind the eye. Cut off the excess.

Ant
> Hook size — 16–22 Mustad 94840

Take a piece of black, brown, or for that matter any other color polypropylene, and tie it in at the bend of the hook. Make a few turns on the rear half of the shank of the hook to give it a humped effect. Now take a black or dark brown hackle, tie it in at the middle of the shank, and make a few turns. Next take the black polypropylene and make another hump on the front part of the shank. To imitate one of the many winged species of ants, add two pale dun hackle tips at the head of the hook and place downwing over the body.

You can use black deer hair also to tie the ant imitation. Tie the deer hair in at the bend of the hook similar to the beetle. Halfway up the shank, tie in the deer hair, leaving some of the smaller, loose hairs as legs. Continue the deer hair to the eye and tie in at the eye. Clip and cement, and you have a realistic, buoyant imitation.

PATTERN SELECTION
(Eastern and Midwestern)

In the following chart I suggest specific patterns that might be best during certain times of the season. I base these selections on the hatches prevalent at different times and days of the fishing months. This chart should help you narrow the number of imitations you carry.

Morning	Afternoon	Evening
APRIL		
Blue Quill — 18	Blue Quill — 18	Dark Brown Spinner — 18
Blue Dun — 16–20	Quill Gordon — 14	Red Quill — 12 or 14
Quill Gordon — 14	Red Quill — 14	
Hendrickson —14 or 16	Hendrickson — 12 or 14	
	Black Quill — 12 or 14	
	Little Black Caddis — 16	
	Grannom — 12–16	
MAY		
Blue Quill — 18	Hendrickson — 12	Red Quill — 12
Blue Dun — 18 or 20	Red Quill — 14	Gray Fox — 12
Blue-Winged Olive Dun — 14	Green Caddis — 14	Grannom — 12
	Grannom — 12–16	Sulphur Pale Evening Dun — 16
	Sulphur Pale Evening Dun — 16	Spotted Sedge — 16
	Spotted Sedge — 16	March Brown — 12
	March Brown — 12	Slate Drake — 12
	Gray Fox — 12	Light Cahill — 12
	Green Drake — 10–16	Green Drake — 10–12
		Brown Drake — 12
		Ginger Quill — 12
		Cream Cahill — 14
JUNE		
Blue-Winged Olive Dun — 14	March Brown — 12	Ginger Quill — 12
Blue Quill — 18	Gray Fox — 12	Green Drake — 10
	Blue Quill — 18	Coffin Fly — 10
	Blue-Winged Olive Dun — 14	Dark Olive Spinner — 14
	Chocolate Dun — 16	Dark Blue Sedge — 12
		Brown Drake — 12
		Sulphur Pale Evening Dun — 16
		Light Cahill — 12
		Yellow Drake — 12
		Golden Drake — 12
		Cream Cahill — 14
JULY		
Blue-Winged Olive Dun — 14	Blue Dun — 20	Slate Drake — 12
Blue Quill — 18	Bluc-Winged Olive Dun — 14	Light Cahill — 12
Dark Brown Spinner — 14		Pale Evening Dun — 16
Trico — 24		Yellow Drake — 12
		Dark Olive Spinner — 14
		Cream Cahill — 14–16
AUGUST		
Blue Quill — 18	Blue Dun — 20	White Mayfly — 14
Trico — 24	Blue-Winged Olive Dun — 14	Slate Drake — 12
		Light Cahill — 12
		Cream Cahill — 14–16
SEPTEMBER		
Trico — 24	Slate Drake — 14	White Mayfly — 14
	Little Blue Dun — 20	Cream Cahill — 14
		Slate Drake — 14
OCTOBER		
Trico — 24	Slate Drake — 14	
	Little Blue Dun — 20	
	Little Blue-Winged Olive Dun — 20	

NATURALS AND IMITATIONS
(Western)

Although I originally suggested using mallard quill sections for wings on many of the Western patterns, I now believe that deer hair, caribou, calf's tail, and hackle tips are much better. Impala should withstand much more abuse on the faster Western waters. Calf's tail is easily dyed. Place the tail in charcoal gray dye for five or ten minutes to achieve the same color as the mallard quill.

For the tail I also recommend the stiffest material available. Dark brown moose mane imitates the tail of the Western Green Drake (*Drunella grandis*) and many other species rather closely. Use this tail material whenever a pattern calls for a dark brown tail.

I also strongly urge you to use the stiffest hackle for the legs of your dry-fly imitations. In fact, on many Western patterns, I use three rather than two hackles. Remember that until late July, most Western waters are higher and faster than their Eastern and Midwestern counterparts.

Many of the species listed in the following pages have no common patterns to match them effectively. Furthermore, many of the species vary considerably in color from river to river. In most cases where color varies, I have so indicated. In some instances, because of color variation, the pattern suggested might be inappropriate for your particular stream.

You'll note that hackle for spinner imitations is optional. If you tie spent winged spinners, don't include the hackle.

Rhithrogena morrisoni	Imitation — Western March Brown
Dun — 8–10 mm	Hook size — 14
	Thread — Brown
Wings — Brown, mottled	Brown mallard
Body — Tan with brown	Tannish brown polypropylene
Legs — Tan	Tan hackle
Tail — Tan	Tan hackle fibers
Spinner	Dark Tan Spinner
	Thread — Brown
Wing — Glassy with brown cross veins	White polypropylene yarn, tied spent
Body — Yellowish	Primrose polypropylene
Legs — Front: brown	Brown hackle
Rear pair: tan	
Tail — Yellowish brown	Dark ginger hackle fibers

Commercial pattern, dun: Western March Brown

If you plan to fly-fish on near-coastal Western rivers from late February to late May, make certain you carry imitations for this mayfly. The Western March Brown is one of the major hatches of the season on the McKenzie, Willamette, Deschutes, and Metolius rivers in Oregon. The hatch lasts for several months on some waters. (See a discussion of this hatch in Chapter 12.)

Baetis tricaudatus and *B. intermedius*	Spinner
Dun — 5–7 mm	Wing — Glassy clear
Wing — Medium gray	Body — Light tan (*intermedius*) to dark rusty brown
Body — Light brown (*tricaudatus*) to tannish gray with an olive cast (*intermedius*)	(*tricaudatus*)
	Legs — Tan
Legs — Tannish cream	Tail — Pale gray
Tail — Pale gray	

Commercial pattern, dun: Blue Dun
Commercial pattern, spinner: Rusty Spinner

I have not suggested one pattern but rather suggest that you carry several patterns with grayish tan, tan, and olive gray bodies in hook sizes from 18 to 22. I've seen hatches of *B. tricaudatus* on the Arkansas River near Salida, Colorado, as early as late April.

These mayflies can be important all season. The duns seem to be most important in the afternoon and the spinners in the evening. Gary Kish says that the

Metolius in central Oregon has a *Baetis* hatch almost every day of the year. Even from January to March you can see these Little Blue-Winged Olive Duns appearing in the early afternoon. The lower Deschutes near Maupin holds a good winter hatch.

Ephemera simulans — see previous section on Eastern patterns

Cinygmula ramaleyi	Imitation — Dark Red Quill
Dun — 7–9 mm	Hook size — 16 or 18
	Thread — Brown
Wing — Dark slate	Dark mallard quills, dark gray calf tail, or hackle tips
Body — Reddish brown, ringed lighter	Dark reddish brown hackle stem, stripped
Legs — Brownish gray	Bronze dun hackle
Tail — Medium gray	Medium dun hackle fibers
Spinner	Red Quill Spinner
	Thread — Brown
Wing — Glassy clear with tan cast	Very pale tan polypropylene tied spent
Body — Reddish brown	Reddish brown hackle stem
Legs — Reddish brown	Brown hackle
Tail — Pale gray	Pale dun hackle fibers

Commercial pattern, dun and spinner: Red Quill

Here is one of the many Western species so ably duplicated by the Red Quill. Most *Cinygmula* species are found on small and medium-sized streams with characteristically colder water temperatures. *Cinygmula* nymphs are found to be extremely abundant on the St. Maries River near Clarkia in northern Idaho.

Ephemerella inermis
Dun — 6–8 mm
  Wing — Pale gray
  Body — Creamish yellow with an olive cast
  Legs — Creamish yellow with an olive cast
  Tail — Creamish yellow

Spinner
  Wing — Glassy clear
  Body — Yellowish olive
  Legs — Dark tan
  Tail — Dark tan

Commercial pattern, dun: Pale Morning Dun
Commercial pattern, spinner: Pale Morning Spinner

This is one of the most common yet diverse species found on Western streams. *Ephemerella inermis* is found on streams as far north as Alaska. The color pattern listed here was taken from a hatch on Henry's Fork in Idaho. The color varies so much, even on the same stream, that it's important to carry imitations with bodies of tan, reddish brown, olive, and the most common color, pale yellow with an olive cast. Since the color is so variable, I have not suggested one specific pattern. Nymphs too vary from light brown to dark brown.

I have seen this species emerging in the morning, afternoon, and evening, so it's important to have imitations available all day. Heavy hatches are found on the Kootenai above Libby, and the Bighorn, both in Montana. Mike Manfredo says that this species produces one of the best hatches on the McKenzie and Willamette rivers in Oregon. This species is one of the most common and most important to match in the West.

Caution: The color of this species varies more than any other mayfly of which I am aware.

Paraleptophlebia bicornuta, P. heteronea,	Imitation — Dark Blue Quill
P. memorialis, P. vaciva, and *P. debilis*	Hook size — 16–20
Dun — 6–10 mm	Thread — Gray
	Dark mallard quills or dark gray hackle tips
Wing — Dark slate	Dark brown polypropylene, ribbed with
Body — Dark slate to dark reddish brown	lighter thread, or peacock herl
Legs — Tannish cream	Ginger cream hackle
Tail — Medium gray	Medium dun hackle fibers
Spinner	Dark Brown Spinner
	Thread — Dark brown
Wing — Glassy clear	Pale gray polypropylene
Body — Dark brown to dark reddish brown	Same as dun
Legs — Creamish gray with dark brown	Pale dun hackle with a turn of dark brown
Tail — Pale gray	Pale dun

Commercial pattern, dun: Blue Quill or Dark Blue Quill
Commercial pattern, spinner: Dark Brown Spinner

Paraleptophlebia debilis duns emerge on Henry's Fork, *P. memorialis* on the Bitterroot River, *P. heteronea* on Rock Creek in Montana, *P. vaciva* on the Gallatin River above Bozeman, Montana, and *P.* *bicornuta* on the Colorado River. Carry Blue Quill imitations with you always. If you plan to fish any North American stream in the morning or afternoon, the Blue Quill is an important pattern.

Epeorus longimanus	Imitation — Quill Gordon or Blue Dun
Dun — 10–12 mm	Hook size — 12 or 14
	Thread — Gray
Wing — Dark slate	Dark mallard quills, dark gray calf tail, or
	dark gray hackle tips
Body — Pale gray; tergites (back) are darker	Pale to medium gray polypropylene or
	muskrat fur dubbed
Legs — Tannish gray with darker markings	Pale tannish gray hackle
Tail — Grayish	Medium dun hackle
Spinner	Red Quill Spinner
	Thread — Tan
Wing — Glassy clear with an amber cast	Pale tan polypropylene
Body — Pale yellowish brown	Pale yellowish brown polypropylene
Legs — Pale yellowish brown with darker	Ginger hackle with a turn of brown
markings	
Tail — Dark brown	Moose mane

Commercial pattern, dun: Quill Gordon or Blue Dun
Commercial pattern, spinner: Brown Drake

Many *Epeorus, Rhithrogena,* and *Cinygmula* species exhibit the general coloration of this species. When B. R. Gilpin and M. A. Brusven conducted a survey on St. Maries River in northern Idaho, they found this mayfly to be one of the three most common species on the river. Rock Creek near Missoula, Montana, also has a good number of these mayflies.

Serratella (Ephemerella) tibialis
Dun — 7–9 mm
  Wing — Pale gray
  Body — Dark reddish brown
  Legs — Creamish yellow
  Tail — Pale gray

Imitation — Red Quill
Hook size — 16 or 18

Spinner
  Wing — Cloudy
  Body — Dark purplish brown
  Legs — Pale yellow
  Tail — Gray

White-Gloved Howdy

Commercial pattern, dun: Red Quill
Commercial pattern, spinner: White-Gloved Howdy

This is another species imitated by the Red Quill. It is found in all Western states, north into Alberta and British Columbia. *S. tibialis* is found on the Willamette, Santiam, and Umpqua rivers in west-central Oregon; it is also found on the San Juan River in New Mexico and the Los Pinos River in southern Colorado. The St. Maries River in Idaho, just southeast of Spokane, Washington, holds abundant numbers of these mayflies. B. R. Gilpin and M. A. Brusven found this species present at twenty-five of twenty-eight stations where they conducted population studies.

Baetis hageni (parvus)
Dun — 4–5 mm

  Wing — Dark gray
  Body — Dark brown
  Legs — Tannish cream
  Tail — Tannish cream

Imitation — Dark Brown Dun
Hook size — 20
Thread — Dark brown
Gray mallard quills
Dark brown polypropylene
Ginger cream hackle
Ginger cream hackle fibers

Spinner

  Wing — Glassy clear
  Body — Dark brown
  Legs — Tannish cream
  Tail — Pale gray

Dark Brown Spinner
Thread — Brown
Pale gray polypropylene
Dark brown polypropylene
Ginger cream hackle
Pale dun hackle fibers

Commercial pattern, dun and spinner: Dark Brown Dun

Don't ever be without this pattern when fishing Western waters. As with *Baetis bicaudatus, B. hageni (parvus)* does not have the typical *Baetis* body coloration. I tried the Little Blue Dun two times during hatches of *B. hageni* and had little success until I switched to the Dark Brown Dun. A heavy hatch of this mayfly appears on Henry's Fork in Idaho in July.

Note the change recently from *Baetis parvus* to *Baetis hageni*.

Hexagenia limbata limbata — see tying description under Eastern and Midwestern patterns

In some areas of the West, the Michigan Caddis or Great Olive Winged Drake is locally abundant. You'll find impressive hatches of this species on Flathead Lake in Montana and some of the near-coastal and coastal lakes in Oregon and northern California. The Williamson River in Oregon contains a good *Hexagenia* hatch.

Caution: Coloration of species varies considerably from location to location.

Heptagenia elegantula	Imitation — Pale Evening Dun
Dun — 9–10 mm	Hook size — 14
	Thread — Yellow
Wing — Gray, slightly barred	Pale gray calf tail
Body — Creamish yellow	Creamish yellow polypropylene
Legs — Cream	Cream hackle
Tail — Cream	Cream hackle fibers
Spinner	Pale Evening Spinner
Wing — Glassy clear	
Body — Cream	
Legs — Pale cream	
Tail — Tannish	

Commercial pattern, dun: Pale Evening Dun
Commercial pattern, spinner: Pale Evening Spinner

Heptagenia elegantula spinners appear on the Colorado River in large enough numbers to consider it important to imitate much of the summer. A size 14 Light Cahill substitutes for the dun and spinner of this species. Since the imitation suggested for the dun works well for the spinner fall, I have not recommended a pattern for the latter.

Callibaetis coloradensis and *C. nigritus*	Imitation — Speckle-Winged Dun
Dun — 6–9 mm	Hook size — 16
	Thread — Tan
Wing — Dark gray with white venation	Dark gray mallard flank
Body — Grayish tan	Grayish tan polypropylene
Legs — Pale grayish tan with darker tips	Pale bronze dun hackle
Tail — Pale tan	Cream ginger hackle fibers
Spinner	Speckle-Winged Spinner
	Thread — Gray
Wing — Glassy clear with heavy gray flecks in the front part of the forewing (male doesn't have as much)	Mallard flank feather
Body — Pale gray	Pale gray polypropylene
Legs — Tannish gray	Pale bronze dun hackle
Tail — Pale tan	Cream ginger hackle fibers

Commercial pattern, dun and spinner: Dark Cahill or Light Hendrickson

The commercial pattern I've listed, the Dark Cahill, does not copy the natural very closely. If your plans include a Western lake or a river like Henry's Fork with some slow water, tie some Speckle-Winged Dun imitations. I have seen *Callibaetis* species on Western waters from early June to late September and on streams with some slow water, like the Blue and the Fryingpan in Colorado.

Al Gretz, Vince Gigliotti, and I fly-fished on a small mountain lake in northern Montana's Bob Marshall Wilderness Area recently. By 10:00 A.M. thousands of *Callibaetis* duns struggled on the smooth surface, and more than a hundred trout rose to this food supply. The hatch lasted for more than an hour. If you plan to fly-fish any of the lakes in the West from late June through September, make certain you carry a supply of speckled-winged imitations with you. (See a discussion of the importance of this imitation in Chapter 11.)

Drunella (Ephemerella) flavilinea Dun — 7–10 mm	Imitation — Blue-Winged Olive Dun Hook size — 14 or 16 Thread — Olive
Wing — Dark gray	Dark gray mallard quills or dark gray hackle tips
Body — Olive green	Olive green polypropylene
Legs — Dark olive brown with creamish tan tips	Dark olive brown hackle
Tail — Dark olive brown	Dark brown moose mane
Spinner	Dark Olive Spinner Thread — Brown
Wing — Glassy clear	Pale gray polypropylene
Body — Dark olive brown	Dark olive brown polypropylene
Legs — Dark olive	Dark olive hackle
Tail — Dark olive	Dark olive hackle fibers

Commercial pattern, dun: Blue-Winged Olive Dun
Commercial pattern, spinner: Dark Olive Spinner

Although the Blue-Winged Olive Dun is an effective pattern, I prefer to mix some green polypropylene with olive to get the desired body color for the pattern.

This species appears in good numbers in early July on the Railroad Ranch section of Henry's Fork in Idaho. It also appears on the Clark Fork in Montana; the McKenzie and Willamette rivers in Oregon; the Green River in Washington; the Firehole and Yellowstone rivers in Wyoming (Yellowstone Park); and the Klamath and Shasta rivers in northern California.

Drunella (Ephemerella) grandis Dun — 14–16 mm	Imitation — Western Green Drake Hook size — 10 or 12 Thread — Dark olive
Wing — Dark grayish black	Impala, dyed dark gray
Body — Dark grayish black with pale yellow ribbing and greenish olive reflections	Olive black polypropylene, ribbed with pale yellow thread
Legs — Grayish black with pale yellow tarsi (tips)	Grayish black hackle
Tail — Base is dark brown, and tip is pale gray	Moose mane
Spinner	Great Red Spinner Thread — Black
Wing — Glassy clear with veining	White polypropylene, tied spent
Body — Black ringed with pale yellow (faint olive cast)	Same as dun
Legs — Dark brownish black	Brownish black hackle
Tail — Dark brown	Moose mane

Commercial pattern, dun: Western Green Drake
Commercial pattern, spinner: Great Red Spinner

The color of this species varies tremendously from stream to stream. The coloration described is taken from hatches on the Bitterroot River in Montana. The species on the Bitterroot River is *Drunella grandis ingens*. This subspecies often appears to be somewhat darker than *D. grandis grandis*. Other rivers with good *D. grandis ingens* hatches include the Alsea in Oregon and the Green River in Washington.

I have seen heavy hatches of *D. grandis grandis* on the Fryingpan River just below the Reudi Reservoir near Basalt, Colorado. This subspecies appears as late as early August on the Fryingpan. Other rivers with good *D. grandis grandis* hatches include the lower Madison in Montana and the Willamette, McKenzie, and Santiam rivers in Oregon. *D. grandis grandis* has a brighter green body than does *D. grandis ingens*.

D. grandis flavitincta is found on Oregon rivers like the Alsea and Yaquina and on the Green River in Washington. This subspecies is found along the Pacific coast from Oregon to Alaska. Gary Kish feels that Oregon's Metolius River has a longer and more consistent Green Drake hatch than any other Western water — from late April until early July.

The pattern I have suggested works well. It works well also when the common *D. doddsi* emerges on Rock Creek in Montana. Some experts feel that a low floating pattern works well early in the season and a fluttering, high-floating fly later in the season.

Caution: Color of duns varies considerably from stream to stream.

Baetis bicaudatus	Imitation — Pale Evening Dun
Dun — 4–5 mm	Hook size — 20
	Thread — Olive
Wing — Pale gray	Pale gray hackle tips
Body — Pale olive	Pale olive polypropylene
Legs — Pale olive	Pale olive hackle
Tail — Pale olive	Pale olive hackle fibers
Spinner	Light Rusty Spinner
	Thread — Tan
Wing — Glassy clear	Pale gray polypropylene
Body — Tan with olive cast	Tan polypropylene
Legs — Tannish	Ginger hackle
Tail — Tan	Ginger hackle fibers

Commercial pattern, dun: Pale Olive Dun
Commercial pattern, spinner: Rusty Spinner

Charlie Brooks said he has seen *Baetis* species on Western streams from mid-January to late October. Although *Baetis* species are small, imitations of them are imperative for fly-fishing in Western waters. Rock Creek outside Missoula, Montana, has a heavy population of this species, as does Henry's Fork just below Box Canyon.

I spotlight *Baetis bicaudatus* first because its coloration is atypical for the species. Many *Baetis* species have bodies of olive gray or olive tan; not so with the pale-olive-bodied *Baetis bicaudatus*. Second, this mayfly is extremely common on many Western streams.

I have witnessed heavy afternoon hatches in mid-July on Henry's Fork in Idaho and have seen many trout surface feeding on them.

Cinygma dimicki Dun — 9–11 mm	Imitation — Light Cahill Hook size — 12 Thread — Yellow
Wing — Tannish cream, barred	Wood duck or imitation flank feather
Body — Pale creamish yellow	Pale creamish yellow polypropylene
Legs — Creamish, with darker markings	Ginger cream hackle
Tail — Tannish	Ginger hackle fibers
Spinner	Light Cahill Thread — Yellow
Wing — Glassy clear	Pale gray polypropylene
Body — Yellowish cream	Yellowish cream polypropylene
Legs — Yellowish cream, with darker markings	Yellowish cream hackle
Tail — Tan	Ginger hackle fibers

Commercial pattern, dun and spinner: Light Cahill

This species is important to imitate because it's fairly common, and the dun and spinner concentrate their activity in a two-hour period in the evening. *Cinygma dimicki* appears on Western waters like the Bitterroot River in Montana for more than a month. The imitation, the Light Cahill, is important when evening fishing.

Male and female spinners are available as food for trout. Imagos of this species characteristically mate just a few inches above the water, similar to *Heptagenia marginalis* in the East.

Cinygmula reticulata Dun — 8–10 mm	Imitation — Pale Brown Dun Hook size — 12 or 14 Thread — Tan
Wing — Yellow	Yellow mallard flank
Body — Tannish brown	Pale brown polypropylene
Legs — Tannish cream	Ginger cream hackle
Tail — Tannish cream	Ginger cream hackle fibers
Spinner	Dark Rusty Spinner Thread — Brown
Wing — Yellow	Pale yellow polypropylene
Body — Dark rusty brown	Dark brown polypropylene
Legs — Dark rusty brown	Dark brown hackle
Tail — Dark brown	Dark brown hackle fibers

Commercial pattern, dun and spinner: Dark Cahill

Spinners of this species concentrate their activity in early morning. The commercial pattern listed is a poor one, so a few copies of the one I suggest might be in order.

Like *Cinygmula ramaleyi*, this species is often found on small and moderate-sized streams with plenty of cold water. I first met *C. reticulata* on the upper section of the Gallatin River in Yellowstone Park. During that first meeting, I recorded a water temperature of 45 degrees—in the middle of July.

Epeorus albertae	Imitation — Light Cahill or Pink Lady
Dun — 9–11 mm	Hook size — 12
	Thread — Cream
Wing — Medium gray	Gray mallard quills or dark gray hackle tips
Body — Grayish cream; female has a pinkish cast	Grayish cream polypropylene
Legs — Cream with darker markings	Cream or badger hackle
Tail — Creamish tan	Cream ginger hackle fibers
Spinner	Salmon Spinner
	Thread — Cream
Wing — Glassy clear	Pale gray polypropylene
Body — Cream gray (female has a pink body)	Female — pinkish red polypropylene
	Male — cream gray polypropylene
Legs — Cream gray with darker markings	Pale blue dun hackle
Tail — Olive brown	Dark brown moose mane

Commercial pattern, dun: Light Cahill or Pink Lady
Commercial pattern, spinner: Salmon Spinner

This is an extremely common species on many Western rivers on summer evenings. I have seen spinners mating on Henry's Fork in the Box Canyon area, on the Buffalo River in Idaho, and on the Madison River in Yellowstone Park.

Siphlonurus occidentalis	Imitation — Gray Drake
Dun — 11–15 mm	Hook size — 12
	Thread — Dark brown
Wing — Brownish gray with distinct veining	Dark gray mallard flank
Body — Brownish black, ribbed lighter	Brownish black polypropylene with tan thread for ribbing
Legs — Pale grayish tan	Pale bronze dun hackle
Tail — Gray	Medium dun hackle fibers
Spinner	Brown Quill Spinner
	Thread — Dark brown
Wing — Glassy clear	Pale gray polypropylene
Body — Dark reddish brown with lighter ribbing	Dark reddish brown polypropylene ribbed with tan thread
Legs — Dark brown	Dark brown hackle
Tail — Dark brown	Dark brown moose mane

Commercial pattern, dun: Gray Drake
Commercial pattern, spinner: Brown Quill Spinner

Duns of this species appear in the afternoon on Henry's Fork and the Bitterroot River in Montana. Since it's a large species that appears late in the season, it's important to carry imitations in July and August.

Caution: The size of this species seems to vary from stream to stream.

Heptagenia solitaria	Imitation — Gray Fox
Dun — 10–12 mm	Hook size — 12
	Thread — Tan
Wing — Pale gray with yellow cast	Pale gray hackle tips
Body — Yellowish tan (top is tan)	Yellowish tan polypropylene
Legs — Tannish gray with darker markings	Bronze dun hackle
Tail — Tannish gray	Bronze dun hackle fibers
Spinner	Ginger Quill Spinner
	Thread — Tan
Wing — Glassy clear	Pale gray polypropylene
Body — Tan ribbed with yellow	Eyed peacock herl, dyed tan and stripped
Legs — Tan with darker markings	Ginger hackle
Tail — Grayish tan	Ginger hackle fibers
Commercial pattern, dun: Gray Fox	
Commercial pattern, spinner: Ginger Quill	

If you plan to fish Western streams after mid-July and especially in early September, don't forget imitations of this dun and spinner. This species, one of the most important of the season, is abundant on the Colorado River near Kremmling in late August.

When you meet this hatch, you'll find rising trout. The Gray Fox effectively copies the dun.

The Ginger Quill is very effective during a spinner fall.

Ephemerella infrequens	Imitation — Pale Morning Dun
Dun — 7–9 mm	Hook size — 16 or 18
	Thread — Yellow
Wing — Pale gray with yellow cast	Pale gray mallard
Body — Creamish yellow with faint olive	Creamish yellow polypropylene, soaked in
cast; can vary to tan	olive dye
Legs — Creamish yellow	Creamish yellow hackle
Tail — Creamish yellow	Creamish yellow hackle fibers
Spinner	Rusty Spinner
	Thread — Tan
Wing — Glassy clear	Pale gray polypropylene, tied spent
Body — Creamish tan	Cream ginger hackle
Legs — Yellow, marked with tan	Cream ginger hackle fibers
Tail — Pale tan	Tan hackle fibers
Commercial pattern, dun: Pale Morning Dun	
Commercial pattern, spinner: Rusty Spinner	

Coloration of this species too varies considerably from stream to stream; in fact, it varies from time to time on the same stream.

The specimen described copies the hatch on the Bitterroot River in Montana and represents the most common color for the species. This species resembles the Eastern *Ephemerella* species, like *E. invaria*. *E. infrequens* is a very common Western species. Idaho waters like the Wood River have good hatches. In Oregon you'll find the species on the Deschutes, Metolius, and McKenzie rivers.

Caution: Color varies considerably.

Rhithrogena hageni Dun — 9–11 mm	Imitation — Pale Brown Dun Hook size — 12 Thread — Olive
Wing — Medium gray	Gray mallard quills or dark gray hackle tips
Body — Tannish olive	Tannish olive polypropylene
Legs — Creamish tan	Cream ginger hackle
Tail — Cream	Cream hackle fibers
Spinner	Dark Tan Spinner Thread — Tan
Wing — Glassy clear	Pale gray polypropylene
Body — Pale olive tan	Pale olive tan polypropylene
Legs — Dark tannish olive with cream tarsi (tips)	Cream, mixed with dark tan hackle
Tail — Gray	Gray hackle fibers

Commercial pattern, dun and spinner: none.

I have seen thousands of these duns emerge on the Madison River above Ennis, Montana. Duns escape rapidly from the surface, but since emergence is fairly concentrated, it's important to have imitations. Imitations of the nymph should work well when this species emerges.

Ameletus cooki Dun — 8–10 mm	Imitation — Dark Brown Dun Hook size — 12 or 14 Thread — Dark brown
Wing — Dark gray, barred	Teal flank feather
Body — Dark brown	Dark brown polypropylene
Legs — Dark brown	Dark brown hackle
Tail — Dark brown	Dark brown hackle fibers
Spinner	Dark Brown Spinner Thread — Dark brown
Wing — Glassy clear with black and yellow markings	Teal flank feather, dyed yellow
Body — Dark brown	Dark brown polypropylene
Legs — Dark brown	Dark brown hackle
Tail — Dark brown	Dark brown hackle fibers

Commercial pattern, dun and spinner: Dark Brown Dun

Duns of this species emerge sporadically during the day, and spinners fall in the afternoon. The species can be important to imitate. The Bitterroot River and Rock Creek near Missoula, Montana, hold good populations.

Rhithrogena futilis
Dun — 9–11 mm

    Wing — Pale to medium gray
    Body — Pale tannish gray with olive cast
         (top of abdomen is much darker)
    Legs — Tannish gray
    Tail — Tannish gray

Spinner

    Wing — Glassy clear
    Body — Black, ribbed lighter
    Legs — Dark gray
    Tail — Dark gray

Imitation — Quill Gordon
Hook size — 12
Thread — Gray
Gray mallard quills or dark gray hackle tips
Tannish gray polypropylene

Rusty dun hackle
Rusty dun hackle fibers

Quill Gordon Spinner
Thread — Black
Pale gray polypropylene
Peacock herl, eyed, stripped
Dark dun hackle
Dark dun hackle fibers

Commercial pattern, dun and spinner: Quill Gordon

This species can be important to imitate. On several occasions on the Bitterroot River while fishing in the evening, I've encountered the spinner mating and laying eggs and have had success with the Quill Gordon Spinner imitation.

Rhithrogena undulata
Dun — 8–11 mm

    Wing — Dark gray
    Body — Dark reddish brown
    Legs — Brown
    Tail — Gray

Spinner

    Wing — Glassy clear
    Body — Light to dark reddish brown
    Legs — Light to dark brown
    Tail — Light to dark brown

Imitation — Dark Red Quill
Hook size — 12 or 14
Thread — Dark brown
Gray mallard quills or dark gray hackle tips
Dark brown hackle stem
Dark brown hackle
Dark blue dun hackle fibers

Red Quill or Dark Red Quill
Thread — Dark brown
White or pale gray hackle tips
Red to dark brown hackle stems
Ginger to dark brown hackle
Ginger to dark brown hackle fibers

Commercial pattern, dun and spinner: Red Quill and Dark Red Quill

---

This species is important on many Western waters like the Blackfoot in Montana. Either color patterns of this species vary considerably from river to river, or I have confused the lighter variation with another species. I think it's probably the former explanation. However, both patterns are important on Western waters.

Caution: Coloration of species varies considerably from stream to stream.

Timpanoga (Ephemerella) hecuba	Imitation — Great Red Quill
Dun — 14–16 mm	Hook size — 10 or 12
	Thread — Brown
Wing — Dark gray	Dark gray impala
Body — Reddish, ribbed lighter	Large reddish brown hackle stem, stripped
Legs — Dark brownish black with cream tarsi (tips)	Dark brown hackle
Tail — Dark brownish black	Moose mane
Spinner	Great Red Spinner
	Thread — Dark brown
Wing — Glassy clear	Pale gray hackle tips
Body — Dark reddish brown, ribbed lighter	Dark brown hackle stems, stripped
Legs — Dark blackish brown	Dark brown hackle
Tail — Dark blackish brown	Moose mane

Commercial pattern, dun: Red Quill
Commercial pattern, spinner: Great Red Spinner

I have observed this species in limited numbers on only one occasion in late July on the Bitterroot River. The few I noted emerging did so in the evening. Other writers suggest this species appears around midday. Nevertheless, carry some large Red Quill dry flies with you on trips in July, August, and September.

I have indicated that the dun has a bright red body. This body color, as with most other species, varies considerably from stream to stream.

Tricorythodes minutus	Imitation — Pale Olive Dun
Dun — 3 mm	Hook size — 24 or 26
	Thread — Pale olive
Wing — Pale gray	Pale gray polypropylene, upright and not divided
Body — Medium to dark olive	Medium olive polypropylene
Legs — Pale cream with dark brown on front legs	Pale cream hackle
Tail — Pale gray	Pale gray hackle fibers
Spinner	Harvey Trico
	Thread — Dark brown
Wing — Glassy clear with dark brown on front edge	Pale gray polypropylene, tied spent
Body — Male: dark blackish with faint lighter ribbing	Dark brownish black polypropylene
Female: cream with faint olive cast	Cream polypropylene
Legs — Cream with gray markings	Cream hackle
Tail — Male: pale gray	Pale gray hackle fibers
Female: cream	Same

Commercial pattern, dun and spinner: Trico Dun and Trico Spinner

I have seen this hatch on many slower silted rivers in the West in late July, August, and September. The Colorado River near Kremmling, Colorado, has a heavy *Tricorythodes* hatch and spinner fall. The Trico spinner fall on the South Platte River near Deckers in Colorado is better copied with a size 20 spent-wing than a 24.

On several occasions I have noted a *Brachycen-*

trus dun emerging also in the morning. In its spinner stage, this latter species has a reddish brown body in both sexes. This species is also somewhat larger than the 3 mm suggested for *Tricorythodes minutus*.

Drunella (Ephemerella) coloradensis
Dun — 12–13 mm

  Wing — Dark gray
  Body — Dark olive brownish
  Legs — Tan
  Tail — Gray

Spinner

  Wing — Glassy clear with heavy brown
      veining
  Body — Dark brown
  Legs — Dark brown
  Tail — Dark brown

Imitation — Dark Olive Dun
Hook size — 12
Thread — Dark brown
Gray mallard quills or dark gray hackle tips
Dark olive brown polypropylene
Ginger hackle
Gray hackle fibers

Dark Brown Spinner
Thread — Dark brown
Pale tan polypropylene

Dark brown polypropylene
Dark brown hackle
Dark brown moose mane

Commercial pattern, dun and spinner: Autumn Green Drake

I have noted members of this species emerging on high-altitude streams well past midday. Since the pattern is not common, it's important to have a few imitations if you plan to fish Western streams in August and September. The Metolius in Oregon has a good population of this species, as does the Wood River in Idaho. You'll find hatches from California north to Alaska and east to Montana, Wyoming, Colorado, and New Mexico.

Ephoron album
Dun — 11–13 mm
  Wing — Pale gray
  Body — White with grayish cast
  Legs — Front: dark
        Rear: white
  Tail — Pale gray

Spinner (male only)
  Wing — Clear
  Body — White (rear may be darker)
  Legs — Same as dun
  Tail — Pale gray

Hook size — 12

Commercial pattern, dun and spinner: White Wulff

The White Wulff in appropriate sizes effectively copies the dun and spinner of this species, so I have not listed any recommended pattern. This species can be important on lower stretches of warmer streams in August. The Humboldt River near Winnemucca, Nevada, holds this species.

WESTERN STONE FLIES

Stone flies appear on Western waters every month of the year. Little Winter Stone flies are especially important on many rivers from February through March. A Little Brown Stone fly in a size 16 copies many of these cold weather emergers.

Pteronarcys californica
    Adult — 35–45 mm

    Wing — Creamish tan with heavy black
           veins
    Body — Burnt orange; underside of thorax
           and head is bright orange
    Legs — Brownish black with small orange
           markings
    Tail — Short and dark brown

Commercial pattern: Troth Salmon Fly

Imitation — Salmon Fly
Hook size — 4 or 6, 8XL, Mustad 94720
Thread — Orange
Creamish tan dyed mallard flank tied
    downwing
Abdomen, burnt orange polypropylene thorax
    and head, bright orange polypropylene
Brownish black hackle

Dark moose mane

This pattern is extremely difficult to tie, and unless you plan to tie many of them I suggest purchasing the commercial pattern recommended. These large dry flies are effective during the egg-laying phase of this stone fly. Don't be on Western waters like the Deschutes in Oregon or the Yellowstone in Montana from late May through early July without several of these imitations.

Gary Kish recommends using the Clarks Stone during this and the following two stone fly hatches. Clarks Stone has a body of gold tinsel over which he ties a piece of loose poly yarn. The poly yarn extends beyond the shank of the hook. Use orange brown to copy the Salmon Fly, and lighter colors for the Willow and Golden Stone flies. Over the poly yarn he ties in a bunch of deer hair. He then adds brown hackle at the front and finishes the fly with a large orange thread head. Gary finds that this pattern consistently works on the Rogue River in Oregon.

Hesperoperla pacifica
    Adult — 25–35 mm

    Wing — Creamish, barred heavily
    Body — Creamish brown
    Legs — Brown
    Tail — Brown

Commercial pattern: Willow Fly

Imitation — Willow Stone fly
Hook size — 6, 8XL, Mustad 94720
Thread — Tan
Creamish mallard flank
Creamish brown polypropylene
Brown hackle
Short brown hackle fibers

This large stone fly is important on many Western streams in June and July. Carry several imitations if you plan to fish water like the Yellowstone River.

Calineuria californica	Imitation — Golden Stone fly (Adult)
Adult — 20–25 mm	Hook size — 8
	Thread — Yellow
Wing — Pale amber	Pale tan deer hair
Body — Pale yellow with wide brown bands	Pale yellow polypropylene ribbed with brown polypropylene
Legs — Pale yellow with brown markings	Cream and brown, mixed
Tail — Dark brown	Moose mane

Heavy hatches of this stone fly appear on many of Oregon's rivers. Tom Neff of Bend, Gary Kish of Oregon City, and I saw a heavy hatch of these in early September on central Oregon's Metolius River. These stone flies appear from June through September.

Family Perlodidae	Imitation — Little Yellow Stone fly
Adult — 7–10 mm	Hook — 14–18

Use the same pattern for this family of stone flies listed for the Little Yellow Stone fly for the East and Midwest. Deke Meyer recently wrote an article about this important family in *Fly Tyer* magazine. Don't fly-fish any trout water in the East, Midwest, or West without a good supply of yellow- and green-bodied stone flies.

WESTERN CADDIS FLIES

Dicosmoecus species	October Caddis
20–25 mm	Hook size – 6
Wing — Brown, spotted	Brown deer hair
Body — Orange to burnt orange	Orange polypropylene, dubbed
Legs — Brown	Brown hackle
Commercial pattern: October Caddis or Orange Caddis	

If you plan to fish the Metolius, McKenzie, or Deschutes rivers in Oregon or the McCloud River in California in October, make certain you have a good supply of October Caddis patterns. This caddis natural brings large rainbows to the surface on the McKenzie. The pupae of this and other Western species seem to produce more trout than a floating copy of the adult.

Hydropsyche species	
7–15 mm	
Wing — Dark brown	Dark brown deer hair
Body — Grayish tan to olive to yellow	Yellow, tan, or olive polypropylene
Legs — Amber to brown	Brown hackle

Hydropsychids are extremely common on Western waters from early June through October. Gary Kish has recorded hatches on the Metolius in Oregon in October.

One of the most common members of this genus is *Hydropsyche occidentalis*. Bob Newell and Wayne Minshall have located this species on the Portneuf and Snake rivers near Pocatello, Idaho. They have also found it on Montana waters like the Beaverhead River, Big Hole River, Clark Fork River, and the Bitterroot River.

If you plan to fly-fish Western waters, make certain you have a supply of imitations copying the gray, green, and yellow adults. Any trip to the Kootenai River below Libby, Montana, would be fruitless without caddis imitations. Every July evening on this river, caddis flies appear and create great dry-fly fishing for the native rainbow population.

Rhyacophila species

George Roemhild of the Department of Biology at Montana State University listed thirty species of this genus probably present in Montana streams and rivers. Bob Newell and Wayne Minshall found thirteen species present in Idaho waters. Is this genus common? Is it important to carry imitations with olive and green in sizes 10 to 16?

PATTERN SELECTION (Western)

To assist you in narrowing the quantity of patterns, I recommend some of the important imitations. These patterns are listed by month and time of day. Remember, these are only a few of the more important imitations; many more mayflies appear, and patterns for many of these have not been included.

The imitations suggested for each month successfully copy many of the mayfly species found on Western waters. I have included one imitation, the Cream Spinner, in July, August, and September. Although this is an *Ephemerella* species, I have never encountered a male of the species and therefore have been unable to have the species correctly identified. Females of this species lay their eggs around 7:00 P.M. on the shore next to the water. Many of the female spinners then fall into the water and become available as food for trout.

Morning	Afternoon	Evening
APRIL		
	Western March Brown — 14	
	Little Blue-Winged Olive Dun — 20	
MAY		
Blue Dun — 18	Blue Dun — 18	Brown Drake — 12
Dark Red Quill — 16	Salmon Fly — 6	Salmon Fly — 6
Light Rusty Spinner — 18	Dark Red Quill — 16	Light Rusty Spinner — 18
Dark Rusty Spinner — 18	Western March Brown — 14	Dark Rusty Spinner — 18
JUNE		
Quill Gordon — 12	Quill Gordon — 12	Brown Drake — 12
Western Green Drake — 12	Western Green Drake — 12	Salmon Fly — 6
Speckle-Winged Dun and Spinner — 14 or 16	Speckle-Winged Dun and Spinner — 14 or 16	Light Rusty Spinner — 18 or 20
Blue-Winged Olive Dun — 14	Pale Morning Dun — 16 or 18	Dark Rusty Spinner — 18
Pale Morning Dun — 16 or 18	Salmon Fly — 6	Great Red Spinner — 12
Salmon Fly — 6	Blue Dun — 18	Pale Morning Dun and Spinner — 16 or 18
Blue Dun — 18	Dark Brown Dun — 20	
Dark Brown Dun — 20	Dark Brown Spinner — 20	
Dark Brown Spinner — 20	Dark Blue Quill — 16 or 18	
Dark Blue Quill — 16 or 18	Dark Brown Spinner — 16 or 18	
Dark Brown Spinner — 16 or 18	Pale Olive Dun — 20	
Pale Olive Dun — 20	Dark Red Quill — 16	
Pale Morning Spinner — 16 or 18		
Dark Red Quill — 16		

Morning	Afternoon	Evening
JULY		
Pale Morning Dun — 16 or 18	Pale Morning Dun — 16 or 18	Pale Morning Dun — 16 or 18
Quill Gordon — 12	Salmon Fly — 6	Salmon Fly — 6
Western Green Drake — 12	Speckle-Winged Dun and	Ginger Quill — 12
Gray Drake — 12	Spinner — 14 or 16	Light Cahill — 12
Speckle-Winged Dun and	Western Green Drake — 12	Pink Lady — 12
Spinner — 14 or 16	Quill Gordon — 12	Salmon Spinner — 12
Blue Dun — 18	Red Quill — 14, 16, & 18	Red Quill — 16
Dark Brown Dun — 20	Dark Red Quill — 14	Dark Red Quill — 14
Dark Brown Spinner — 20	Dark Blue Quill — 18	Red Quill — 16
Dark Blue Quill — 18	Dark Brown Spinner — 18	Cream Spinner — 16
Dark Brown Spinner — 18		Blue-Winged Olive Dun — 14
Pale Olive Dun — 20 and 24		
Dark Brown Spinner — 24		
Trico Spinner — 24		
Salmon Spinner — 12		
Pale Brown Dun — 12		
Dark Brown Dun — 14		
AUGUST		
Dark Blue Quill — 18	Dark Blue Quill — 18	Pale Evening Dun — 14
Dark Brown Spinner — 18	Dark Brown Spinner — 18	Gray Fox — 14
Gray Drake — 12	Gray Drake — 12	Pale Evening Spinner — 14
Pale Olive Dun — 20 and 24	Blue Dun — 18 or 20	Ginger Quill — 14
Trico Spinner — 24	Red Quill — 14 and 16	Brown Quill Spinner — 12
Dark Brown Spinner — 24	Pale Morning Dun — 16 or 18	Cream Spinner — 16
Pale Morning Dun — 16 or 18	Gray Fox — 14	Gray Fox — 14
Ginger Quill — 14		
Red Quill — 14 or 16		
SEPTEMBER		
Dark Blue Quill — 18	Gray Fox — 14	Gray Fox — 14
Dark Brown Spinner — 18 and 24	Pale Evening Dun — 14	Ginger Quill — 14
Blue Dun — 18 and 20	Dark Blue Quill — 18	Brown Quill Spinner — 12
Pale Olive Dun — 24	Blue Dun — 18 and 20	Dark Rusty Spinner — 20
Trico Spinner — 24	Dark Brown Spinner — 18	Pale Evening Spinner — 14
Speckle-Winged Dun and	Speckle-Winged Dun and	Cream Spinner — 16
Spinner — 14 or 16	Spinner — 14 and 16	
Ginger Quill — 14		
OCTOBER		
Trico — 20–24	October Caddis — 6–10	

Tying a caddis imitation is fairly simple whether it's intended for Eastern, Midwestern, or Western streams. The pictures demonstrate the process.

Figure 17. Dub a small amount of poly material onto the waxed tying thread.

Figure 18. Wrap the dubbing toward the eye of the hook, then backward toward the bend, and finally forward toward the eye. Tying the dubbing in this manner produces a well-tapered body. If you plan to include hackle, leave plenty of space at the eye.

Figure 19. Tie a small bunch of deer hair (light or dark depending on the wing color of the natural) near the eye after removing all short hair. The length of the deer hair wings should be slightly longer than the length of the body.

Figure 20. Trim the base, and tie in firmly.

Figure 21. If you prefer more buoyancy, add hackle to the imitation. Tie one or two hackles in front of the deer hair and wind.

Figure 21A. Finished caddis or stonefly imitation with hackle.

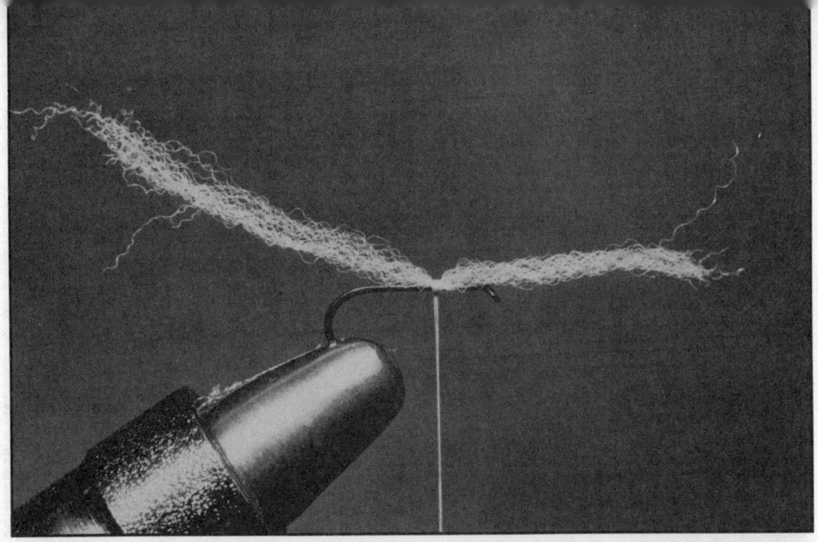

Figure 22. Tie in a strand of polypropylene material near the eye of the hook. Remember to leave plenty of room for the hackle, and add a few strands of Krystal Flash or sparkle yarn.

Figure 23. Clip and shape polypropylene. Tie in several pale dun hackle fibers at the bend of the hook for the tail. Dub a small amount of cream poly material for the rear half of the abdomen.

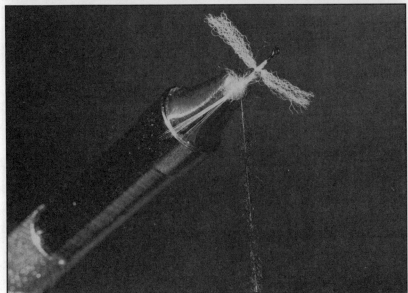

Figure 24. Finish body by dubbing dark brown poly material for the front half of the body.

Figure 25. Body, wings, and tail complete.

Figure 26. Tie in one or two pale dun hackles and wind. Most fly tiers omit this stage.

Figure 27. Finish with a whip finish, and lacquer.

MEETING AND FISHING THE HATCHES

CHAPTER 6

FISHING THE MORNING HATCHES (Eastern and Midwestern)

In the following list, (A) indicates that hatches or spinner falls also often occur in the afternoon and (E) that they often occur in the evening. Dates listed are approximate. An M in front of the species indicates an important Midwestern hatch. If you see (*vagans*) or (*Ephemerella*), the species was changed recently. The old classification is contained in parentheses.

DUNS

M *Baetis tricaudatus (vagans)*[1] (A)—Little Blue-Winged Olive Dun; 10:00 A.M.–6:00 P.M.; April 1[2]

M *Paraleptophlebia adoptiva* (A)—Dark Blue Quill; 11:00 A.M.–4:00 P.M.; April 15

M *Baetis phoebus* (A)—Little Blue-Winged Olive Dun; morning and afternoon; May 10

M *Stenonema fuscum* (A & E)—Gray Fox; 4:00–8:30 P.M. (some days hatches may occur earlier); May 15

M *Baetis quebecensis* (A)—Little Blue-Winged Olive Dun; morning and afternoon; May 15

M *Stenonema vicarium* (A & E)—American March Brown; 10:00 A.M.–7:00 P.M.; May 20

Eurylophella (Ephemerella) bicolor (A)—Chocolate Dun; late morning and early afternoon; May 25

Drunella (Ephemerella) cornuta (A & E)—Blue-Winged Olive Dun; morning and afternoon with a peak sometimes around 11:30 A.M.; May 26

M *Ephemerella needhami* (A)—Chocolate Dun; late morning and early afternoon; May 30

M *Paraleptophlebia mollis* (A & E)—Dark Blue Quill; 10:00 A.M.–4:00 P.M. (sometimes hatches occur into the evening); June 3

Attenella (Ephemerella) attenuata (A)—Blue-Winged Olive Dun; sporadic during the day; June 5

Paraleptophlebia strigula (A)—Blue Quill; 9:00 A.M.–4:00 P.M.; June 5[2]

Leptophlebia johnsoni (A)—Iron Blue Dun; 11:00 A.M.; June 9

M *Stenonema pulchellum*, Pulchellum Group (A)—Cream Cahill; sporadic around midday and evening, June 15[2]

M *Dannella (Ephemerella) simplex*—Little Blue-Winged Olive Dun; morning and afternoon; June 15

M *Baetis brunneicolor* (A)—Little Blue-Winged Olive Dun; morning and afternoon; June 15

M *Siphlonurus alternatus* (A)—Gray Drake; morning and afternoon; June 15

Paraleptophlebia guttata (A)—Dark Blue Quill; sporadic during day; June 25[2]

M *Drunella (Ephemerella) lata* (A)—Blue-Winged Olive Dun; sporadic during day; June 25

Drunella (Ephemerella) cornuta (A)—Blue-Winged Olive Dun; sporadic in morning but mainly around 11:00 A.M.; June 25[2]

M *Paraleptophlebia debilis*—Blue Quill; morning; July 2

M *Tricorythodes stygiatus*—Pale Olive Dun; 7:00–9:00 A.M.; July 15[2]

Tricorythodes attratus—Pale Olive Dun; 7:00–9:00 A.M.; July 15[2]

M *Baetis pygmaeus* (A)—Little Blue-Winged Olive Dun; morning and afternoon; August 1

SPINNERS

M *Baetis tricaudatus (vagans)* (A & E)—Rusty Spinner; 10:00 A.M.–6:00 P.M. (and later); April 3[2]

Epeorus pleuralis (A)—Red Quill Spinner; 11:30 A.M.–2:00 P.M. (sometimes later); April 20

Eurylophella (Ephemerella) bicolor—Chocolate Spinner; afternoon; May 26

M *Paraleptophlebia mollis* (A & E)—Dark Brown Spinner; morning and afternoon (and sometimes evening); June 4

---

[1]Species may produce several broods per season.
[2]Hatches appear for many days.

Paraleptophlebia guttata (A & E)—Dark Brown Spinner; morning and afternoon (and sometimes evening); June 26
Paraleptophlebia strigula (A & E)—Dark Brown Spinner; morning and afternoon (and sometimes evening); June 6
M *Paraleptophlebia debilis*—Blue Quill; morning and afternoon; July 2
M *Tricorythodes stygiatus*—Reverse Jenny Spinner (female), Dark Brown Spinner (male); 8:00–11:00 A.M.; July 15
Tricorythodes atratus—Reverse Jenny Spinner (female), Dark Brown Spinner (male); 8:00–11:00 A.M., July 15

CADDIS FLIES

Rhyacophila species—Green Caddis; morning; July 15

I take a rather uncommon approach to fishing the hatches and spinner falls. Most writers have categorized aquatic insects according to the time of season they emerge—that is, early, middle, or late. This method is useful and follows one of the four rules set forth for meeting and fishing the hatches: emergence dates. But no matter how good you are at predicting the season an insect emerges, you'll likely miss the hatch if you aren't on the stream at the proper time. Therefore, I prefer to utilize another one of the four rules to group aquatic insects: time of day. Using this latter approach, I have divided the hatches into those that normally appear in the morning, afternoon, or evening. There is nothing sacred about this type of grouping, however, since many insects listed in one category may emerge in fishable numbers during another time of the day. For example, the Green Drake,

normally an evening hatch, sometimes appears in heavy numbers in the afternoon. Another evening emerger, the Slate Drake, often appears in the morning or afternoon on cloudy days in June or July. Many other mayflies fall into this exception-to-the-rule category. Furthermore, many mayflies and caddis flies that appear in the afternoon in May emerge later, usually in the evening, in June or July. In addition, many *Paraleptophlebia* species that begin appearing in the morning continue through the afternoon and on into the evening.

I enjoy fly-fishing in the morning probably more than at any other time of day. In direct contrast to the problems associated with late-evening fishing, you don't have to worry about changing imitations in almost total darkness and locating rising trout from distant sounds. No reflex casting is needed here, just pinpoint casting to clearly visible rises.

Morning is not without its disadvantages, however. As the fly-fisherman sees better during the day, so too does the trout, making new demands on the angler. It requires a more refined approach to the stream, a better presentation of the artificial, and a finer leader, among other things, to achieve success.

When I think of morning fly fishing, I think of Blue Quills, which effectively copy most *Paraleptophlebia* species; Blue-Winged Olive Duns, which imitate some important *Drunella* species; and the Pale Olive Dun (and of course the spinners of this species), which imitate several of the *Tricorythodes* species.

Figure 28. The Blue-Winged Olive Dun imitates many of the morning-emerging *Drunellas*.

Figure 29. The Reverse Jenny Spinner duplicates the *Tricorythodes* species appearing in the morning in the East, Midwest, and West.

Figure 30. A stretch of Spring Creek in central Pennsylvania that contains good hatches of *Tricorythodes* and *Drunella cornuta*, both morning emergers.

THE TIME TO USE THE BLUE QUILL IS NOW

I had just tied a dozen size 18 Blue Quills and presented them to a friend. After he thanked me for the dry flies, he asked the all-important question: "When should I use these artificials?"

"If you plan to be on the stream any morning or afternoon, the time to use the Blue Quill is now," I urged.

"What do you mean?"

"Well, the Blue Quill effectively copies many *Paraleptophlebia* species, and members of this genus can be found on most waters from early morning until late afternoon almost every day from mid-April until late October."

Yes, the Blue Quill and Dark Blue Quill imitate rather closely species like *P. adoptive, P. mollis, P. strigula,* and *P. guttata* in the East and Midwest and *P. debilis* and *P. packi* in the West, and many other members of this common genus. Most of these subimagos have dark slate gray wings, dark grayish brown bodies, dark gray tails, and pale tan to pale gray legs.

Not only are the duns similar in appearance, but so are most spinners (especially females). Because of their body coloration, females are sometimes called Dark Brown Spinners. This is an appropriate common name for this genus, and although there are few commercial imitations that adequately copy the natural, the one suggested in Chapter 3 does extremely well during a spinner fall.

In addition to similarity in size and general coloration, most species emerge at corresponding times—mainly mornings (but remember, they can continue into the evening). Even in April, when mornings can be extremely cold, some brave *Paraleptophlebia adoptiva* duns appear by 11:00 A.M., but the largest number of this species usually appears around 2:00 P.M.

Probably the most important subimago is *Paraleptophlebia mollis*, with *P. adoptiva* a close second. Both duns are often sluggish and drift on the surface some distance before taking flight.

But there are two other *Paraleptophlebia* species: *P. strigula* and *P. guttata*. Both have proved to be important to meet and fish during June, July, and August on many Eastern streams. Although neither has been mentioned often in fly-fishing literature, both species produce rising trout while emerging.

I first met *Paraleptophlebia strigula* on Big Fishing Creek in mid-June more than a decade ago. I arrived at a stretch above Lamar called the Narrows at 7:00 A.M. This stream contains fertile limestone water with a good, steady flow throughout the season. The water temperature seldom rises above 60 degrees even on the warmest summer days on this section of the stream.

When I arrived at the stream, I was greeted by a heavy morning fog, typical here because of the difference in air and water temperatures. A few Blue Quills (*P. strigula*) already had appeared on the surface, and several trout rose but not enough to motivate me to cast to them. I spent the first two hours collecting duns and taking photographs.

It was now 11:00 A.M., and hundreds of the motionless duns rode the surface of the pool in front of me. Most had emerged in the fast water at the head of the pool and traveled possibly 300 feet without taking flight. The legs of this species are extremely pale, so I searched in my Blue Quill compartment until I found an imitation containing very pale dun hackle. I tied the artificial onto the 6X tippet and waded into the pool just below a half-dozen rising trout. I disturbed the first two fish and now moved toward a third fish that was still feeding. More trout now joined the half-dozen surface feeding, and all actively gulped in the small slate-colored duns passing near them.

A major hatch was underway, and the trout seemed to sense it.

The first cast barely landed on the surface in front of a heavy trout, and the dry fly immediately disappeared with a huge swirl. The rainbow showed his annoyance with the strike by leaping out of the water and then heading upstream past two boulders. My leader caught on one of the rocks, but I successfully mended it. After a few minutes of following the rainbow up through the pool, I turned it, and it headed toward me. I scooped my net under the trout and proudly lifted the 3-pounder out of the water. It had probably gained some of that weight that day feeding on the thousands of mayflies available to it.

Duns emerged and trout rose until 2:00 P.M., when the hatch finally subsided. Coincidentally, while subimagos appeared, thousands of imagos from yesterday's hatch undulated in their mating flight so characteristic for most *Paraleptophlebia* species.

Another important species in the dun stage is *Paraleptophlebia adoptiva*. Although it most often appears in greatest numbers in the afternoon rather than the morning, we'll discuss it here.

Jim Heltzel and I arrived at Cedar Run in north-central Pennsylvania just before 11:00 A.M. A brisk breeze chilled the late April morning. It had rained, drizzled, and flurried for the past three days, but at last the leaden gray color had given way to a bright blue sky.

My thermometer registered a 55-degree air temperature and a 45-degree water temperature—both poor indicators of the tremendous mayfly hatches that were to follow shortly. We had stopped at a long, deep, eroded pool on Cedar Run, which was probably created by water unendingly pounding a huge rock ledge for years. A small stream cascaded in as a miniature waterfall on the far side of Cedar Run. The pool was 50 to 60 feet long and 10 feet deep at its deepest spot.

Only a few gray midges dotted the surface when we arrived, and no trout rose, so I tied on a Lady Ghost streamer. The water seemed void of trout. For two hours I methodically cast that streamer without success.

Around 1:30 P.M. several Blue Quills braved the cold water and air temperatures and appeared on the surface. However, they were too dazed to fly and after several abortive attempts floated aimlessly around and around in an eddy near the far shore. Now more Blue Quills emerged. Two dozen or more immobile duns rested in the small eddy. Occasionally a small native brook trout rose to capture one of the motionless duns.

By 2:00 P.M. hundreds of Blue Quill duns had appeared, and now ten to fifteen trout actively fed on the surface. I tied on a size 18 Blue Quill and cast toward what appeared to be a large trout now feeding in the fast water at the head of the pool. The first cast adequately covered the feeding fish, and it gulped in the imitation almost immediately. I struck. Too late! Don't forget, it had been six long months since I had last had a strike on a dry fly. I was more successful with the next four trout, all taken in the fast water at the head of this picturesque pool.

About 2:30 P.M. another species, the Quill Gordon, began emerging in large numbers, and about 3:00 P.M. enough Hendricksons appeared to encourage trout to switch a third time. With each imitation I caught more than ten trout.

Who would believe that all this activity, all this dry-fly fishing, occurred on a cold blustery April late morning and afternoon? I had been conditioned not to expect a sizable mayfly hatch until the water temperature neared 50 degrees.

The Dark Blue Quill imitation effectively duplicates other species that also appear in the morning. For several years I met and fished a small mayfly that habitually emerged at 11:00 A.M. I was confident it was a *Paraleptophlebia* species. However, after I examined it under a microscope, I was surprised to find out it was *Serratella deficiens*. This species appears on Elk Creek in central Pennsylvania for weeks, always at 11:00 A.M. A Dark Blue Quill tied on a size 20 hook effectively copies this species. I have had other reports that this species is important to duplicate.

Don't overlook the Blue Quill on Midwestern rivers. *Paraleptophlebia adoptiva* appears on most Michigan and Wisconsin rivers in late April and is important to fish. I've seen Blue Quills on the Little Manistee near Frederick until late September.

When should you use the Blue Quill? If you're fly-fishing any morning of the season from mid-April to October—the time to use the Blue Quill is now.

WHEN BLUE-WINGED OLIVES EMERGE

Recently I fly-fished the Junction Pool on the Beaverkill near Roscoe, New York. As I headed for the stream, I met a fellow fly-fisherman returning to his car.

"Anything happening?" I asked.

"There was a pretty good hatch of Blue-Winged Olive Duns earlier this morning," he said.

"What size?"

"A size 14 or 16. A size 12 wouldn't work."

Blue-Winged Olives present a dilemma. The hatch that appeared that morning on the Beaverkill could have been a bright olive *Drunella cornuta* or the darker olive-bodied *D. walkeri*.

When someone says he saw a March Brown, Gray Fox, Slate Drake, Quill Gordon, or Green Drake hatch, you know the fly to use and approximately the size the fly should be. This is not the case with the Blue-Winged Olive Dun. Some species are greenish olive, others are bright olive, and still others are tannish or yellowish olive. Some can be imitated with a size 14 fly, while others require a size 16, 18, or 20 hook.

Blue-Winged Olives are common in three regions of the United States. In the East, you'll find them on the Beaverkill and the Delaware in New York, the Connecticut in New Hampshire, and on Penns and Big Fishing creeks in Pennsylvania.

Blue-Winged Olives loosely refer to about seven different mayfly species in the East, three in the Midwest, and three in the West. Most of these mayflies belong to the Genus *Drunella* (part of *Ephemerella* until recently). They range from a size 12 to a size 20. All have various shades of olive as their body color.

Blue-Winged Olive Duns usually emerge most heavily in the morning and early afternoon. Spinners of most of the species lay their eggs near dusk and often form concentrated spinner falls. Most of the spinners have dark olive black bodies and are called Dark Olive Spinners. Emergence for many of the species occurs from late May to late July. Since many of them appear through mid-season, these mayflies offer the last opportunities for meeting and fishing a sizable hatch in daylight.

In the East you'll see *Drunella cornuta* and *D. longicornus* appear around the end of May on many streams. Like the Hendrickson (*Ephemerella subvaria*), *D. cornuta* probably has several subspecies. From New York north at the same time *D. cornuta* appears, *D. walkeri* emerges. *Serratella simplex*, a size 20, emerges about mid-June. This Blue-Winged Olive Dun makes up for its small size by producing heavy hatches on some of the larger Eastern and Midwestern rivers. At about the same time in June, *Attenella attenuata* appears on New York and New England trout streams.

The last heavy hatch of Blue-Winged Olives on the Manistee and Au Sable appears when *Drunella lata* emerges in mid-July. This same species also appears on Eastern streams such as Penns Creek about two weeks earlier.

Most Blue-Winged Olives escape rapidly from the surface when emerging. If, however, you meet and fish one of these hatches on a cool, overcast, drizzly day, you'll have memorable fishing. Fish the Au Sable when duns can't escape, and you're in for some great fly-fishing. I fished the North Branch near Lovells one mid-July morning, preparing to fish a Trico spinner fall. The fall occurred but was preceded, coincided, and followed by a spectacular Blue-Winged Olive hatch. A cool drizzle fell all morning. Duns attempted to escape, but their normally rapid escape

rapidly slowed at takeoff. Trout readily took the stragglers on the surface. For more than three hours, duns struggled and fish rose. A size 16 Blue-Winged Olive Dun worked well on the risers.

If you plan any morning fishing trips on Eastern and Midwestern waters from late May through late July, carry a good supply of Blue-Winged Olive Duns in sizes 14 to 20. If you do meet a hatch of Olives, return to the same location in the evening for a spectacular spinner fall. Again carry Dark Olive Spinners in sizes 14 to 20 for some exciting meeting and fishing the hatches and spinner falls.

Next time you hear someone saying that they saw a Blue-Winged Olive Dun hatch, don't reach for the first olive fly you find in your fly box. Check the hatch for size and color. Then you'll be properly prepared when Blue-Winged Olives emerge.

TRICOS COAST TO COAST

It's 8:00 P.M. on August 5 and you're fly-fishing on the Battenkill near Arlington, Vermont. What spinner fall can you expect to see within the next hour? The Trico. Let's say you're on the McKenzie near Eugene, Oregon, on the same day. What spinner fall will you see? The Trico. The same goes for dozens of Midwest streams like the Au Sable and its North Branch near

Figure 31. A male *Tricorythodes* spinner.

Lovells and the Namekagon near Hayward, Wisconsin.

The Trico is one of the most common mayflies in the United States. Several Trico species can be found on Western, Midwestern, and Eastern waters from mid-July into early September, and even later on some waters. These species are so similar that you can use the same pattern on the McKenzie or the Callapooia rivers in Oregon that you use on the Au Sable in northern Michigan, on the Delaware River between New York and Pennsylvania, and on the Musconetcong in New Jersey.

A size 24 pattern copies most of these mayflies. However, on some Colorado rivers, I've fished over a Trico spinner fall using a size 20 imitation.

Ken Walters and Ed Exum of Denver and Bob Newell of Anchorage, Alaska, took me to their favorite Trico spot on the South Platte River near Deckers, Colorado. Ken operates Flyfisher Limited, an Orvis store in Denver. He fishes Trico falls weekly throughout the season at Deckers or South Park on the South Platte. On that first trip to meet the South Platte's Trico fall I caught some heavy browns up to 3 pounds and 20 inches long. Trout fed voraciously on the spent spinners and readily took that size 20 spent wing. The Trico on the South Platte often falls in heavy numbers until mid-October.

In some regions of the country, few fishermen bother with this diminutive hatch. Several years ago I visited the McKenzie River near Eugene, Oregon, in early October. At 10:00 A.M. I saw thousands of Tricos in their familiar mating flight 20 feet above the water. Near the city limits of Eugene, I saw more than a dozen trout feeding freely on the spent spinners. On the four occasions that I've seen the hatch and spinner fall on the McKenzie, I've never seen another fisherman meeting and fishing the hatch.

All over the West you'll encounter great Trico hatches. Fish Montana's Bitterroot or the Missouri, and you'll see Tricos. Fish Henry's Fork or the Wood River in Idaho, and you'll see Tricos. Al Smeraglio of Levittown, Pennsylvania, spends several weeks annually on the Wood River just to fish the Trico. Mike Manfredo of Illinois fishes the North Platte near Cowdrey, Colorado, when the Trico appears on that river.

In the East I've found the Trico on at least fifty Pennsylvania streams. The Beaverkill in New York and the Battenkill in Vermont also contain respectable hatches.

I'd seen only a feeble hatch on the Au Sable in the Midwest. When I returned to Grayling, Michigan, in mid-September to fish the Trico once more, fall

Figure 32. A section of the North Branch of the Au Sable near Lovells, Michigan. Here you'll see heavy Trico and Sulphur hatches.

had appeared early. The Grayling area had already experienced a frost, which usually signals the end of heavy Trico falls for the season.

Rusty Gates at the Gates Au Sable Lodge said the hatch intensity had dwindled considerably in the past two weeks. That was confirmed when Rusty and I fished the South Branch early Friday morning. He said that the heaviest hatches on the river and its branches occur from July 20 to August 10. Did I have to wait another year to meet and fish a decent Trico spinner fall on the Au Sable?

The next day I decided to head up above Lovells to the North Branch, which also exhibits a heavy Trico hatch in August. Would it still appear in September? When I arrived at the stream at 9:00 A.M., the air temperature was 45 degrees. By 10:00 A.M. the water temperature registered only 46. Only a handful of Trico spinners hovered in the air above me. I almost left the river when hundreds and then thousands of pale olive green female Trico duns began emerging from the water ahead of me.

Maybe the hatch today would be fishable. By 10:45 A.M. a few Trico spinners landed on the surface. I glanced at a 100-foot stretch below me and saw five rising trout. I reentered the water about 30 feet below the pod of rising trout. Soon three more trout joined those already surfacing. In minutes I had more than a dozen trout unrestrainedly gorging themselves just upstream from me. Soon more than thirty trout fed in front of me. It looked as if someone upstream had tossed trout pellets into the water.

With each cast I covered rising trout. I didn't cast to any specific rise; each drift with the spinner pattern covered four or five trout. I saw several swirls and short strikes to my Harvey Trico pattern, so I tied on a new 3-foot piece of Dai-Riki .005 tippet material. Now I had a better float and less drag with the longer, finer tippet. Finally, a strike—a heavy 12-inch brook trout took the pattern. A few casts later a 10-inch native brown took the Harvey Trico and then a brook trout. By 11:45 A.M. dark brown male Trico spinners appeared on the surface. The action continued for two hours with little let-up from the trout. Fifteen of those rising trout took my size 24 Harvey Trico that day.

I left the water after two hours of continuous action.

Figure 33. Rusty Gates of Grayling, Michigan, fishing the Au Sable during a Trico hatch.

Still a half-dozen trout rose to a steadily dwindling supply of spinners. I had many refusals that day.

The Trico can be spectacular in September and even into October on the McKenzie in Oregon and the South Platte in Colorado. The fall occurs later in the day. Normally in July and August, Tricos fall onto the surface from 8:00 A.M. to 10:00 A.M. The water on the North Branch was low and clear, and these trout had been fished over during this hatch for more than two months. But what a day! What a hatch! What great fall fishing!

Whether you're on the McKenzie in the West, the North Branch of the Au Sable in the Midwest, or the Delaware in the East from mid-July to late September, look for a Trico spinner fall. This small mayfly might turn an uneventful no-hatch day into an explosive, unforgettable meeting and fishing the hatch day.

CHAPTER 7

FISHING THE AFTERNOON HATCHES (Eastern and Midwestern)

In the following list, (M) indicates that hatches or spinner falls also often occur in the morning and (E) that they often occur in the evening. Dates listed are approximate. An *M* in front of the species indicates that the species is common in the Midwest.

DUNS

M *Baetis tricaudatus (vagans)*[1] (M)—Little Blue Dun; 10:00 A.M.–6:00 P.M. (sometimes with heavy emergence around 1:00 P.M.); April 1

M *Paraleptophlebia adoptiva* (M)—Dark Blue Quill; 11:00 A.M.–4:00 P.M. (heavy emergence often from 2:00–4:00 P.M.); April 15

Epeorus pleuralis—Quill Gordon; 1:00–3:00 P.M.; April 18

M *Siphloplecton basale*—Great Speckled Olive Dun; 1:30 P.M.; April 18

M *Ephemerella subvaria*—Hendrickson (female), Red Quill (male); 2:00–4:00 P.M.; April 23

M *Leptophlebia cupida*—Black Quill; 2:00–4:00 P.M.; April 27

M *Ephemerella rotunda* (E)—Pale Evening Dun; 2:00–8:00 P.M.; May 8

M *Stenonema fuscum* (M & E)—Gray Fox; 4:00–8:30 P.M. (many days hatches occur earlier); May 15

M *Pseudocloeon* species[1,2] (E)—Little Blue Dun; afternoon and evening; May 10

M *Ephemerella invaria* (E)—Pale Evening Dun; 3:00–8:00 P.M.; May 20[3]

Ephemerella septentrionalis (E)—Pale Evening Dun; appears mainly in the evening but does emerge sporadically in the afternoon; May 18

M *Stenonema vicarium* (M & E)—American March Brown; 10:00 A.M.–7:00 P.M.; May 20

M *Stenacron interpunctatum canadense* (E)—Light Cahill; sporadic during afternoon with a concentration at dusk in June; May 25[3]

M *Litobrancha recurvata* (E)—Dark Green Drake; 1:00–8:00 P.M.; May 25

M *Ephemera simulans* (E)—Brown Drake; sporadic in afternoon; May 25

Ephemera guttulata (E)—Green Drake; mainly evening, but many smaller streams have heavy hatches in the afternoon; May 25

M *Siphlonurus alternatus* (M)—Gray Drake; morning and afternoon; June 15

M *Dannella (Ephemerella) simplex* (M)—Little Blue-Winged Olive Dun; morning and afternoon; June 15

Eurylophella (Ephemerella) bicolor (M)—Chocolate Dun; late morning and early afternoon; May 25

Drunella (Ephemerella) cornuta (M)—Blue-Winged Olive Dun; morning and afternoon; May 26

M *Ephemerella needhami* (M)—Chocolate Dun[4]; late morning and early afternoon; May 30

Eurylophella (Ephemerella) minimella (M & E)—Chocolate Dun; afternoon; June 1

M *Paraleptophlebia mollis* (M & E)—Dark Blue Quill; 10:00 A.M.–4:00 P.M. (often continues into early evening); June 3

Attenella (Ephemerella) attenuata (M)—Blue-Winged Olive Dun; morning and afternoon; June 5

Leptophlebia johnsoni (M)—Iron Blue Dun; 11:00 A.M. (sporadic in the afternoon); June 9

M *Stenonema pulchellum* (M)—Cream Cahill; sporadic around midday; June 15[3]

Paraleptophlebia guttata (M)—Dark Blue Quill; sporadic during day; June 25[3]

Drunella (Ephemerella) cornuta (M)—Blue-Winged Olive Dun; sporadic during morning and afternoon (often around 11:00 A.M.); June 25[3]

M *Pseudocloeon* species—Little Blue Dun; afternoon; September 20

Isonychia matilda (E)—Slate Drake; afternoon and early evening; September 20

SPINNERS

M *Baetis tricaudatus (vagans)*[1] (M)—Rusty Spinner; 10:00 A.M.–6:00 P.M. (and later); April 3[3]

M *Paraleptophlebia adoptiva* (E)—Dark Brown Spinner; 4:00–7:00 P.M.; April 17

Epeorus pleuralis (M)—Red Quill Spinner; 11:30 A.M.–2:00 P.M.; April 20

M *Ephemerella subvaria* (E)—Red Quill Spinner; 3:00–8:00 P.M.; April 28

M *Leptophlebia cupida* (E)—Early Brown Spinner; 1:00–6:00 P.M.; April 28

Eurylophella (Ephemerella) bicolor (E)—Chocolate Spinner; afternoon and evening; May 27

M *Ephemerella needhami* (E)—Chocolate Spinner; afternoon and evening, May 30

M *Paraleptophlebia mollis* (M)—Dark Brown Spinner; morning and afternoon; June 4

Paraleptophlebia guttata (M)—Dark Brown Spinner; morning and afternoon; June 25

CADDIS FLIES

M *Brachycentrus numerosus*—Grannom; morning to evening; April 18

Psilotreta species—Cream Caddis; morning to evening; April 25

M *Chimarrha atterima* (M & E)—Little Black Caddis; 11:00 A.M.–6:00 P.M., April 26

M *Brachycentrus fuliginosus* (M & E)—Grannom; 3:00–7:00 P.M. (sometimes in the morning); May 10[5]

Rhyacophila lobifera (M & E)—Green Caddis; 4:00–9:00 P.M.; May 10[5]

Symphitopsyche (Hydropsyche) slossanae (M & E)—Spotted Sedge; 1:00–6:00 P.M.; May 23

STONE FLIES

Strophopteryx fasciata (M)—Early Brown Stonefly; afternoon; April 10

Isoperla signata (E)—Light Stonefly; afternoon; May 8[5]

Isoperla bilineata—Yellow Stonefly; morning and afternoon; June 5

Alloperla imbecilla—Little Green Stonefly; morning and afternoon; June 5

Many anglers believe that afternoon is a poor time to be on the stream. Fly-fishermen plan to be on their favorite water while a comforting morning fog still

---

[1]Species may produce several broods per year.
[2]Species are not listed in the Insect Emergence Chart, but can be important on occasion.
[3]Hatches appear for many days.
[4]Color may vary.
[5]Dates are approximate. Emergence may begin earlier in the season.

covers waters, cooled by the darkness before. Even more anglers schedule their trips to meet sunset and the well-known hatches and spinner falls this period produces. But how many credible anglers fish trout waters in mid-afternoon—especially in mid- and late season?

Anglers might qualify their degradation of afternoon fishing by saying: "Sure, this is the time when the Quill Gordon, Hendrickson, Black Quill, American March Brown, and some Gray Foxes emerge—but these hatches occur only the first month and a half of the season. After June, it's useless to cast over waters heated by a hot afternoon sun. Certainly you wouldn't waste an afternoon in July or August in uncomfortable, sweaty waders with temperatures hovering around 90 degrees. Besides, no hatches appear on these midsummer afternoons."

To these comments I say, "Try this time slot before you condemn it to oblivion." Sure, fishing in the afternoon can be hot and uncomfortable. Yes, afternoon is a notoriously poor time to try for lunker trout because they characteristically don't feed during daylight hours. But as you'll see, or as you already know, this is not a time necessarily void of emerging insects or, for that matter, rising trout.

A visit to your favorite stream in June, July, or August might surprise you. There can be sporadic hatches of several *Drunella* species, many of which are effectively duplicated by the Blue-Winged Olive Dun. Many *Baetis* species also choose hot, humid summer afternoons to appear. These, of course, are imitated by the Little Blue Dun.

In addition, there are other little-known but significant *Eurylophella* species that appear on many afternoons in late May and June. A lot of these afternoon emergers are effectively matched with the Chocolate Dun. On any given June afternoon, enough of these lethargic duns can appear to encourage trout to feed.

Many of these species are members of the Genus *Eurylophella*. One of these, *E. bicolor*, begins emerging around noon and continues throughout the afternoon. Another species, *E. minimella*, appears on Pine Creek in Pennsylvania in early June from late morning until early evening.

Both species, plus others like *Ephemerella needhami*, are all effectively copied by a size 16 Chocolate Dun. *Always* include several Chocolate Duns in your selection of artificials for use in afternoon fly-fishing.

Not only does afternoon have its own insect hatches, but it also harbors holdovers from the morning and premature appearances from the evening. This is only natural since this time span is a connecting link between the other two time periods. Holdovers and premature hatches and spinner falls most often occur in April, May, or June, but some (*Paraleptophlebia, Baetis*, and *Drunella* species) spill over into July and August.

Holdovers from the morning are aquatic insects that initially appear in the earlier time slot but many times continue into the afternoon in profuse or limited numbers. Many of the Blue Quills (*Paraleptophlebia* species) often appear heaviest in the morning but often continue emerging in more limited numbers through mid-afternoon. I've noted *Paraleptophlebia mollis* duns emerging on Cedar Run in late May as late as 6:00 P.M. and in large enough numbers to produce many rising trout. At least one *Paraleptophlebia* species, *P. adoptiva*, appears in heaviest numbers in the afternoon rather than the morning.

The other large group of holdovers comes from the genus *Drunella*. These Blue-Winged Olive Duns begin their emergence in the morning, sometimes with a concentration between 11:00 A.M. and noon. Many continue well into the afternoon, often in sparser numbers. Still, enough can appear on some days to encourage trout to feed on escaping duns.

Premature hatches of species that usually emerge in the evening occur in late May and early June. The Pale Evening Dun (both *Ephemerella rotunda* and *E. invaria*) and Light Cahill (*Stenacron interpunctatum canadense*) commonly appear in the afternoon during May and June, and they sometimes appear in heavy enough numbers to encourage trout to feed.

What about July? No decent mayfly would emerge during the afternoon in this month? Wrong again! Hatches aren't as frequent, but several species of *Baetis* appear almost daily on hot July afternoons. One *Baetis* species, as yet unidentified, appears almost daily on central Pennsylvania streams in July. Other *Baetis* species appear in August and September in the afternoon. Don't overlook afternoon fishing in September and October. In early fall you'll encounter spectacular hatches of Slate Drakes and Little

Blue Duns (*Pseudocloeon* species).

Caddis flies, too, appear in the afternoon. One of the most important I have met and fished is the Green Caddis. In early May it emerges in the afternoon as well as the evening.

Afternoon fishing is lousy? Bunk! Sure, it's not the most productive time, but it's still a good time to meet and fish some of the hatches and often a good time to fly-fish over feeding trout.

DRY FLIES IN APRIL

What a time to be alive! A beautiful warm spring afternoon in late April or early May. After months of snow, just plain cold weather, and patient waiting, I thrive on outside activities at this time. Fly-fishing over rising trout is a bonus. Some of the best-known and heaviest hatches appear on these cool (and sometimes downright cold) afternoons. Who hasn't heard of the Quill Gordon or the Hendrickson? These species, *Epeorus pleuralis* and *Ephemerella subvaria*, emerge on many Eastern and Midwestern streams in late April. Some afternoons during this early season, air temperatures barely rise above 40 degrees and water temperatures barely above 45 degrees. On many of these days, these two species brave the elements and announce the coming of a new fly-fishing season.

Since the Hendrickson usually follows the Quill Gordon by less than a week and since both hatches appear about the same time, it's logical to discuss them together. On some fertile streams I've noted Quill Gordon duns emerging around 1:30 P.M., shadowed by a Blue Quill (*Paraleptophlebia adoptiva*) peak at 2:00 P.M., and Hendrickson at 3:00 P.M. The peak emergence of the Quill Gordon is usually a week ahead of the Hendrickson, and the two hatches never seem to appear in equal numbers on the same day.

Emergence dates can vary from year to year by as much as several weeks. Recently we experienced an extremely warm April. All early hatches, including the Quill Gordon and Hendrickson, emerged well before the season began in the Northeast. All artificials tied to meet and fish these hatches had to be placed aside for another year.

For four years, as if part of an enforced ritual, Jack Conyngham, Guthrie Conyngham, Dick Mills, and

I planned annual trips to coincide with either the Quill Gordon or Hendrickson. We planned these treks to the productive streams like the Loyalsock Creek in north-central Pennsylvania and to the Beaverkill and Willowemoc in New York because these waters have heavy hatches of both species. We scheduled these trips so we would be on the water any weekend that falls between April 20 and April 27. On these trips, we usually meet either or both of the hatches. Sure, we agree after four years of meeting these hatches that it's extremely risky to expect many rising trout on some of the cold, blustery days often encountered then, but we're anxious to be on the stream to meet and fish while the first species appear.

Of all these planned trips, the third was by far the most memorable to date. We arrived in separate cars and met at a section of the Loyalsock near Barbours at 1:00 P.M. Predictably, a cold north wind blew downstream. Our only asset for meeting and fishing the hatch that afternoon was the semipleasant 55-degree air temperature.

Only two or three mayflies appeared in the first half-hour, so I backed out of the snow-chilled water to survey the entire stretch for any signs of a major hatch. While impatiently waiting (I never wait patiently), I checked the water temperature and recorded the 46-degree reading in my notebook. Still no hatch. But the elements improved. The north wind slowed to a breeze, the air temperature rose several degrees, and the water temperature neared 50 degrees.

By 1:20 P.M. several duns abruptly appeared in front of me on the high spring waters. I followed their path on the water's surface for more than 100 feet, through the entire length of a pool, but none was seized. Within a half-hour, more than a hundred newly emerged duns appeared on the fast stretch several feet upstream. As the dazed, motionless duns entered the pool below, eight to ten trout took up feeding positions and occasionally fed on the laggards.

As we witnessed the emerging Quill Gordons and concomitant feeding, all four of us scattered out quickly in the large pool to fish over rising trout. I selected an area where four trout occasionally rose to the dark duns. I tied on a fresh Quill Gordon imitation with dark slate wings and cast toward two trout closest to me. After a half-dozen or so casts, I made

the first catch of the year. The trout was barely 6 inches long, but I get excited every new season when I experience success with dry flies in April. Several other trout also seized the artificial before the hatch began to wane.

The Quill Gordon subsided as quickly as it had begun a half-hour before. Quite a few half-drowned subimagos still floated past, but these had probably emerged earlier on stretches several pools upstream.

That afternoon the four of us had a half-mile section of the productive Loyalsock to ourselves. Not one other fisherman had planned to meet and fish the hatch in this area of the stream. We decided to go to our cabin for the evening and on the way anxiously entered into a discussion of the next day's tactics to meet and fish the hatch.

There's no need to arise early on these spring days, since little emergence activity occurs before 10:00 or 11:00 A.M. However, when we awoke in midmorning, we were greeted by a freak 2-inch snowstorm. By noon most of the snow had melted, but the temperature had risen to only 40 degrees, and scattered snow flurries still fell from the leaden gray skies. Even with the tremendous uncertainty of the weather, we decided to travel to the stream to see if another hatch might appear. We arrived on the stream just in time to be greeted by snow squalls and immediately built a fire to warm ourselves from the chilling winter wind. By 2:00 P.M. only a couple of dazed, bewildered, frozen duns had appeared. No hatch appeared, and no trout showed.

I describe this unsuccessful experience because weather often affects one's chances of meeting and fishing the hatches in April and early May. Changeable spring weather conditions often affect the quantity of mayflies appearing and the quality of fly-fishing.

The Red Quill Spinner, or the imago of *Epeorus pleuralis*, has been of little consequence in my experience. I have noted several mating flights around noon or later but have seen little or no feeding on the spinners. The same Red Quill used to imitate the male dun of *Ephemerella subvaria* can be effective should the need ever arise to imitate the *Epeorus pleuralis* spinner.

The Hendrickson is one of the most common and fishable mayflies. I have recorded this species on large streams like the Beaverkill and Loyalsock; on small streams like Cedar Run and White Deer Creek; on medium-sized streams like Bowman Creek; and on slightly acid streams like the Lehigh River. Midwestern rivers like the Au Sable and Rifle in Michigan and the Wolf and Brule in Wisconsin host heavy Hendrickson hatches. You'll find one of the heaviest hatches of this species on the Delaware River near Hancock, New York.

Since emergence for this species is usually concentrated into a two-week period on most streams and since duns most often appear from 2:00 to 4:00 P.M., dense hatches are the rule (except on smaller streams). Furthermore, the late afternoon–early evening spinner fall, unlike that of the Red Quill Spinner (*Epeorus pleuralis*), sometimes produces rising trout.

Coloration of male and female duns of *Ephemerella subvaria* varies substantially, so a separate imitation for each sex is in order. From above (dorsal), both appear similar, but a ventral view portrays the difference; the female has a dark pinkish tan abdomen, whereas the male has a reddish body that is slightly ringed. Some writers have indicated that males and females emerge from different stretches of water. On many occasions during an emergence, I have checked the male and female ratio on a particular stretch rather than fish. From my observations, the sexes emerge together. This suggests that trout might do one of two things: they may be selective and take only male or female, or they may take male and female indiscriminately.

Size also varies from stream to stream. Many hatches in the East and Midwest can be copied with size 16 Hendricksons. Caucci and Nastasi indicate that they found several subspecies of *Ephemerella subvaria*. I agree with this finding.

I have had more success with the Hendrickson imitation than with the Red Quill. Since the female is slightly larger than the male, it might be that trout are selective in taking the more substantial piece of food, the female dun. Nevertheless, make certain you have Red Quill artificials with you, since they effectively copy the female spinner (the female spinner imitation should have spent wings).

The spinner fall for *Ephemerella subvaria* usually occurs late in the afternoon or early in the evening.

The imago can be an important source of food on these otherwise-void early-season trips. The spinner is fairly easy to identify on wing because of the orange egg sac it carries under its curved abdomen.

For many years I reserved my dry-fly fishing for June, July, and August. Not now! Now I prepare myself so I can fish dry flies in April.

CADDIS IMITATIONS CAN BE EFFECTIVE

The Little Juniata River in central Pennsylvania is a fantastic stretch of trout water. Large brown trout abound in every pool. Annually fly-fishermen take many 3- and 4-pounders. The river is 80 to 90 feet wide, and it is almost impossible to wade from one shore to another. Until a few years ago, the stream was heavily polluted from an upstream paper mill and from raw, untreated sewage. Now all that's changed. Before the cleanup, the dark brown water had a pungent, nauseous odor. Now there is no odor near the chalky green water.

Since its comeback (and possibly before), the river has had some profuse mayfly hatches. But probably more common than the mayflies is the almost daily emergence of several caddis fly species. From early May until the end of July, on many afternoons and evenings, there are enough Green Caddis (*Rhyacophila* species) on or near the water to encourage the large browns to feed on the surface.

Several years ago on these same productive waters of the Little Juniata, I learned the value of meeting and fishing the hatch when caddis flies appeared. I traveled with Larry Wilson to the Barn Pool at the lower end of the Espy Farm on a chilly mid-May afternoon. As we approached the deep pool, I noted hundreds of mothlike insects moving upstream in unison 2 or 3 feet above the surface. I quickly waded into the cold water and positioned myself below three surfacing trout. For a minute or two I searched for insects resting on the surface. I scooped at several riding past me, caught one of them, examined the abdomen, and concluded it was a Green Caddis. Soon more caddis floated past, and dozens of trout began surfacing for some of the partially emerged caddis.

A major hatch was underway. I had prepared for this circumstance by tying a half-dozen downwing artificials of the Green Caddis a few days before. With the first cast, I caught an overhanging bush on the far shore. But that wasn't the only problem: there were several current speeds between me and the feeding fish, and the caddis imitation floated only a foot or two before severe drag set in. Finally, a good cast, a mend upstream, and the Caddis drifted drag-free directly over a trout that had been casually sipping in naturals. The brown sucked in the artificial, and I struck. The trout swam toward the center of the stream, leaped into the air, and headed upstream. A gentle nudge on the fly rod moved the fish back downstream toward me. In ten minutes I landed the 3-pound trout that had gorged itself on the easily accessible food.

In the Preface, I said rather assertively that I prefer dry-fly fishing and most often choose not to use wet flies. On many occasions, during a hatch of stone flies, and to a greater extent caddis flies, however, trout seem to refuse surface imitations. On one of these instances on the Little Juniata, I noted caddis fly after caddis fly float directly over what I thought were rising trout. Not one of these naturals was seized, however. Trout seemingly surfaced throughout the pool that day, but few actually took naturals on the surface.

During this frustrating experience, my caddis dry fly sank and became a wet fly drifting a few inches beneath the surface. On the first drift I noted a huge swirl at the "wet fly" as it made the turn at the end of the natural drift. I roll-cast in the same direction again, letting the imitation sink a few inches. This time a brown rose to the fly, and I hooked it. Trout after trout that afternoon took the imitation only when it was fished a few inches beneath the surface.

During an emergence of the Light Stonefly in early May, I tried the same tactic. During this hatch too, trout easily succumbed to a dry-fly imitation stone fly fished just under the surface.

Why does an imitation of either of these two orders prove so effective when fished in this manner? Several fishermen I know theorize that stone flies and caddis flies usually escape rapidly from the surface, and were trout to seize these surface naturals, they would expend more energy on them than they would gain from the food value. Furthermore, the easiest time to capture the caddis is when it is escaping to the surface to emerge.

The Spotted Sedge is a common caddis fly on many streams the third or fourth week in May. Several years ago John Hagan, Dick Mills, and I arrived at Bowman Creek four hours after it had been stocked. Close to a hundred newly introduced trout formed a tight school in front of me. Spotted Sedges soon appeared directly over the school, and the fish seized them with little apprehension. Ten or more sedges now skittered above the trout. I tied on an imitation and made the same movement that the natural did. Cast after cast with the imitation produced trout after trout. John Hagan used a size 16 Light Cahill, which is almost identical to the natural except for the upright wings. For every trout John caught, I caught and released five. After a frustrating hour of saying, "These trout shouldn't notice the difference," John switched to a downwing Spotted Sedge imitation. His rate of success immediately increased. Were the upright wings the problem with these relatively unsophisticated trout?

I have used downwing patterns for caddis flies and stone flies for about twenty years. They're important to include in any dry-fly assortment (in fact, in any assortment). Why? First and foremost, these downwing imitations more accurately copy the natural. When the caddis fly rests on the surface, its wings are folded tentlike back over the body, and the downwing imitation copies this pose correctly. Second, I feel that caddis flies and caddis fly patterns, which have been overlooked for years, are important as a source of food for trout and are therefore important to imitate. I once met an expert fly-fisherman on the same Little Juniata River. He took more trout and larger trout than any other fisherman on the stream. On several occasions when he was fishing, I sat back and watched. He was not one to come over and converse, but he mechanically went on with his expert skill of casting, catching, and releasing trout. Finally, on about the third or fourth meeting, I asked him what pattern he used. "Caddis—nothing but caddis. Day in, day out they catch more fish for me," he said as he showed me his Green Caddis imitation.

If you learn nothing more from this book than the fact that caddis imitations on Eastern, Midwestern, and Western streams have been neglected but are extremely important, you'll probably be a more successful fly-fisherman.

We discussed in Chapter 5 methods of tying the caddis fly and stone fly. I prefer the first of the two recommended methods—with a body of polypropylene and deer hair wings. (I strongly recommend an imitation with two hackles for all Western patterns.) It's important, however, to select the color of deer hair that best matches the wings of the insect. Light deer hair, for example, effectively copies the wings of the Light Stonefly and Spotted Sedge, whereas darker deer hair is used for the Grannom. These suggested patterns don't ride as high on the surface as do regular dry flies but apparently are much more effective during a hatch of the naturals.

Include some emerger patterns in your selection. Earlier I wrote how effective the floating caddis pattern became when I purposely sank it. This wasn't a fluke. Trout chase emerging caddis during a hatch. I tie my caddis emergers with an appropriate body and three turns of partridge or woodcock hackle. This imitation is deadly during a caddis hatch.

Although I've discussed only a couple of caddis fly species, many others are important to match. Tie caddis imitations with cream, yellow, tan, brown, dark brown, gray, green, olive, and black in sizes 12–20. This range of colors and hook sizes should prepare you to meet and fish most caddis fly and also most stone fly hatches.

You haven't tried a downwing caddis imitation yet? Try one; it might make a potentially uneventful trip into a successful one.

THE CREAM DUNS ARE COMING

The Pale Evening Duns (*Ephemerella rotunda, E. invaria*, and *E. dorothea*), the American March Brown (*Stenonema vicarium*), the Gray Fox (*Stenonema fuscum*), and the Light Cahill (*Stenacron canadense*) have many things in common as mayfly hatches.[1] All begin appearing in mid-May—some earlier and some a little later—and all are moderate sized. More important, all species have cream, creamish yellow, yellowish cream, or tannish cream bodies (some have an orange or olive cast also).

Rather than discuss all together, we'll look at the Pale Evening Dun, then the Gray Fox, then the American March Brown, and finally the Light Cahill. Remember, although we're discussing these as afternoon hatches, most tend to appear in heaviest numbers in the evening and could be examined under that heading. Most, however, initially appear in the afternoon (and morning for the Gray Fox and American Brown), and as warm weather arrives and June approaches, most species appear in larger numbers in the evening.

On May 8 several years ago, I visited the Barn Pool on the Little Juniata River to look for a hatch of Green Caddis. Caddis flies were already in the air and on the water then I arrived. By 4:00 P.M. a few Pale Evening Duns (*Ephemerella rotunda*) rested on the surface with the Green Caddis. I thought this was only a premature emergence and didn't expect the hatch to last very long. But by 5:00 P.M. the hatch became heavier; hundreds of duns rode the surface. Trout now

---

[1]*Sulphur* and *Pale Evening Dun* are used interchangeably in this story and throughout the book. More recent fly-fishing literature calls *Ephemerella rotunda* and *E. invaria* Sulphurs.

Figure 34. A *Heptagenia* species well represented by the Pale Evening Dun. This species most often appears near dusk.

Figure 35. A good cream dun imitation is the Light Cahill shown here.

Figure 36. The Pale Evening Dun is another effective cream dun imitation.

switched their surface feeding from the Green Caddis to the more plentiful Pale Evening Dun. Thirty feet from me, at the head of the pool, a huge trout devoured every dun in his path. From its characteristic "slurp" I knew it was a lunker. On the third cast, I successfully covered the rise; the monster took the fly, and I set the hook. The brown immediately leaped out of the water, displayed its golden brown belly, and broke free. This was the biggest trout I had ever seen take a dry fly, especially this early (5:00 P.M.) in the day. I conservatively estimated the trout I had just lost to be about 26 inches long.

I rested for a while after the episode (and I still trembled fifteen minutes later). While resting on the bank and trying to regain my composure, I surveyed the pool once again, hoping that monster would feed again on some of the hundreds of duns still floating downstream. He did not; and he was now more difficult for the next angler to catch. But there were several smaller trout working. I waded back into the pool again but not with the same enthusiasm I had earlier. Losing that large trout still haunted me.

A week later I visited the same stretch of the Little Juniata with Jim Heltzel. I had described to him the previous week's hatch and the huge trout I had lost, and he was anxious to meet and fish while a hatch progressed.

For the middle of May, the day was chilling, with a wind blowing out of the north at about 15 to 20 miles per hour. The temperature hovered around 45 degrees all afternoon. A few duns already greeted us as we arrived at the Long Pool at 3:00 P.M.

MEETING AND FISHING THE HATCHES

Figure 37. The American March Brown, a cream dun imitation.

Figure 38. The Gray Fox, which imitates a cream dun. Although the Gray Fox pictured here is tied with badger hackle, I recommend cream variant.

No trout rose to the few Sulphur duns on the Long Pool, so I moved downstream several hundred yards to see if there was any surface feeding in the pools below. Hundreds of dazed subimagos now floated on these pools, but still few trout showed. On my return trip to the Long Pool, Jim Heltzel motioned for me to hurry to the middle section. When I arrived, I knew why he wanted me: ten or more trout now methodically took these pale duns, seemingly too cold to take flight. Four fish rose 15 feet from where we stood. I entered the water, false cast the Pale Evening Dun several times, and landed the artificial 2 feet in front of the closest trout. A heavy rainbow hit and broke loose after a couple of leaps. Another cast above a rising trout and another rise to the artificial. More

casts, more trout—in all, six large trout struck the imitation within ten minutes.

The Pale Evening Dun appeared on the Little Juniata River that year until the middle of June. As the season progressed, the duns emerged later and later, until early June when the species appeared at dusk.

Pale Evening Duns or Sulphurs aren't limited to the Pennsylvania. The North Branch of the Au Sable at Lovells, Michigan, has a tremendous Sulphur hatch in late May. You'll also find a good hatch on the Battenkill near Arlington, Vermont.

A few days after the Pale Evening Dun first appears, the Gray Fox (*Stenonema fuscum fuscum*) emerges. Although the Gray Fox is likely to appear morning, afternoon, or evening, hatches most often occur

Figure 39. Afternoon on the Au Sable in Michigan.

between 4:00 and 8:00 P.M. Earlier I suggested that the Gray Fox might not emerge in the numbers that the Pale Evening Dun does. However, on one stream (and I'm sure there are others), the Gray Fox emerges in large numbers. When it appears in the quantity it does on Bald Eagle in central Pennsylvania, it can be the most impressive hatch of the season.

Stenonema fuscum first arrives about May 15 (earlier or later depending on location and weather conditions), but the most profuse hatches occur from May 20 to June 5. On some streams, especially headwaters, the species continues in limited numbers into July.

Several years before, someone had reported to me that a brown and cream mayfly emerged in mid- and late May on the Bald Eagle. On May 20 I arrived at the stream, curious to see if the species would

appear and which species it was. I arrived at the stream at 3:00 P.M. and decided to take an exploratory trip. I followed a well-traveled path upstream a couple hundred yards to a clearing. Flycatchers perched at vantage points on many of the elms and willows near the stream. Barn swallows too made their characteristic low, swerving flight just above the middle of the stream. Occasionally a flycatcher took off, headed for the stream, hovered, and then returned to its perch. Several times two flycatchers from opposite sides of the stream met in the center and fought over an insect. I observed the surface carefully now and saw that the birds were feeding on *Stenonema fuscum* subimagos. I stared at the same stretch and noted possibly thirty duns emerge in a twenty-minute period but saw only one make it to the safety of a nearby tree. I wondered how mayflies have any chance to multiply when they are taken freely as nymphs by fish, captured on the surface by trout and birds, and taken in flight by many winged predators.

Some of the duns floated 10 to 20 feet on the surface before their fateful escape. Not once did I observe a trout rise for these lethargic mayflies. Since there was no action, I returned to my car for photographic equipment and sat by a pool at the bridge, capturing duns and taking pictures of them.

An old fisherman wandered by about 5:30 P.M. and watched carefully as I took photos of the mayflies. He complained at the apparent lack of trout in the stream. I shook my head in agreement as I looked through my single-lens reflex and snapped one final shot. I had to agree with the old man since I had been on the stream more than two hours, experienced a fairly sizable hatch, and observed not one feeding trout.

The old man left in a few minutes, certain that the fishing would not improve later. I decided to stay until dusk. About 8:15 or 8:30 P.M. every Gray Fox dun in that section of the stream must have decided to emerge. Hundreds and hundreds of brown and cream subimagos appeared in the air, and still more rested on the water after breaking free from their nymphal cases. These duns appeared only minutes after the last flycatcher and barn swallow left the area for the day. The mayflies seemed to realize they were now free from attack from above. In a short, fast stretch at the head of the pool, fifteen trout now actively gulped resting duns. This action occurred in an area that, for the past several hours had seemed to contain no trout at all. Earlier I had tied a Gray Fox onto the leader in case any hatch appeared but not really expecting anything like this. Almost every cast produced a rise to the artificial. Trout after trout hooked and then released. The hatch continued through the half-light and on into darkness; the trout continued feeding in unison with the hatch. Finally I quit because I no longer had any idea whether trout were rising to the imitation or the natural.

Here, in a pool that I had sworn earlier had no trout, in a stream that was heavily fished, I met and fished a spectacular Gray Fox hatch. While all this action occurred, not one other fly-fisherman was in sight, enjoying the rewards of meeting and fishing the hatch.

Hatches of this species are impressive on the Delaware River near Hancock, New York. Bob Sentiwany and I have been in the middle of spectacular hatches of Gray Foxes on the Delaware River in early June, where huge native rainbows rose freely to the duns.

The Gray Fox is one of the most common *Stenonema* species on many Wisconsin streams and rivers. Sporadic hatches occur in the afternoon on the Namekagon just above Hayward.

A day or two after the dun emerges, it changes into a completely different-looking imago, the Ginger Quill. The spinner fall also provides memorable flyfishing. Females fall spent to the surface around 8:30 P.M.

For years I had not experienced a sizable, fishable hatch of American March Brown (*Stenonema vicarium*) duns or spinners. After all of these observations, I was convinced this species was truly a sporadic emerger and not important to meet and fish.

Then one June 1 I traveled to the diminutive but fertile Big Fill Run in central Pennsylvania. On this 10-foot-wide mountain stream, I saw hundreds of American March Brown duns appear. Sure, they emerged sporadically, but duns were continuously on the water from noon until after 4:00 P.M. They rode the surface for great distances before struggling free of the surface film. Hundreds of March Browns rested on rocks by the stream, presumably too tired to reach safety in nearby trees.

More important than experiencing a sizable hatch, I observed trout rising to the duns all afternoon. Upstream and downstream in fast water, pockets, and pools, trout fed eagerly on the large duns. All afternoon I fished over trout rising to the naturals, and all afternoon I caught trout. Don't let anybody tell you that sporadic hatches can't be important.

A year later I encountered a good hatch of March Browns on the Beaverkill. It was June 8, and several of us had traveled to this hallowed stream to meet and fish while the Green Drake appeared. We arrived at Mountain Pool at 6:00 P.M. and were greeted by an early-evening hatch of March Browns. It was a sparse hatch, but several trout rose to take the duns. Since we still had an hour and a half before any Green Drakes might appear, I tied on an imitation of the March Brown. I selected what I thought was the largest trout rising to the naturals and waded toward the center of the stream. Several casts, and the trout took the artificial. I landed the 16-inch brown in a few minutes. Three more heavy trout took the artificial that night before the Green Drake appeared.

The imago, the Great Red Spinner, might be important on evenings in late May and early June. I say "might be" because although I have seen heavy flights, I have rarely seen the spent spinners on the water. The spinner appears over fast water around 8:00 P.M.

The final cream dun performer is the Light Cahill (*Stenacron interpunctatum canadense*). This large-stream species appears before May has ended and continues well into July. Many Michigan and Wisconsin rivers hold respectable hatches of it. As with other cream duns, the Cahill appears sporadically in the afternoon in late May, when it often emerges with the Pale Evening Dun (*Ephemerella rotunda*). In late June and until the species has ended its annual appearance in mid-July, the Light Cahill emerges at dusk in an explosive hatch. During the latter half of this species' emergence, the Cahill often coemerges at dusk with the Yellow Drake (*Ephemera varia*). Trout during this latter period often indiscriminately take either species. Therefore, it's imperative to use imitations that correctly copy the yellowish cream body of both species (this color copies only the male *Stenacron interpunctatum canadense*).

Figure 40. Hatches of the cream dun *Ephemerella invaria* (Pale Evening Dun) are common on many Eastern and Midwestern streams.

Figure 41. The *Ephemerella rotunda* (Pale Evening Dun) is a cream dun of the East and Midwest.

I place *Stenacron interpunctatum canadense* as one of the best hatches of the season for several reasons. First, it has an extremely lengthy appearance. I have encountered fishable hatches as early as May 25 and as late as July 15. Furthermore, when the Cahill appears, it often does in numbers large enough to produce rising trout. Finally, because the species often appears sporadically, duns on any given day might emerge for four to five hours, providing plenty of time for rising trout to gorge themselves.

Spring Creek in central Pennsylvania was rated in 1954 as one of the top one hundred trout streams in the nation. Shortly after this rating, the stream experienced some bad times. First, excessive organic material was pumped into an upper branch as a result of an overload on a municipal sewage system. This material lowered the oxygen content of the stream and killed much of the aquatic life. Additionally, in the last twenty years, the stream has suffered from chemical spills, gasoline spills, and other catastrophes, all with a detrimental effect on the benthos of the stream. Huge hatches of Green Drakes were common prior to 1957; now there are none. Only recently has the stream made a gallant attempt to return to its original fertile condition. Along with this recent revitalization, some mayfly species have reappeared. Heavy hatches of *Ephemerella rotunda, S. interpunctatum canadense*, and some *Baetis* species have returned.

I recently heard a Bellefonte angler say that mayfly hatches had returned to the lower end of Spring Creek. In late May and early June, the stream had a large hatch of large pale yellow mayflies. I traveled to a section below Fisherman's Paradise on a chilly late May evening. By the time I arrived, several yellow duns were already emerging. I captured a dun still riding the surface and assumed from its coloration, size, and two tails that it might be the Light Cahill (*Stenacron interpunctatum canadense*).

I rested on a bank by a large pool, waiting for trout to surface to the sparse hatch. A trout at the lower end of the pool casually took the cream duns, but to reach that fish I might disturb the entire pool. More duns appeared on the fast stretch at the head of the pool, and trout surfaced for them. I noticed one large swirl to the duns and cast above what I thought was a large trout. The trout seized the imitation immediately and swam downstream toward the center of the pool. As I guided the heavy brown toward my net, I heard two boys, who had been watching this whole episode from behind, say, "Boy, is that a big trout!"

"Would I like to catch a trout like that!" one of them said.

"Do you really want the fish?" I asked.

"Yeah," the smaller boy said as his mouth opened wide.

I waded to the shore and handed the 18-inch brown to the older boy with outstretched arms. He quickly grabbed the fish and ran up a steep hill through shoulder-high briars to his parents' house, screaming words of excitement. I dislike keeping trout, and I detest even more keeping trout for friends—but here were two youngsters who might take more interest in fishing if they experienced success. Besides, their parents owned the farmland through which this stream flowed, and one should be courteous to the landowner.

This *Stenacron* imago produces heavy, concentrated spinner falls in June and July. Mating activity usually occurs after 8:00 P.M. On many evenings I've seen thousands of spinners available to trout.

Female duns have a decided orange cast to their creamish yellow bodies. I've tied artificials with this orange cast to the body, and they have proved extremely effective.

There are four other cream duns that can be important to meet and fish. All again are placed under the heading of Pale Evening Duns or Sulphurs for the fisherman, since they too have pale yellow or orangish yellow bodies. *Ephemerella dorothea* and *Ephemerella invaria* I discussed briefly. To these two I can add *Heptagenia aphrodite*, *Heptagenia hebe*, and *Ephemerella septentrionalis*. *H. hebe* is especially abundant on Wisconsin rivers.

To the Light Cahill list I can add *Stenacron interpunctatum interpunctatum, S. interpunctatum heterotarsale, Heptagenia marginalis, Stenonema pulchellum*, and others that appear mainly during the late season. These species too can be extremely important on those late-season days when few hatches or falls occur. I list here subspecies of *Stenacron interpunctatum*. The Light Cahill (*Stenacron canadense*) is also considered a subspecies of *S. interpunctatum* and should properly be listed as *Stenacron interpunctatum canadense*.

For the first month or so, we witness the emergence of several dark species. But when mid-May arrives in the East and Midwest, we can be assured that the cream duns are coming.

CHAPTER 8

FISHING THE EVENING HATCHES
(Eastern and Midwestern)

In the following list, (M) indicates that hatches or spinner falls also often occur in the morning and (A) that they often occur in the afternoon. Dates listed are approximate. An *M* in front of the species indicates that the species is common in the Midwest.

DUNS

M *Ephemerella rotunda* (A)—Pale Evening Dun; 3:00–8:00 P.M.; May 8

M *Stenonema fuscum* (A)—Gray Fox; 4:00–8:30 P.M.; May 15

Heptagenia aphrodite (A)—Pale Evening Dun; 8:00 P.M.; May 18

Ephemerella septentrionalis—Pale Evening Dun; 8:00 P.M.; May 18

M *Ephemerella invaria* (A)—Pale Evening Dun; 3:00–8:00 P.M.; May 20[1]

M *Stenonema vicarium* (A)—American March Brown; 10:00 A.M.–7:00 P.M.; May 20

M *Stenacron interpunctatum canadense* (A)—Light Cahill; 6:00–8:30 P.M.; May 25[1,2]

M *Litobrancha recurvata* (A)—Dark Green Drake; 1:00–8:00 P.M.; May 25[3]

M *Ephemera simulans*—Brown Drake; 8:00 P.M.; May 25

Ephemera guttulata—Green Drake; 8:00 P.M.; May 25

Stenonema modestum—Cream Cahill; evening; May 25

M *Epeorus vitreus*—Light Cahill (male), Pink Cahill (female); 8:00 P.M.; May 25[1]

M *Isonychia sadleri*—Slate Drake; evening; May 25

Stenonema ithaca—Light Cahill; evening; May 25[1]

M *Stenacron interpunctatum interpunctatum*—Light Cahill; evening; May 25

M *Siphlonurus quebecensis*—Gray Drake; evening; May 25

M *Isonychia bicolor*—Slate Drake; 7:00 P.M.; May 30[1]

M *Ephemerella dorothea*—Pale Evening Dun; 8:00 P.M.; June 1[1]

Serratella (Ephemerella) deficiens—Dark Blue Quill; 6:00 P.M., June 1

M *Hexagenia limbata*—Michigan Caddis or Great Olive-Winged Drake; dusk; June 5

Heptagenia marginalis—Light Cahill; 8:00 P.M.; June 15[1]

M *Stenacron interpunctatum heterotarsale*—Light Cahill; evening; June 15

M *Heptagenia hebe*—Pale Evening Dun; 8:00 P.M.; June 22[1]

M *Ephemera varia*—Yellow Drake; 8:00–9:15 P.M.; June 22[1]

Potamanthus distinctus—Golden Drake; 9:00 P.M.; June 28

Potamanthus rufous—Cream Drake; 9:00 P.M.; June 28

M *Isonychia harperi* (M & A)—Slate Drake; 7:00 P.M.; July 20[1]

M *Ephoron leukon*—White Mayfly; 7:00 P.M.; August 15

M *Hexagenia atrocaudata*—Big Slate Drake; 8:00 P.M.; August 18

Isonychia matilda—Slate Drake; 3:00–7:00 P.M.; September 15

SPINNERS

M *Paraleptophlebia adoptiva* (A)—Dark Brown Spinner; 4:00–7:00 P.M.; April 17

M *Ephemerella subvaria* (A)—Red Quill; 3:00–8:00 P.M.; April 28

M *Leptophlebia cupida* (A)—Early Brown Spinner; 1:00–6:00 P.M.; April 28

M *Ephemerella rotunda* (A)—Pale Evening Spinner; 6:00–8:00 P.M.; May 10

M *Stenonema fuscum*—Ginger Quill Spinner; 7:00–9:00 P.M.; May 18[1]

---

[1]Hatches usually appear for many days.
[2]Formerly *Stenonema*.
[3]Most appropriate imitation.

Heptagenia aphrodite—Pale Evening Dun;[3] 8:00 P.M.; May 20

Ephemerella septentrionalis—Pale Evening Dun;[3] 8:00 P.M.; May 20

M *Ephemerella invaria*—Pale Evening Spinner; 7:00–8:30 P.M.; May 22[1]

M *Stenonema vicarium*—Great Red Spinner; 8:00 P.M.; May 22

Stenonema modestum—Cream Cahill Spinner; evening; May 25

M *Stenacron interpunctatum canadense*—Light Cahill;[3] 7:00–9:00 P.M.; May 27[2]

M *Litobrancha recurvata*—Brown Drake; 7:00–9:00 P.M.; May 27

M *Ephemera simulans*—Brown Drake; 8:00 P.M.; May 27

Ephemera guttulata—Coffin Fly; 8:00 P.M.; May 27

M *Epeorus vitreus*—Salmon Spinner; evening; May 26[1]

M *Isonychia sadleri*—White-Gloved Howdy; evening; May 26[1]

Stenonema ithaca—Light Cahill; evening; May 26

M *Stenacron interpunctatum interpunctatum*—Light Cahill; evening; May 26

Drunella (Ephemerella) cornuta—Dark Olive Spinner; 7:00–9:00 P.M.; May 27

M *Isonychia bicolor*—White-Gloved Howdy; 8:00 P.M.; May 31[1]

Leptophlebia johnsoni—Blue Quill Spinner; 6:00–8:00 P.M.; June 11

M *Siphlonurus alternatus*—Gray Drake; evening; June 15

Heptagenia marginalis—Olive Cahill Spinner; 8:00 P.M.; June 16[1]

M *Stenacron interpunctatum heterotarsale*—Light Cahill; evening; May 26

M *Dannella (Ephemerella) simplex*—Dark Olive Spinner; evening; June 16

M *Stenonema pulchellum*—Cream Cahill Spinner; 8:00 P.M.; June 16

M *Drunella (Ephemerella) lata*—Dark Olive Spinner: 8:00 P.M.; June 20

M *Heptagenia hebe*—Pale Evening Dun;[3] 8:00 P.M.; June 23[1]

M *Ephemera varia*—Yellow Drake; 8:00 P.M.; June 23[1]

Potamanthus distinctus—Golden Spinner; 9:00 P.M.; June 28

Potamanthus rufous—Cream Spinner; 9:00 P.M.; June 28

Drunella (Ephemerella) cornuta—Dark Olive Spinner; 7:00–9:00 P.M.; July 3[1]

M *Isonychia harperi*—White-Gloved Howdy; 8:00 P.M.; July 21[1]

M *Ephoron leukon*—White Mayfly; 7:00–8:00 P.M.; August 15

M *Hexagenia atrocaudata*—Dark Rusty Spinner; 6:00–7:00 P.M.; August 19

Isonychia matilda—White-Gloved Howdy; 3:00–7:00 P.M.; September

CADDIS FLIES

M *Chimarrha atterima* (A)—Little Black Caddis; 11:00 A.M.–6:00 P.M.; April 26

M *Brachycentrus fuliginosus* (A)—Grannom; 3:00–7:00 P.M.; May 10

Rhyacophila lobifera (A)—Green Caddis; 3:00–9:00 P.M.; May 10[1]

Symphitopsyche slossanae (A)—Spotted Sedge; 1:00–6:00 P.M.; May 23

Psilotreta frontalis—Dark Blue Sedge; 8:00 P.M.; June 8[1]

Evening...that time of huge drake hatches and resultant, ranging trout. Evening is that period of daylight, sunset, half-light, and darkness—vying for recognition and only the last one prevailing. Evening fly-fishing can be more rewarding or more frustrating than any other part of the day. It can be more rewarding because this is the time to match the Green Drake, Light Cahill, Yellow Drake, and many other productive hatches. It can be satisfying too during one of the hundreds of spinner falls that seem to occur almost every summer night over fertile fast-water stretches. It can be more fruitful also because this is typically the time of day that the lunker trout lose their timidity and range freely in their search for food.

But fly-fishing in the evening can be profoundly frustrating. The fly-fisherman has to fight darkness, praying for a few more minutes of enough light to view his imitation float flawlessly over a methodically feeding trout. Evening fishing is especially trying when the angler hurriedly attempts to test one more pattern over one more feeding trout. In the process he has extreme difficulty holding the rod, dry fly, and line overhead toward the last hint of daylight and trying to place the leader through the eye of the hook.

Evening fly-fishing is not consistently productive during all months of the season. Few duns emerge and spinners fall until after mid-May. Most mayflies in April and early May appear during the warmest part of the day—from noon until 4:00 P.M. But midway through May a noticeable shift occurs; duns and spinners now appear more often in the evening hours.

Late May, June, July, and August harbor the bulk of the evening hatches and attendant spinner falls. The emergence of the Gray Fox and the subsequent Ginger Quill Spinner herald the advent of premier evening fly-fishing. This select angling begins around May 18 (a few days earlier or a few days later) and continues through June with the emergence of Brown Drakes (*Ephemera simulans*), Green Drakes (*E. guttulata*), Great Olive-Winged Drakes (*Hexagenia limbata*), and Yellow Drakes (*E. varia*). This outstanding time to meet and fish while the hatches appear wanes in August after the appearance of the White Mayfly (*Ephoron leukon*), the Big Slate Drake (*Hexagenia atrocaudata*), and some late Light Cahills (*Stenonema* species).

Although evening fishing can be productive throughout the summer, the greater part of the hatches appear near the beginning of June. Within a couple of weeks we see the likes of the Green Drake, Gray Fox, Slate Drake, Light Cahill, Brown Drake, Great Olive-Winged Drake, and others.

Caddis flies during this early part of June can produce exciting action on selected streams during the evening. Species like those imitated by the Green Caddis and the Dark Blue Sedge engender prolific hatches during early June.

In June, with many mayflies and caddis flies emerging concurrently, it's important to determine what food item (insect) trout are selecting. On these multihatch nights, it's imperative to "fish the hatches and not the hatch." Make certain you have imitations of all species that might emerge. Predicting which hatch will be the major one can be difficult, and forecasting which species trout will prefer can be downright frustrating.

Spinners too are productive at dusk. Imagos associated with the duns, plus many others where the subimago appears sporadically during the day, can create productive spinner falls. Spinners of many species meet, mate, lay eggs, and fall spent on the water just at dusk.

If you're not certain which spinner will fall spent onto the water on a given night, try this strategy. Most females mating at dusk do so over fast water, perhaps to ensure that the fertilized eggs, when deposited on a fast stretch, will be well distributed. Just before dark, if emerging duns are absent, move upstream to a moderate or fast stretch where mating imagos

Figure 42. The Light Cahill is an excellent pattern for all areas. (Photo by Jeff L. Katherman)

are likely to be present. Try to identify what species is present in the largest formation (try to catch a female spinner), and match it with an imitation you have with you. It's of value to know what method of egg laying the spinner uses, for if the species never touches the surface in its ritual, the fall might be unimportant. Furthermore, if the female drops the eggs from a foot or two above the surface or if she dies away from the water after egg laying, the fall will be unproductive. Return downstream to the head of the pool and wait for the spent spinners to appear on the water.

This advice has made fishing spinner falls more meaningful and much less frustrating for me. These falls can be baffling, because by the time you decide on the proper imitation, the fall and the feeding have subsided. Many times I have wasted fifteen or twenty minutes during an explosive fall on the Beaverkill trying unsuccessfully to match the actual spinner with the correct imitation in almost complete darkness. With the method I'm suggesting, you'll be prepared well ahead of the spinner fall.

On many of our better streams like the Beaverkill, Big Fishing Creek, and Penns in central Pennsylvania, and the Willowemoc, spinner falls occur almost every evening. Many duns that appear sporadically throughout the day produce fantastic, concentrated falls. Often

Figure 43. The common Light Cahill of the East and Midwest, *Stenacron interpunctatum canadense.*

Figure 44. A *Drunella lata* spinner. This species often produces a heavy spinner fall in late June or July in the East and Midwest.

the imagos appear on the water in great quantities for a very short period in the evening. Several species of the genus *Drunella*, commonly imitated by the Blue-Winged Olive Dun, emerge in a less than explosive manner as a subimago. Their emergence is usually diffused throughout the day, with a possible peak around 11:00 A.M. Most imagos of these species appear over the water in the evening to mate and fall in huge numbers at a time when lunker trout are more readily likely to feed.

In this chapter, we'll look at three of the evening hatches and their spinner falls: the Green Drake, Yellow Drake, and Slate Drake. All three are important, but other species listed at the beginning of this chapter can also be productive.

FISHING THE GREEN DRAKE HATCH ON PENNS CREEK

Were the reports we had heard true? Did the annual appearance of the Green Drake really excite the big trout on Penns Creek as much as we had been told? Or was it another exaggerated tale of an overzealous fisherman? It had been ten years since I had last seen the hatch. Was it as prolific as ever? We would soon find out!

Three of us arrived at Penns Creek at 6:00 A.M. Why so early, when the Green Drake usually doesn't appear until the evening? First, we didn't want to take any chance of missing the hatch, and second, we wanted to put in a full day on this productive limestone

Figure 45. Two popular imitations of the Green Drake hatch.

stream. During the first five or six hours, we caught and released thirty trout, though few of them, were large. We caught most of these trout on Light Cahill dry flies fished wet with a fast retrieve.

We fished only half-heartedly that morning in anticipation of the Drake hatch later in the day. Shortly after noon we moved downstream, several miles below the village of Coburn. This area is apparently ideal for the *Ephemera guttulata* nymph, since the stream contains large stretches of slow to moderate water and a bottom of mud and silt.

At 3:00 P.M. we arrived at an old railroad tunnel. During the next four hours, we experienced little success and were about ready to call it a day. Only one thing kept us at the stream: the largest hatch of duns usually occurs after 8:00 P.M. We did see a few duns emerging during the day but only sporadically.

It was now 7:00 P.M., and fishermen started arriving in droves. They hurriedly assembled their gear and took their positions on the stream. It was reminiscent of the scene on opening day of trout season. Dick Mills, Tom Taylor, and I kept on fishing, while twenty to thirty other fishermen in our immediate area just sat there and watched. When I asked one of the natives why he wasn't fishing, I received the same reply I had several years ago when I first saw this unforgettable hatch: "You gotta wait until the fish start working."

It was now 7:45 P.M. No trout were rising, and all fishermen were still waiting. One of the natives across the stream collected naturals (duns) from some of the low-lying trees and placed them in a paper bag. He'd use these duns later when the hatch began. I couldn't wait for the hatch to begin and continued to fish. Since we had had so much success during the day using a Light Cahill dry fly fished wet, I decided to tie on an extended-bodies Green Drake and fish it wet also. After several casts and quick retrieves I noted a huge swirl. The line tightened, and I knew I had on a heavy trout. The fish stayed deep and started swimming downstream away from the fast water toward a large, deep pool. Twenty hectic minutes later and 100 yards downstream, I netted one of the finest orange-bellied brown trout I had ever caught.

Now it grew darker. The sun moved behind some tall oak trees to the west of the stream, and the lengthening shadows brought a slight chill to the air. Large white mayfly spinners met over the water and formed a cloudlike cover. These white spinners were dull-colored Green Drake duns a couple of days before but had cast away their subimago skins in preparation for their final and most important act of the life cycle: mating.

Up to this point, only a few dark green duns rested on the chalky water before they took flight. However, the deepening shadows of evening seemed to remind

Figure 46. The Coffin Fly spinner.

the large tannish gray nymphs that it was time for them to emerge. . .and the famous Green Drake hatch at Penns Creek began. Upstream and downstream fishermen started casting, while they bellowed in nervous anticipation, "They're working, they're working," as hundreds of duns appeared on the water. As I looked upstream at a stretch of about 100 yards, I saw at least twenty large trout now methodically and brazenly feeding on the newly emerged duns. Nearer to me, five large fish, oblivious to all the fishermen near them, devoured dun after dun. On my first cast, I hooked a heavy fish. It went to the bottom, shook several times, and left me with the artificial hanging in a nearby bush. Quickly I retrieved the fly and cast just above a second rising trout. It immediately struck, and in a few minutes I netted a 14-inch rainbow. Now almost complete darkness had come to the stream. To the west a faint glow lingered in the sky, and as I looked upstream toward that glow, I saw ten to twenty duns float past me. I quickly cast for a third trout which I heard gulping in subimagos directly in front of me and only a few feet out from the bank. The fish struck the imitation, turned upstream, plunged deep toward the center of the pool, and broke my 4-pound leader.

The hatch continued until well after dark, and when we decided to quit at 10:00 P.M., fishermen still fished, duns still emerged, and trout still rose. We hated to leave the stream, but our casting arms were numb from the almost steady sixteen-hour ordeal.

The emergence of the dun at any given spot on the stream lasts for a few evenings and constantly moves upstream nightly. You can stretch your meeting and fishing of this particular hatch by being on the stream for the spinner falls. The falls occur simultaneously with the dun emergence in the evening and last a couple of days after the dun has dissipated. Although the dun lasts only a few days in the same area, on any given evening it is capable of emerging for three or four hours.

The Beaverkill in New York's Catskills has a memorable *Ephemera guttulata* hatch. On this fertile stream, the Green Drake appears several days later than on Penns Creek. Although the mayfly numbers are not as heavy as on Penns Creek, the trout seem to be more numerous and the fishermen more successful.

If you enjoy catching lunker trout or get a thrill hearing them splash, don't miss the unforgettable experience of the Green Drake hatch.

Figure 47. The Slate Drake imitation effectively copies many of the *Isonychia* species.

THE SLATE DRAKE: A FLY FOR ALL SUMMER

The American March Brown emerges about the third week in May and is present on most fast waters for the next couple of weeks. The Gray Fox appears about the same time, and duns of this species continue to emerge well into June. Imitations of either of these mayflies are especially effective during emergence time. Most mayfly species, as we have seen throughout this book, follow this pattern: annually emerging for a few weeks out of the year.

However, there are several mayflies, all imitated by the Slate Drake, that begin appearing in late May and continue to appear until late September. *Isonychia bicolor* is the first of the trio to emerge, usually in late May, followed closely by *I. sadleri*. Finally, in

mid-July and until September, *I. harperi* and *I. matilda* appear. These homogeneous species, all effectively imitated by the Slate Drake, appear for four months of the fishing season. If artificials imitating the American March Brown and Gray Fox are effective in late May and June, an artificial imitating the three *Isonychia* species (as the Slate Drake imitation does) should be "a fly for all summer."

But wait: decent Slate Drake hatches appear on Eastern waters into late September and early October, often in the afternoon. Recent studies indicate that some species of this genus might produce more than one brood a year.

Present imitations of the *Isonychia* species are few, and those existing don't do an adequate job. The pattern most fly fishermen use when a hatch of bicolors appears is the Leadwing Coachman or the Dun Variant. Let's look at the Coachman versus the natural:

Leadwing Coachman
   Tail — None
   Body — Peacock
   Wings — Gray quill
   Hackle — Brown

Isonychia species
   Tail — Medium gray
   Body — Dark slate gray
   Wings — Dark slate gray
   Legs — Front, dark brown
           Rear, cream

Schwiebert, in his classic *Matching the Hatch*, has suggested that the Leadwing Coachman does not duplicate closely enough the hatch when it appears. Perplexed by the need for a closer imitation but frustrated by the lack of a more realistic pattern, I designed an artificial and dubbed it the Slate Drake after the

Figure 48. A male *Isonychia* dun.

nomenclature from Donald DuBois' comprehensive book, *The Fisherman's Handbook of Trout Flies*. I attempted to make the artificial as lifelike as possible by using medium gray hackle fibers for the tail, stripped peacock quill for the body, dark gray mallard quill for the wings, and one cream hackle in the rear and one dark brown hackle in front for the legs.

How effective is the Slate Drake as an artificial? I tied about a dozen of the new imitations and put them in my "frustration box"—a box containing a hundred or so seldom-used patterns. Early in July that year, several of us traveled to the Loyalsock Creek in north-central Pennsylvania. We hit the "Sock" on one of those evenings when no artificial, large or small, seemed to work.

Evening had arrived, and the pool I waded into was now in complete shadow. The pool was a deep one about a quarter-mile long with plenty of fast water at its head. Large dark gray mayflies began emerging profusely along the edges. I captured an emerging dun and recognized it as a Slate Drake. Now I had my chance to go to my frustration box and select a realistic pattern to fish the hatch. On the second cast, a large rainbow sucked in the dry fly almost imperceptibly in the fastest water in the pool. When I netted the 15-inch trout, I was smiling, elated with the initial feeling of success a new pattern always produces. Meanwhile, Dick Mills had a large hook-jawed rainbow rise to the same artificial 2 feet away from him, but when he lifted his rod to cast again, he lost the

large fish. That evening we caught three additional trout—none larger than a foot—but this was the beginning of success with the pattern.

In early August of that same year, I fished the fabled Willowemoc in New York. It was the middle of the afternoon, and I had fished for two hours without even one strike. Finally I tied on a fast-water version of the Slate Drake, which contained pale gray calf for the tail and dark grayish brown calf for the wings. In less than an hour I had five nice brown trout—all caught on the Slate Drake and all this action in the middle of an extremely hot afternoon in August when most trout are supposedly inactive.

The imitation is productive in September too. On White Deer Creek, a small but productive trout stream in central Pennsylvania, I saw hundreds of "bicolor" duns appear one early September afternoon. Shortly after noon, I entered the stream and began casting the Slate Drake. I casually made one or two casts in a small pool and was ready to move upstream when I saw a flash beneath the artificial. A few casts later to the same area—a strike, and I netted a 15-inch brown trout. Twenty feet upstream, I saw another trout working, and on the first cast it hit—but I promptly lost it. For most of the rest of the day, I had similar success—hole after hole, riffle after riffle, pocket after pocket—with the Slate Drake.

In my position at Penn State University, I travel quite a bit, registering adults in continuing-education classes. Recently, in September, I had an hour before a scheduled registration in Tunkhannock in northeastern Pennsylvania. On my way to the registration, I stopped off at Bowman Creek, an excellent but heavily fished stream. I had only a short time to fish, so I left my car with rod, net, and a box of Slate Drake imitations. I had no time to change clothes but arrived at the stream with a bright orange shirt, tie, and new shoes. As I approached the stream, I realized how I was dressed and how I must have appeared to any passer-by. On about the tenth cast, I hooked a rainbow about 13 inches long, released it, and proceeded to the next pool—one with a large hole under a root. After five fruitless casts I was ready to quit, but like most other fly-fishermen, I had to make one more cast. The fly landed an inch from the root and immediately disappeared. When it disappeared, I heard a noise that sounded as if somebody had thrown a large log in the creek. Nervously I set the hook and played what I now realized was a large fish. After fifteen minutes and two wet shoes, I landed the 18-inch brown trout, which too had succumbed to the Slate Drake.

Since the method of emergence of the *Isonychia* species is unusual, a brief look at the life cycle is important. The nymph is almost always found in fast water. When it's ready to emerge, it swims to shore or a partially exposed rock, crawls completely out of the water, sheds its nymphal skin, and flies to a nearby tree to rest. The method of emergence portrays one distinct disadvantage to imitating this mayfly: the emerging dun is usually not readily available to trout. After a day or two resting on a bush or tree, the dun sheds its skin and becomes the White-Gloved Howdy spinner.

Few duns are normally on the water; however, on windy evenings or during periods of high water, many nymphs apparently don't swim to shore but emerge in the stream.

The spinner too can be important throughout the summer, and the imitation of it is effective. I've had more success with the Slate Drake or dun pattern, although I must confess I've used that imitation more than the White-Gloved Howdy.

Several years ago when I first used the Slate Drake, I placed it in an inconspicuous compartment of my seldomly used patterns. Now it is one of the most important artificials I have.

THE YELLOW DRAKE EMERGES

We've all heard many success stories about the Green Drake and probably even the Brown Drake. But who's ever apprised you of the Yellow Drake? If you haven't had the opportunity to fish during an emergence of this impressive mayfly, you're missing a lot of late-season sport.

The Yellow Drake is an important hatch from the angler's and trout's points of view for several reasons. *Ephemera varia* appears in late June and July, well after the last Coffin Fly has deposited its eggs. A full two or three weeks after the Green Drake has ended its annual appearance, the Yellow is just beginning its emergence. The species arrives in small numbers by June 20, and within a couple days, enough duns are present to produce a fishable hatch.

The Drake is significant also because it emerges for a protracted period and because it's extremely common on many streams and rivers. The Yellow Drake is unusually common for a mayfly so neglected. I have seen hatches on large streams like the Beaverkill and the Loyalsock and on rivers like the Little Juniata but also on small mountain creeks like Six Mile Run in north-central Pennsylvania. The hatch is atypical on the last stream, since most of its stretches are swift, and nymphs of *Ephemera varia* require less rapid stretches to endure. However, there are ample beaver dams and man-made impoundments on Six Mile Run to create the slow-water habitat needed by the nymph. The best hatches on other fast-water streams also seem to occur in sluggish areas.

Finally, the dun of the species commands attention because of its often sluggish takeoff when emerging. Because of this characteristic, I gave the dun a rating of 3 on the Insect Emergence Chart in Chapter 2. This quality, coupled with moderate size, universality, and appearance at dusk, encourages large trout to capture emerging duns.

With so many advantages to fishing this hatch, you'd think many fly-fishermen would plan trips to meet the Yellow Drake. Few anglers, however, do. In all my years of fly-fishing, I have seen only a dozen or so anglers who actually fished while this hatch progressed. From these observations and because this species is common, large, and lethargic, it is probably

Figure 49. The Yellow Drake artificial.

the most overlooked hatch of the season in the Eastern and Midwestern United States. I've often wondered why the Yellow Drake and other late-season species are neglected by most anglers. Probably low water, fewer trout, marginal water temperatures, and less numerous hatches discourage many from fishing in July and August. Certainly fishing while the Green Drake emerges is impressive, and meeting and fishing the Great Olive-Winged Drake (*Hexagenia limbata*) can be awe inspiring, but we continue to disregard the Yellow Drake.

I first met this hatch on Mom's Pool on the same Fishing Creek I mentioned earlier. This pool is one of at least three artificial dams created many years ago for milling purposes. Fishing Creek, and especially Mom's Pool, has huge hatches of *Ephemera varia*. My first visit to this stream was ten years ago on a hot July evening. Since it was an extremely warm day, I decided to cool off by wading in this exceptionally cool mountain water. Mid-July water temperatures barely reach 60 degrees, even during the hottest summer days. More times than I'd like to remember, I've had to back out of the pool during the height of a hatch and rest on the bank to warm up. Several times I've worn long underwear in the middle of summer to keep warm while wading this water.

As I entered the water, I saw only an occasional dun emerge. All were taken readily by a dozen or so barn swallows flying 2 or 3 feet above the surface in a swerving flight. As I watched, these acrobatic birds captured two duns still resting on the surface.

About 8:00 P.M. three trout began working above me, so I waded upstream within casting distance of the lowest feeding fish. My first cast covered the lowest trout, about 2 feet above it. A bird—it looked like a cedar waxwing—swooped down from a nearby tree, grabbed the artificial, and flew away with it. There I was holding the fly rod in my right hand and looking at the other end of the line, now 10 to 15 feet in the air, propelled by an ambitious but disillusioned waxwing. I guess this is the ultimate in imitations: one so deceptive that it duped a keen-sighted, insect-eating bird.

By 8:30 P.M. a major hatch had commenced and a large trout fed consistently on slow-moving duns directly across from me. The lunker rose just a foot or two from a high, rocky ledge on the far shore. My first cast caught a rock on the ledge, and I lost my Yellow Drake artificial. I quickly tied on another imitation, cast above the rising fish, and covered the rise. He struck almost immediately, and I set the number 12 hook. The fight was on, and the heavy trout ran downstream rapidly, taking out precious line from my reel. I waded through the chilled water downstream with the fish until it stopped, hesitated, and then swam back upstream toward its lair under the rock ledge. I knew that if it reached the jagged rocks I'd lose it, because there it could easily fray the 5X leader. I put as much pressure on the fragile leader as I could and successfully turned the heavy trout toward me. It ultimately tired and moved to the surface near me. I scooped the net under it and triumphantly lifted an 18-inch golden brown trout out of the water. Now I really felt the chill of the water. Besides, darkness had encompassed the stream, and the imitation was hopelessly soaked, so I decided to quit.

Tom Bean of Noxen, near Bowman Creek in northeastern Pennsylvania, is one of those few fly-fishermen who consistently plans his fishing trips around the Yellow Drake emergence. He visits nightly a section of Bowman called Botnick's Pool. Here is an ideal stretch for the *Ephemera varia* nymph. Botnick's is about a quarter of a mile of very slow water formed by a 2-foot-high breast of stream-gathered rocks. Nightly, from late June until early August, Tom fishes this deep, slow water with much success.

Recently Tom returned home one night and asked me to duplicate the dry fly he had in his hand. The only problem was that the imitation he showed me no longer had wings or hackle but just a piece of yellow yarn. He had just caught several large trout on the artificial, and now the fly was mutilated beyond recognition. When Tom described the original dry fly and the hatch he had met, I surmised that the fly was the Yellow Drake and the hatch was *Ephemera varia*.

I tied a few imitations for Tom and accompanied him on his next trip to Botnick's Pool. When we climbed down the steep cliff leading to the stream, we saw a few Yellow Drakes already emerging. Several small trout seized some of the naturals, but Tom suggested we wait until some of the lunkers fed. In a few minutes, a huge fish began gulping the yellow mayflies under a hemlock about 15 feet away from Tom. He immediately cast toward the rising trout. On the second attempt, the trout rose to the artificial, seized it, and swam to the bottom of the pool. The fish stayed deep and headed downstream toward the breast. Tom waded along the shoreline, following the fighting trout. After 15 minutes, the huge brown trout lost much of its strength and now swam aimlessly near the surface. I quickly got in position with my net, lowered it into the water, and lifted up a 23-inch beauty. Night after night Tom does well with the Yellow Drake imitation.

Spinner falls for this species occur about the same time or a little earlier than the dun. Since the spinner resembles the dun, one imitation will work double duty.

Don't overlook the Yellow Drake if you want some late-season action.

Figure 50. The McKenzie River near Eugene, Oregon, is an example of a low-altitude river.

MEETING AND FISHING THE HATCHES

CHAPTER 9

FISHING THE UNHATCHES

You've arrived at your favorite stream on a good average date to fish when a common mayfly species is supposed to emerge. Although you've planned every detail thoroughly and have followed the four rules for meeting and fishing the hatches, the expected hatch doesn't appear—or the predicted hatch does emerge but in very limited numbers. What do you do now? There are several options. First, you might wait until dusk for a spinner fall. Second, you might use a dry fly imitating a species that recently emerged from the stream. Third, you might want to try an attractor pattern. Fourth, imitations of terrestrial insects like the ant, beetle, grasshopper, and cricket can be effective on these days of sparse hatches. Sure, there are other alternatives—you could use a wet fly, streamer, or nymph—but suppose you want to rely on dry flies.

A Wulff Royal Coachman used on Western streams. Note the heavy body and dense hackle.

We'll exclude option 1—waiting for a spinner fall—and examine the latter three. Using an imitation of a species that possibly emerged the past couple of days is a valid suggestion. If trout have been feeding on the Pale Evening Dun for the past couple of weeks, that pattern might be effective even though no naturals appear that night. Imitations of a species are often productive long after the hatch has ended.

The second option is using an attractor pattern. What? You say it's sacrilegious to discuss attractor patterns in a text devoted to matching hatches with exact imitations? Not when a hatch is absent. Furthermore, attractor patterns are often very effective.

Attractors do not copy specific insects. They may or may not have the proper shape and form of a mayfly, stone fly, caddis fly, or another insect (or spider, etc.), and often the artificials are bizarre. The patterns might be so outlandish that they possibly irritate trout into striking—or they might even suggest an unusually juicy morsel.

Two attractors, especially the Wulff Royal Coachman and the Patriot, can be very productive dry flies during an unhatch. These two patterns even succeed, sometimes impressively, during hatches.

Several years ago I fished while thousands of *Tricorythodes* spinners fell spent on Falling Springs. The imitation I used for the female spinner was virtually ineffective, though it was difficult to distinguish it from the natural. In a frustrated moment during the spinner fall, I tied a size 16 Wulff Royal Coachman onto the tippet and cast the dry fly above trout rising to *Tricorythodes* naturals. These naturals, of course, are appropriately duplicated by a size 24 Reverse Jenny Spinner. On many occasions, trout approached

141

the Coachman, nudged it or swirled under it, and returned to their feeding positions. Other trout followed the attractor on its drift downstream for 3 or 4 feet, and these too returned to their original feeding spots without touching the dry fly. But several trout followed the artificial for some distance and slowly gulped it in. Why would a trout take an oversized pattern like a size 16 Coachman during a fantastic *Tricorythodes* spinner fall? Sometimes the Coachman works well during a hatch or spinner fall, but it and the Patriot also are effective during the unhatches. The Patriot is a new attractor pattern. Let's study it in more detail.

THE ONLY ATTRACTOR PATTERN YOU'LL EVER NEED

"No attractor pattern works in central Oregon's Metolius River," said a number of fly-fishermen. But ask Tom Neff of Bend, Oregon, or Gary Kish of Oregon City, Oregon, about the Patriot. "Attractors don't work well on Pennsylvania streams," either, but ask Art Gusbar, Pat Docherty, Bob Foor, Bob Panuska, or John Randolph about their experiences with the Patriot. All these fly-fishing friends realize the value of this unique attractor pattern. Let me explain.

Ten years ago I developed a new attractor pattern. About that time I visited a specialty fly shop near Sunbury, Pennsylvania. Owner Jim Hepner experimented dyeing marabou various shades of blue and

Figure 52. A new attractor pattern—the Patriot.

gray. Before I left his store, Jim handed me several marabou feathers dyed with Veniard's fluorescent blue dye.

At about the same time I read an excellent article "Flies That Resemble Nothing But Really Work," in *Fly Fishing the West* (now *Flyfishing*). The article referred to a study by Larkin and Ginetz of British Columbia, "Choice of Colors of Food Items by Rainbow Trout." The scientists examined which salmon egg colors were most often selected by rainbow trout. Some general conclusions from this important experiment have merit for fly-fishermen. The study suggested that in high light intensities, blue and red were preferred by rainbows. Against a blue background (blue sky), blue again was the most preferred egg color.

After reading the article on attractors and experimenting with color preference, I tied some new floating patterns using the blue marabou Jim Hepner gave me. The pattern I settled on contained a red floss midsection with light blue ends of dubbed marabou, a tail of deer hair, white wings made of calf tail, and medium brown hackle for legs. I dubbed the new dry-fly pattern the R(Really) B(Blue) Coachman. I showed the finished product to several friends, and they laughed at the bizarre color combination.

But the important question was, Would it work? The day before I headed for some favorite Western rivers, I decided to test the RB on the Little Juniata River in central Pennsylvania. It was July, and no mayflies appeared that evening. The dry fly looked good on the water. It was easy to follow with its white wings and high profile, partly because of the stiff deer hair tail. In one short boulder-strewn moderate stretch of water, I enticed four heavy browns to the surface with the RB—beautiful streambred brown trout sucked in that ugly new pattern! But would I experience the same kind of success on Western waters? I'd soon find out.

The next day I landed at Jackson Hole, Wyoming, and traveled to Canyon Lodge in Yellowstone Park. I had tied a half-dozen RBs—size 12s—for testing on these Western rivers. The next morning I met Vince Gigliotti of DuBois, Pennsylvania, and Mike Manfredo of Mahomet, Illinois. Vince is a teacher in Pennsylvania and spends the summer months fishing the great Western streams. Both Vince and Mike were anxious casts, another brown took the attractor. Vince and Mike looked on, bewildered. Downstream, a couple of hundred feet to a long, moderate stretch of what looked to be productive water with a deep pool below, I caught eight heavy browns and lost three more on that pattern.

Vince, Mike, and I planned to meet the next day at the Railroad Ranch of Henry's Fork in eastern Idaho. We hiked downstream to the middle part of the ranch. Vince showed me a size 18 RB he had tied the evening before. Since he had no blue body material in his portable fly-tying kit, he and Mike had ripped apart a blue canvas hiking bag and used that material for the body of the attractor.

Shortly after we began casting, Vince casually waded upstream toward me.

"I hope nobody catches that 18-inch rainbow down there," Vince said.

"How do you know there's an 18 incher down there?" I asked.

"Well, I just had a trout on that large or larger, and he took my RB."

The RB has also worked well on Midwestern waters like the Manistee, Pigeon, Rifle, and Au Sable rivers in Michigan. The RB day after day outperformed ten other attractor-type patterns I tested. On pool after pool on the Pigeon and Manistee rivers, the RB took trout. Even brook trout on Michigan's fabled Au Sable succumbed to that blue pattern. Many trout had probably never seen an attractor quite that color before.

Recently I used the RB on trips to the Bighorn in south-central Montana and on several rivers on New Zealand's South Island. On both trips the RB was hands down the leading trout catcher, taking more than a dozen trout in the 4- to 6-pound category. On the Bighorn, during a lackluster week of fly-fishing, the RB saved the trip for me with several fish over four pounds.

On the Waikaia and the Oreti rivers on the South Island of New Zealand, the RB took both risers and nonrisers up to 7 pounds—heavy browns and rainbows that had been rising to size 16 Dark Red Spinners grabbed that darned attractor. On the upper Eglinton River, Mike Manfredo caught a 6½-pound rainbow on the RB that had been rising to a black stone fly.

Figure 53. Gary Kish fishes on the Metolius River in central Oregon using a Patriot.

to take me to their favorite stretch of the Lewis River in the Park. Vince said that the last couple of days, thousands of large crane flies bounced across the surface, and browns reacted strongly to the new supply of surface food. As is often my luck, the day we arrived, only a few of the crane flies appeared. However, each one that rested on the surface too long soon disappeared into the mouth of a large brown. Soon the few crane flies that had appeared were gone and the surface was quiet—a great time to test my RB.

After several casts with the RB, a heavy brown glided downstream closely behind the attractor just under the surface and sucked it in. In a couple of more

Clear water, extremely wary trout, and the RB proved an effective pattern on many of the South Island's waters. Fifteen of the twenty heaviest trout that Mike Manfredo and I caught on that latest trip to New Zealand were taken on the RB.

Within the last few years, a new type of fluorescent material, Krystal Flash, has entered the market. I replaced the blue marabou with Orvis's smolt blue Krystal Flash color for the body of the revised attractor.

When I visited the Youghiogheny River in southwestern Pennsylvania, I gave one of these new attractors to Art Gusbar and another to Pat Docherty. Immediately Art dubbed the new attractor the "Patriot." He felt the name was appropriate when he saw the bright red floss midsection, white wings, and the blue Krystal Flash body. Seconds after Art began fishing the Patriot, he hooked a heavy rainbow. Within a short time, the heavy fish broke his tippet. Pat now tied on his Patriot. On his first cast with the Patriot, Pat too hooked a heavy rainbow that broke his tippet.

I tied up several dozen of these new Patriots and gave my son, Bryan, several to test on the East Branch of the Clarion River in Pennsylvania. When no one else caught trout, Bryan caught ten heavy browns on this attractor.

I recently gave John Randolph, Bob Panuska, and Vince Gigliotti this attractor to test on the Bald Eagle near Milesburg, Pennsylvania. All had unusual success with the new pattern. Even when trout rose to a size 24 Trico, some took the Patriot.

I met Tom Neff of Bend, Oregon, and Gary Kish of Oregon City on the Metolius in central Oregon in early September. Gary, who spends his summers guiding, tying, and casting for the Camp Sherman Store, has developed an excellent emergence chart for the Metolius River.

We met at the Camp Sherman Store, talked about strategy, and headed upriver a couple of hundred yards to fish. Dozens of Golden Stoneflies returned to the Metolius surface to deposit eggs, a few late Green Drakes even appeared, and several caddis flies also were active. But there weren't enough insects to create a hatch, so I decided to try the Patriot.

By the end of the day, both Tom and Gary were using Patriots. When no heavy hatch appeared on the Metolius, the Patriot took rainbows—heavy rainbows.

If you have only one attractor pattern in your selection, make certain it's the Patriot.

I tie the attractor in sizes 12 to 18 but use a size 14 RB 90 percent of the time. On extremely selective trout, I often lean toward a size 16 or 18.

Try the Patriot, especially on those hatchless days. Whether you're on the Little Juniata River or Penns Creek in the East, or the Au Sable in the Midwest, or on the Bighorn or the Metolius in the West, the Patriot will prove to be a great selection. It could well be the only attractor you'll ever need.

Patriot Tying Description
Size 12–18
Tail: Light deer body hair
Wings: White polypropylene yarn upright and divided
Hackle: Brown
Body: Three strands of smolt blue Krystal Flash wound around the shank of the hook. Make a mid-rib with two to three turns of red floss.

OTHER POPULAR ATTRACTOR PATTERNS

The unhatch occurs more often than the hatch on many streams. Here's where an attractor pattern can be important. Look at small mountain streams. Have you seen any profuse hatches on many of these small brooks? Look also at marginal water—those located just outside large metropolitan areas. These streams are stocked heavily early in the season only because of their proximity to many anglers. Many streams are almost void of nymphal life. Few hatches occur on many of these waters, and those that do appear do so in limited numbers.

In the West too, the unhatches are often more important than the hatches. On many occasions I've seen streams void of mayflies, caddis flies, and stone flies. What patterns are effective on these trips?

The Wulff Royal Coachman has produced some exciting fly-fishing for me on Western streams. I entered the Madison River on the lower end of Yellowstone Park one hot July afternoon. No insects emerged, and of course no trout surfaced. I immediately checked the water temperature and noted a

73-degree reading. At this point I almost backed out of the water and returned to the car, but this was only the second opportunity I had had to fish this productive section of water, so I decided to stay and try the Coachman. The Coachman I used had three stiff hackles (I recommend three rather than two when fishing many of the faster Western rivers).

The stretch of water I entered contained all moderate to fast water. During the first fifteen minutes, I had no strikes and again almost decided to retrace my steps back to my car. But before I did, I wanted to cast over one more deep pocket of water upstream a few feet.

On the second cast over this deep pocket, the artificial floated directly over a submerged boulder and promptly disappeared. I set the hook on the attractor and for a few seconds didn't know whether I had hooked concealed debris or a fish. Suddenly the snag began to move downstream slowly—no rapid movement but rather a planned retreat toward the rapids below. The heavy fish stayed deep, not once showing its color. Finally I turned the trout upstream toward me and urged it to follow me to the shore with as much pressure as I felt the 4X tippet could withstand. I beached the 4-pound brown and gently unhooked the Coachman from its lower jaw.

On another occasion with the Wulff Royal Coachman, I had phenomenal success. This occurred on the Buffalo River near Island Park, Idaho. During the first few hours of morning fishing, I noted only a few *Epeorus albertae* spinners above the water; none touched the surface. Several large *Hesperoperla* (Willow Flies) stone flies fluttered to the surface to lay their eggs and were captured almost immediately by trout. I decided to stay with the Coachman and caught more than twenty trout in two hours of fishing.

Are there other attractor patterns that are productive on Western waters? We saw earlier that the Patriot works well on Western waters. The Goofus (also called the Goofus Bug and Humpy), Royal Humpy, and Renegade also take trout during the unhatches.

Recently I watched a local fisherman use the Renegade on the Buffalo River near Box Canyon. On almost every cast, he caught a rainbow—some of them 2 pounds and heavier. This pattern seems to work equally well as a wet or dry fly.

The Humpy or Goofus reminds me of a high-riding Coachman. The difference is the deer hair back on the Goofus. Body colors on these dry flies vary from red to green to yellow, and all are effective.

During the next unhatch, whether you're fishing Eastern, Midwestern, or Western streams, you can use an imitation of a dun or spinner that recently emerged. Or you can try an attractor pattern like the Goofus, Wulff Royal Coachman, or the exciting new Patriot.

CHAPTER 10

MEETING THE WESTERN HATCHES

In Chapter 1 I set out four rules to follow if you plan to meet any of the mayfly hatches: to fish while a common mayfly (or caddis fly or stone fly) emerges, at an appropriate date and time for the species, and on a good stream where this species occurs. But to meet Western hatches, other factors are important: water temperature, altitude or elevation, water discharge, and weather.

If these are the only additional rules (or variables) and if we recognize and understand them, why is meeting Western hatches risky? Mainly because the West, especially the Rocky Mountain area, is a land of contrasts. Water temperatures, stream elevations, and water flow vary considerably from river to river, and they can vary substantially from stretch to stretch on the same water. Stream flow, water temperature, and weather also affect Eastern and Midwestern hatches, but these regions often lack the extreme variability of the West. Water temperature, altitude, water flow, and weather may influence the dates and times a mayfly emerges and the stream on which it emerges.

Steve Jensen in his excellent master's thesis, "Mayflies of Idaho," suggests that some Western mayfly species often emerge within predictable temperature, elevation, and stream-flow limits. Many authors writing about Western hatches have indicated that *Epeorus longimanus* replaces *E. albertae* on higher elevations of the same stream. Others have mentioned that *Drunella coloradensis* replaces its sister species *D. flavilinea* on higher sections of the same streams.

If we take a closer look at the Blue-Winged Olive Dun, *Drunella flavilinea*, using all the variables, we'll more fully understand the ingredients necessary to meet the hatches. Jensen suggests that this species usually appears when the water temperature is between 45 and 65 degrees, on moderate stretches of water, on elevations ranging from 4,000 to 6,500 feet.

I first met this species on Henry's Fork near Island Park, Idaho. The altitude of Henry's Fork at this point is 6,150 feet, well within the prescribed range. During this initial meeting and at the beginning of the emergence, I recorded a water temperature of 59 degrees. What would have happened if I had been fishing a stream at an elevation below 4,000 feet or in water warmer than 65 degrees? I might not have met the Blue-Winged Olive Dun.

Therefore in addition to approximate time of day (usually in the evening for *Drunella flavilinea*), the time of year (late June or July), a good stream (Henry's Fork), and a common species, elevation and water temperature are also important.

But just when we've pinpointed the variables necessary to meet the Western hatches, we're confronted with another problem: diversity. Water temperatures vary tremendously from stream to stream. To illustrate, look at the Madison River. On the Madison in Yellowstone Park I recorded a temperature of 73 degrees at 4:00 P.M. one day. The next day, 20 miles below Hebgen Lake, on the same Madison River, I noted a 57-degree water temperature, again at 4:00 P.M. Why this difference? The upper Madison is influenced extensively by the geysers and thermal waters of Yellowstone Park, whereas the section below is fed continuously by melting snow and water from the bottom of Hebgen Lake.

Following is a further indication of this water temperature variability. These are water temperatures recorded on various rivers from July 7 to July 12

Figure 54. Colorado's Blue River is an example of a high-altitude stream—8,120 feet at the area pictured here.

between 4:00 and 7:00 P.M.:

Gallatin River, Specimen Creek area, July 11: 47 degrees
Bitterroot River, Florence, Montana, July 7: 54 degrees
South Fork of the Madison River, West Yellowstone area: 54 degrees
Yellowstone River, Corbin Springs area, July 9: 56 degrees
Henry's Fork, Island Park, Idaho, July 12: 60 degrees
Clark Fork, Deer Lodge, Montana, July 8: 64 degrees
Gibbon River (lower section), Yellowstone Park, July 10: 72 degrees
Madison River, Yellowstone Park, July 10: 73 degrees

This is diversity! In a matter of 25 miles in the west Yellowstone area, we have the warm upper Madison River and the cold Gallatin River. The Gallatin River had afternoon temperatures in the middle to upper 40s, whereas the Madison registered 73 degrees.

Why does the water temperature vary so greatly? Melting snow affects many Western stream temperatures much of the summer. The Bitterroot is typical; every few miles, another feeder stream pours in additional cold water from melting snow from the Bitterroot Range just a few miles away. Temperatures on this stream remain cold throughout July. Any river flowing any distance without these colder feeder streams often warms considerably; this is what happens to Clark Fork in northwestern Montana.

If mayfly species emerge at fairly specific water temperatures and Western streams are highly diverse in these temperatures, then predicting emergence dates for many Western species is impossible. Wrong! Sure, it will be more of a hit-and-miss proposition than in the East and Midwest, but many hatches can be met with some degree of accuracy—especially

Figure 55. A slow section of the Colorado River near Kremmling, Colorado. Good hatches of *Callibaetis nigritus, Tricorythodes minutus,* and *Heptagenia solitaria* occur here in early fall.

hatches on the same stream from year to year. Other hatches, like *Tricorythodes* species and *Heptagenia solitaria* (Gray Fox), which appear over much of the season, are also fairly easy to meet.

But many Western species also exhibit a preference for fairly specific elevation ranges. *Callibaetis coloradensis* is usually found on lakes of streams with slow water above 5,000 feet, whereas *C. nigritus* is found on the same type of water but below 4,500 feet.

Let's look at some typical Western streams and the elevations they attain at various locations:

Blue River, Dillon, Colorado: 8,760 feet
Colorado River, Kremmling, Colorado: 7,300 feet
Firehole River, Grand Loop Area, Yellowstone Park: 7,154 feet
Henry's Fork, Box Canyon area: 6,300 feet
Bitterroot River, Victor, Montana: 3,400 feet
Clark Fork River, Tarkio, Montana: 2,900 feet
McKenzie River, Eugene, Oregon: 300 feet

Again we have extreme diversity. If many mayfly species inhabit only waters at specific elevations, then many streams will be void of many species or contain them on only limited stretches. Over the years, I've found altitude to be the least dependable variable. If all other conditions except for elevation are appropriate for a given species, then a mayfly might be found at a higher or lower altitude than that listed in the Insect Emergence Chart in Chapter 2.

Western streams also vary considerably in their velocity and discharge. Many waters are extremely fast, especially during spring and summer runoff. By mid-July most waters finally subside and become fishable (especially for the dry-fly fisherman). Again, the West has contrast. Some of the streams in Yellowstone Park are fishable in April, May, and June. Streams also vary in velocity. Velocity seriously affects which mayfly species inhabit a stream. Flow varies from very slow, like portions of Henry's Fork in Idaho

MEETING AND FISHING THE HATCHES

and the Colorado River in Colorado, to moderate-flowing rivers, like the Bitterroot River in Montana and the Blue River in Colorado, to rapid rivers like the Arkansas in Colorado and the Gallatin River in southwestern Montana.

Another factor that affects hatching activity is weather. The West, especially the Rocky Mountains, has weather extremes. Weather too affects the predictability of meeting the hatches. Charlie Brooks of West Yellowstone had fished many times in snowstorms in June, July, and August, but this is not typical since daytime temperatures often near 90 degrees in midsummer. A sudden cold snap, a heat wave, a cold rain, a late-summer snowstorm—all affect tremendously the fly-fisherman's ability to meet the hatches.

There is another set of variables with the coastal and near-coastal rivers of Oregon, Washington, and California. Hatches on these rivers can occur in late February while rivers in Yellowstone Park still contain a heavy layer of ice.

Thus, variations in water temperature, elevation, water discharge, and weather make it difficult to meet the hatches. However, if we keep all these cautions in mind, we can often meet and fish Western hatches—not always but often. Since temperature, elevation (to a limited degree), and velocity affect the appearance of many mayfly species, I have listed them in the Insect Emergence Chart for Western species.

Because of the added variables, it's important to consult local fishermen for stream conditions, current hatches, hot spots, and so on. Following is a list of reputable sporting goods stores near Western streams.

These stores, and many others not mentioned, have competent personnel to keep you aware of needed information. Since hatches are not as predictable in the West as they are in the East and Midwest, I strongly urge you to stop in at one of these or any other to ascertain emergence activity:

Anglers All
5211 South Santa Fe Drive
Littleton, Colorado 80120

Dan Bailey—Flies and Tackle
209 West Park
Livingston, Montana 59047

Bud Lilly's Trout Shop
West Yellowstone, Montana 59758

Camp Sherman Store
Camp Sherman, Oregon

Streamside Anglers
501 S. Orange
Missoula, Montana 59801

Will's Fly Fishing Center
P.O. Box 68
Island Park, Idaho 83429

The Flyfisher Ltd.
315 Columbine St.
Denver, CO 80206

Let's look at three hatches I met recently and compare the information on these variables with those listed in the Insect Emergence Chart.

Species	Date	Time	Water Temperature[1]	Elevation[2]	Flow[3]
Drunella flavilinea	July 10	8:00 P.M.	59	6,150	M
Chart data	June 15 and later	Evening	M&C	M&H	M
Paraleptophlebia memorialis	July 18	1:00 P.M.	64	3,450	S
Chart data	July 1 and later	Morning and afternoon	M&C	A	A
Drunella grandis	July 6	11:30 A.M.	54	3,450	M
Chart data	June 5 and later	Late morning and afternoon	M&C	L&M	M

[1]Cold (C) is below 55 degrees; moderate (M) is from 55 to 65.
[2]Low (L) is below 4,000 feet; moderate (M) is from 4,000 to 7,000 feet; high (H) is above 7,000 feet; (A) means all elevations.
[3](S) means slow; (M) means moderate.

These hatches and many, many more were major hatches, and all were met because emergence dates, times, water temperatures, elevations, and water flows were appropriate for the species.

One other important ingredient I have not mentioned is the size of the stream or river. Some species are found in small streams, others in larger streams, others in rivers, others in lakes and ponds, and a few species are found in all of these.

With all these cautions in mind for meeting the hatches, we'll look at fishing the Western hatches in the next three chapters. We'll look at the Red Quill and its effectiveness as an imitation in the morning, afternoon, and evening. We'll study the Western Green Drake and the Speckle-Winged Dun through stories about morning fishing. The story about the Western March Brown should give you insight on an exciting hatch from late February to May. Then we'll examine an afternoon emerger, the Little Dark Brown Dun. Finally, we'll scrutinize evening hatches by looking at the downwings, and a story about an evening spinner fall on the Colorado, and the Brown Drake. Don't miss the discussion of the Trico hatch in Chapter 6.

CHAPTER 11

FISHING THE MORNING HATCHES (Western)

In the following list, (A) indicates that hatches or spinner falls also often occur in the afternoon and (E) that they often occur in the evening. Dates listed are very approximate (remember that Western dates are even less precise than Eastern and Midwestern). If you see (*vagans*) or (*Ephemerella*) the species or genus was changed recently. The old classification is contained in parentheses.

DUNS

Baetis tricaudatus (A & E)—Little Blue Dun; late morning, afternoon, and early evening; April to November[1]

Baetis intermedius (A & E)—Little Blue Dun; late morning, afternoon, and early evening; April to November[1]

Ephemerella inermis (A & E)—Pale Morning Dun[1]; late morning, afternoon, and early evening; May 25[1]

Cinygmula ramaleyi—Dark Red Quill; late morning; May 25

Pteronarcys californica (stone fly)—Salmon Fly; emergence often occurs in the morning, but egg laying can happen almost any time of the day or evening; May to August, depending on the stream

Acroneuria pacifica—Willow Stonefly; egg-laying phase can occur almost any time of day or evening; June and July

Callibaetis nigritus (A)—Speckle-Winged Dun; late morning; June to October[1]

Baetis bicaudatus (A & E)—Pale Olive Dun; late morning, afternoon, and early evening; June through October[1]

Paraleptophlebia heteronea (A)—Dark Blue Quill; morning and afternoon, June 1

Drunella (Ephemerella) grandis (A)—Western Green Drake; late morning and afternoon; June 5 (hatches appear in mid-June on the Upper Madison and Henry's Fork)

Serratella (Ephemerella) tibialis (A)—Red Quill; late morning and afternoon; June 5

Callibaetis coloradensis (A)—Speckle-Winged Dun; late morning and early afternoon; June 12[1]

Epeorus longimanus (A)—Quill Gordon; late morning and early afternoon; June 12

Drunella (Ephemerella) flavilinea (E)—Blue-Winged Olive Dun; midmorning and evening (evening hatch seems to be more important); June 15

Drunella (Ephemerella) doddsi (A)—Western Green Drake; late morning and afternoon; June 15

Baetis hageni (parvus) (A & E)—Dark Brown Dun; late morning, afternoon and early evening; June 20

Ephemerella infrequens (A)—Pale Morning Dun;[1] late morning and afternoon; July 1 (hatches occur until mid-August on colder streams)

Paraleptophlebia memorialis (A)—Dark Blue Quill; morning and afternoon; July 1

Rhithrogena futilis (A)—Quill Gordon; late morning and afternoon; July 1[2]

Cinygmula reticulata (A)—Pale Brown Dun; late morning and afternoon; July 5[2]

Paraleptophlebia vaciva (A)—Dark Blue Quill; morning and afternoon; July 5

Paraleptophlebia debilis (A)—Dark Blue Quill; morning and afternoon; July 5[1]

Siphlonurus occidentalis (A)—Gray Drake; late morning and afternoon; July 5 (hatches occur well into August)

Rhithrogena hageni (A)—Pale Brown Dun; late morning and afternoon; July 10

Ameletus cooki (A)—Dark Brown Dun; late morning and afternoon; July 10[2]

Rhithrogena undulata (A)—Quill Gordon;[3] morning and afternoon; July 10[2]

Tricorythodes minutus—Pale Olive Dun; morning (duns sometimes appear as late as 11:00 A.M.); July 15[1]

Paraleptophlebia packii[4] (A)—Dark Blue Quill; morning and afternoon; July 20

Drunella (Ephemerella) coloradensis (A)—Dark Olive Dun;[3] midday; August 1

Paraleptophlebia bicornuta (A)—Dark Blue Quill; morning and afternoon; September 10[2]

SPINNERS

Baetis tricaudatus (E)—Light Rusty Spinner; early morning and evening (evening seems to have the larger spinner falls on many occasions; this goes for many of the *Baetis* species); April to November[1]

Baetis intermedius (E)—Dark Rusty Spinner; early morning and evening; April to November[1]

Ephemerella inermis (E)—Pale Morning Spinner; morning and evening; May 26[1]

Cinygmula ramaleyi (A)—Red Quill Spinner; late morning and early afternoon; May 28

Baetis bicaudatus (E)—Light Rusty Spinner; morning and evening; June through October[1]

Callibaetis nigritus (A)—Speckle-Winged Spinner; late morning; June to October[1]

Paraleptophlebia heteronea (A)—Dark Brown Spinner; morning and afternoon; June 2

Callibaetis coloradensis—Speckle-Winged Spinner; late morning; June 13[1]

Drunella (Ephemerella) flavilinea (E)—Dark Olive Spinner; morning and evening; June 16

Baetis hageni (parvus) (E)—Dark Brown Spinner; morning and evening; June 21

Ephemerella infrequens (E)—Rusty Spinner;[3] morning and evening; July 2

Paraleptophlebia memorialis (A)—Dark Brown Spinner; morning and afternoon; July 2

Epeorus albertae (E)—Salmon Spinner (male is Light Cahill); morning and evening (morning spinner fall seems to be more protracted, but evening fall might be heavier); July 6

Cinygmula reticulata—Dark Rusty Spinner; early morning; July 6[2]

Heptagenia solitaria (E)—Ginger Quill Spinner; late morning and evening (evening seems to be heavier); July 6[1]

Paraleptophlebia debilis (A)—Dark Brown Spinner; morning and afternoon; July 6[1]

Siphlonurus occidentalis (E)—Brown Quill Spinner; morning and evening (evening seems to be heavier); July 6[1]

Rhithrogena hageni (E)—Dark Tan Spinner; morning and evening; July 11

Tricorythodes minutus—Reverse Jenny Spinner (female), Dark Brown Spinner (male); morning (can continue into early afternoon in September); July 15

Paraleptophlebia packii (A)—Dark Brown Spinner; morning and afternoon; July 21

Paraleptophlebia bicornuta (A)—Dark Brown Spinner; morning and afternoon; September 11[2]

---

[1]Hatches or spinner falls may occur for many days.
[2]Hatches or spinner falls may occur before date listed.
[3]Color varies and common name may be inappropriate.
[4]Not listed in Emergence Chart, but may be important.

Morning fishing in the West—the time of the Pale Morning Duns, the time of the Western Green Drake, the time of the Speckle Wings, and yes, the time of the Pale Olive Duns (*Tricorythodes*). Morning fishing, especially fly-fishing, can be rewarding if you plan to meet and fish while one of the almost endless early-day hatches occurs.

We meet some spectacular hatches in the morning, none probably more remarkable than the Western Green Drake (*Drunella grandis*). These mayflies, which are likely to appear on some streams as early as late May, begin their daily emergence as early as 10:00 A.M. These Drake duns always amaze me because they habitually emerge on moderate to fast stretches, still extremely high from spring runoff. The duns are awkward in their takeoff and consistently rest on the surface for long distances. On many occasions I've noted hundreds of subimagos on the water but none in the air. Most duns were either victims of the fast water or of rising trout. Although rivers are high during the time the duns emerge, trout eagerly take the struggling duns.

At about the same time the Green Drake appears, so does *Rhithrogena futilis*. This moderate-sized mayfly is also slow in its takeoff from the water and can be important to meet and fish. I've dubbed the dun and spinner of this species Quill Gordons because they remind me so much of the Eastern species *Epeorus pleuralis*. I've noted this dark gray dun on the water many days during late June and early July from 10:00 A.M. to 2:00 or 3:00 P.M.

The morning sector contains some other important hatches to meet and fish. In late May *Ephemerella inermis* begins its annual appearance on some Western rivers. This species is often called the Pale Morning Dun and usually initially appears daily about 10:00 A.M. On streams like Henry's Fork, the Pale Morning Dun continues appearing until 7:00 P.M. Duns are on the water for many weeks and often, especially after late June, produce fishable hatches for hours on rivers like the Bighorn and Kootenai in Montana. *Ephemerella inermis* is extremely variable in color, especially body color. I've seen tan, olive, reddish brown, and pale yellow mayflies—and all have been identified as members of this species.

Concomitant with *Ephemerella inermis* is its sister

Figure 56. The Western Green Drake with a hair wing.

Figure 57. The famous Western Green Drake, *Drunella grandis*.

species, *E. infrequens*. These subimagos too are commonly dubbed Pale Morning Duns. *E. infrequens* also varies tremendously in color. Body color of duns ranges from tan to pale yellow with an olive cast. Duns usually begin appearing around 11:00 A.M. in early July on the Bitterroot in Montana.

The list of morning emergers goes on and on. If you fish slow streams, lakes, or ponds, you're likely to encounter one of the Speckle Wings that consistently appear around 11:00 A.M. *Callibaetis* species

(Speckle Wings), many multibrooded, appear from mid-June through much of September. The Colorado, and to a lesser extent the Blue River, has respectable *Callibaetis* hatches. Henry's Lake in Idaho and many of the smaller mountain lakes in the Bob Marshall Wilderness Area just east of Kalispell, Montana, have spectacular *Callibaetis* hatches in early July.

Morning is also the time for the Dark Blue Quill to start its appearance. *Paraleptophlebia* species appear from late May until September or October, almost

Figure 58. A Western Blue Quill, *Paraleptophlebia memorialis*.

without interruption on many Western rivers. *Paraleptophlebia heteronea* is one of the earliest of the Blue Quills to appear, often emerging in early June. The genus continues to appear in July with *P. debilis* and *P. memorialis* emerging, and on into September and October when *P. debilis* and *P. bicornuta* appear. Most species of this genus emerge from mid-morning until mid-afternoon, and spinners are active at the same time.

Morning is also the time for several species to complete their life cycle by mating and laying eggs. On any morning in July, you might encounter active spinners of *Epeorus albertae* (Salmon Spinner) or *Siphlonurus occidentalis* (Brown Quill Spinner). Both species also mate in the evening, and the latter time seems to harbor the heavier falls. There are other spinners that can be seen mating in the morning. *Ephemerella infrequens* and *E. flavilinea* can produce fishable morning spinner falls. *E. infrequens* is often imitated with the Rusty Spinner (because of color variation this common name might not be appropriate) and *E. flavilinea* with the Dark Olive Spinner. Spinners of *Heptagenia solitaria* also can be observed in the morning and evening. As with the Salmon Spinner and Brown Quill Spinner, more Ginger Quills seem to fall in the evening.

Even into September, many mayfly species emerge and fall in the morning. *Tricorythodes minutus*, which first appears in mid-July, continues well into September almost every morning on many of the slower, silted

rivers in the West like the Colorado in central Colorado. Idaho's Wood River and Oregon's McKenzie also produce good Trico hatches.

Want to fish while some excellent hatches appear? Try morning fishing in the West. Almost any month of the season, you can fish while morning hatches and spinner falls occur.

SPECKLE-WINGS AND GRAYLINGS

Vince Gigliotti and Al Gretz live in Punxsutawney, Pennsylvania. That's also the home of the famous groundhog, Punxsutawney Phil. The two Western travelers met me in Kalispell, Montana, in early July recently to go on a fishing trip. Vince and Al spend a month or more in Montana, Wyoming, and Idaho each year in quest of ultimate fly-fishing.

Vince suggested that we head toward Glacier National Park and then up the South Fork of the Flathead River. The paved road ended just beyond the dam breast of the Hungry Horse Reservoir. The ranger station on the Bob Marshall Wilderness Area lay 40 miles ahead. The picturesque trip up the valley would take a couple of hours to reach the river above the dam. By the time we had traveled 50 miles on the jolting, bumpy, winding road, we took a narrow trail to the southwest and headed for a lake within a mile of the reservoir.

"Looks like grizzly country," Vince complained, as he got out of the car.

Figure 59. A Speckle-Winged Spinner, *Callibaetis nigritus.*

All Al and I saw was a blue, pristine, 20-acre lake full of rising trout. Rising trout? The three of us scanned the late-morning surface of the lake and verified that trout rose throughout the width and breadth of the dam.

We hurriedly gathered our gear, including a noise-maker Vince took with him to scare unwanted grizzlies away. As we got to the shoreline, I netted a few of the duns and spinners that caused the trout to feed on the surface. The wings of these 9 mm mayflies quickly helped me identify them as *Callibaetis nigritus*, or Speckle-Winged Spinners.

While I was still examining the mayflies, Vince and Al started casting to more than a dozen rising fish in front of them. Each hooked a couple of trout in a short time.

"I got a grayling," Al yelled.

"I got one too," said Vince.

I hurriedly tied on a size 16 imitation of the Speckle-Winged Spinner and cast toward what I thought was the largest fish rising in front of me. The dry fly landed a foot or two in front of the last rise, but it soon disappeared. I had my first grayling—a 12-inch beauty.

The action continued almost uninterrupted for more than an hour. Until noon, spinners returned to the surface and fish rose. Vince kept looking over his shoulder for a grizzly and suggested we leave the area.

Here was the first time I had fished the elusive

Speckle-Winged Spinner—on its home territory, a lake. Many of the lakes in the Bob Marshall Wilderness Area contain trout and a bountiful supply of Speckled-Winged Duns. Fly-fish the area from early June through July in mid-morning, and you should meet the hatch and spinner fall. Vince, Al, and I did with Speckle-Wings and graylings.

A DRY FLY FOR ALL DAY AND ALL SUMMER IN THE WEST

There's an imitation that effectively matches many Western mayfly species. This dry fly duplicates mayflies that emerge in May, June, July, August, and September. This same dry fly copies species that appear in the morning, afternoon, and evening. Furthermore, this artificial is productive on many of the Western rivers. It has provided success on the Bitterroot and Blackfoot in northwestern Montana, the Box Canyon Area of Henry's Fork in Idaho, and the Colorado, Blue, and Eagle in Colorado.

What dry fly is so effective, so many days of the year, on so many waters? It's the Red Quill. If this artificial imitates so many mayflies so closely and is productive almost any time of day, on many streams, then it should be an extensively used pattern on Western waters. But let me cite an experience I had in trying to obtain more Red Quills one day. A year before I had mutilated my last three Red Quills—or

Figure 60. The Red Quill, so effective in the East and Midwest, is also an effective Western pattern.

rather a few heavy trout did—and I visited two well-known sporting goods stores to replenish my supply. Neither store had any Red Quills on hand; in fact, one never stocked the imitation. A salesman tried to sell me some Quill Gordons, which he said were very close to the Red Quill. In desperation, I returned to my motel room, unpacked my fly-tying supplies, and tied several of the red-bodied imitations. I needed them the next day for a planned fishing trip to the Bitterroot River.

The Red Quill is productive in the morning. One morning, around 10:00 A.M. in mid-July, I fished the Bitterroot River just south of Florence, Montana. I entered the tail of a long pool that had been formed by a huge, half-submerged pine tree. As I scanned the surface, I noted four trout rising to a sporadic hatch. Although there were few naturals on the water, those that did appear rested a long time before taking off. I quickly captured several duns and saw that they had tannish red bodies and could be correctly imitated with a size 16 Red Quill. I tied a Red Quill onto the tippet and cast above one of the four fish now surfacing. Each trout rising to the naturals in that pool quickly seized the imitation. All four of the trout were heavy rainbows that had been feeding on that red-bodied morning hatch.

This productive morning mayfly was later identified as *Ephemerella inermis*, the Pale Morning Dun.

As I have suggested many times before, members of this species vary considerably in body coloration.

The Red Quill is also effective in the afternoon. A few miles upstream from Florence, I met an exciting prolific spinner fall one late July afternoon, again on the Bitterroot. Little feeding occurred before 1:00 P.M. A few Gray Drakes and Dark Blue Quills appeared on some slow water in a nearby sandbar, but no trout fed on these. Suddenly several trout began feeding voraciously on spent spinners directly in front of me. I stood at the head of a pool where the fast water channeled into a narrow but deep, fast stretch. I searched the eddy near the fast water and observed a few and then a hundred or so bright red spinners spent on the surface. These red imagos *Rhithrogena undulata*) too could be appropriately matched with the Red Quill.

I hurriedly tied on a size 14 imitation and cast directly upstream into the fast water in the channel. Five trout now freely fed on these red spinners and quickly seized the imitation. But trout that I didn't see taking naturals also took the artificial. Spinners fell and trout fed until almost 3:00 P.M., when the last available spent female was captured near my feet by a small trout.

During that hot Montana afternoon, in the middle of the summer when fly-fishing is supposed to be poorest, I had met and fished while a great spinner

Figure 61. A section of the Blackfoot River in northwestern Montana. Hatches of *Rhithrogena undulata* are common on this stream.

fall occurred. In the two-hour period of the spinner fall, I had hooked and released fifteen trout on a Red Quill. The Red Quill is an effective afternoon pattern, especially when a spinner fall occurs.

But the Red Quill is also an excellent choice for evening fishing. I remember an evening on the Blackfoot River near Potomac in Montana. When I arrived at the river in early July, I stood near a cliff overlooking a long, fast stretch. I wondered what mayflies would inhabit this rapid section, but I did observe several trout already feeding.

By the time I had climbed down to the stream, thousands of caddis flies had begun to abandon nearby bushes and trees and moved toward the center of the river to lay their eggs. About 7:30 P.M. I noticed hundreds of *Rhithrogena undulata* spinners hovering near trees where they had recently shed their pellicle (sub-

imagal skin). I captured several males and quickly concluded that these adults too (females may be lighter) could be copied with the Red Quill. The *R. undulata* spinner on the Blackfoot is somewhat darker than the same species on the Bitterroot, but I felt confident that the same Red Quill that had proved so successful on the latter stream would suffice here on the Blackfoot.

A trout surfaced barely a foot from the shore. I covered it on the second cast, and the foot-long rainbow hit immediately. Every tenth or fifteenth cast seemed to produce a trout on that fast section—and all this action happened with the effective, productive Red Quill. Although trout rose intermittently throughout the evening, I never noted one natural, especially one looking like the Red Quill, on the water.

I quit that evening on the Blackfoot about 9:00 P.M.,

but only after a dozen or more trout had seized that Red Quill dry fly.

The Red Quill is effective in August and September. I remember the first evening I met the *Heptagenia solitaria* imago, on the Eagle River in Colorado. This spinner is better imitated with the Ginger Quill, but I didn't have any Ginger Quills with me on that meeting. The Red Quill proved to be an excellent substitute.

Morning, afternoon, or evening—May, June, July, August, and even September—the Red Quill is an imitation that can be productive in the West. If the Slate Drake is an imitation for all summer in the East, the Red Quill is an imitation for all season in the West.

A MORNING ON THE BITTERROOT WITH THE WESTERN GREEN DRAKE

I arrived on the Bitterroot River one midmorning in late June. Spring runoff still created fast, extremely high water. The water temperature barely reached the 50-degree mark. Pine trees, uprooted by the tremendous force of the purging water, lay in the slower areas of the stream. The river appeared to be 3 or 4 feet above its normal late-summer flow. How would I ever catch trout on dry flies under these circumstances?

Rather than fish, I sat by the stream, mesmerized by the rapid, churning water. A good hatch of *Ephemerella infrequens* duns appeared shortly after I arrived. Nothing, however, rose for these moderate-sized mayflies, although the hatch became heavier. By 10:30 A.M. Quill Gordons (*Rhithrogena futilis*), a larger mayfly, joined the smaller *Ephemerella infrequens* (Pale Morning Dun). Both species rested on the surface for protracted periods before flying to nearby trees. But no trout rose to either species. At this point I seriously doubted that any trout would surface feed under these adverse conditions.

Then, about 11:00 A.M., a much larger mayfly appeared. Two of these mayflies fluttered aimlessly in an eddy created by two uprooted trees. Then three of these large mayflies appeared, then four.

I stood below the uprooted trees to catch and identify these mayflies. While I waited for the duns to reach me, three separate trout surfaced for the duns before I could capture one of them. I soon collected a couple of male duns and assumed from the dark grayish black coloration and green cast that these were Green Drakes (*Drunella grandis*).

Weren't these duns supposed to have bright green bodies? I knew that they lost the green cast rapidly, but I captured several and studied them within seconds of their appearance. These duns, as well as some duns I saw on the upper section of the Gibbon River, had a distinct greenish cast, but they were not green. Evidently here's another example of the tremendous color variation the same species exhibits on various different Western streams.

But I had only a bright green imitation with me that morning. I tied one on anyway and cast above one of the three rising trout. On the first drift over one of the trout, I noticed a rapid movement directly beneath the artificial but no strike. On the third or fourth cast, that movement became a strike as a heavy rainbow sucked in the Green Drake imitation. The fish leaped out of the swollen water and then headed deep, winding my leader around some submerged debris.

Four trout hit that Green Drake fly that morning before I decided to quit. That's not an unusually high number, but under the extremely poor early-summer stream conditions, I was satisfied.

It was now 2:00 P.M., and I headed back to my car. As I did, an occasional trout still rose to the sporadic Green Drakes. Plenty of Pale Morning Duns and Quill Gordons still appeared, but not once did I see a trout take either.

I hurried back to my motel that afternoon; I had a lot of fly tying to complete before I fished again the next morning. I wanted to copy the Bitterroot version of the Western Green Drake more closely. I tied a half-dozen imitations that had bodies of dark grayish black polypropylene mixed with a small amount of the same material but green. I ribbed each body with pale yellow thread. Now I was prepared to fish the hatch the next day. The question that went through my mind that evening was, Would the hatch appear tomorrow, or was it finished for the year? Only a visit to the stream could tell.

The next morning proved to be even more successful on the Bitterroot. I arrived at the same pool, sat on the same bank, and waited for something to happen. Almost immediately, around 10:30 A.M., the first Green Drakes appeared. It was not a sudden or heavy appearance—just a few duns emerging at the head of the pool every five or ten minutes. But almost every time one of these large mayflies attempted to leave the surface, the fluttering action attracted trout.

One trout rose near the head of the pool, two or three were in the center, and one took laggards that had floated the length of the hole near the tail. This is great fly-fishing. You know that though the hatch is less than concentrated, the duns drift on the surface for an extended period, and this encourages fish to rise. And you realize that the species will probably continue to emerge well into the afternoon.

Methodically I selected one trout, then another, and another, until I had covered, caught, and released most of the trout in that pool that had risen to the Green Drake naturals.

The Western Green Drake continued to appear on the Bitterroot until the second week in July that year. As stream conditions improved, so did the success with an imitation of the Green Drake. *Drunella doddsi* is a common sister species, and it also appears on many streams in the morning and afternoon, possibly a week or two later than *D. grandis*.

The Western Green Drake is extremely common on Western waters. You'll find hatches from southern California to southeastern Alaska east to the eastern slope of the Rockies.

If you get the opportunity from late May to early July to fish while this large *Drunella* species appears, you'll never forget it. Mornings, especially when fishing during a hatch of Western Green Drakes, can produce exciting, memorable fishing experiences.

CHAPTER 12

FISHING THE AFTERNOON HATCHES (Western)

In the following list, (M) indicates that hatches or spinner falls also often occur in the morning and (E) that they often occur in the evening. Dates listed are approximate; remember that Western dates are even less precise than their Eastern and Midwestern counterparts.

DUNS

Rhithrogena morrisoni (W)—Western March Brown; afternoon; late February to late May

Baetis tricaudatus (M & E)—Little Blue Dun; late morning, afternoon, and early evening; April to November[1]

Baetis intermedius (M & E)—Little Blue Dun; late morning, afternoon, and early evening; April to November[1]

Ephemerella inermis (M & E)—Pale Morning Dun;[2] late morning, afternoon, and early evening; May 25[1]

Cinygmula ramaleyi (M)—Dark Red Quill; late morning (may continue into the afternoon); May 25

Baetis bicaudatus (M & E)—Pale Olive Dun; late morning, afternoon, and early evening; June through October[1]

Paraleptophlebia heteronea (M)—Dark Blue Quill; morning and afternoon; June 1

Drunella (Ephemerella) grandis (M)—Western Green Drake; late morning and afternoon (see Chapter 11 for more information); June 5

Serratella (Ephemerella) tibialis (M)—Red Quill; late morning and afternoon; June 5

Callibaetis coloradensis (M)—Speckle-Winged Dun; late morning and early afternoon; June 12[1]

Epeorus longimanus (M)—Quill Gordon; late morning and early afternoon; June 12

Drunella (Ephemerella) doddsi (M)—Western Green Drake; late morning and afternoon; June 15

Heptagenia elegantula (E)—Pale Evening Dun; late afternoon and evening; June 20[1]

Baetis hageni (parvus) (M & E)—Dark Brown Dun; late morning, afternoon, and early evening; June 20

Ephemerella infrequens (M)—Pale Morning Dun;[2] late morning and afternoon; July 1

Paraleptophlebia memorialis (M)—Dark Blue Quill; morning and afternoon; July 1

Rhithrogena futilis (M)—Quill Gordon; late morning and afternoon; July 1[3]

Cinygmula reticulata (M)—Pale Brown Dun; late morning and afternoon; July 5[3]

Paraleptophlebia vaciva (M)—Dark Blue Quill; morning and afternoon; July 5

Paraleptophlebia debilis (M)—Dark Blue Quill; morning and afternoon; July 5[1]

Siphlonurus occidentalis (M)—Gray Drake; late morning and afternoon (heaviest hatches seem to occur around 3:00 P.M.); July 5 (hatches occur well into August, especially on colder streams)

Heptagenia solitaria (E)—Gray Fox; late afternoon and evening; July 5[1]

Rhithrogena hageni (M)—Pale Brown Dun; late morning and afternoon; July 10

Ameletus cooki (M)—Dark Brown Dun; late morning and afternoon; July 10[3]

Paraleptophlebia packii[4] (M)—Dark Blue Quill; morning and afternoon; July 20

Drunella (Ephemerella) coloradensis (M)—Dark Olive Dun;[1] midday; August 1

Paraleptophlebia bicornuta (M)—Dark Blue Quill; morning and afternoon; September 10[3]

SPINNERS

Cinygmula ramaleyi (M)—Red Quill Spinner; late morning and early afternoon; May 28

Paraleptophlebia heteronea (M)—Dark Brown Spinner; morning and afternoon; June 2

Epeorus longimanus (M)—Red Quill Spinner; late morning and early afternoon; June 16
Paraleptophlebia memorialis (M)—Dark Brown Spinner; morning and afternoon; July 2
Paraleptophlebia vaciva (M)—Dark Brown Spinner; morning and afternoon; July 6
Paraleptophlebia debilis (M)—Dark Brown Spinner; morning and afternoon; July 6[1]
Ameletus cooki—Dark Brown Spinner; early afternoon; July 11[3]
Rhithrogena undulata (E)—Red Quill or Dark Red Quill;[2] afternoon and evening; July 11[3]
Paraleptophlebia packii (M)—Dark Brown Spinner; morning and afternoon; July 21
Paraleptophlebia bicornuta (M)—Dark Brown Spinner; morning and afternoon; September 11[3]

CADDIS FLY

Dicosmoecus species (M & E)—October Caddis; afternoon; October 15

STONE FLIES

Pteronarcys californica—Salmon Fly; morning and afternoon; June and July
Calineuria californica—Golden Stonefly; afternoon; June through September
Hesperoperla pacifica—Willow Fly; variable; June and July

---

[1]Hatches or spinner falls may occur for many days.
[2]Color varies and common name may be inappropriate.
[3]Hatches or spinner falls may occur before date listed.
[4]Not listed in the Emergence Chart, but may be important.

As in the East and Midwest, afternoon fly-fishing in the West can be the least rewarding time of day to fish. Afternoon is not the most propitious time to see free-ranging lunker trout feeding. But add an afternoon hatch or spinner fall to the picture, and the fly-fisherman can have an exciting experience—the waters can come alive with rising trout. Indeed, afternoon in the West is blessed with some excellent hatches and spinner falls.

We have many holdover subimagos in the afternoon. These are mayflies that initially appear in the morning but continue into the afternoon, often in heavy numbers. The two species that make up the Western Green Drakes (*Drunella grandis* and *D. doddsi*), the Pale Morning Duns (*E. inermis* and *E. infrequens*), and the Red Quill (*Serratella tibialis*) are only a few of the Ephemerellidae species that appear in the morning and continue into the afternoon.

Baetis species, commonly imitated by the Little Blue Dun, or Little Blue-Winged Olive Dun also continue into the afternoon from the morning. With many species of this genus, the heaviest hatches often occur in the afternoon. *Baetis hageni (parvus)* (Dark Brown Dun), *B. bicaudatus* (Pale Olive Dun), and *B. intermedius* (Little Blue Dun) are three *Baetis* species that can be important to meet and fish on many summer afternoons. As we'll see later, *B. hageni* is one of the most important hatches I have ever experienced in the West.

Figure 62. The *Baetis hageni (parvus)* dun is an important mayfly to meet on many Western streams.

Figure 63. The Dark Brown Dun on a size 20 hook is a productive imitation of the *Baetis hageni (parvus)* dun.

Members of another genus, *Paraleptophlebia*, so ably imitated by the Dark Blue Quill, are also holdovers from the morning. *Paraleptophlebia debilis* and *P. memorialis* can be productive many July afternoons, and *P. bicornuta* is important because it appears in early September.

Spinner falls also occur in the afternoon. Some of the best afternoon fishing I have experienced happened while spinners of *Ameletus cooki* (Dark Brown Spinner) and *Rhithrogena undulata* (Red Quill) fell.

Afternoon also is the time of the sporadic emerger, the Gray Drake (*Siphlonurus occidentalis*). When you fish this hatch in late July and early August, if trout are feeding you can have an extremely productive afternoon.

Don't overlook the Western March Brown on near-coastal waters. This important species emerges on the Willamette and McKenzie rivers every afternoon from late February until late May. If you're fortunate enough to hit a Western March Brown (*Rhithrogena morrisoni*) near the Pacific coast, you'll see how productive afternoon fishing in the West can be. (I've included a story about this fantastic hatch later in the chapter.)

Caddis patterns can be important on these afternoons. The orange-bodied October Caddis *Dicosmoecus* found on many California rivers like the McCloud and Sacramento and Oregon rivers like the Deschutes and McKenzie produces some late season action.

Afternoon fishing in the West can be exciting—especially if you've prepared yourself to fish while one of the many hatches appears.

THE THREE-MONTH HATCH— THE WESTERN MARCH BROWN

April 28 was a cold, blustery, rainy day on the McKenzie River near Eugene, Oregon. Mike Manfredo boasted continually about the great hatch on the river this time of year. The hatch, the Western March Brown (*Rhithrogena morrisoni*), appears on Willamette Valley rivers in late February and continues every afternoon into late May. This size 14 mayfly brings scores of rainbows to the surface during the hatch on the river.

Long before many Western fly-fishermen think of hatches, this mayfly appears. Why does it begin appearing in February? Spring often comes early to the Willamette Valley—much earlier than to the Rocky Mountain area.

Ken Helfrich of nearby Springfield, Oregon, would be our guide for the 6-mile float trip down to the Willamette River. Ken, like his grandfather and father, has guided on the river for more than eighteen years. He also guides on Oregon's Rogue River and Idaho's Middle Fork of the Salmon River. He not only handles the McKenzie Boat well on the river but he's also an excellent fly-fisherman and knows the hatches

Figure 64. Ken Helfrich on the McKenzie River during the October Caddis hatch. The river comes alive at this time with rising rainbows.

the McKenzie holds. He's a member of the McKenzie River Guides Association and the Oregon Guides and Packers.

In late February to late April, Ken often drifts the river near Eugene to meet the March Brown hatch. In May you'll find him 30 miles upriver above Vida fishing the same hatch. Just about the time the March Brown peters out, a heavy Western Green Drake appears on the river. Ken also regards this latter hatch as a great time to meet and fish the hatch.

Annually the state stocks 150,000 trout in the McKenzie. You're not allowed to kill any trout over 14 inches on the river. Ken says that restriction placed on the McKenzie twenty years ago has saved the river.

We entered the river that morning just across from a state park near Eugene. As I do so often when I

first begin to fly-fish, I took a few seconds to check the water temperature. The thermometer rose to 50 degrees. I say rose because the air temperature never got out of the high forties. Ken, Mike, and I had adequately prepared for the inclement weather with heavy jackets and rainwear.

I hadn't done much float fishing before so Ken had to teach me quickly the refloat method he uses for dry fly-fishing from a McKenzie boat. First, you cast your dry fly 45 degrees downriver from the boat; then you lift the fly upriver the distance of your leader and let it float back downriver. We tied Ken's favorite pattern, a parachute Western March Brown dry fly, onto the tippet and a wet-fly version of the imitation on the dropper.

Ken drifted us through several sets of rapids, possibly two miles down from our point of entry. Only occasionally did we see any March Browns. Then we reached a moderate but deep rapids followed by a long, flat pool. As we approached the rapids from above, we saw thousands of March Brown suddenly emerge onto the surface. With the cold air and drizzle, only a small percentage of the duns successfully struggled free from the water and became airborne. What seemed like hundreds of rainbows rose to this early spring bonanza throughout the upper part of the pool. With Ken's expert guidance, Mike and I caught a dozen trout before we exited the pool. Each riffle and pool downriver contained a good number of rainbows eager to surface feed. At several pools, the surface action became so intense that we left the boat and fished to risers from the shore. Duns first appeared in massive numbers at 2:00 P.M. Even at 4:00 P.M. a few duns still appeared.

Downriver 4 miles, we entered the cloudy Willamette River where few trout rose. What a day this had been! What a spectacular hatch! Within a few miles of Eugene, Oregon, Mike, Ken, and I caught more than fifty trout on that dismal, overcast day.

Mike and Ken fish the Western March Brown from the end of February until late May on the McKenzie. The river is difficult to access and to fish from shore, so drifting with a McKenzie-type boat is the only suitable alternative.

Ken has guided fly-fishermen over trout rising to an abundant supply of Western March Brown duns.

Figure 65 — A parachute pattern tied by Ken Helfrich to copy the Western March Brown.

He's seen this same hatch on the river thousands of times. Fishermen on his boat have caught as many as a hundred trout during a March Brown, Green Drake, or October Caddis hatch on the river. You'd think by now Ken would lose some of his enthusiasm for the hatch, the river, and his success, but he still gets excited about meeting and fishing this tremendous extended Western hatch.

THAT GREAT AFTERNOON HATCH ON HENRY'S FORK

It was my third trip to the fabled Henry's Fork in Idaho. On my previous trips I had seen many *Ephemerella inermis* (Pale Morning Dun) subimagos and many trout rising to these mayflies. I saw many more *D. flavilinea* (Blue-Winged Olive Dun) duns and correspondingly more fish feeding on these. I even met and fished while thousands of Blue Quills (*Paraleptophlebia debilis*) began their annual emergence. And I noted some precursory Gray Drakes (*Siphlonurus occidentalis*) emerge along the edges in mid-afternoon. But nobody ever told me that one of the greatest hatches I would ever experience—that includes the East, Midwest, and West—would be the diminutive Dark Brown Dun, *Baetis hageni (parvus)*. Here on this water noted for its great hatches, I experienced the Dark Brown Dun every afternoon for more than a week.

I had gone to Idaho in mid-July with plenty of imitations to match the Blue-Winged Olive Dun, Brown Drake, Blue Quill, and Western Green Drake. The Green Drake (*Drunella grandis*), however, had emerged around June 20 (and usually does so on this stretch); the Brown Drake (*Ephemera simulans*), which I had met earlier that year on Pine Creek in Pennsylvania, had appeared on the lower Railroad Ranch about June 25. I was afraid I had missed most of the major hatches by this mid-July meeting.

I planned to fish the section just above the Railroad Ranch and arrived there about 9:00 A.M. At 10:00 A.M. a few Blue-Winged Olives (*Drunella flavilinea*) appeared but not enough to create any frenzied surface feeding. An hour or so later a few Pale Morning Duns (*E. inermis*) emerged, but again few trout rose to this sparse hatch. I sat back on the shore next to the water and collected male duns of the six or so species sporadically emerging. As many other writers have said before, this stream, and this section in particular, is a veritable insect factory. By noon I was convinced that no hatch would probably occur before evening—but I decided to remain and collect and photograph more insects.

Around 1:00 or 1:15 P.M., I noticed a few small dark brown mayflies emerging. I hoped the species wouldn't emerge in any great numbers, since I didn't have any imitation for it. The closest artificials I had to imitate this little mayfly were a size 18 Dark Blue Quill and Blue Dun. Things didn't work out the way I had planned. This was the hatch of the day—no, of the week! By 2:00 P.M. literally millions of these dazed duns floated past me—and not one took flight. Trout that had been inactive quickly became active. Fish moved out of the weed beds into feeding channels in the stream, and a major afternoon hatch was underway. In a 100-yard section more than a hundred trout rose to these small duns. All of this action occurred in the middle of a hot Idaho afternoon.

Great, but I had no imitation that I felt adequately matched the hatch. I quickly tied on the size 18 Dark Blue Quill and started casting over ten rising fish. Ten casts, twenty casts—still no success. Too many trout rose to the naturals, and I found myself covering three, four, and even five trout on one cast. Finally a large fish swirled at the imitation, and then a second and third trout did the same. I was confused, frustrated, and angry. Why hadn't someone told me about this important Western hatch?

Accepting defeat for the moment, I headed back to my car 100 yards away. I had my fly-tying gear in the car and decided to tie several Dark Brown Duns on size 20 hooks. While I was tying these diminutive imitations, wind gusts scattered some of my feathers yards away, and I spent precious time retrieving them. I did not dare look back at the water I had just fished; I was fearful that the hatch would end by the time I had completed tying three imitations.

But the hatch had not ended. Thousands and thousands of motionless Dark Brown Duns still drifted on the surface, and more than a hundred trout still methodically fed as I reentered the area I had left twenty minutes before. Now, with much more confidence, I was prepared to meet and fish the hatch. I cast to the first rising trout just a few feet from shore. After ten or more casts, the feeding trout finally seized my artificial rather than a natural. The foot-long rainbow leaped several times to show its displeasure before I netted and released it. Then a second trout, a third trout, and on and on until I caught more than fifty fish during that afternoon hatch.

From 2:00 to 4:00 P.M. there were so many duns on the water that there was hardly any chance for a trout to take the imitation. But by 4:00 P.M. the hatch had diminished just enough that catching rising trout became easier. Trout still fed and duns still appeared at 5:00 P.M. The hatch had continued without interruption for more than four hours.

Certainly this was an outstanding afternoon hatch—one that emerged in heavy numbers, occurred all afternoon, encouraged hundreds of trout to rise, and produced many rises to appropriate imitations. The hatch appeared from July 12 through July 15 (and probably before and after those dates) and always began between 1:00 and 1:30 P.M. On each of these days thousands of duns emerged and hundreds of trout fed on them.

Interspersed with the Dark Brown Duns were many Pale Olive Duns (*Baetis bicaudatus*). Enough of these subimagos appeared on the water every afternoon to produce rising trout.

Want to meet and fish while an excellent hatch appears? Try Henry's Fork when the Dark Brown Dun emerges.

CHAPTER 13

FISHING THE EVENING HATCHES (Western)

In the following list, (M) indicates that hatches or spinner falls also often occur in the morning and (A) that they often occur in the afternoon. Dates listed are very approximate; remember that Western dates are even less precise than Eastern and Midwestern.

DUNS

Ephemerella inermis (M & E)—Pale Morning Dun;[1] late morning, afternoon, and early evening; May 25[2]

Ephemera simulans—Brown Drake; evening; May 25 (appears on Henry's Fork, Idaho, in late June)

Hexagenia limbata[3]—Michigan Caddis; late evening; June 12

Drunella (Ephemerella) flavilinea (M)—Blue-Winged Olive Dun; morning and evening (evening seems to be heavier); June 15

Heptagenia elegantula (A)—Pale Evening Dun; late afternoon and evening; June 20[2]

Heptagenia solitaria (A)—Gray Fox; late afternoon and evening; July 5[2]

Epeorus albertae—Pink Lady (male can be imitated by the Light Cahill); evening; July 5

Cinygma dimicki—Light Cahill; evening; July 5[4]

Timpanoga (Ephemerella) hecuba—Great Red Quill; evening; July 5

Ephoron album—White Mayfly; evening; August 15

SPINNERS

Baetis tricaudatus (M)—Light Rusty Spinner; early morning and evening; April to November[2]

Baetis intermedius (M)—Dark Rusty Spinner; early morning and evening; April to November[2]

Ephemera simulans—Brown Drake; evening; May 26 (usually later than date listed)

Ephemerella inermis (M)—Pale Morning Spinner; morning and evening; May 26

Baetis bicaudatus (M)—Light Rusty Spinner; morning and evening; June through October[2]

Drunella (Ephemerella) grandis—Great Red Spinner; evening; June 6 (usually later than date listed)

Serratella (Ephemerella) tibialis—White-Gloved Howdy;[5] evening; June 6

Hexagenia limbata—Michigan Spinner; dusk; June 13

Drunella (Ephemerella) doddsi—Great Red Spinner; evening; June 16

Baetis hageni (parvus) (M)—Dark Brown Spinner; early morning and evening; June 21

Heptagenia elegantula—Pale Evening Spinner; evening; June 21[2]

Rhithrogena futilis—Quill Gordon; evening; July 2[4]

Ephemerella infrequens (M)—Rusty Spinner;[1] morning and evening; July 2

Epeorus albertae (M)—Salmon Spinner (male can be imitated by the Light Cahill); morning and evening; July 6

Timpanoga (Ephemerella) hecuba—Great Brown Spinner; evening; July 6

Cinygma dimicki—Light Cahill; evening; July 6[4]

Siphlonurus occidentalis (M)—Brown Quill Spinner; morning and evening; July 6

Heptagenia solitaria (M)—Ginger Quill Spinner; morning and evening; July 6

Rhithrogena hageni (M)—Dark Tan Spinner; morning and evening; July 11

Rhithrogena undulata (A)—Red Quill or Dark Red Quill; afternoon and evening; July 11[4]

Drunella (Ephemerella) coloradensis—Dark Brown Spinner; evening; August 2

Ephoron album—White Mayfly; evening; August 15

---

[1]Color may vary, and common name may be inappropriate.
[2]Hatches or spinner falls may occur for many days.
[3]Generally considered a Midwestern species but may be locally important in the East and West.
[4]Hatches or spinner falls may occur before date listed.
[5]Name taken from *Isonychia* spinner.

Figure 66. *Cinygma dimicki* looks like the Gray Fox found in the East and Midwest.

When I think of evening fishing, I remember vividly one of my trips to the Bitterroot River in Montana. It was an early July evening, and for the two hours that I had scanned the stream, not one trout surfaced. I doubted whether this would be a good evening to meet and fish while any hatch or spinner fall occurred.

At 8:00 P.M. several *Cinygma dimicki* duns emerged from slow water just upstream from where I stood. A few minutes later, spinners of the same species met over the water. But still no trout fed.

Now it was almost dark, and several trout took up feeding positions in fast water noticeably slowed by a partially submerged evergreen. Soon the several trout became twenty hungry, feeding fish.

I noticed hundreds of *Rhithrogena futilis* now mating and tied on a Quill Gordon to match the spinner. Rainbow after rainbow took the Quill Gordon imitation before I quit that evening.

But that's not the only memorable fishing experience in the evening. I recall meeting and fishing while thousands of Blue-Winged Olive Duns (*Drunella flavilinea*) duns appeared one late June evening on Henry's Fork and while Pale Evening Duns (*Ephemerella inermis*) continued to appear in the Box Canyon Area of Henry's Fork.

Figure 67. A *Rhithrogena futilis* spinner, copied by a Quill Gordon, works well when the spinner is active in the evening.

FISHING THE EVENING HATCHES

Figure 68. A Blue-Winged Olive Dun found on many Western rivers in the evening, *Drunella flavilinea*.

Among the most productive evenings is the one I spent on the Yellowstone River when I fished while thousands of downwinged caddis flies and stone flies returned to that river to lay their eggs. And that too was the evening I was to meet and fish at the time when the huge stone fly the Salmon Fly (*Pteronarcys californica*) reappeared.

Evening caddis activity is common on other Western waters. Montana rivers like the Clark Fork near Deer Lodge, the Blackfoot River near Bonner, and the Kootenai River just below Libby produce spectacular evening fly-fishing over caddis flies in early July. All three produce exciting matching-the-hatch opportunities with downwings.

Evening is also the time that the widespread but ephemeral Brown Drake (*Ephemera simulans*) appears on some Western rivers.

There are many other evening hatches and spinner falls that can engender memorable fishing experiences. Both *Epeorus albertae* duns and spinners are on the water many summer evenings. *Heptagenia* species like *H. elegantula* (Pale Evening Spinner) and *H. solitaria* remind me of many Western trips that were successful because I fished while spinners of these species fell. The latter adult is appropriately imitated by the Ginger Quill.

A SEPTEMBER EVENING ON THE COLORADO RIVER

It was early September. I had an unexpected opportunity to fish several streams in Colorado. But what about the hatches? Would I encounter any? Would any be heavy enough to produce rising trout?

I stayed overnight in Kremmling, Colorado, and awoke to a light frost and a temperature of 29 degrees. I arrived on the Colorado River around 10:00 A.M. and scanned the surface for emerging duns, falling spinners, and feeding trout. There were plenty of mayflies in the air and a few on the water. *Tricorythodes minutus* spinners that had emerged not much more than an hour before already fell spent onto the water. *Callibaetis* and *Paraleptophlebia bicornuta* duns and spinners dotted the surface. The former are imitated by the Speckle-Winged Dun or Spinner and the latter by the Dark Blue Quill and Dark Brown Spinner. Although there were many species on the water, none appeared (except for *Tricorythodes*) in heavy enough numbers to encourage trout to rise.

I did little fishing that morning but sat back on the shore much of the time watching the hatching characteristics of the various mayfly species. Around 10:30 A.M. hundreds of Ginger Quill Spinners (*Heptagenia solitaria*) took positions a few inches above the surface. Little did I realize that this same species would create one of the greatest evening spinner falls that I have ever witnessed.

At 2:00 P.M. I still sat there by the Colorado searching the water and the air for signs of new mayfly species. I bent over my reflex camera and took several shots of *Callibaetis* duns and spinners. A state fish warden came by and asked how I had done fishing. I told him I had done little fishing and seen very few trout rise. He urged me to try the Gore George section of the Colorado a few miles below Kremmling. So

Figure 69. A *Heptagenia solitaria* female spinner. This species produces excellent spinner falls on many Western streams during August and early September.

at 4:00 P.M. I traveled to that section of the river.

Above the gorge, the Colorado is a slow, silted, meandering river, but as it enters the gorge, it becomes a rapid, rampaging torrent with long, fast stretches and short, deep holes. As I entered the gorge area, I noted *Baetis* spinners already mating. I also noted a fairly sizable (10–12 mm) dun emerging in good numbers. Trout near the far shore fed freely on subimagos that waited too long before taking flight. I captured several duns and assumed that they were *Heptagenia solitaria* subimagos from their yellowish tan coloration (and because I had seen spinners of this species upstream in the morning).

By 6:30 P.M. thousands of tan spinners appeared a few inches above the water. These spinners were the same species as the emerging duns and had probably emerged the night before.

Few trout rose to the duns or spinners—at least any that I could easily reach. I was ready to quit for the day and moved upstream through the gorge to the first large pool above it. Here thousands of Ginger Quill spinners hovered inches above the surface. Occasionally trout jumped completely out of the water to capture one of the fluttering adults. Now hundreds of male and female imagos drifted on the surface, and more than twenty trout rose to the newly found food supply.

The Ginger Quill is an excellent imitation for the *Heptagenia solitaria* spinner, so I quickly tied on a size 12 pattern and cast above a large trout feeding not more than 10 feet from me. On the first cast, the trout hit, and I set the hook. Without ever jumping once, the heavy fish headed downstream toward the first fast stretch entering the gorge. I turned the trout, and it headed back upstream. I netted the 18-inch rainbow, released it, and cast above another fish rising to imagos. That trout too took the imitation on the first pass. Now on to another rising trout, then another, and so on until I had caught and released more than twenty trout in less than an hour during that spinner fall.

As is often the case in the East and Midwest, no other fishermen were there to meet and fish the spinner fall. Again, as with so many other Western species, no one had prepared me for this important mayfly. No one had emphasized that *Heptagenia solitaria* is extremely important to meet and fish. No one had prepared me for that evening spinner fall on the Colorado River in September.

The next morning I headed for the Eagle River, 50 miles to the south. I spent the entire morning locating ranchers who owned land adjacent to the Eagle River and asking their permission to fish on their property. This brings up an important point to remember when fishing Western waters: much of the good water is on private land. The ranchers who own this land jealously guard their legal right to private property. I've discovered that most ranchers will allow you to fish if you ask. Always ask for permission, especially in the West.

I was fortunate that morning. I located a rancher who owned a 5-mile section of the Eagle River. He indicated that I could fish any part of the stream he owned. I thanked him and traveled to the stream.

When I arrived at the river around 3:00 P.M., I noted hundreds of *Baetis* duns emerging along the edges of a large pool. No trout, however, rose to these diminutive mayflies. Since the Ginger Quill had worked so well on the Colorado River the night before, I decided to try it on the Eagle. On my second or third cast in a large, deep hole, a heavy trout sucked in the imitation and promptly broke the 5X tippet.

I tied on a second Ginger Quill imitation and cast above a trout that had surfaced just a minute before. This fish hit on the first pass, and I netted and released a 15-inch cutthroat.

I waded downstream 200 feet to the next good pocket of water. Here too many *Baetis* duns emerged, but again no trout rose to these Little Blue Duns. Within a half-hour, six trout took the Ginger Quill in this second pool. All this action occurred on a hot September afternoon while few trout rose to naturals.

It was now 6:30 P.M. *Baetis* and *Ephemerella* spinners became active, but so did another spinner, *Heptagenia solitaria*. Now I understood why trout had so readily taken the Ginger Quill. The spinners that are so effectively imitated by the Ginger Quill had been on the Eagle for a number of days, and these hungry trout fed even when few *Heptagenia* naturals were apparent and even in the middle of the afternoon.

More than ten trout now fed on spent spinners, and by 7:00 P.M. I had caught more than twenty trout, fifteen of them 15 or more inches long.

Do you have time in September to spend an evening on the Colorado—or for that matter, many other Western streams? Then fish in the evening while Ginger Quills effectively copy the mating spinners of *Heptagenia solitaria*.

DOWNWINGS ARE FOR THE WEST—ESPECIALLY IN THE EVENING

On many occasions when I have fished Western waters, I have encountered more emerging and egg-laying caddis flies and stone flies than mayflies. One evening in early July on the Yellowstone River, just below Corwin Springs, I noted only three mayflies emerge. During that same six hours, I saw thousands of downwings perform their egg-laying flight. Each downwing species seemed to take its turn over the water—first a pale yellow stone fly; then a dark brown caddis; then the huge Willow Fly (*Hesperoperla pacifica*); and last, the giant of giants, the Salmon Fly (*Pteronarcys californica*).

As is common in early July, the Yellowstone River was high and discolored from melting snows in nearby Yellowstone Park. The river was impossible to wade, and no trout surfaced. John Bailey had warned me earlier that day that the river was high—certainly no place to use dry flies. As I walked along the shore, I saw thousands of mating Salmon Flies clinging firmly to the willow trees. Wind gusts of 30 or more miles per hour were common during that hot day in the canyon. Occasionally, the breeze dislodged several stone flies from their resting place and forced them prematurely to the water. A few trout fed on these occasional visitors. Other dislocated Salmon Flies landed on my hat, face, or fishing vest in an attempt to escape the winds. I noticed some Willow Flies also in the air and on the trees. If things went well, I might be on this highly productive river while one of these species landed in numbers on the water and became available as food for hungry trout. I hoped that one of these unpredictable females chose tonight to lay eggs.

It was now 9:15 P.M. I had stayed for six hours at the water—still no movement by the female *Pteronarcys*. I was ready to return to the motel; I had not fished during the six-hour stay but patiently waited for the return of the Salmon Fly.

About 9:20 P.M. one, then two, then a hundred, then several thousand females decided to fly toward the river to deposit their eggs. They flew almost 100 feet above the water and then down toward and onto

Figure 70. The Salmon Fly tied by Al Troth.

the surface. As these huge fluttering orange-bodied stone flies floated on the surface, large trout everywhere seized them; many fed within inches of the bank. I cast that awful-looking dry fly above what I thought was a heavy trout. The imitation had barely hit the cloudy water when a heavy fish sucked it in. Now the fight was on. The trout headed for the center of the river, and I couldn't turn it with my 4X tippet. Within seconds the leader snapped, and I found myself hurriedly tying another Salmon Fly onto the tippet. Ten trout took this unsightly imitation before I quit. When I left the river, trout were still feeding on the spent females, but darkness had made fishing impossible. The six-hour wait had been worthwhile, for I had finally experienced an egg-laying episode of the Salmon Fly.

If you ever have the opportunity to fish while *Pteronarcys californica* returns to the water, you'll never forget the action. Carry several imitations of the giant Willow Fly also, for this imitates a stone fly species, which also can be important in June and July.

The time to fish the downwings is when they return to the water to lay their eggs. Local authorities state that *Pteronarcys* females can return almost any time of day, but sometimes noon is preferred. I was successful in meeting and fishing the stone fly at dusk.

Imitations of the Salmon Fly are extremely difficult to tie; I recommend you buy imitations rather than tie them. Probably the best Salmon Fly pattern I have ever seen is the one tied by Al Troth of Dillon, Montana. He uses buoyant elk hair dyed orange to duplicate the body of this large stone fly. This imitation floats better than any other pattern I have tested, and I have heard many stories of success with it.

Pteronarcys californica is found on many Western waters. Emergence of this species often occurs in the morning, and the hatch normally moves upstream daily, for example, to the Green Drake on Penns Creek in the East. Bud Lilly lists the following streams as having good *Pteronarcys* hatches. The Salmon Fly usually appears first on Henry's Fork in May or early June. Shortly after, it emerges on Rock Creek in northwestern Montana, then Clark Fork, the Blackfoot, and the Madison. Hatches occur on the last two waters in middle to late June or early July. One of the last waters on which this large stone fly appears is the Yellowstone River. It often occurs on the Yellowstone in early to middle July. Water temperatures are often in the high 40s and low 50s, and streams are often discolored when this species appears. Both conditions prevent, or at least inhibit, dry-fly fishing. You'll also find a great hatch of these stone flies on the Deschutes in central Oregon near the end of May.

Earlier I said I tied my Eastern and Midwestern

caddis and stone fly patterns with deer hair and no hackle. I strongly recommend including two hackles on each Western downwing pattern. Eastern patterns usually do not float well on the faster Western rivers. However, my Eastern pattern did work well one evening on Clark Fork, near Deer Lodge, Montana. This water is much slower in its upper reaches than it is 20 miles below.

Here again, no mayflies appeared. About 8:00 P.M. thousands of caddis flies (Family Philopotamidae) skittered on the water. Since color, especially body color, of caddis flies is very misleading in the air, it's important to capture a natural and duplicate it with an appropriate imitation. Always carry sizes from 12 to 20 with cream, olive, tan, brown, gray, dark brown, green, and black bodies. The species laying eggs that evening on Clark Fork could be appropriately copied with a size 16 Dark Brown Caddis. Twenty heavy brown trout took that caddis pattern that evening on this highly productive stream.

The Kootenai near Libby, Montana, also hosts many caddis hatches throughout the year. I've had exceptional success a few miles downriver from Libby on a size 14 Green Caddis.

Many of the Trude patterns (Black, Blonde, etc.), Sofa Pillow, and others with downwings effectively imitate many stone fly and caddis fly species.

On many occasions, especially in the evening, I have encountered downwings on Western waters when no mayflies emerged. If you want to meet and fish while some dramatic, spectacular surface feeding occurs, use downwing imitations. Downwings indeed are made for the West.

THE BROWN DRAKES OF THE WEST

Just a month earlier I had fished on the Delaware River while the ephemeral Brown Drake (*Ephemera simulans*) appeared. Nine days later I hit the same hatch on the Pigeon near Vanderbilt in Michigan. Now I headed to Henry's Fork in Idaho to meet the Western Green Drake in late June.

Al Gretz, Terry Carlson, and I fished the upper end of the Railroad Ranch for three days while huge olive-colored Green Drakes appeared late in the morning. The third day the hatch subsided after 2:00 P.M., and Al suggested that we come back in the evening to see what hatches might appear.

We reentered the water about 7:00 P.M. and didn't have to wait long for hatching action. Within minutes a major Blue-Winged Olive Dun (*Drunella flavilinea*) commenced. The three of us tied on size 16 medium olive–bodied patterns and caught several rising trout. Blue-Winged Olives continued to appear for an hour until the hatch petered out.

Al suggested we head down the fork a mile to see if any mayfly activity appeared there. Here we waited until nearly 9:30 P.M. before anything happened. First a few and then dozens of dark brown duns appeared in front of us in the half-light of those long summer evenings in Idaho.

The duns appeared slightly darker but very similar to the same species found on the Pigeon in Michigan and on the Delaware in New York. I took a pattern fashioned after the Eastern Brown Drake and tied it on the heavy tippet.

Rainbows began feeding on the lethargic duns almost immediately as if they had waited for the hatch. I faced upriver toward the last trace of light from the long-past sunset. Looking toward the light, I could faintly see my pattern float downriver. Several times I mistook a rise for a natural as a strike at my fly and set the hook. Then a heavy rainbow hit the Brown Drake imitation, and I horsed the green fish in trying to cast to another rising fish before I lost all available light. Al too caught trout on the Brown Drake dun. The hatch continued past 10:00 P.M., but we quit.

Brown Drakes on Western streams? Yes, the hatch on Henry's Fork is a heavy impressive one. But Brown Drakes appear on other nearby rivers like the Woods and the Firehole and Madison in Yellowstone Park. Brown Drakes appear from Idaho east to the Housatonic in Connecticut and across much of Canada. This species normally appears for only a few days a year; be prepared with patterns and plenty of fast action.

CHAPTER 14

A PLEA TO ALL FISHERMEN

Every time I cast a dry fly on Hendrickson's Pool on the Beaverkill, I am amazed at the number of trout this and every other pool on these waters contain. Try being on these stretches almost any evening around dusk; the rises during a spinner fall are difficult for the mind to comprehend. I find myself many times during these emergences or falls casting over not one rising trout but twenty or thirty. As Guthrie Conyngham and his brother, Jack, have said many times, these rises at dusk remind them of Pennsylvania's Lehigh River and how it used to be thirty years ago.

But let's look at the Beaverkill in midmorning during late July or August. The Beaverkill has a fairly adequate *Tricorythodes* emergence and associated spinner fall occurring from 7:00 to 11:00 A.M. On Barnhart's Pool during the fall, fifty or sixty trout might be feeding freely on the spent imagos.

Falling Springs in south-central Pennsylvania is similar to the Beaverkill although much smaller. Try to arrive on this highly fertile limestone stream around 8:00 A.M. in August. You'll see *Tricorythodes* duns already appearing in good numbers. The hatch isn't as impressive as it once was, but still enough spinners fall to bring trout to the surface. By 9:00 to 9:30 A.M., the spinner fall commences, and although the pools in this stream are extremely small, you'll see a few trout feeding in almost every one.

Now let's look at the Loyalsock Creek in north-central Pennsylvania. The Loyalsock is an excellent freestone stream—not quite as large as the Beaverkill nor as fertile as Falling Springs but still noted for some fantastic hatches and excellent trout fishing. The Loyalsock, in its middle section at least, has an adequate *Tricorythodes* hatch. The species is not as dense as on Falling Springs but is still heavy enough to encourage trout to surface feed. However, on a good day you'll see only five or ten trout rising to the spinner fall in the long pool just below Hillsgrove. Why this discrepancy in numbers of rising trout compared with the previous two streams? This area of the "Sock" is open water where all kinds of hardware and bait can be used. The legal limit on this stream is eight, and most anglers remain until they kill their limit (if they're lucky). The Loyalsock is also a marginal summer stream with temperatures often above 70 degrees. Areas of the Beaverkill and Falling Springs described earlier are so-called no-kill areas where trout caught must be promptly returned to the water. Stretches or streams where trout must be released contain more trout later in the season—more trout to catch, release, and enjoy many times by many fishermen.

Oregon has adopted an excellent policy on some of its streams—a slot limit. On the McKenzie River you can't keep any trout over 15 inches long. The state stocks thousands of foot-long rainbows in the river and encourages anglers to keep some of these. Larger trout, streambred or holdovers, must be returned. Ken Helfrich of Eugene said this regulation has been the salvation of the McKenzie River.

If we want better fishing, we have to encourage fishermen to release trout so they can be enjoyed another time. But before we encourage anglers to release more, we must be ready to answer compelling questions. Here's part of the rationale some fishermen use for keeping fish.

1. *The trout will die anyway, so why should I release them?*

Several years ago I discovered a fabulous trout stream, the Little Juniata River in central Pennsylvania. I fished the water daily for weeks after a friend had told me about the huge native browns in the stream. After a few weeks of these solitary trips, I decided to invite another friend to experience the success that is so frequent on this stream. We had no success that evening, and I apologized time and time again to my friend. (I should have known better. On the way to the stream, I was bragging about the number and size of the trout, and it seems every time I do this, I have no success.)

I revisited the Little Juniata River a week later, and as I hiked to a pool a half-mile downstream from the Espy Farm, I saw the friend whom I had invited to the stream a week earlier. With him were four other anglers he had invited. When I asked if they had had any success, two of them opened their creels and displayed eight heavy browns that ranged from 15 to 18 inches long and must have weighed 2 to 3 pounds each. My mouth dropped in disgust and dismay when I viewed these large trout, now killed, never to challenge another angler.

"Why didn't you release them?" I asked rather angrily.

"Oh, we caught others and released them, but these would have died."

They were using soft-shelled crabs, and they were probably correct. Trout often take live bait voraciously and swallow bait and hook. Usually with flies, trout can be released unharmed. I guess this is why I rely on artificials. This is also a good reason for all of us to encourage others to take up fly-fishing. I can recall catching the same unusual-looking brook trout on Bowman Creek three times within a two-week span. How many other fishermen also had the pleasure of hooking this same trout?

2. *Who'd believe that I caught all these trout if I released them?*

Most sportsmen believe that keeping trout, not releasing them, is the proper thing to do. And it is

Figure 71. The fabled Beaverkill in New York. In the foreground is Hendrickson's Pool and in the background Barnhart's Pool.

a way to display to all one's fishing expertise. It'll be difficult to release trout the first couple of times—maybe others won't believe you—but give it a try. Besides, releasing trout can be contagious among your peers.

John Hagan, Lloyd Williams, and Dick Mills guard jealously the trout in the "fly-fishing only" area of Bowman Creek. They've seen many incidents of greed on this stretch when fishing is good. One day after the state released some trout, they saw one "sportsman" catch and keep two limits. When he caught his first limit, the angler furtively walked back to his car, emptied the contents of his creel into his truck, and calmly reentered the stream and started fishing again. By the time he had caught a second limit of six trout, John Hagan had had enough and waded over to the fisherman and asked him to stop. The angler ceased only after three fishermen converged on him. This

Figure 72. A sign on the McKenzie in Oregon indicating that a slot limit is in effect on the river.

man probably went home that evening and bragged to his friends about his expertise, when almost anyone could have done as well.

3. *I promised the trout to a friend.*

Let the friend go catch his own fish. He doesn't fish? Let him buy some at the local fish market. I can't argue with anyone who really enjoys trout and takes a few for his own benefit.

Certainly there are some times when you can and should keep trout: late in the season on a marginal stream, large lunkers that take many small trout, and artificial situations, such as private streams that are overstocked with trout.

As your fly-fishing progresses from beginner to expert, I hope a metamorphosis will occur. Your attitude toward your prey will become one of deep respect. I say "I hope" because as you advance through the stages, you'll probably experience more and more success and fewer and fewer failures—from few trout to many trout. Somewhere along the way evolves admiration for the quarry as a highly selective creature so revered that the mere thought of killing one after successfully enticing it to the dry fly is revolting. Returning the trout to its native haunt becomes natural, and keeping an occasional trout hooked too deeply or the rare lunker is the exceptional bonus.

APPENDIX

DISTRIBUTION MAPS OF
SELECTED MAYFLIES

Following are distribution maps showing where species of selected mayflies may be found throughout the United States. The species are located within the borders of the areas delineated. Page references in the captions refer the reader to further information about that species.

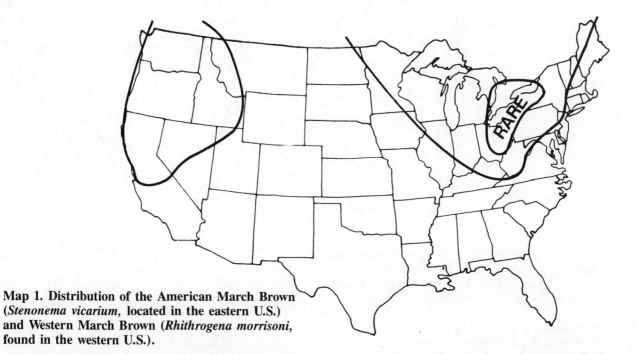

**Map 1. Distribution of the American March Brown
(*Stenonema vicarium,* located in the eastern U.S.)
and Western March Brown (*Rhithrogena morrisoni,*
found in the western U.S.).**

[Adapted from Lewis, *Taxonomy and Ecology of
Stenonema Mayflies,* Environmental Protection
Agency, 1974.]

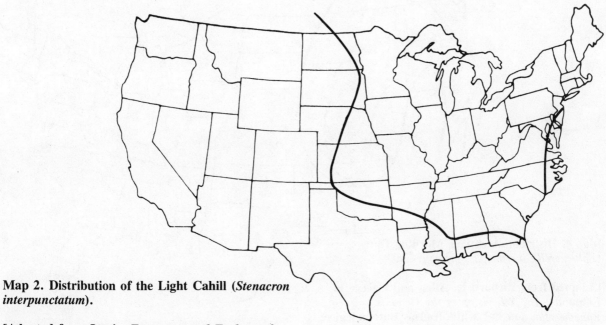

**Map 2. Distribution of the Light Cahill (*Stenacron
interpunctatum*).**

[Adapted from Lewis, *Taxonomy and Ecology of
Stenonema Mayflies,* Environmental Protection
Agency, 1974.]

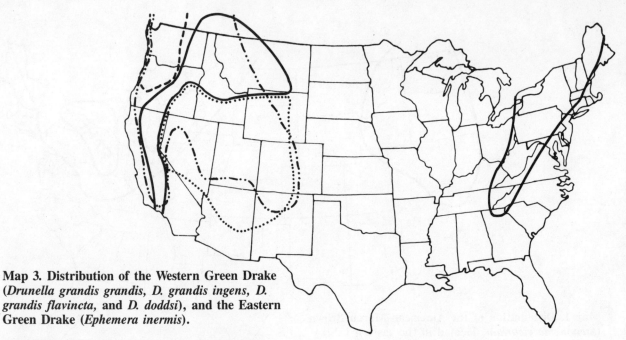

Map 3. Distribution of the Western Green Drake (*Drunella grandis grandis, D. grandis ingens, D. grandis flavincta,* and *D. doddsi*), and the Eastern Green Drake (*Ephemera inermis*).

[Adapted from Richard K. Allen and George F. Edmunds, Jr., *A Revision of the Genus Ephemerella,* Journal of the Kansas Entomological Society, 1961, and W.P. McCafferty, *The Burrowing Mayflies of the United States,* Trans. American Entomological Society, 1974.]

_ _ _ _ _ _ *D. grandis flavincta*
_____ *D. grandis ingens*
. . . . *D. grandis grandis*
___ . . ___ *D. doddsi*
_____ *E. guttulata* (in the eastern U.S.)

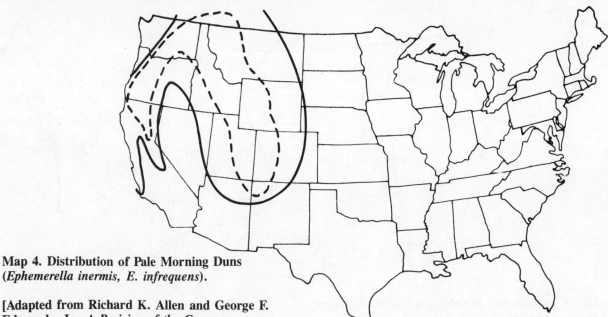

Map 4. Distribution of Pale Morning Duns (*Ephemerella inermis, E. infrequens*).

[Adapted from Richard K. Allen and George F. Edmunds, Jr., *A Revision of the Genus Ephemerella,* Journal of the Kansas Entomological Society, 1961, and W.P. McCafferty, *The Burrowing Mayflies of the United States,* Trans. American Entomological Society, 1974.]

_____ *E. guttulata*
_ _ _ _ _ _ *E. infrequens*

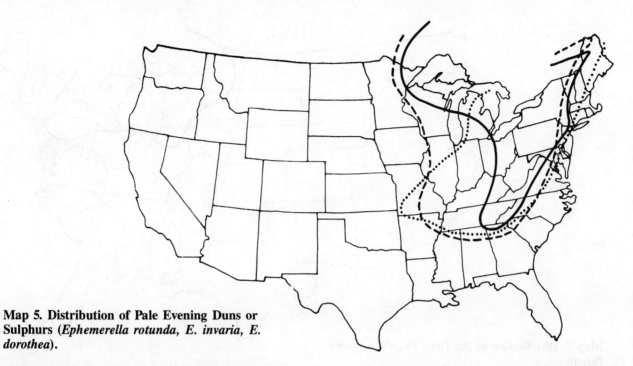

Map 5. Distribution of Pale Evening Duns or Sulphurs (*Ephemerella rotunda, E. invaria, E. dorothea*).

[Adapted from Richard K. Allen and George F. Edmunds, Jr., *A Revision of the Genus Ephemerella,* Journal of the Kansas Entomological Society, 1961.]

＿ ＿ ＿ ＿ ＿ ＿ *E. invaria*
＿＿＿＿＿＿＿ *E. rotunda*
· · · · · · · · · · *E. dorothea*

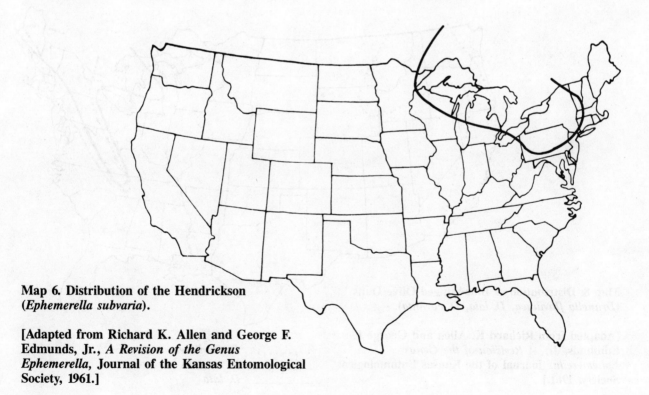

Map 6. Distribution of the Hendrickson (*Ephemerella subvaria*).

[Adapted from Richard K. Allen and George F. Edmunds, Jr., *A Revision of the Genus Ephemerella,* Journal of the Kansas Entomological Society, 1961.]

Map 7. Distribution of the Gray Fox (*Stenonema fuscum*).

[Adapted from Lewis, *Taxonomy and Ecology of Stenonema Mayflies,* Environmental Protection Agency, 1974.]

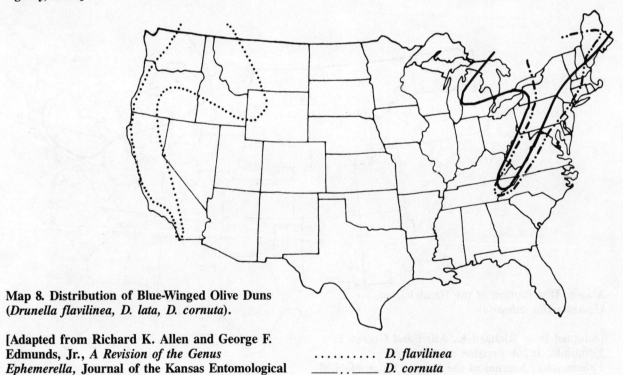

Map 8. Distribution of Blue-Winged Olive Duns (*Drunella flavilinea, D. lata, D. cornuta*).

[Adapted from Richard K. Allen and George F. Edmunds, Jr., *A Revision of the Genus Ephemerella,* Journal of the Kansas Entomological Society, 1961.]

.... *D. flavilinea*
____ .. ____ *D. cornuta*
_____ *D. lata*

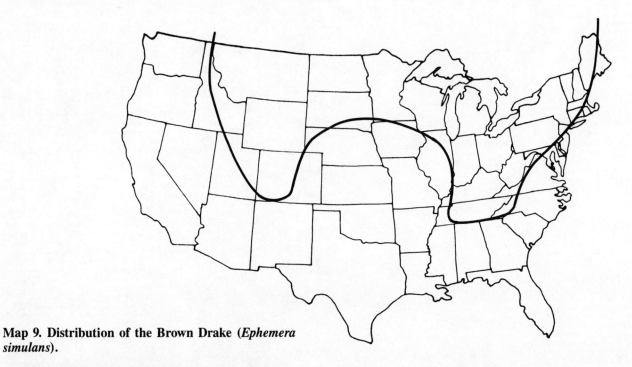

Map 9. Distribution of the Brown Drake (*Ephemera simulans*).

[Adapted from W.P. McCafferty, *The Burrowing Mayflies of the United States,* Trans. American Entomological Society, 1974.]

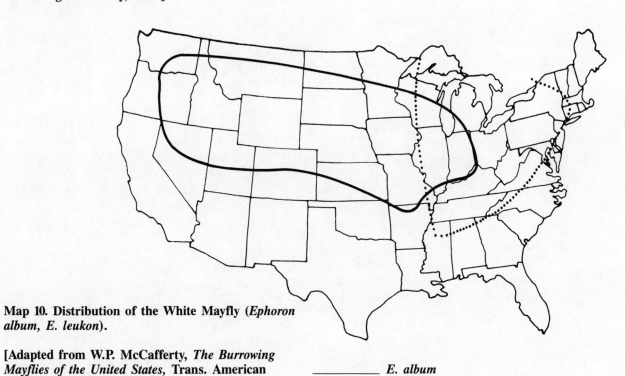

Map 10. Distribution of the White Mayfly (*Ephoron album, E. leukon*).

[Adapted from W.P. McCafferty, *The Burrowing Mayflies of the United States,* Trans. American Entomological Society, 1974.]

_____ *E. album*
.... *E. leukon*

SELECTED
BIBLIOGRAPHY

BOOKS

Burks, B.D. *The Mayflies, or Ephemeroptera, of Illinois*. Urbana: State of Illinois, 1953.

Caucci, Al, and Nastasi, Bob. *Hatches II*. Piscataway, N.J.: Winchester Press, 1986.

Colorado Fishing Guide. Colorado Recreation Guides, 1977.

Edmunds, George F., Jr. *The Type Localities of the Ephemeroptera of North America North of Mexico*. University of Utah Biological Series. Salt Lake City: University of Utah, 1962.

Edmunds, George F., Jr., Jensen, Steven L., and Berner, Lewis. *The Mayflies of North and Central America*. Minneapolis: University of Minnesota Press.

Hafele, Rick, and Dave Hughes. *The Complete Book of Western Hatches*. Portland: Frank Amato Publications, 1981.

Leonard, Justin W., and Leonard, Fannie A. *Mayflies of Michigan Trout Streams*. Bloomfield Hills, Mich.: Cranbrook Institute of Science, 1962.

McCafferty, W. Patrick. *Aquatic Entomology*. Boston: Jones and Bartlett Publishers, 1981.

Needham, James G., Traver, Jay R., and Hsu, Yin-Chi. *The Biology of Mayflies*. Hampton, England: E.W. Classey Ltd., 1935.

Needham, Paul R. *Trout Streams*. New York: Winchester Press, 1969.

Schwiebert, Ernest G., Jr. *Matching the Hatch*. Toronto: Macmillan, 1955.

———. *Nymphs*. New York: Winchester Press, 1973.

Swisher, Doug, and Richards, Carl. *Selective Trout*. New York: Crown Publishers, 1971.

Usinger, Robert L., ed. *Aquatic Insects of California*. Los Angeles: University of California Press, 1956.

DISSERTATIONS

Jensen, Steve. "The Mayflies of Idaho." Ph.D. diss., University of Utah, 1966.

Driear, Ralph E. "A Comparative Study of the Aquatic Insect Populations of Rock Creek, Montana and Its Major Tributaries," Ph.D. diss., University of Montana, 1974.

ARTICLES

Allen, R.K., and G.F. Edmunds, Jr. "A revision of the genus *Ephemerella* (*Ephemeroptera, Ephemerellidae*). The subgenus *Attenuatella* IV. The subgenus *Dannella*." *J. Kans. Entomol. Soc.* 34 (1961), 161–173.

———. "A revision of the genus *Ephemerella* IV. The subgenus *Dannella*." *J. Kans. Entomol. Soc.* 35 (1962), 333–338.

———. "A revision of the genus *Ephemerella* V. The subgenus *Drunella* in North America." *Misc. Publ. Entomol. Soc. Amer.* 3 (1962), 1474–1479.

———. "A revision of the genus *Ephemerella* VI. The subgenus *Serratella* in North America (*Ephemeroptera: Ephemerellidae*)." *Ann. Entomol. Soc. Amer.* 56 (1963), 583–600.

———. "A revision of the genus *Ephemerella* VII. The subgenus *Eurylophella* (*Ephemeroptera: Ephemerellidae*)." *Can. Entomol.* 95 (1963), 597–623.

———. "A revision of the genus *Ephemerella* VIII. The subgenus *Ephemerella* in North America. *Misc. Publ. Entomol. Soc. Amer.* 4 (1965), 243–282.

Bergman, Edward A., and William L. Hilsenhoff. "*Baetis Ephemeroptera: Baetidae*) of Wisconsin." *Great Lakes Entomologist* 11 (1978).

Edmunds, G.F., Jr. "The type localities of the Ephemeroptera of North America north of Mexico." *Univ. Utah Biol.* Ser. 12 (1962).

Lewis, P.A. "Taxonomy and Ecology of Stenonema mayflies (*Heptageniidae: Ephemeroptera*, Environ. Monit. Ser. Nat.)." *Environ. Res. Cent. (Cinci).* EPA 670/4-74-006 (1974), 81.

McCafferty, W.P. "The Burrowing Mayflies (*Ephemeroptera: Ephemeroidea*) of the United States." *Trans. Amer. Entomol. Soc.* 101 (1974), 447–504.

Newell, Robert L., and G.E. Minshall. "An Annotated List of the Aquatic Insects of Southeastern Idaho. Part I. Plecoptera." *Great Basin Naturalist*, December 31, 1976.

Newell, Robert L., and G. Wayne Minshall. "An Annotated List of the Aquatic Insects of Southeastern Idaho, Part II: Trichoptera." *Great Basin Naturalist* 37 (June 1977).

PAMPHLETS AND BULLETINS

Emergence Schedule: A Complete Guide to Matching the Insect Hatches of Michigan Trout Streams. Challenge Chapter of Trout Unlimited, Bloomfield Hills, Mich., 1987.

Hilsenhoff, W.L. "Aquatic Insects of Wisconsin with Generic Keys and Notes on Biology, Ecology, and Distribution." Wisconsin Department of Natural Resources. Technical Bulletin 8. 1975.

Newell, Robert L., and David S. Potter. "Distribution of Some Montana Caddisflies (Trichoptera)." Proceedings of the Montana Academy of Sciences 33: 12–21 (1973).

INDEX